JOHAN BORGEN (1902-79) was a central figure in Norwegian cultural life in the twentieth century. He was popular as a journalist, especially during the second World War, when his satirical articles under the pseudonym of Mumle Gåsegg poked fun at the German occupying forces. He was also for some years a successful playwright, but it is his novels and short stories which are his most important literary achievement. His postwar fiction in particular often investigates the problem of identity; he believed that what we call our personality is a fictional construct, a fine name for the cage we have constructed for ourselves. *Little Lord* (*Lillelord*, 1955) is the first volume of a trilogy which follows the life of Wilfred Sagen, a boy growing up in the privileged environment of upper-class Kristiania, but struggling with dark forces within himself. It was followed by *De mørke kilder* (The Dark Springs, 1956) and *Vi har ham nå* (We've Got Him Now, 1957).

JANET GARTON is Emeritus Professor of European Literature at the University of East Anglia, Norwich. She has published books and articles about Nordic literature, including *Norwegian Women's Writing 1850-1990* (1993), *Contemporary Norwegian Women's Writing* (1995), *Elskede Amalie* (2002) and most recently a biography of Amalie Skram, *Amalie* (2011). She has also translated Bjørg Vik, Cecilie Løveid, Paal-Helge Haugen, Kirsten Thorup and Henrik Ibsen.

Some other books from Norvik Press

Kjell Askildsen: *A Sudden Liberating Thought* (translated by Sverre Lyngstad)

Jens Bjørneboe: *Moment of Freedom* (translated by Esther Greenleaf Mürer)

Jens Bjørneboe: *Powderhouse* (translated by Esther Greenleaf Mürer)

Jens Bjørneboe: *The Silence* (translated by Esther Greenleaf Mürer)

Hans Børli: *We Own the Forest and Other Poems* (translated by Louis Muinzer)

Peter Fjågesund: *Knut Hamsun Abroad: International Reception*

Arne Garborg: *The Making of Daniel Braut* (translated by Marie Wells)

Sigurd Hoel: *A Fortnight Before the Frost* (translated by Sverre Lyngstad)

Jonas Lie: *The Family at Gilje* (translated by Marie Wells)

Amalie Skram: *Fru Inés* (translated by Katherine Hanson and Judith Messick)

Amalie Skram: *Lucie* (translated by Katherine Hanson and Judith Messick)

Amalie and Erik Skram: *Caught in the Enchanter's Net: Selected Letters* (edited and translated by Janet Garton)

Helene Uri: *Honey Tongues* (translated by Kari Dickson)

LITTLE LORD

by

Johan Borgen

Translated from the Norwegian
and with an essay
by Janet Garton

Norvik Press
2016

Originally published in Norwegian by Gyldendal norsk forlag under the title of *Lillelord* (1955)

A catalogue record for this book is available from the British Library.

ISBN: 978-1-909408-17-3

Norvik Press gratefully acknowledges the generous support of Stiftelsen Fritt Ord and NORLA (Norwegian Literature Abroad) towards the publication of this translation.

Norvik Press
Department of Scandinavian Studies
University College London
Gower Street
London WC1E 6BT
United Kingdom

Website: www.norvikpress.com
E-mail address: norvik.press@ucl.ac.uk

Managing editors: Elettra Carbone, Sarah Death, Janet Garton, C. Claire Thomson.

Cover illustration: Detail from *Nydalsrendet 1917*, Nydalen, Oslo (Nasjonalbibliotekets bildesamling, Oslo). Photographer: Sigurd Kristiansen.

Layout: Elettra Carbone

Cover design: Marita Fraser and Elettra Carbone

Printed in the UK by Lightning Source UK Ltd.

Contents

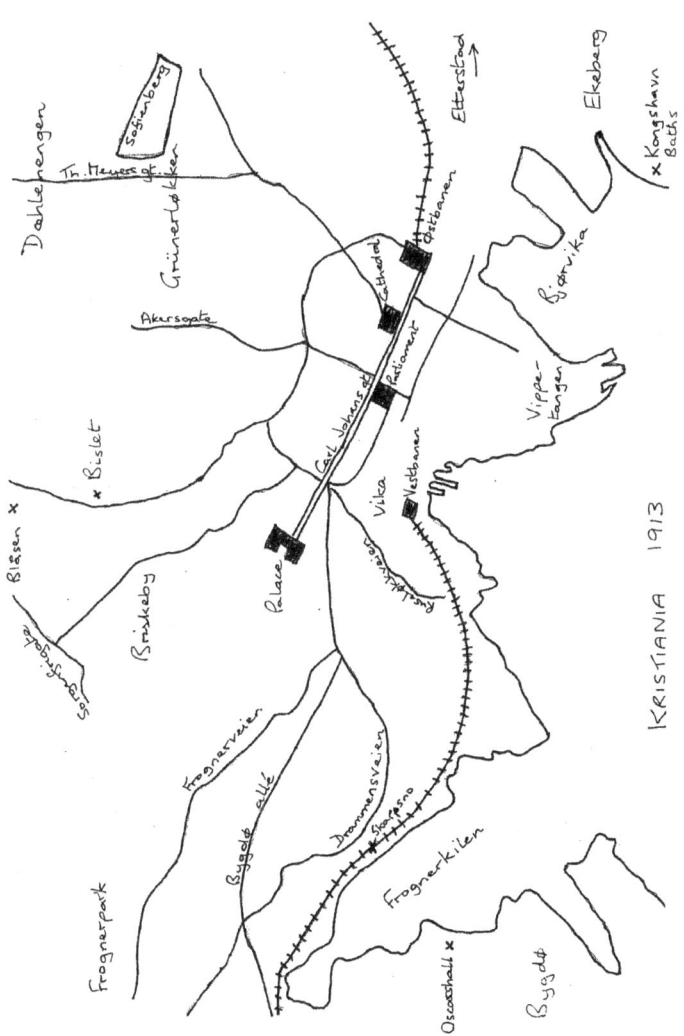

KRISTIANIA 1913

Dahlenengen
Sofienberg
Th. Meyers gt.
Grünerløkken
Akersgate
Ostbanen
Ekeberg
Kongshavn Baths
Bjørvika
Vippetangen
Cathedral
Etterstad →
Bislet
Bislet ×
Blåsen ×
Briskeby
Sørligbyskoge...
Parliament
Carl Johans gt.
Vika
Vestbanen
Palace
Frognerveien
Bygdø allé
Drammensveien
Storgata
Raadhus...
Frognerkilen
Oscarshall ×
Bygdø
Frognerpark

I

LITTLE LORD

1

The uncles and aunts came in snorting from the cold. Their breath looked like smoke coming out of their mouths as they passed through the narrow porch, where the maid was waiting to receive them. Then they came in, stamping, to the large square hall with the elk's head over the fireplace opposite and tapestries on all the walls. There it was warm. There it was inside.

Little Lord was standing on the carpet in the middle of the drawing room, listening to their arrival through the closed door. He was aware of exactly what was happening as they entered in turn and breathed in the aroma, an aroma of wood and carpets and the discreet hum of an imminent family dinner, asparagus soup, trout, venison steak. He knew where and how the housemaid Lilly would help them out of their overcoats, how Uncle René would say with mild coquettishness: 'No thank you, young lady, I'm not that old …' and walk over with his sable-lined coat and hang it in the cloakroom to the left of the front door, whilst tubby Uncle Martin – despite the fact that he was much younger – would let himself be assisted with straightforward pleasure: anything to make life easier … and the aunts, how they would say hello quickly to one another in front of the mirror, say hello to a reflection as it appeared – and then shake hands properly just after with the real person, and how someone would say something about the cold and that there was snow in the air. Little Lord could see it more clearly than if he had seen it and hear it more fully and richly in his imagination as he stood there in the middle of the room, exactly where he should be when they came in, to play the little host who just happened to be standing there when the housemaid opened the door a moment later. A ritual each time – so that Mother could then emerge as if slightly surprised from the interior of the house, just a moment too late, the busy housewife … He stood in the middle of the floor, enjoying it. A nervous pleasure at the festivities to come made him tingle. He heard the train pass – an outgoing train to Skarpsno – just below the windows facing towards Frognerkilen bay. On any other day he would have run to the bay window, which was a step higher than the rest of the drawing room, in order to see the shower of sparks from the tall chimney of the locomotive come dancing out into the dark winter's afternoon, and slowly fade in the air or along the banks of snow on both sides of the railway line, often right into the garden, between the summerhouse and the old fountain with the walnut tree standing proudly beside it.

Not today, no sparks today. Nothing other than to be standing in the middle of the floor because that was where he should be, and because he enjoyed it, and someone would say 'the little man of the house' – it was Aunt Kristine who would say it: 'the little man of the house, already at his post', she would say, and there would be an intoxicating scent of cocoa and vanilla around her – or perhaps that was just something he imagined because she produced 'home-made confectionery' in her tiny little kitchen, and had her own shop in Kongens gate, and everyone said she was 'admirable'; at one time she had played the lute and sung in elegant restaurants abroad, and once someone had said that she was admirable, but perhaps a little, you know … and then one of those quick sideways glances from Mother which indicated that there was a child listening. But Mother knew that the child knew that Aunt Kristine's eyes became as soft as velvet after dinner, and her voice became melodious, and she quietly kicked off her shoes under the sofa and leant forward with her plunging décolleté.

And he could *see* through the closed door how Uncle René folded his thin hands which could disappear into each other as he came back from the cloakroom, and briefly inspected his moustache which was waxed at the points as he passed the mirror, and with a diminutive comb which appeared and disappeared in his magician's hands – as everything could appear and disappear in those hands – smoothed his thin grey-blond hair, smoothed it down across his forehead, with one of those lightning movements his hands were created for, and how a moment later he would be standing in the doorway on the point of entering, in order to – at the last moment and with exaggerated politeness – make way for Aunt Charlotte, who in contrast would come foaming in with the silken rush of her many skirts – and Uncle René would say 'mon petit garçon' and raise the dark brown eyebrows which Mother had once said he dyed, and twinkle down at him with a playfulness which didn't really have any special meaning, but was agreeable, and formed part of the occasion as well …

After that Uncle Martin with his tight-fitting striped trousers, which spread out grandly from the prison of his waistcoat, would say his piece about 'masculinum'; but that would not be until after Mother had come in.

Not until then – a good while after the others – and he knew it was in order to make a point of her lack of importance – would Aunt Klara come in, black-clothed and flat-chested, and excuse herself more and more, the more heartily Mother welcomed her …

Little Lord stood in the middle of the floor, listening to the sound of the train receding. Soon the incoming train from Skarpsno would pass, and for a moment throw its long light beams out over Frognerkilen, where the ice gleamed dully and there was hardly any snow. And this clamour from a world outside merely increased the tingling pleasure at being *here*, being *inside*, at the many people, at the smell of roast venison, at the memory of the gentle plop of the bottles of red wine which had been opened a good hour ago … at the shimmer of coloured light from the oriental lamps in the bay window. It flickered over brass trays and scary Bengal masks which looked friendly now – and dancers in Meissen porcelain, who stood gracefully frozen in the uneven light, dancing brilliantly to the end of time on the dresser, unremarked by the grown-ups who walked past them or glanced at them distractedly, but not by him who had made their flowing movements, poised to leap, identical with a movement in himself: poised on the brink.

He knew each one of them as they would enter, and what they would say, and their clothes and their scent above all; he knew each of his aunts by their perfume. And yet the moment before the tall white door opened – that door with the decorated panels in soft blue and brown – that moment was almost unbearable with anticipation. Once he had wet himself at that precise moment, out of pure excitement, and had been forced to receive them in his warm, wet velvet trousers, but that was long ago; that was when he was eleven, three years ago. Now he stood there in his navy-blue outfit with the white linen collar and with his ash-blond curls cascading down over it, in his smooth patent leather pumps and with shining clean nails – stood there straight as a candlestick in order to be present and be the one to welcome them to the house; each time as if by chance, but equally full of celebration and anticipation.

The incoming train came snorting along over by Skarpsno. Straight after that the thunder beneath the windows grew as the train rushed past. Now the sparks would be dancing. He knew it. He stood with his back to the windows and watched it through the three glass panels, watched it with his back. Then the noise receded towards the town. The door opened. Lilly's arm came into view against the door panel and disappeared again. Uncle René stood in the doorway and then – slightly surprised – made way for Aunt Charlotte who came foaming in with the silken rush of her skirts!

He disappeared into them. Little Lord did not mind being caught in order to disappear into Aunt Charlotte's swishing silk, which sounded like a tinkling of bells close up when she hugged him to herself, tightly to her body. Her rapture as she did so was overwhelming, and when he looked up Aunt

Charlotte had tears in her eyes, and Mother had said that she would have loved to have children. Uncle René was standing behind her during this rapture. He came forward, bowed ceremoniously, shook hands and said: 'Mon petit garçon …' . Then he raised his all-too-brown eyebrows humorously and let his hands disappear into each other as he went over towards the bay window and looked out towards Oscarshall. Soon – at table – there would be time to study his amazing fingers as they bewitched everything he took hold of, the thin stem of the glass, a fork, or when he raised his hand, almost transparent but for that reason doubly commanding, in order to 'say a few words' … . Everything Uncle René touched came to life and shone. For a moment his hand caressed the icon over the arched entrance to the oriental bay window. 'Ridiculous place to put it,' he muttered, as so often before.

Uncle Martin came in. At the same moment Mother stood in the other doorway. Little Lord had speculated whether it was agreed between them – once they had been brother and sister, said Mother – well, they still were, but how could that fat man be her brother? Uncle Martin came over to him. Everything about him was striped and curved, like on that blue lady by Matisse on the wall ('Is that supposed to be art?'). Uncle Martin came over to him and said hello to Mother over his head, tugged briefly at his curls and said: 'Good God, Sussie, is it not about time to trim the curls off this young Samson and let him appear as masculinum?'

He knew just what Mother's face looked like then, even though his own eyes were fastened on a patch on Uncle Martin's trousers where the stripes gathered into a straining centre and then fell vertically downwards. Mother's eyes were smiling then, they were smiling in welcome and irritated and full of tenderness as she looked down on him standing there knowing about those eyes, even though his glance was stiffly fastened on the straining patch on Uncle Martin's trousers.

And Uncle Martin said lightly, dismissing the topic: 'Well, Good Lord, if you want to carry on letting the lad play Little Lord Fauntleroy until he's in his dotage …' .

But now Aunt Valborg had come in behind her portly husband. She was tiny and the only one who met Little Lord's eyes on a level with his own; she said: 'Martin - !' in that mild and authoritative tone which made Uncle Martin stretch absent-mindedly and say: 'Everyone to their own taste' and in a fit of comradeship go over to Uncle René and look in some confusion at the pink statuette standing all alone on the black pillar under the palm. Under Uncle Martin's gaze it became small and meaningless, but when Uncle René lifted the statuette and turned it around in his thin hands it grew and turned into a story about a lady struggling with a swan, struggling, yes, but she liked it … that was one of the exciting things.

Aunt Valborg gave him her chubby hand and held his for a moment. Aunt Valborg's gaze did not come down from above. In that way she seemed like a child. She laughed and said: 'You're growing taller than I am, my boy – not that it takes much.' Aunt Valborg laughed at herself good-naturedly.

Little Lord stepped quickly up onto the raised step, took his place with his back to the window and said: 'Welcome, everyone.'

'Too soon, dear child!' called Aunt Kristine, who only now came hurrying through the door. She hugged him briefly, filled him with the scent of cocoa. It was as if they were drowning him one after the other: Aunt Charlotte in her thunderous silk skirts, Aunt Kristine in her scent of cocoa, Uncle Martin just at the sight of his grandly curved stomach … .

'Besides, Aunt Klara - !' said Mother, looking nervously at the door where Aunt Klara was now making her entrance, black with a white jabot, flat-chested, calculatedly late, with her lorgnette on a cord, straight away wetting her lips with the tip of her tongue, which was almost white and looked like ash.

Little Lord left his raised position in the window and went to meet her, asking winningly, as he knew was expected of him: 'Oh, Aunt Klara, let me see your brooch!'

'Later on, child, not so impatient.' But she said it with a friendly little pat on the cheek which demonstrated both that she was mollified and that she was now and always a teacher. She was a teacher of German and French and was upright in both body and opinions ('Like a grammar book,' said Uncle Martin to Uncle René behind the fan palm – 'except that she doesn't let any of the irregular verbs show.')

Aunt Klara took out her little lace handkerchief at once and dabbed her nose with it. That white, gently curving nose and the little handkerchief belonged together for Little Lord; and the scent of Maria Farina which at that moment flew like a refreshing spray through the sultry room. The veins on the backs of her hands formed an entrancing landscape, like a picture in geography with rivers and mountains – they too were lightly perfumed with Maria Farina … so different from the beloved heavy perfume of Mother's own Beylie's Es Bouquet. *That* was kept in the next-to-top drawer of Mother's dressing table; when he was smaller he could just reach the drawer with the tip of his nose if he pulled out the bottom drawer and stood on it. Then Mother was closer to him than even here in the drawing room where she was now filling the space between the aunts and uncles.

Her perfume was generous and perceptible everywhere, not fresh and ephemeral like Aunt Klara's perfume, of which there was just a hint every time she opened her little pearl-embroidered Bohemian purse, leaving Maria Farina to escape from her lace.

And he felt a sense of well-being at these contrasts, a secure balance between all things in his protected world. Now was the time for them to mingle with one another a little restlessly, and inspect one another absent-mindedly, until the tall double doors to the dining room were flung wide by an invisible force, which he knew very well was the housemaid Lilly, and Mother would say: 'Please be seated, everyone!'

Now was the concentrated time of pleasure and anticipation. They were here. All of them. And he would make someone happy by making another childish appeal to Aunt Klara – for it was expected of him – and saying: 'Let me see your brooch now, Aunt Klara!'

He said it. And she said, as she was supposed to: 'But my dear boy, don't you ever get tired of looking at this brooch …'. And she pulled the thin gold chain carefully over her head and opened the outermost brooch, which contained another exactly the same but a little smaller, and opened that; and that contained another one exactly the same. And he said: 'Ooo!' But even the innermost brooch had a hinge which made it look as if you could open it. Once Mother had said that it contained a photograph and that was Aunt Klara's tragedy. And Little Lord knew that he shouldn't know that and shouldn't ask whether it too could be opened. He knew that just as he knew a thousand accepted things. A lot of things were just given.

Far, far off he knew in this moment of happiness that there was also a world outside – the ice at Frognerkilen, the street, his school … and that the boys in his class wore different clothes when *they* had visitors. He knew that. He knew that they knocked things over and broke windows and got holes in their trousers. He knew that at Andreas' house there were no cabinets with dancers on them, and that they ate herring on Saturdays and didn't drink wine from cut crystal glasses. He knew that some of the boys called him 'girlie' because he had curls and wore different clothes. He knew that Uncle Martin's 'masculinum' was a reference to this.

On one occasion long ago, when he was ten – it was over coffee, as Uncle René's fingers were busy playing with the thin glass that came with the coffee – Little Lord had suddenly said: 'Then 'e fell on 'is bum and slid down …'. And Mother had looked as if she was going to faint and Aunt Klara's tongue popped in and out of her mouth like the cuckoo in the cuckoo clock on the dining room wall, but Uncle Martin had broken into noisy laughter and called out: 'Bravo, young man!' and squeezed a flushed hand down into the waistcoat pocket under his round stomach and fished out a ten-øre coin; and the scene had been interrupted by panicky intervention because the coin had to be disinfected with ammonia before he could have it to put in his piggy bank.

Little Lord had been ashamed then. Not because of the

word, but because he had given them a glimpse of a secret.

For he knew something the boys did not know, and neither did the aunts and uncles, and neither did Mother: he had a lot of such words. He had a lot of such thoughts. He had a whole existence which was *like that* – and not at all how they believed it to be …

The double doors to the dining room were opened as if by magic. No hands could be seen. Mother said: 'Oh, please be seated …' as if she herself were slightly surprised. And they were set in motion, all of them in front of him, all heading for the door and the lovely smells which wafted heavily towards them. And he went last and as it were steered them in to the good land of Goshen with small hand directions they couldn't see. Almost without knowing it he imitated Uncle Martin's waddling gait, then Uncle René's gliding elegance, and Aunt Klara's erect grammatical walk, and he swung along behind Aunt Charlotte's mild silken thunder. He danced behind them with loving scorn, and felt himself brimming with happiness at this double mood of pleasing and mocking. And right in the doorway, as he passed the housemaid Lilly, he stuck his tongue a little way out of his mouth and at the same time made a gesture as if to embrace her, whilst he pretended to drive the flock in front of him to the table, where the light from the candelabras fell mildly over blue porcelain.

'Baa-aa-aa-aa!' Little Lord bleated soundlessly behind his beloved family as they went in to dinner.

2

Little Lord stood by the east-facing window in the dining room, deliberately letting the sharp morning sun shine directly into his eyes. He hadn't eaten, and felt a sick distaste for the very room, its smells, the thought of going to school. He heard the cuckoo clock ticking behind him, and let the stroke of each second go though him like a stabbing pain. On the high-backed gilt leather chair in front of Mother's writing desk lay his sealskin satchel with its straps hanging down. Even the acrid smell of leather was noticeable this morning and it bothered him. He heard Mother coming down the stairs and knew that in the next moment she would be standing in the doorway. Flames of irritation leapt up inside him.

'But Little Lord, aren't you going to school?'

'Call me Wilfred,' he said coldly, without turning round. It took even him by surprise.

'But my dear …'. Now he could hear her footsteps coming towards him. His mood changed abruptly. He went towards her with tears in his eyes.

'Forgive me, Mother.'

'But it's half-past eight – past that.'

'Mother …'. All at once he let tears come into his eyes – not running freely, but just so that he could feel the pressure which made his throat ache agreeably. 'Mother, I can't go to school today.'

She put her arm protectively around his shoulders and they went to the window together. 'Look, Mother,' he said, nodding towards the dark wet branches which filtered the sunlight. 'Mother, I need several flowers for my herbarium, blue anemones … several plants with their roots as well – no, it's not too early in the year, I can dig them up from under the melting snow on Bygdø.'

'But then I'd have to write a note tomorrow that you were ill,' she said. 'That would be a lie.'

He knew that she was won over. He knew it from her eyes. He knew it from everything, from her black dress, that she was having one of her subdued days, one of the days she was going to go to the cemetery and remember Father. He shrugged:

'Lie – not if you write that I have a sore throat.'

Then she shrugged too, with exactly the same movement of her grown-up round shoulders as he had made with his thin childish ones, a movement expressing wilfulness and frivolity.

'And Mother –' he followed her from the window into the

room. 'Call me what you want, call me Little Lord.'

Mother turned round, she looked concerned. 'Perhaps my brother Martin is right, it's time we started to call you by your proper name.'

He was gripped by a strong sense of discomfort, discomfort because unsettling realities were looming up. He reached out his arms to her in appeal and said: 'Call me Little Lord!'

She sighed happily. 'Well, if that's what you want, my dear.' Then she went back to her writing desk: 'You need money for the boatman.'

She reached for the blue china cup, the farthest right of the row along the ledge, took out the key and unlocked the desk. The curved sliding top glided upwards in a marvellous way; he loved to see things function so smoothly and easily. From the little top drawer on the left she took out her brown purse, and then took two five-øre coins from the middle section which you could close with a little brass clasp. A sweet smell came from the purse, from the tiny book with thin leaves of powder which lay in the open back compartment together with two small pink pencil ends, the remains of 'ball pencils', hoarded in greedy sentimentality from her youthful triumphs at great balls. Then she closed and locked the desk again and put the key back in its place in the cup on the ledge.

'And you haven't eaten anything either?'

She rang the bell beside the dresser with its carved cupboards and the extravagant silver stand set in the centre of a display of silver goblets and bowls of Bohemian glass.

'Mother, I waited to eat with you. I don't have any appetite when you're not there.'

And that became true the moment he said it. He felt hunger surge through him as if he had achieved something difficult. And he felt restless at the thought of everything to come – but now as a sweet sensation along his back and up through his legs. Mother had the hot coffee brought in, and mother and son attacked the breakfast table with secret joy, in tacit agreement to put off anything unpleasant.

'Mother, I don't think you should wear black today,' he said.

She looked at him in confusion. He had expressed her own thoughts, he often expressed her thoughts at the very moment they occurred. 'The weather is so lovely. You can change, I think.'

And this 'I think' was like a secret pact, the remnants of a childhood language which had once meant something.

He stood up politely as soon as she got up. He heard her going upstairs and into the room on the first floor. Quickly he went across to the desk, climbed on a chair, fished out the key and unlocked it. A moment later he was standing there with four twenty-five-øre coins and five ten-øres in his hand. Then, just as he was about to put everything back, he was seized by a new thought. He took out one 'ball pencil' from the back compartment in the purse, found a small note in the same place with a list of purchases and wrote – in an exact copy of Mother's neat backward-sloping writing – three items of expenditure which came to exactly one and a half kroner altogether. Then he put everything back as it had been, got down from the chair and went over to the window, whistling, just as the housemaid Lilly came in to clear the table.

She stopped in surprise. 'Aren't you at school?' she said.

'As you see, Lilly dear,' he said, turning towards her beaming.

'Does Madam know you're playing truant again?'

'Lilly, what a word – .' He went towards her, smiling. 'I'm going to Bygdø to collect plants today, the weather's just right.' She puffed out her cheeks scornfully. He went closer: 'You know, Lilly, after Mother, but she's so much older, you are the prettiest lady I know.'

'Lady,' puffed Lilly, vanquished.

'Yes, lady,' he insisted, standing close to her and looking at her with narrowed eyes. 'You know, I think you're the daughter of someone – someone high-up, a minister or a wholesale merchant. Your hands … the way you walk … .'

'Are you starting on that again,' said Lilly, collecting the plates with her plump red hands. 'You know what I think you are, you've got a screw loose, up here.' She pointed up at the golden curls at the front of her maid's cap. 'A screw loose all right,' she confirmed happily and felt the minister's daughter coursing through her veins.

'Now you must give me a cuddle,' he said challengingly; she was standing quite close to him. She turned round quickly and bent down to him with a sudden warmth. And with a passion she was not expecting he buried his face in her firm breasts and quickly drank her in. She freed herself, embarrassed, and straightened up. 'I think you're mad,' she said softly.

'Yes, or perhaps I have a screw loose – let's say that.' He walked away from her, but turned back to her again, with eyes that were shining with restless desire.

At that moment Mother came in, in a pale beige dress and grey shoes.

'Haven't you gone yet?' she said. He said: 'Mother, I wanted to wait for you, so you could wave to me from the window. Yes, that's what you should wear today,' he said quickly, 'don't you think, Lilly?'

The two women exchanged a quick, confused glance. He said: 'Now I'm off - - Lilly dear, could you please butter me three slices, I don't mind what's on them, although one with smoked salmon and two with Swiss cheese would be splendid.' He went out into the hall to get his coat and cap. From there he ran quickly up to his room, where he pocketed the French electric torch Uncle René had given him for Christmas. Mother and Lilly avoided each other's eyes awkwardly whilst he was out.

He walked slowly down towards Skarpsno in his new grey coat. The boatman was sitting on the quay, smoking. He wanted to see the money before he set off. He was used to young lads. When they were half-way across and just at the point where they could be seen from the drawing-room window at home, Little Lord stood up in the boat and waved. He couldn't see Mother, but he knew she could see him. He waved for a long time and said to the boatman: 'It might be that I'll come back with you too.' He put another five-øre coin in the box on the seat in front of him.

'All the same to me,' answered the man. His fingers holding the oars had the strangest foreshortened claws. The whole man looked like a well-trained animal, the like of which had never existed in natural history. All year round, except when the ice lay thickest in the winter, he rowed to and fro and ferried the traffic from Skarpsno to the small bay on the other side.

Little Lord went ashore quickly and stood in full view on the stone quay for a moment. There were four grown-ups waiting to travel back to town. He slipped down into the boat behind them and sat down out of sight of the house back home in case anyone was still at the window. When he came ashore on the town side again he walked quickly out along Drammensveien to the first stop for the Bygdø tram. He gave the conductor a ten-øre coin and was given five øre change. At Atheneum he got off and crossed over to the Grand Hotel, where he got on a green tram which said Grünerløkken; he stood at the front by the driver and tensely watched the tracks which were sucking them in. All his restlessness flared up again. He could feel it as a delightful tingling in his limbs. He stood there singing loudly to accompany the noise of the tram. The day was new and strange in all ways. And this was one of his secret expeditions to places and areas Mother and his aunts knew nothing about, to lads and grown-ups they perhaps did not really believe existed. Dangerous, unknown places full of dangerous, strange smells, and people who talked differently, walked differently, were different, yes, were something completely *other* …

Little Lord got off at Olaf Ryes plass. He had been here before – four times – and on the same errand. He went into a doorway in Markveien, gathered his curls carefully on top of his head and pressed his cap down over them. Then he walked over to Thorvald Meyers gate. There, and in the muddy streets up towards Dæhlenengen, he knew that he would meet the boys, either on the waste ground or going along the street with soup pails or carrying parcels. Here he would meet up with his unknown friends who spoke differently and were something *other*. Here he would undertake one of the adventures which had been so costly a couple of times, but which he couldn't do without.

He didn't have to search in vain. He had entered a dingy,

filthy street which ended in some gloomy piles of planks; behind them lay a building with buckets of whitewash and scaffolding. He had registered that they were there, in the dark entryways, the moment he passed. Now he could hear the threatening and teasing calls behind him of boys who were gathering into a mob. 'Oily snob!' 'Ladyboy!' And the ubiquitous funny remarks about something to do with 'yer ma', which he didn't really understand. He swallowed, dry-mouthed in terror, as he walked along – straight-backed, not looking round – and heard the gang behind him growing.

These boys spoke a different language from him, they went to school in the afternoons, to something called elementary school. They were different in every way, and he detested them gleefully every time he met them. Today he chose to walk ramrod-straight in his new grey coat and let them tease him until they themselves were at bursting point.

Soon the voices sounded more threatening behind him; the boldest drew closer, a couple of them had already reached out and twitched his coat, one tried to trip him up as if by accident as he ran past; it was a little lad they called Ratty who smelt of acrid pepper; it must be trousers stained with pee.

'Daren't turn round. Daren't turn round!' they yelled behind him, louder and louder. He didn't quicken his steps, stopped himself doing it; wanted to run a bit, but resisted it. He walked right towards the towering piles of planks which opened up in front of him with a sombre cavern inside. It led into the darkness. He walked into the cavern in front of them with dignity. Here there was no way back. Here there were no grown-ups he could appeal to. Here he had to take what was coming, or win at once.

The gang was close behind him now. Someone was in the lead and treading on his heels with every step. It got darker and darker deeper into the cavern, and the calls behind him acquired an undertone of fierce hostility.

Just as he could make out the end of the cavern he turned round suddenly, grabbed the electric torch from his pocket and directed the blinding light straight at the gang.

The effect was more powerful than he had calculated. The ones in front staggered backwards. Those at the back stood still, gawping. There were nine boys, a motley crowd of poor clothes and tousled hair, dirty fists and thin white faces, full of intensity and hunger.

A groan passed through the group. He extinguished the light. The darkness invaded them in red flames which blinded them. He switched the light on again – then off, and put it in his pocket.

They stood facing each other in the thick darkness. One boy from *his* world, and nine boys from *theirs*. He had a momentary advantage. None of the boys had seen an electric torch before. He knew it. He had counted on it. It was his card. Now he had played it. There was a groan of pent-up expectation around him.

'How much d'you want for tha' light?' one of them asked. Another said, almost reverently: 'Let's hold it a bit?'

Little Lord passed the torch to the hand held out in the darkness. The boy couldn't switch it on. 'Like this,' said Little Lord, pressing the button. The cavern of planks flamed up like a fairytale grotto around them and all the faces were flickering and strange. It was as if the boys didn't know each other any longer; their solidarity was broken. Little Lord switched the light off. The boy stood there with the magic wand in his hand, a magic wand with no magic power for him. The faces shivered with excitement in the dark.

'Let's see,' came a voice from the darkness. The torch was passed on. Little Lord knew that now – now he'll make it light. The power is broken. Perhaps I won't even get the torch back again. 'Well lads,' he said out into the darkness: 'what's to do?'

He heard the foreign note in his own voice, he could hear that this was the voice of an unknown lad, a Wilfred perhaps, someone he met now and then, and he felt this lad's power within him, his desire to be the leader.

'Gi's the light,' he said, and reached out his hand at random in the darkness.

A hand fumbled for his and found it. Once again he held the

torch in his hand, switched it on in a short flash. In the darkness he quickly unscrewed the magnifying cap and removed the bulb, then screwed the cap back on.

'Here,' he said. 'Anyone want to try?'

Eager hands reached out, struggled with the button and the little push switch, passed it from hand to hand. They couldn't switch it on, they argued, they blamed each other for having broken the light. All solidarity was destroyed in what had been a crowd of friends, a gang. He stood there feeling their faces turned eagerly towards him, waiting for a suggestion, for an order.

'All right, give it here,' he said tersely, screwed the bulb in again quickly and switched it on for a second. He looked into boys' faces which had become the faces of war-hungry men, streaked with lust for adventure. Once he had suffered a defeat amongst them. Someone had suggested a game of catch-in-your-cap, but he knew that if he took off his cap his long hair would come tumbling down. It had ended in a fight which he had lost before it started – and a flight along the long muddy streets, where his pursuers had all the advantages.

It was important to suggest something which would catch on.

'What if we had a go at the milk shop on the corner,' he said coldly.

'What, Jonsa's?' someone said.

'Or the Jewish cigar shop?' he threw out blindly. He knew there was a tobacconist which ended in *vitsj* somewhere down in Toftes gate. He was taking many chances – on there being animosity towards 'the Jew', a hunger for tobacco which he could only imagine, a desire for adventure or love of sweet things, a childish or adult urge to break out and change the everyday into something different.

'We'll take the Jew,' said a husky voice in the darkness. There was a thrilling smell of rotten wood inside the vault where they were standing. Unwashed clothes and the odours of excited boys increased the atmospheric pressure. For a brief intoxicated moment he knew that here and now he could make nine boys do anything at all, everything they didn't want to.

'Follow me,' he said curtly and made his way through them. They moved aside warily, and followed him muttering. And when they came out into the light he knew, full of inner jubilation, that the transformation would remain even when they emerged into a familiar scene – or precisely then: everything would be transformed for them, even the streets, the houses they looked up at on both sides, him – especially him, provided he was in the lead, with two or four supporting him closely. He had a sudden idea. 'You can be adjutants,' he said to the closest ones on both sides.

Who did he mean? They began to call out between themselves. Stronger lads, who had got left behind a little, pushed forwards in front of the entrance to the cavern of planks and asked: 'And me? And me?'

'You're a guardsman,' he said carelessly to the hulking lad with the husky voice; he was the one who'd trodden on his heels, who'd had a go with the torch. He heard the husky voice repeat: 'Guardsman.'

Someone at the back of the group asked what they were going to do with the Jew. Little Lord had the answer ready. 'To start with we'll help ourselves to a few things.' Someone in the group said 'to start with' reverently. They knew that must mean there was worse to come.

At the corner across the street from the tobacconist's he realised they couldn't all go in. He turned quickly to the lads, who formed a circle around him. 'Four of us'll do this. The rest spread out in the park for a while.'

The faces shone dully towards him, he didn't see them, not as faces. He saw them as oval discs in the sharp light, the mouths red, open for his orders. They all wanted to be one of the four. Or none of them wanted to. He shivered nervously at the knowledge, knowing that those who were chosen would tremble with delight and wish themselves far away at the same time.

'You,' he said and let his hand fall heavily on the husky one's shoulder.

The one they called Ratty was already shrinking back, but too late.

'And *you*,' he said, catching Ratty with a hand which was heavy with power.

There was one left to choose. Every pair of eyes was looking down, except for the eyes of a pale little lad, which were worshipping, hypnotized …

'All right, you then,' said Little Lord as if he was letting himself be persuaded to do a good deed; the pale little lad sank under the grip of the hand on his shoulder. This was the beginning of everything. And the end.

He jerked his head at the rest of the group. 'We'll meet in the park – later,' he said. 'Have these anyway!' He tossed a few ten-øre coins to them.

They threw themselves at the money, fought over it. Then they left, departing reluctantly, relieved and unhappy, doubting and believing all at once.

The four of them had a hurried conference, then they wandered separately and nonchalantly past the shop on the lower corner and glanced in. Little Lord kept watch until the customer who was in the shop came out. Then he made a sign with his head and strolled in casually.

The tobacconist turned politely from his shelves and looked enquiringly at his young customer.

'I'd like to see some cards,' he said, going up to the counter. 'And then I need four Batschari for my father. Four Cypriennes.'

'I'm sorry, young man,' said the shopkeeper politely, 'I think you're too young to be buying cigarettes.'

'I've brought a note from my father,' said Little Lord, reaching for the inside pocket of his grey coat. He could hear them in the doorway now, they were coming in.

'Those cards on the shelf over there, I'd like to see those,' he said.

The tobacconist turned his back and limped heavily over to the shelf at the back of the shop.

Little Lord turned commandingly towards the husky lad.

'Take 'im,' he whispered. 'Hold 'im.'

The lad stood there uncomprehendingly. The tobacconist was standing on a low stool now, in order to reach the cards.

'Do as I say,' whispered Little Lord. 'When I say *now*. And you – ' he looked at Ratty, 'take the till behind the counter, *there*, and grab what you can. When I say "now": *now*.'

The big lad was over the counter like a cat and grabbed the old tobacconist from behind. Ratty ran behind the counter and grabbed money from the till. The third lad – the little pale one – backed towards the door, white in the face. 'Take this and run!' whispered Little Lord, and fished out a ten-øre coin. The lad ran out of the door. His large shoes clattered down the street. Little Lord turned round towards the shop. No-one was coming in from outside. The sun had deserted the area. It had begun to drizzle.

'Get out. Share with the lads,' he said harshly to the two shaken boys who were coming towards him from inside. Behind the closed door he turned alone towards the tobacconist, who came stumbling forwards round the counter. For a moment they faced each other, the fourteen-year-old in defiant panic and the sixty-year-old furious and frightened. Then Little Lord lifted his hand to strike. Twice. The tobacconist slumped back on the counter, stunned. Little Lord walked quickly to the door and passed an older workman on the way in. He held the door open for him politely, then walked quickly up the street towards Dæhlenengen, away from the park where they were to meet.

He hesitated for a moment on the corner, knew that now – *now* the alarm would come, the shouts would begin, people would stream out of doors and stairways. They would search northwards and eastwards, out towards the waste ground where the boys usually hung out.

Quickly he crossed the street; there was a chance, but it was the only one. He was across in the next side street when he heard the shouts. He ran into a gateway, through into the yard which ended in a fence of planks with two dustbins next to it. He jumped up onto one of them, hoisted himself heavily over the fence and found himself in a new back yard. He walked out of the gateway and was in a new street, searching for the right direction. He could hear the shouts now, several voices without words. He went to the left, crossed the street, walked over the waste ground there and came to an open area behind high blocks of flats. He found a gateway and entered a square between some old wooden houses with a pump in the centre. He pumped water onto his hands, which had blood on them. He pulled his cap firmly down on his head and allowed himself to reflect briefly. A bent old woman came out of one of the wooden houses with a green metal container, making for the pump. 'Excuse me,' he said and bowed politely, 'could I possibly have a drink of water?' He bowed so deeply that she could not see his face. She was overcome by the unexpected tone, and wanted to fetch a cup. She limped in to get one. All at once he didn't have the heart to abandon her. And when she came out with the cup and he'd had a drink, he fished out one of the twenty-five-øre coins and handed it to her.

'Many thanks. Please take this for your kindness.'

The woman stood staring after him open-mouthed as he walked between the wooden houses and through a long narrow passage between walls of damp wood. He emerged into a street he'd never seen before. He couldn't hear the shouts any more. It was all far behind him, a place in a world. But that world could reach him if he wasn't smart. He carried on walking south and slightly to the east. He could feel in his body which direction he was walking in. He came out by the fence of Sofienberg cemetery and went in through the gateway, since there was a deserted street along the fences on both sides. The drizzle had thickened into a dark fog. A little way into the cemetery he crouched down by a grave. Now he could hear shouts again. It could be those shouts. It could be him they'd seen. He lay down by the grave and bored his fingers into the cold earth and said: 'Don't let them come. Not this time.'

The shouts faded away. It was as if he'd become a different person. He read on the gravestone: *Rakel Jensen* … . He knelt down by the grave and said: 'Thank you, dear Lord.'

He got up and scurried between the graves, bent double in

order to come out on the other side of the cemetery. Through the railings along Sofienberggaten he could see the black helmet of a police constable. The shiny point on his helmet shone unfamiliarly amongst all the grey-brown, treeless branches around him.

The helmet approached steadily, giving him an unexpected feeling of security. A policeman – he was there to protect decent citizens even in this unsafe and impoverished district … .

Little Lord stood up to his full height and walked smartly out of the cemetery, straight towards the police constable, as if he were looking for protection.

This was the tense interval when he was neither fighting nor running, but surrendered everything to chance. If things went well now, then everything went well. And if they went wrong – that was something he had never thought about; that was the dark unknown to which he had surrendered.

The policeman took no notice of him. He continued at his measured pace along the grey walls of the houses. The boy straightened up all at once and felt an expression of scorn flit across his face. He was still on a knife-edge between the fright which possessed all his limbs with happiness and the longing for his own world, for the hidden security which he could not enjoy without having something to balance it against. As he walked he was already imagining that warm, lighted home on Drammensveien with all the enclosed comfort which he loved; and imagined having a secret, a new secret – evil deeds which he was the only one to know about.

He walked quickly across the square at Schous plass to take the tram home. New ideas proliferated in his head as he went. He acknowledged them, took them up and rejected them. He had done something now, struck a poor old man with his own hands. He didn't feel the slightest touch of sympathy or conscience. For the danger was not past. He had to look out for himself now. He had to protect himself against *something*. He had to create that *something* himself in order to protect himself against it, and he felt a great happiness at the thought, that thing which set him free from everyone knowing everything.

Soon, he knew, it would be just Mother and home which constituted complete reality, and this … was something other, something he had put behind him.

But only for a time, until exciting new ideas had to be admitted, so that all his assured security would be put at risk in his world which had to be rich in excitement and contain things only *he* knew.

And as he walked slowly southwards through the lower part of the town centre, a good and benevolent feeling of calm descended on him. He was going towards something positive and wanted to do a positive act. By a stationery shop on Øvre Slottsgate he went in and bought paper and an envelope and a ten-øre stamp. He stood at the tall desk for customers and wrote in Frøken Wollkwarts' neat hand, which made every letter into a friendly creature full of smiles:

Fru Susanna Sagen.
Drammensveien.
Kristiania.

I am writing these few lines to inform you that your son Wilfred is making exceptional progress in all subjects, and is remarkable for his pleasant demeanour.

Yours sincerely
Signe Wollkwarts.

He posted the letter at the corner of Carl Johans gate before he got on the tram by Atheneum. Mother really had deserved such a pleasure, he thought as he let his curls drop into place below the edge of his cap.

3

The doorbell rang.

Mother lowered *Morgenbladet* over her coffee cup and listened.* Together mother and son heard the door from the corridor to the hall open and Lilly walk across the floor to the narrow entrance porch.

The door opening. The postman's throaty morning greeting, and Lilly's high voice full of laughter … Little Lord felt a warm sense of well-being at these ritual sounds. It was in their own home, everything was in their own home – that was how the world was. This certainty was something which at the same time excluded everything else, made it distant and prevented it becoming reality in order to tip the scales in his nervously balanced world. This was the place where nothing could happen.

Lilly knocked lightly and placed the post on the corner of the table. Mother looked absent-mindedly at the letters over the edge of her paper. Letters with company crests, from a world which sought her out, but without breaking into her existence, amusing recommendations she could be tempted by or turn down. The Silk House or Steen and Strøm who were advertizing their new creations before the forthcoming court ball.

Then she fished out the only letter without a crest. The neat, slanting handwriting on the envelope awoke just enough curiosity for her to open it and read it quickly.

Little Lord examined his soft-boiled egg closely. For each mouthful he took, he made sure to include exactly the right amount of yolk and exactly the right amount of white, together with exactly the right-sized bite of his toast, with exactly the right amount of salt on his egg-spoon. The grown-ups always laughed a little at how carefully measured his enjoyment of his food was. Then he felt his mother's glance resting on him, and reached out for his teacup, whose contents were mixed half-and-half with milk and a spoonful of sugar.

'Oh, my dear boy,' said Mother. He looked up with exactly the right amount of surprise. 'What is it, Mother?' he asked. He looked slightly concerned now, and knew it.

'It's … it's … no, I can't tell you what it is.' Mother assumed a solemn expression.

'Is there something wrong?' he asked. He felt his eyes watering slightly. He was in fine form.

'No, wrong … no, my dear, there's nothing wrong, you can be sure of that!' said Mother. Her eyes were shining. She was so pretty. He felt a sweet joy running through him at the feeling that he had made her happy.

'But then you can tell me, surely, Mother – I mean if there's nothing wrong?' he said.

She got up and went over to the window, humming. She was filled with such happiness that she had to hide it from him. But no, a letter like that was something between her and the school, it was surely not Frøken Wollkwarts' intention that she should make the boy a party to their secret correspondence. No, she would write a letter, that's what she would do. She would write a letter to the teacher and tell her how pleased she was, and that Frøken Wollkwarts should continue to take good care of her clever little son. She would do more, she would send Frøken Wollkwarts a gift, something discreet, perhaps a brooch – but something genuine, something exclusive.

And suddenly she felt herself to be irresponsible and incompetent in comparison with such a teacher – a person with education and experience and solid knowledge, all the things she had neglected in her sheltered life. She was seized by pedagogic earnestness, by a desire to communicate something which would have an improving effect.

'Just look here in the newspaper,' she said with a sudden change of subject, 'think what a difference there is in the homes, the backgrounds – yes, it would do you good to know a little about these things now, Little Lord …'

She sat down purposefully with *Morgenbladet* in between

them. 'Just look what it says here … about some boys in a place called Grünerløkken … no, I don't know exactly where it is, somewhere far away – and just think, they broke into a poor tobacconist's – look, in the middle of the day, my dear – and *struck* him – and *stole* his money – and … yes, as I said, it's important for you to know that things like this happen – just think, boys your own age, younger than you: aged ten to twelve it says in the paper … Oh my poor little boy!'

She had stood up again, overcome by the atmosphere she had created. She bent over him and hugged him close. 'Those poor, poor boys,' he heard her say.

He heard the words as if through cotton wool. Nausea surged up in him. It had come so unexpectedly. That it was all in the paper. That she took it the way she did, perhaps that more than anything else.

Nausea surged up in him. Everything turned inside out. And before he could prevent it he vomited onto the plate in front of him: egg, milk, tea.

'Oh no, Little Lord!' She stepped backwards in horror. 'I didn't mean – '

'I'm sorry, Mother,' he said through the tears which had been forced out by pure physical impotence.

'Oh no, my dear boy, it was my fault – how could I know … did it upset you so much …' She was mopping him with a clean napkin, rang the bell for the maid … 'Little Lord has been sick suddenly. Could you please …' She pointed at the plate. 'It was all my fault,' she explained unhappily. 'I was reading something horrible and brutal from the newspaper, about some boys …'

But Little Lord didn't want to have the day off school, not that day. 'It's all over now, Mother,' he said, getting up.

'My brave boy,' she said proudly. 'But don't you think it will be too much for you …'

All at once he could see in his mind's eye the coloured print of Lord Nelson which hung in his bedroom. The admiral stood firm, bleeding and one-eyed by the foot of the mast, whilst black cannonballs were frozen in mid-flight 'Mother,' he said, standing up, 'it's not worth mentioning.'

He stopped near the table on his way out of the room. There, on the edge, lay the newspaper; a dirty sheet of paper against the snow-white tablecloth, looking like an intrusion into the ivory-coloured purity of the porcelain; an unforeseen echo of the world which was not permitted to exist when he was at home where everything was good. 'No, Mother,' he said again, 'it's nothing, I'm fighting fit. I don't want to miss out on school for such a little thing.'

That brought her back to where he wanted her, to the letter. She took it in her hand again and stood for a moment, weighing it like something good and cheering in the midst of a world which sent them such terrible messages.

'I hope it goes well, my dear,' she said as he left. 'And give Frøken Wollkwarts my regards – for the present!'

There were sixteen boys sitting round the table in the fifth year at Frøknene Wollkwarts' private school.* Frøken Signe and Frøken Anette Wollkwarts divided the subjects between them. Frøken Signe Wollkwarts, who taught Norwegian and religion, was sitting at the head of the table looking with concern down the rows of blond and dark boys' heads, heads with spiky short hair or with wavy fringes, boys with ragged dirty nails and boys with hands like kid gloves placed neatly on the table surface in front of them. Today there was a collective air of absent-mindedness which she found more of a strain than anything else; more than ignorance and outspoken defiance, more than a wilful nature. Wilful natures were in fact Signe Wollkwarts' speciality.

But most of all her worried thoughts circled around the well-behaved Wilfred Sagen. He never played any sly tricks, he was well-dressed, well-behaved, talented, but with a tendency to exaggerate which seemed to turn all his charm into parody. Was it possible that all this derived from the fact that he had begun with a couple of years' private tuition and had come under her correction too late?

She sat looking along the row at the yellow curls which fell right down over the white collar. She had considered whether she should write and ask his mother if it was sensible to let the boy go around looking so eccentric, she had discussed it with her sister. But together the FrøkneneWollkwarts had concluded that the hairstyle of pupils lay outside the competence of Frkn. Wollkwarts' well-reputed Institute for the Junior Education of Boys, as it was still called on the school's leaflets; they were 'distributed in advance of the school year to a circle of educated families to whom it might be of interest.'

The air in the schoolroom was heavy. The window on the opposite side of the room was ajar behind the tall woven blinds. But it was as if there was no life in the early spring weather outside. It was mild and still and a little hazy. The words came and went in Frøken Wollkwarts' thoughts: mild and still and a little hazy – exactly like the intellectual atmosphere in her own schoolroom that day.

It was time to move on to 'written work', which inescapably included hand-writing practice, even for the higher classes in Frøknene Wollkwarts' institute.

The pens scraped in all the exercise books. The pens scraped in elegant handwriting according to the precepts of Olsen & Wang, short sentences with a specific moral content: 'With laws shall the land be built. North Pole 90' stood on one line. And on the two following: 'Bear burdens, they said to the camel bird. I cannot for I am a bird, it answered. Fly, they said to it. I cannot for I am a camel (Arabian proverb).' The pens scraped. Frøken Wollkwarts looked at the time on a fat silver watch which hung on a thin chain around her neck and was concealed in a pocket in her white blouse.

'Has everyone finished the page?'

The boys looked up, expectant, shy, relieved … It felt as if a hidden obstruction was weighing on the whole class on such a day.

'Hands up those who have finished!'

Small, ink-stained hands waved in the air. A small number ducked and reached for their pens in mild panic.

'Wilfred, have you not finished?'

'No, Frøken Wollkwarts,' he answered politely. And all at once she knew that it was this self-assured politeness which got on her nerves. None of the other boys called her by her name, as if to put her in her place, in a distant place, with their correctness.

'And why have you not finished?' she asked with unusual irritation. The boys looked up at her frightened, they were sensitive to unusual changes of tone.

'Because I haven't started, Frøken Wollkwarts,' Wilfred answered in a loud clear voice. Some of the boys giggled, others stared straight ahead, terrified.

Signe Wollkwarts had learnt during her course at the teacher training college that she should count to five before she lost her temper. When the ritual was over, she asked with determined friendliness: 'Why have you not begun?' And when he did not answer: 'Let me see!'

Wilfred got up obediently and walked quietly along the table. He passed her his exercise book with the blank page. The perfect text samples shone out in all their loneliness.

'But what in all the world have you been doing all this time?' she asked.

'Thinking.' It was said without reflection, without any sense of guilt.

'Thinking about what?'

'I really can't tell you, Frøken Wollkwarts. I regret it. I regret it most sincerely.'

But his head was not bowed, like those of other boys when they admitted something; his glance did not waver. And she was not used to hearing that they 'regretted'.

'I don't understand, Wilfred, you were writing?'

'I *pretended* I was writing.'

Was there a tiny ironic smile deep down in that clear blue gaze? Was all this finely chiselled innocence a cover for depravity and defiance? She couldn't believe that. Wilfred was generally speaking a dutiful boy, quick-witted and with an unusual facility for expressing himself. Her sister praised his abilities in zoology and botany particularly warmly. But he had a dislike of pressing flowers.

Frøken Wollkwarts took a grip of herself. 'We'll take a break now. After that we'll have Bible study.'

The sound of boys tumbling out with repressed mirth, the hum which changed into laughter and shouts as soon as they had reached the bottom of the stone steps and were out in the gravelled yard which was bordered by ancient lime trees and a green plank fence … she loved that sound. It bore witness to natural high spirits and suitable respect. Frøknene Wollkwarts were known for their liberal pedagogic principles, which allowed the pupils to play freely in the schoolyard, so long as there was no violence. The teacher peered unobtrusively out from behind the window blind and secretly watched Wilfred. It struck her that he resembled one of Raphael's angels; the soft, regular profile, the curving eyelashes, slightly too long, strikingly dark against the blond sweep of the curls, his proud and yet graceful carriage as he stood there beneath the lime tree. There was something ethereal over the whole figure, and yet – she could not make it out: a species she did not know, lacking all submission, yet charming and obedient – though without really conforming. Something almost brutal within a model of refinement …

She couldn't master the idea in her thoughts, more than that: she didn't want to acknowledge it, that something could elude her experience and her imagination.

Should she write a letter to this Fru Sagen? She had seen her once at a concert. She had been together with Wilfred then, and a sister and her husband. A friend of hers had pointed them out to her, out of interest in this man – an old dandy, as far as she could see, of that French type which passed for men-of-the-world here in Kristiania, a man surrounded by scandal and gossip. And she had thought: how strange, there's a certain likeness, no, not likeness, but a kind of spiritual kinship between this older gentleman and young Wilfred. And she remembered now – almost shame-faced – that she had made it clear to her friend that she knew these people as well; the young angel was her pupil, one of her very best!

Frøken Signe stood behind the blind and felt suddenly abandoned; abandoned by the Wollkwarts and by a world *she* had never belonged to, indeed which she despised, but which her inner being inhabited. Professor Wollkwarts had been one of those radical Darwinists who could afford to find a position for his daughters outside the best society. Afford intellectually, that is – not economically. He left them the best inheritance, a good education; but nothing else. They had devoted themselves to their pedagogic duties with a resignation which over the years had blossomed into quiet happiness …

Frøken Wollkwarts went out onto the steps and rang the brass bell. The games ceased instantly. She noticed that Wilfred had not joined in. He was still standing under the large lime tree, watching the tumult with an expression of absent-minded irony. On the other hand, he did not break off his activity as quickly as did the others. He lined up facing the steps, as if aware he was being watched, and walked calmly up and in. She watched him pass. He bowed formally as he went past. One of the maxims from training college popped into her head with blazing clarity: never persecute a pupil! Neither with suspicion nor with exaggerated interest.

The class proceeded at its steady pace with the gaps in knowledge and small comic misunderstandings which ought to be easy to bear in a teacher's working day.

Signe Wollkwarts was aware of that. She was quite happy to be patient with the odd mistake concerning Jairus' daughter or Abraham's sacrifice. She was personally not an adherent of this popularization of difficult topics in Bretteville Jenssen and Sven Svensen's version.* But then again on the other hand – if they were to absorb the information which was demanded in religious knowledge … Frøknene Wollkwarts' Institute could still claim the honour of having sent the best contingents over to secondary school.

It was time for an oral test. The exam was not far away. The questions were on the subject of the Annunciation. They had arrived at the ticklish question of the angel Gabriel. Automatically her glance fell on Wilfred, who would be able to answer tactfully.

'So he said unto Mary: I am the angel Gabriel …'

'That stand in the presence of God,' replied Wilfred.

'Correct. And then – ?'

'And then they cast him into the lion's den.'

She looked hard at him, trying to see if it was deliberate sabotage: 'Wilfred, that was someone else.'

Wilfred met her gaze candidly.

'I thought it was the angel Gabriel,' he said.

'That was Daniel. The prophet Daniel. He was the one cast into the lion's den.'

'Miss,' said a boy eagerly, waving a grey hand in the air: 'In our picture Bible it says that they cast him into the lion's *liar*.'

'Yes, well, den or *lair* …' Frøken Wallkwarts fingered her silver watch-chain nervously. 'It's the same thing.'

'But miss, how could they cast him into a liar?'

All eyes were turned on her in eagerness and confusion. She was about to explain the difference between *lair* and *liar* …

'It even says so under the picture!'

'Under Doré's sketch,' said Wilfred.

An anger she could not account for surged up in Frøken Wollkwarts. 'Wilfred,' she said, 'that is not relevant. It is true that the picture you are thinking of which depicts Daniel in the lion's den, or lair, was drawn by the Frenchman Gustave Doré, 1833 to 1883. But that has nothing to do with the angel Gabriel.'

She saw his face turned towards her now. It was as if it grew into a different face, into a picture she had seen somewhere, at the Pinakotek in Munich, the Vatican gallery …

Wilfred said in a clear and unashamed voice: 'I was wrong. I hope you will excuse me, Frøken Wollkwarts.'

She thought, as she continued with the oral test: I must write that letter, it is not pleasant, but I must do it. These people are full of arrogance. The whole of her mild being was suddenly permeated by a spirit of rebellion she hadn't felt for a long time. She thought to herself in dismay: is it because they're rich?

The door to the next classroom opened. Frøken Anette Wollkwarts stood in the doorway. She walked a few paces towards her sister. 'I hope you will excuse me, Signe,' she said, 'I need a pupil from your class – from your fifth form – to explain to my fifth-formers about vertebrates, sub-section mammals.' She looked towards the open door with a meaningful smile – she had spoken loudly on purpose. 'May I please borrow your Wilfred for a quarter of an hour?'

Wilfred rose obediently, looking modestly at Frøken Signe: 'If Frøken …' – he made a slight bow – 'Wollkwarts would allow it, it would be a pleasure.'

The peaceful school was like a primed grenade. Even in the junior classes with the assistant teacher in the next room, the rhythmical reading faltered for a few moments, as though everything were communicated through the walls by thought alone. Everything on that peaceful house's ground floor was as if transformed. Frøken Signe noticed it, and thought that there were days when God was absent. Distractedly she allowed her pupils to repeat the same answers, as she thought – and now she thought it with clear malice: I shall write that letter, and I shall not show it to my sister. She was already drafting the letter in her thoughts. She knew that it was her duty to warn that some mischief was brewing.

But it was one of those days when thoughts pass through walls, and cause strings to vibrate which guess thoughts and put them into words. As Wilfred was standing by the board and holding forth to the fifth-formers in the next classroom in an authoritative voice about the poster which was hanging there, he thought: she'll send a letter home, I know she will. She'll write it this evening and post it on the corner of Løvenskjoldsgate and Frognerveien.

He knew it with an inner calm which carries the seeds of decision within itself. He was used to thoughts going through walls, they did that at home too. They guessed. It was just a matter of knowing when it happened. You could know it through an internal restlessness which alerted you, he was used to being tuned in to it – a restlessness which was succeeded by calm. He stood on the other side of a wall and knew – without surprise – she'll write a letter home. And a blissful sense of triumph spread through him because he knew more than they knew that he knew. For this set him apart. That letter, he knew, she'll write it this evening. He smiled with satisfaction at the poster about vertebrates and cast a calm glance into the hateful eyes of the boys who were humiliated by being put in their place by his matter-of-fact knowledge.

And the same happy feeling of calm filled him that evening in the drawing room with Mother. She was leafing through *Die Woche*, he was reading about the physiology of angels in *Skillings Magazin*.* He had thrown a quick, horrified glance into the spacious, matt blue kitchen where the housemaid Lilly was making repairs to his new grey spring coat. She had two hot irons ready on the stove. He closed the door quickly and let the servant think what she would. He just had time for a polite greeting to Madam Frisaksen, who was on a visit from the country with the maids and was drinking a cup of coffee with the kitchen maid Oleanna on a corner of the kitchen table.

'I can't understand,' Lilly was saying to the kitchen maid, 'how that boy manages to get himself so filthy out there on Bygdø, he must have been lying on his stomach digging plants. It's torn as well.'

Oleanna was sitting on a stool at the table next to Madam Frisaksen, commenting on concerns raised by the *Christiania Nyheds- og Avertissementsblad*,* her private paper.

'It's awful about these lads from Grønnerløkka,' she said to Madam Frisaksen. 'Now they're blaming a stranger who turned up. The only trace he left is some sandwiches which fell out of his pocket when he pulled out a torch near a pile of planks. There was one with smoked salmon, it says, and two with Swiss cheese.'

Lilly looked up from her work. She said nothing. Thoughts swirled around her head. An ominous feeling came over her.

And she said nothing the next morning when the postman rang and the house's golden boy was on the spot before her; he must have been standing in the hall and seen the postman coming.

'There's just something for Mother,' he said, quickly sorting through the letters. Then his mood changed abruptly and he looked at her appealingly.

'Is Lilly cross with her Little Lord this morning?'

The housemaid tossed her head and walked off.

She didn't want to lose that postman for anything in the world.

She didn't notice Wilfred pushing a letter into his pocket and going in to his mother, humming, with the rest of the post.

4

Little Lord opened the letter with completely steady hands. He sat down on the edge of his unmade bed. Without the slightest stab of conscience he felt his way into a mother's state of mind as he read. Not *his* mother's – some other one. The experiment gave him the good feeling of rocking on a thin cloud in a room full of transparent light which made things dangerous.

Fru Susanna Sagen,

I feel that it is my duty to write to you regarding your son Wilfred. His behaviour has aroused deep concern in both my sister and myself in recent weeks.

As you and I both know, your son's abilities leave nothing to be desired. In most respects he is far more mature than his fellows. He is also a year or two older than most of them.

But there are times when your son is so markedly different from his fellow pupils that his conduct is quite foreign to our experience. It is as if he does not really understand what it means to be a pupil at a school. Just today one of those situations arose which place him painfully outside the pupil group. It would no doubt be best if Wilfred himself explained to you what it was that happened. But this situation was not an isolated occurrence. It has more the air of hidden opposition to the necessary discipline or perhaps to school as a whole. I do apologize for having to refer this matter to you, but I would ask you as urgently as possible to investigate the difficulties which have arisen. Nothing would please me and my sister more than if a conversation between you and your son could result in an improvement in Wilfred's attitude to his school.

Yours respectfully
Signe Wollkwarts.

He lifted the single lined sheet of paper carefully to his face and breathed in a faint smell of school. Pleasure at something forbidden made him quiver, it filled the room and made it different. The portrait of his father looked detachedly out into the room from the wall, indifferent, a little tired, mild and yet stern with his short beard over the high uniform collar. Quietly and gleefully he tiptoed across and locked the door, then he cleared the books on the table into piles and got his pen out of his pencil case, all the time listening warily to the sounds from the house.

Fr. Signe Wollkwarts.

I have read your letter about my son Wilfred with much concern.

I can assure you that I will spare no efforts in my attempts to bring about the change in his attitude towards his school which you are so kind as to suggest.

I hope I may beg you for the time being not to mention our exchange of letters either to my son or to anyone else.

Yours sincerely
Susanna Sagen.

When Little Lord had posted the letter in the postbox he walked down the street with a feeling of relief. The light afternoons had really become noticeable now. That always made him feel happy and light, as if he had a song in his legs. With a tiny little jump he had gone beyond the bounds of the permissible – a tiny little jump, but precisely so far that he could not jump back, that no explanation could rescue him. He was exactly where he wanted to be; something had been done which could not be undone.

The streets smelt sweetly of fresh pollen after the heavy days of rain just past. Everything around him seemed calculated to please, to please him especially, because he had embarked on something which hung in the balance. He decided to drop in on his friend Andreas who lived in Frognerveien, in one of the furthest blocks of flats almost right up by the park.

There was a piano in Andreas' sitting room, a sad black instrument. Once they had asked him to play on it, for he was good at it, wasn't he? And he had wound down the piano stool, which was far too high and had no doubt been used for something else, and played a Chopin mazurka on the instrument, which was so heart-rendingly out of tune that he felt extra pleasure at the implausible performance. And Andreas' father and mother and his two brothers had listened devoutly, until Andreas' mother got up shortly afterwards and said: 'I'm afraid it needs tuning. There's never anyone who plays here … '. And he had answered that the piano had an excellent sound, perhaps one or two strings could be tightened a little when the opportunity arose … And her glance was dark with gratitude at this breath from a world where people lied out of kindness.

On the way he amused himself by peering in through all the windows on the ground floor, where he could see men sitting in shirt sleeves, reading at dining-room tables underneath paraffin lamps which cast a melancholy glow over both man and table. In some places he could also see children creeping on tiptoe through the rooms, and the points of the leaves of fan palms which stood hidden in a corner. He knew that the one sitting bent over the table reading was *the father*.

He was the one they were tiptoeing for. And the stern men whose pictures hung on the walls just at the periphery of the light from the hanging lamps, that was perhaps *their* fathers; they hung on the walls and demanded continued sternness.

He was filled with a cool happiness as he walked along at the fact that he had no father. He felt it as gratitude towards his mother, that she had let him be alone with her. When he looked at the old photograph of his father hanging over the dining table in the smoking room, it told him even less than the painted portrait in his own room. The short beard over the high collar gave a clearer impression of the strength which he was pleased he had escaped having around him. Was there also something else in that picture – something almost the opposite? It occurred to him when he thought about it, but he always forgot to look more closely, he avoided it. Instead he stole glances at other fathers behind the windows he passed and at other pictures on stern walls. It must have a fateful effect to have such men in the house every day.

Little Lord remembered his father only as a thin cloud of cigar smoke in the hall in the mornings. It was a good and agreeable smell which dissipated in the course of the day. It grew fainter, as the memory of his father had grown fainter. He would always remember his father as a veil of fragrance, ephemeral and non-demanding. And he would remember it with gratitude because it disappeared and didn't remain hanging there like a threat of return and catastrophe.

He wandered in lazy happiness along the long, melancholy street in the spring afternoon. He liked these sad streets, they made him happy. There was something in their long-drawn-out dreariness which called forth the gladness within him, much more than things which existed in order to make him glad, more than the circus.

Now he knew, as well, why it had occurred to him to visit Andreas. He was going to ask him about geography homework for the next day, but he wanted to steal a peep at his father. He was usually sitting in a dark brown rocking chair in the dining room during the afternoons; it was their only living room. When the boys came in he would smile cheerfully, wink one eye and pull gently on his thin brown moustache which had a habit of hanging down. And then he would ask how things were at home and how he was getting on. Suddenly he felt it was so inexpressibly sad, everything up at Andreas' place. He would go over and drink it in for a short time, and then he would have the good, rich walk home all to himself afterwards. The tired smell of a stuffy dining room would hang in his nostrils and remind him of all the misery he did not have to be part of. Then he would be able to surrender himself completely to his good mood, which would make him forget that there was anything to worry about.

As soon as he picked up the smells in the stairway in Frognerveien he was filled with a delight which made him moan. Here it didn't smell of poverty as it did in the doorways in Grünerløkken, which he had frequented like a thief in his own existence. Here it smelt *boring*. He let the word sink into him with a thrill. Every single door into the hallways with frosted glass and grey curtains on brass rods inside, the rectangular brass plates with worn edges from all the polishing around the engraved names in a sloping hand which was meant to look elegant – they radiated boredom, which entranced him because it implied the possibility of flight. This time, as so often before, he didn't seriously think that he was going to ring the bell at Andreas's. Panic in the face of all this strangeness would overpower him before he got so far. But then all at once he was there, was standing there, had rung; he was standing in front of the entrance in happy fright, staring at the grey pattern of the curtain on the inside. He could hear muffled steps in the long corridor within, the one with the resigned brass hooks where the dead coats hung straight up and down in an eternal dusk.

He could still run. Once he had done just that: run in gleeful panic, further up the stairs whilst a rumpled old woman's face appeared and looked around bewildered; after which the old woman had shuffled out onto the landing in her slippers and peered down the stairwell – just as he had calculated. He himself was standing safely behind the next curve of the bannisters, watching the scene, until the woman padded in again, muttering.

But when he was out on the street again that time he felt a little sorry for the old woman in felt slippers.

This time he stood there as the footsteps approached. The same old head – now it was called Marie – appeared furtively in the crack. The security chain was fastened. He took off his cap and bowed deeply. 'Good day, Marie. I'm sorry to disturb you, but I just wondered whether Andreas is at home?'

He looked into a face which suddenly was no longer old. It dissolved into an open child's smile, where all the wrinkles contradicted the expression itself, like in a Frans Hals they had at home in the smoking room. 'Well good day to you, is it a young gentleman coming calling?' said the old woman happily and closed the door for a moment in order to release the security chain. ('None of Andreas' friends has such good manners as that Wilfred, mum.') – 'Yes, Andreas is doing his homework, please come in.'

It was exciting in Andreas' room. The three brothers used it, with everything shared out precisely: books, instruments, cut-out pictures. Andreas' brother did taxidermy. Wilfred breathed in the intoxicating smell of formalin the moment he entered the room.

'Does it smell awful?' asked Andreas. 'I don't notice it.'

'Great!' said Wilfred, sniffing it in deeply.

'Oskar is mad. Now he's selling things to the museum.' Andreas looked up at Wilfred through his round steel glasses, proud and ashamed at once, full of eagerness. Andreas was Wilfred's closest friend in class, a devoted and slightly fearful henchman. He exuded goodness like a feeble warmth.

The boys finished off their geography homework. They sat facing each other over the worn table. Then came that silent moment when each tries to guess the other's intentions.

Wilfred felt a wave of shame pass through him. But he didn't intend to leave with unfinished business.

'Your mother – is she still ill?'

'Came home yesterday. But she's in bed.'

'I ought to say hello to your father… '

The boys stood facing each other uncertainly. Wilfred knew what was going through Andreas' mind: why does he always have to 'say hello' to my father?

'I mean say goodbye – or good afternoon?'

'He's having his afternoon nap in the dining room.'

'We could just have a look, we can tiptoe.'

And once again that same ceremony. Two boys stealing on

tiptoe through a pantry with an oil-cloth-covered bench and tall, pale blue cupboards with glass doors, through which the remains of the best dinner service from days past stare out sluggishly and unsymmetrically through the narrow panes … the door to the dining room which is silently opened a crack.

'He's asleep …'

That picture – ah, yet again! – of a man sitting in the solitary rocking chair, pushed into the corner under the palm, with his left hand hanging loosely over *Christiania Intelligenssedler,** which has fallen on the floor. His head tilted forward with his chin hidden in a greyish starched shirt, his moustache – which is meant to point assertively upwards – hanging down slightly, onto the chin which disappears into the collar. Above him – half concealed by the palm with the tips of its leaves yellowing – the framed photograph of someone who might have been *his* father … .

'Let's go!'

A whispering voice behind him. They must go, mustn't wake him up. But Wilfred shook it off, he *had* to stand here a few seconds longer, to drink in the whole picture: on the little three-legged coffee table with a white cloth stood a moustache cup with a worn gold rim, on the saucer the stump of a cigarillo, carefully extinguished the moment before falling asleep; the white cloth still on the table ('We might as well leave it on until supper time!') with the brass pendant light over it, not lit just now, but with its innate melancholy humming in every curve of the looped candelabra and the mysterious arc of the brass bowl.

A tap on his back. A low whisper: 'We must go!'

The dresser! A miniature stabbur,* mirroring a proper dresser's extravagant tastelessness in a poor reflection which made the exaggerated outlines ugly and meaningless.

Wilfred felt a nervous joy streaming through him, the beginnings of fear: that it *was* like that, that it could be like that. He gave in to the pressure from his friend behind him, closed the door and said: 'I just wanted to say hello to your father, but I can see he's asleep.'

He looked into his friend's helpless face. There was a mute prayer behind the glasses, a prayer that he would not believe that this was all.

'I really like being at your place,' said Wilfred. 'You're all so cosy here.'

A single questioning glance which found confirmation in Wilfred's open child's eyes. All at once it was as if the glance and the glasses fused in happiness. Andreas said: 'We get on fine.'

They went out onto the street together. It had grown almost dark.

'So you'll come round and see me soon,' said Wilfred. He was Wilfred now. His eyes were hard boy's eyes.

'Sure thing!' said Andreas happily. 'You know, Wilfred,' he said, 'I'll tell you something. It's just rubbish when some of the boys say they're afraid of you, I can tell you that … '

Wilfred raised his hand lightly.

The long street was like a ravine with lonely islands of gaslight along it. The brown pavement of hardened earth seemed black and cold.

'My uncle René says that when you really want to say something – you should *wait*, that's what my uncle says.'

'I don't care about your uncle. I like you. That was what I wanted to say.'

Was that Wilfred? Andreas saw a thin white hand in the gleam of the gaslight. It raised itself above him, to one side, became like a secret sign. Then it struck – lightly, on his cheek. It felt half like punishment, half like a caress.

Then he saw his friend's back a little way down the street. A sombre anger boiled up in Andreas against his will. And against his will he called out softly: 'Little Lord!' It could have been a curse, it could have been a pet name.

His friend didn't turn round. Soon he appeared in the gleam of the next gaslight. But he didn't turn round. Andreas thought: if he turns now … but he didn't turn. Had he heard?

'Little Lord!' he called more loudly. But now his friend was far distant.

Andreas wet his fingers with his tongue and stroked his cheek. Then he spat. The lenses of his spectacles misted over, he tore them off. Then he clenched his fist and turned towards the door. A moment ago they had been standing there, the two of them. He clenched his fist and struck his flaccid cheek twice. Then he put his glasses on again and stroked his face gently. With heavy tread he stumped up the three steep steps.

Wilfred walked quickly along Frognerveien. At every square patch of light thrown on the pavement by the gaslights he measured his steps, and each time he made sure he did not step on the edge of the shadow.

He did it automatically, but nonetheless consciously. He was aware of the precise moment when his friend stopped looking at his back. He knew within himself that this time he had not done anything wrong, not gone too far, just put things in their proper places. He had done something preposterous, but only what he had wished. His whole mind was filled by a peace which all at once grew so enormous that it gave birth to new tensions, to an anticipation of unimaginable sensations.

He didn't want to offend Andreas, not in any way. He wanted to make him into a friend – without initiating him, to give him something, a gift, charity – but he didn't want to know about him. He had seen his father now. He had breathed in the smell of formalin in the boys' room. He would send Andreas' mother flowers. He would fill himself with the happiness of making pity into an asset. He knew that the maid Marie – an ancient oil painting who opened the door and laid cloths on the tables – that she would help him with his good deeds.

He knew too that he would have drunk his fill of this pleasure once it was carried out. 'Bloody hell, Uncle Martin!' he said aloud to the air. 'Bloody hell, Uncle Martin. You're a fan of Napoleon. You despise Talleyrand …'

What he was saying wasn't important. But he was hopping as he said it. He hopped along Elisenbergveien and felt a rush of joy beneath the birch trees there. He carried on hopping, but in silence now, along the whole street – until he passed the postbox. He pulled a face at it for a long moment.

At home he rang the agreed signal: one short and one long. He could hear Lilly's steps and his mother's – the race to reach the door. Mother was last. She beat Lilly by letting her win.

And he could sense the sudden switch in his mother's mood: so pleased that he had come – so dutifully stern because he was so late.

'Thank you, Lilly. Mother, you must excuse me. You know I went to see Andreas. But his mother had just come out of hospital. She wanted so much to see me.'

'Oh, what a good boy you are …'

And the housemand Lilly's quick glance as she went towards the door in the passage.

'Oh Lilly, by the way – thank you so much for cleaning my coat, I climbed over a fence at Bygdø, you understand.'

Lilly's glance, which passed over him, half appeased, half frightened.

And as they went into the drawing room – through the other door, *their* door: 'You know, Mother, there's something about coming home when you've been round at a friend's – you know … just the – atmosphere … that is what you call it, isn't it?'

*

But when he was standing in his nightshirt under the portrait of his father he felt a freezing sensation in his back. The whole room seemed to be distorted. He climbed up on the chair by the bed and took the picture off its hook. He put it down on a chair with its back to the room.

He couldn't sleep, though he was not afraid of anything right now. He just couldn't sleep because of everything that was going on.

He lit the bedside lamp and got out of bed bare-legged. He was freezing. He went over to the writing desk and pulled out the right-hand drawer where the big family album lay. He leafed through the thick pages and found a photograph of a man with a moustache, sitting holding a child on his knee. *Father and Little Lord,* it said underneath it.

He picked up the soft yellow pencil from the writing tray on the desk and drew a short beard on the man on the photo. He looked over at the picture on the chair, standing there with the grey-brown canvas side out. But he could see it more clearly now than before he had turned it round.

Father and son he wrote in his mother's hand under the picture in the album.

5

Could it be such a long time between three Thursdays?

Little Lord often felt sick with excitement for the whole day before Uncle René's musical evenings. Once Borghild Langaard had been there.* After Little Lord had played the little piece by Gluck, she had said: 'That boy gets so intensely involved in everything.'

He wasn't meant to hear that. Or was he?

They often had visitors whose pictures had been in *Morgenbladet*. Every third Thursday – but could it be such a long time between three Thursdays? Little Lord was always unsure of the calendar. He measured it by Thursdays. It was also important to keep anything threatening at a distance. Thursdays were good for that.

Yes, it was important to keep it at a distance, everything which threatened. Don't let it happen, dear God, dear Mother, dear Anyone and Anything, don't let it happen.

Or let it happen! Let it happen with a bang. Let the police stand in the middle of Uncle René's music room with gilded legs on all the chairs. Let the police stand in the middle of the room – two stern men with forked beards and helmets atop their uniforms: '*Is there someone called Wilfred here? We've come to pick him up now.*'

He could see them in front of him. He could see the whole

thing in front of him. He could see the open mouths, see them half rising from their chairs, feel the glances from each one of them – like blades of steel through his body, and he would get up from the narrow piano stool and say: 'That's me, may I please play my Mozart first?'

The music room was a high room with white walls. White and yellow was the colour of everything in Uncle René's music room. Once Wilfred had believed that it was heaven – the real one. Ever since then he had the firm conviction that it must look something like that where God was.

There were no fan palms in Uncle René's music room, and no pictures on the walls, just the bust of Beethoven on the white bureau with decorated drawers protruding like rounded bellies. And curved gilded legs on that too, as on everything; those legs which seemed to strut with a sumptuous well-being in which they had been permitted to stiffen one day when they were at their best: ro-co-co – it sounded like cooing doves, a sound of comfort, of good humour, a festiveness which spread to everyone's consciousness as they came streaming in.

Dinner was not served at Uncle René's. They had tea and toast in the interval. Before the interval it was usually Bach and Brahms and everything with B. But afterwards came the exciting moments with Debussy and César Franck, or some of the correct and slightly tame sonatas of unknown origin which everyone knew were written by Uncle himself. But that was a secret, and God help the person who mentioned it … . There were three permanent musicians from the orchestra of the National Theatre; a viola, a cello and a violin. The piano was played by various different guests, but never by Uncle himself: he kept to the violin or flute. And Little Lord knew well that they sometimes made fun of Uncle a little, even though he was a very good player. He believed that Uncle was aware of it himself. The strange thing with Uncle René was that it didn't seem as if anything affected him. He was just the way he was.

Once a poet was to come, and Little Lord had been dreading it for the whole day. He knew grown-ups who wrote music, but no-one who wrote words. He thought it must be so unnatural. But that poet had been like a piece of music himself, when he read in the interval.* He had broad cheek-bones and piercing blue eyes which looked at you for a long time. And when he read 'Gobelin' in the interval, and afterwards about a girl called Elvira who was going to a ball, then Little Lord thought that words could be even more than music, because it was both music and words.

On other occasions it was music that seemed to tell a story; once they played the sonata in B minor by Chopin, and when they came to the Funeral March – then the world came to an end.

Mother had been reading out so much from the paper just at that time about a ship called *Folgefonnen* which had been wrecked somewhere at sea.* And Little Lord sat by himself in the dusk and heard the music telling of the water rushing in over the sloping deck, swallowing up the people in its sorrowful thunder. And he knew as he sat there by himself that nothing which happened in the world, no reality, could be as great as the expression it was given in notes which became words.

Words became notes, and notes words, but it was more than that: they became everything. Everything was contained in the vault which words and notes built up around him, and in that vault he knew he was alone amongst everything that existed, and that nothing could touch him. They could come then, Frøknene Wollkwarts and the police and all the old women in Grünerløkken – they couldn't touch him in his vault, but would continue to circle around him, bewitched, according to a law which governed all things and made everything good in the end …

'And here is a young man who would like to present his Mozart!'

He was to play 'with an orchestra'. For the first time he would feel the solemn undertow when the others began, and then he would join in, and from then on take over the lead from three adult musicians who played for a living. He had imagined it to himself many times, each time filled with terrified triumph at the moment, and at what succeeded, when he felt he stood on top, alone, and was the one the others led up to or followed.

But it was all so different. He could dream as much as he liked when the others played, find words or pictures for the notes and make them mean something all the time. Not now.

He wasn't standing on any bridge. He was part of a calculation which they all had to work together to solve. And when he joined in on the keys, it was not him who led, it was hardly him playing at all. It was not the others and him and certainly not him and the others. It was *them*.

Together they acted and counted according to laws none of them could control. And he embroidered his Mozart according to a pattern in which he himself could neither choose nor evaluate, just do it right or wrong. And he was not at all nervous of making a mistake, as he had expected. He was obeying a law.

His fingers followed, but there was something in him too which followed, a kind of accompanying certainty about everything which was happening then and there. For the first time he was not floating around in a vault between other creatures; he was part of an instrument, which itself was part of a closed circle of instruments where the expectations of one released music from the other, following a pattern which could continue on into eternity.

And when they had finished, and the fat little viola player from the theatre stood up and applauded to his face, and when the thin first violinist seized his hands and held them out in the light from the candelabra as if to study them, then he was neither tired nor happy nor proud, but just full of a soft warmth which wanted to escape from his hands and his head, or from his throat. He quickly kissed his mother on the cheek. Then he walked out of the music room and ran as if in panic to the toilet, where he locked the door. He sank to his knees, trembling, by the toilet bowl and cried. But when he got up and had blown his nose properly he had sufficient presence of mind to pull the porcelain handle of the chain, so that if anyone heard the water they would just assume he had been to the toilet. For he dared not share this emotion with anyone.

And the remarkable thing was that when the water foamed into the bowl it was as if it took the whole of Mozart down with it; he himself was left standing, hard, cold and a little ashamed. This had never happened to him!

This had never happened to him. He would never again play when anyone else was listening. In there they were a closed club, a communion, and no-one revealed the misdeeds of others. He knew all at once that there was a border somewhere, between the run-of-the-mill and the really good, and that he hadn't even approached that border, and would never approach it. He didn't know where the border was, or who belonged on one side or the other. He just knew that *he* would never reach the border to the good. And it didn't cause him any pain. It was almost a release.

He tiptoed out into the hall and took his coat and plaid cap. He quickly threw his coat over his arm, so that no-one should come out and catch him. Very quietly he dropped the latch behind him and walked close to the railings down the veranda steps of Uncle René's fantastic old villa. Now he could hear them playing again in there behind the yellow blinds. It was Debussy now. The notes from Uncle's flute sent their muted plaint out to him on the road leading to town.

It was dark and pleasant on the road beneath the trees. Soon he saw the light of the gas lamps from town. Everything was quiet. Everything was good. He had sinned against someone or something, perhaps against Mozart. He would not commit that sin any more. He didn't regret it. But he wouldn't do it any more.

All other sins … a lust for *all things* blazed up in him and made him start running and leaping, moaning softly with delight and longing. A whole world of forbidden things and things which possibly were forbidden and things which were almost allowed – a whole world of possibilities was waiting; full of sin, of sins. And he was looking forward to all of them. He wanted to do everything to people's faces and behind their backs. He saw a tall striking woman on her own in front of him. He felt a desire to lay her down on the road and take her then and there, and he walked more quickly in order to catch up with her. But when he was just behind her he didn't even dare do that. He stopped and bent down to tie his shoelace in order to let her get ahead of him.

But he knew that he could have done it, that he *could* do it, and that all things contained a sweet pain.

With glowing cheeks and a dry throat he reached the streets of the town and calmed down. The fear of everything he had done and of being discovered began to make itself felt a little again. But he banished it; he drove it away with dreams of lust which he gorged on and let his being be absorbed into and disappear. Cautiously he then measured the possibilities, felt himself to be small and weak, but also full of defiance and good strong will. He would do everything. No less than everything.

But not play Mozart again when anyone was listening.

6

Fru Susanna Sagen lowered her *Morgenbladet* and looked timidly up at the clock which stood on the mantelpiece under its glass dome. The tea tray with all its trappings in porcelain and antique silver was standing ready on the round table. Contrary to her normal habit she had smoked an Egyptian cigarette whilst waiting for her brother. 'Martin,' she had said on the phone, 'is it necessary to be so conspiratorial? We can have a chat when we have dinner together on Sunday.'

But Uncle Martin had insisted. He wanted to talk to her when Wilfred was not at home. So it must be Little Lord he wanted to talk about, 'as the boy's godfather and guardian in place of his father'. It didn't bode well when he called him Wilfred. It was as if her brother wanted to take her little boy from her when he was on such a mission.

She remained seated when the bell rang. For the last few seconds of being alone she revelled in the self-contained atmosphere of these rooms where she had lived most of her adult life. This *was* her life – with everything that involved – and she felt herself inwardly like a slumbering lioness when she became aware of a threat to the slightest part of these surroundings; and in them Little Lord was included, and also included was the steady tick-tock of the clock on the shelf and every scent, even the unchanging temperature of the rooms.

Martin came towards her, smiling: grey tweeds, double collar, with a large pearl in his tie. So today we're the successful businessman of an English cut, she thought involuntarily. She knew her dynamic brother's various phases. Every role contained an incontrovertible reality which beneath all the disguises was one and the same: a positive view of life which was incarnated in set phrases like *common sense, looking at things practically, keeping your feet on the ground* … . She knew it off by heart, knew it from a childhood which had not been a bed of roses, through a long adult life which was reckoned to have been almost too much a bed of roses.

'A cup of tea – ?'

'Thank you.' He picked up the unfolded newpaper from the chair he was about to sit in, glanced at the part of *Morgenbladet* which had clearly just been the object of perusal, and read, still standing, in an official voice which was meant to express all possible irony to the sister living in her own little world:

> The king danced the first *française* with fru Lindvig, wife of the minister, vis-à-vis Admiral Dawes and fru Inga Schjelderup, the first waltz with the wife of the proprietor P. Anker, Rød, the second waltz with the wife of Captain L'Orange, the second *française* with Madame Terras Rivas, wife of the Mexican minister, vis-à-vis Mr. Blehr, the prefect, the third waltz with frøken Hagerup, the third *française* with fru Scheel, wife of the High Court Judge, vis-à-vis Mr. Heyerdahl, solicitor and mayor of Christiania. The dinner dance with fru Møller, wife of the proprietor Kai Møller …

'Do sit down, don't stand there being impossible,' said his

sister. 'Is it really so ridiculous that a person looks through the account of a court ball? Once upon a time I actually had the pleasure myself …'

'Who says it's ridiculous?' he said good-humouredly and refolded the newspaper in its proper folds. 'But I dare swear you haven't checked the latest recorded figures of the number of dead from the *Titanic*.'*

'What you call realities, my dear Martin,' she said, pouring out his tea, 'actually always means the miserable things, and nothing else. What good is it to me to know exactly whether it was one thousand or fifteen hundred who perished with that dreadful ship?'

'What you say is very true. But what is interesting is whether these people were driven to their deaths by the frenzy to break records or to make a profit, and to what extent the notorious false reassurances that the boat was still afloat and all were safe were sent out so that certain people might have time to manoeuvre on the London and New York stock exchanges.'

'Now I'm sure you've been reading *Social-Demokraten* again,'* she said lightly. 'Really it's a little odd that you with your views are so open to all kinds of persuasion from these people as soon as anything happens in the world! Anyway, I doubt it was to talk about the court ball or the wreck of the *Titanic* that you have allowed yourself a pause in your hectic office schedule and come to see your lonely sister in her widowhood in the middle of the morning?'

A little ruffled, he surveyed her smooth face, which in some way looked far too young. He helped himself to the regulation two sugar lumps, whilst he fought to hold fast to his train of thought in these surroundings which always undermined him, at the same time as they fulfilled all his requirements for comfort.

'In a way it is actually related matters I should like to discuss,' he said, 'if you will allow: to be precise, the unpleasant world of reality *contra* pleasant illusions. To put it bluntly, my dear, I am concerned about Wilfred.'

'About Little Lord?' It sounded almost like a correction.

'About our Wilfred, yes, your Little Lord. You know, we are so fond of the boy, all of us, – you, his mother, me, his uncle by blood, Valborg, his aunt, René, his uncle by marriage … I'm sure I don't need to assure you of how highly we regard him – each in his own way, yes, indeed, each in his own way … well, let me try to explain to you, let me, since I see matters in a more practical light …'

'Martin,' she said, 'you have an irritating way of behaving as if you've been interrupted whenever you can't express what you mean.'

He looked seriously into his sister's mocking face. It was as if childhood had remained unchanged in the relationship between the two of them: always devoted, always at a distance, always on either side of an invisible border.

'It's actually not so easy to express either,' he said weakly, and fortified himself with a whole cup of tea at once. 'The thing is, I'm not at all sure of what it is I want to say, but if you will hear me out – well then … Take for example René with all his splendid interests: one day it amuses him to fill the boy with a complete course in French Impressionists – with the result that today Wilfred knows off by heart everything about the development from Claude Monet to Gauguin, via van Gogh and Cézanne, right up to this Henri Matisse who …' – he glanced nervously over towards the painting over the sofa; it was a constant torment to him that that kind of thing should be so remarkable. And now this monstrous Edvard Munch was going to fill the university with his daubings.* 'Would you be so kind as not to interrupt me?'

She sat there with her teacup, self-assured, with the same mocking smile.

'You're right, you didn't interrupt me. It must be a bad habit of mine …' He took his silk handkerchief out of his breast pocket and wiped his forehead with it. 'But what I want to say is this: you stuff him full of art, of music, even with lectures on the finest vintages of Bordeaux wine. You let his curls grow freely like a girl's, you call him – yes, yes, I am well aware that a lot of this is both touching and – all right, educational as well. His aunt Kristine stuffs him with sweets and more than that, with the whole of her sugar-coated presence which – you will excuse me for saying so – is somewhat alien to us. What I want to say is that in a busy world which demands a pragmatic attitude to life from the coming generation, and – believe me – to an increasing degree as the society in which you and I live so comfortably will be transformed, and *not* to our advantage, believe me as I said … in the midst of this busy world you are creating around the lad an atmosphere of unreality, of eagerness to please all and sundry. Yes, you must excuse me now that I have broached the subject; the fact is that everyone loves him, everyone finds him attractive and talented, but each and every one of us – and we are after all so different from one another – likes him from their own particular standpoint, never for one moment from *his*. One could almost be tempted to ask: where is the lad himself, where is *Wilfred* under all this pleasing, all these winning ways, all this perfect behaviour and adaptability? Where is he, do you think? *What* is he? And what is perhaps more important: what will he be suited for …'

Fru Susanna sat for a while, looking straight ahead. The mocking smile had vanished. For a moment she was overcome by a feeling of inadequacy, the same she had experienced at the thought of the teacher Frøken Wollkwarts. But just as this feeling announced itself, something else occurred to her, and her eyes filled with a silent triumph which possessed her more and more strongly as her brother spoke, and which shone out from her to such an extent that it made him pause, unused as he was to talking for a long time about more abstract topics.

'Do you know what I think?' she said at length, getting up. 'You have earned one of those light pre-lunch whiskies which you Anglo-Saxons like to press on your business associates.'

*

She walked calmly through into the sitting-room and returned with a bottle, siphon and glass. Uncle Martin looked with a feeling of relief at what she was carrying, and happily poured himself a drink, of which he immediately downed half. He also saw a piece of paper, an ordinary sheet of writing paper which his sister was holding in her hand when she returned. She passed it to him after he had taken a drink. 'Read this,' she said quietly. Her hand holding the letter shook slightly.

'Fru Susanna Sagen … these few lines to inform you that your son Wilfred is making exceptional progress … '

He read it twice to gain time. Then he drank the rest of his drink and read the short letter one more time.

'I'm very pleased,' he said in a subdued voice. 'Do I need to say that I'm extremely pleased that the lad is making progress at school and that his teachers are satisfied with his behaviour?'

'Then it's perhaps not such a bad thing if his own mother and a few other people are also interested in promoting his – aesthetic education?'

It was said mildly, without triumph this time. It was not necessary.

Martin stood up, pulled out his gold watch in its hinged case and looked relieved. He had delivered his message, and he had been – to some extent – routed. He ought to be satisfied.

'Sussie, my sweet,' he said, leaning over his sister to give her a light kiss. 'I can't tell you how happy and relieved this makes me. Thank you for being prepared to listen to my views, which I must admit seem right now to carry less force. On the other hand you know that as the lad's godfather and guardian in place of a father …'

'… and as a man of practicalities,' she affirmed, with that mocking smile.

He stood for a while, feeling worried again. There was always something about the whole atmosphere in which she breathed which worried and irritated him, at the same time as he worshipped it.

'Susanna,' he said, suddenly serious again. 'There's something I've never got round to asking you – there are normally so many people around when we meet, and besides …'

'I didn't interrupt you,' she said. She was standing in front of him, happy and confident. She put the little letter from the teacher back in an envelope with extremely neat handwriting on it. His glance rested for a moment on the writing on the envelope.

'You don't have to answer if you don't want to,' he went on, 'but what does the boy really know about his father?'

She stepped back a pace, then turned and walked towards the window. For a moment she stood looking out over Frognerkilen, where the ice had recently thawed and the waters of the fjord gleamed like oil in the warm April sunshine.

'He knows what everyone knows,' she said lightly, walking towards him, serious now, but not concerned. 'He knows that his father was one of the noblest people who has ever lived, and a man who succeeded in life, who gave society and his family all they could wish for and who left behind a sense of loss which is difficult to overcome for those who were closest to him.'

She spoke the last words with tears in her eyes, but with a determination which seemed challenging.

'Does he remember him?' asked Martin quietly.

'I don't know how much or how little. He was no more than five when …'

Brother and sister were standing quite close to each other now. He touched her cheek gently. 'Strictly speaking it's none of my business either. Well, we have managed to have a talk about something which concerned me. You have allowed me to talk, and I'm grateful to you. At the same time you have reassured me – in a way …'

He broke off and went towards the door, looked once more at his watch in its hinged case, turned at the door and said: 'Is Little Lord not a fan of Oscar Mathisen?'*

She laughed briefly. 'Why on earth did you suddenly think of that?'

'Well – I just thought it would be normal. Are you aware of the fact that he has won all the races down in Davos again and improved on his own world records from Hamar and Frogner for the 500 and 1500 metres?'

'You really are the most astonishing person,' she said. 'No, I'm not really aware of that. And why should Little Lord and I think about this Mathisen?'

'Everyone does,' he said. He turned towards the door again, slightly uneasy now. 'Everyone does, all normal people. They're talking about it, they call him Oscar. Well, bye for now – no, you don't need to ring for the maid, I can find my own way out.'

Out on Drammensveien Martin got in behind the wheel of his new Peugeot automobile, after starting the engine with the starting handle. He drove cautiously towards the town centre, sounding his klaxon constantly as he went. People would still walk out into the street without thinking, so it was not a risk-free enterprise to be a driver of one of the modern speed machines in Kristiania.

He drove down towards Carl Johans gate. It struck him how these people here at home lived phlegmatically in their own little world; they went about in their own comfortable thoughts, sorting out their own little affairs with no trace of the passion and anxiety which had been evident in the people in Berlin, Leipzig and Paris when he had visited those countries on his business trip last winter. And had anyone been worried by B.W. Nørregaard's thoughtful article in *Morgenbladet* recently,* in which he demonstrated that despite Britain's continuing superiority at sea, Germany would soon have caught up with her when it came to those dreadful war machines, dreadnoughts and the so-called super-dreadnoughts? According to Nørregaard's calculations, they would have reached parity in two years' time, and that would coincide with the completion of the excavation of the Kiel Canal to its full depth.* It would be to Britain's advantage, he wrote, to go to war now and not wait until 1914, if the politicians had decided that war was inevitable, and it certainly looked that way …

Nothing of this seemed to worry the citizens of this well-fed town, which nevertheless was full of people who were far from well-fed, especially in the East End. What did his sister Susanna know of such things, for example? Was she even aware that the East End existed? Was Little Lord? He probably had no idea that there were boys in a completely different world so close to his own, boys who didn't eat off damask tablecloths or find their clean underwear hanging neatly folded over the back of a chair twice a week …

He tried to think about the letter his sister had shown him. But the thought of it could no longer sweep aside his vague feeling that something was wrong.

In Stortingsgaten he had to slow down because of the volume of pedestrians, and it got really bad in Prinsens gate after he had passed Atheneum. He was making for his office on the corner of Tollbodgaten and Skippergaten, where his solid export and import firm was based. Solid – how long for? It was as if anxiety about *everything* derived from his worries about this nephew whom he found incomprehensible.

On the corner of Nedre Slottsgate it became impossible to drive on. He had to stop the automobile because of the crowds of people. He took the opportunity to light a cigar, and looked around intently from his high seat. The vehicle shook violently beneath him and made it difficult to get his cigar lit.

Surrounded by a whooping crowd and drawn by four horses, a red-painted monster was moving slowly towards him. He realized almost at once what it was: the fire service's new automobile, their first one, he had read about it in the papers.* From his elevated observation post in his own automobile he watched with interest as the wondrous vehicle advanced slowly, pulled by four strong horses, and paralysed all the traffic in its advance through the exultant crowd.

There was something about the sight which corresponded with Martin's recent thoughts – something about all this horsepower which was still not harnessed here at home, something about a crowd which was celebrating the dawning of a new age without in any way being conscious of what it involved.

The jubilation died away through the streets. Uncle Martin knocked the ash off his cigar and moved forward again in his own vehicle.

Yet again he saw clearly in his mind's eye the address on the letter to his sister, which intruded into his thoughts. There was something about the ink, that greenish-black official ink which was used in the *city* – it looked quite different from the mild blue ink used at school. He didn't want to think about it, but it bothered him. Wilfred bothered him.

Different thoughts met him on the corner to his own offices, thoughts of goods, of exchange rates, of a world which *also* existed; and – it seemed to him – existed with greater clarity than the hazy world here in his home town. The fragrance from the roasting coffee in Skippergaten tickled his nostrils agreeably. *That* was reality.

Susanna Sagen was standing in the bay window looking out over Frognerkilen; she too was plagued by worrying thoughts. Not about this matter of Little Lord; she even allowed herself a small triumphant smile as she walked through and put the letter back in her writing desk – but always this air of something foreign and disturbing which came along with her brother, with all his trips and contacts, with his *world*.

Two widely differing trains of thought came and went in her mind. Unease at being reminded too strongly of this *world*, of life in general – was she not letting it slip away from her altogether, day after day, year after year; on the one hand simply a useless being, and therefore superfluous, on the other hand without the courage – or even sufficient appetite – to take part in this life, hardly even in its pleasures. Once upon a time she had at least travelled …

And then: the other thing, that which always disturbed her about this *world* which she found more and more unendurable, that which her brother – and other people as well, as far as that went – allowed his carefree thoughts to be disturbed by: the fact that this much-debated world was not behaving according to the rules. Her glance fell on the newspaper.

It wasn't that a trifling Turkish-Italian war was unsettling people's thoughts up here in this blessed far north;* or the

hunt for the brutal automobile bandits through fertile France;*
or that Messrs Amundsen and Scott were undermining all
geographical concepts by bringing the poles into the picture*
– but there was something in the very atmosphere, something
which reached all the way here to her home and, as it were,
suspended the isolation which had always been taken for
granted; an isolation which you broke out of only when you
yourself wished it, that is when you decided to travel … and
then the fact that you had to take on board these matters here
at home where it had always been so good to be; that the
Germans, the English and the French were set up in opposition
to one another and you yourself had to choose: if you approved
of one you had to condemn the other. These countries with
their marvellous cities and their entrancing little villages, these
nations with different characteristics which you could praise or
condemn … suddenly they emerged from a satisfying context
which until now had been known as 'abroad'. And now – all at
once – they were a matter of personal concern. Just as this talk
of a coming war had been promoted from a conversational
topic at dinner parties to the kind of debate which made the
gentlemen raise their voices over a glass of whisky, and indeed
could even make them forget they were in polite society …
That had happened. And that was despite the fact that she
could remember that the topic had been something so distant
and unconnected with them as this Kiel Canal …

Abruptly her concern shifted to domestic matters … Yes,
it was at the same dinner party that the ladies had begun to
debate *the housemaid question* – whether they should have
an education, and all this leisure time which was suddenly
available. It had occurred to her to take a liberal stance. It was
true that she did have her two good full-time maids, Oleanna
the cook and Lilly the housemaid, as well as the little extra
maid Åse, a transparent little creature who came to help when
they had guests. She had been lucky – in this matter as in
everything. Now who was it who had put it like that?

Kristine – of course. Yet another disturbing phenomenon,
dear Kristine, the widow of her weak and refined little brother

who had died before he was thirty. She too was one of those competent people, whatever else you might say about her – all these things which were really nothing to do with you, which all at once could crowd in on you and break into your sheltered world. She had been lucky. With maids. With everything. And yet – all these disturbing worries. Even the maids, as a matter of fact.

One day this Lilly had shown herself to be a saucy little miss; it was something about what was to be done with Little Lord's clothes, some socks – and the pert miss had actually suggested that this 'golden boy' made more than a little work, or whatever it was she said, and that it wasn't so certain he was so much better than all the others.

Utter nonsense of course, nothing to get upset about. And the little creature had retracted what she had said at once.

Nevertheless, as fru Sagen stood there she began to have an uncomfortable feeling that all this upset was in some way or other focussed on Little Lord, her beloved boy: the Kiel Canal, the distant lands which seemed to be getting closer, the maid question, all this talk about the working classes which *were coming* … Well, of course it was because he was a child, he was the future, the one who would come to experience whatever it was that adults at present were almost fearful of.

And yet: could her Little Lord have anything to do with class conflict and the Kiel Canal –?

She dismissed the question. Was that the doorbell?

'Mama!' he called from the doorway. 'Didn't you hear me?'

She didn't recognise him at once, even though the light was falling on him.

'Yes, Mama,' he said, coming quickly towards her. 'I did it myself, or actually I got Reinskou the barber in Tostrupgården to do it …'

It was only now that it dawned on her. Little Lord's hair was cropped – no, not cropped, but his long locks had gone, and almost all of his curls.

He pouted at her in a childish manner: 'Don't you think it looks good?'

She had his head right up close now, and was running her hands through his rough hair. A thought struck her: he looked like his father as he stood there in the doorway. She had been so deep in her own thoughts at that moment that she thought it was him standing there.

He turned his childish face up towards her, waiting to be kissed.

'Yes, it's nice,' she said, bending down to kiss him. 'Lovely!' she said.

'Lilly said I looked like a plucked chicken,' he said, delighted.

She pushed him away a little, stood looking at that beloved head lit from above.

'Lovely!' she said with conviction: 'If it had to be done …'

He turned abruptly to the tea table with its empty cups.

'Uncle Martin's been here,' he said, 'I could tell by the cigar smell … Mama, are you upset?'

'No, my dear,' she said. 'Not upset.'

Suddenly she was thinking about the Kiel Canal again.

'You know we've talked about it, Mama, that one of these days I'd have to get rid of my curls.'

Of course – they had talked about it, as about so many things. It struck her that you talked like that about a great many things without actually thinking they could happen.

'He asked whether I wanted to take my hair home, the barber …'

'Did you bring it then?' A silly little hope flared up in her.

'No, really, Mama – what would we want with that hair? It feels good to have got rid of it, you know.'

Of course it was good to have got rid of it. Her brother Martin would approve of this, it matched his ideas about masculinum. Long curls on a big boy – that was not hard facts, it was a dream.

'I think it suits you really well, darling,' she said. It didn't sound entirely convincing.

'I'm not a child any longer,' he said, disappointed.

She was lost in her own thoughts. She heard what he said, but it stayed hanging in the air around her – like so much else. The Kiel Canal. It was just a word, a disturbing word.

72

'It will be your first ball without curls,' she said suddenly.

'Ball? Oh …'

'I hope you haven't thought of cancelling that – even though you think you're so grown-up!'

Now her bitterness was noticeable. He felt caught off guard, sad, he daren't disappoint her in that too.

'No, of course,' he said, 'if you think we should do it … we can say this will be the last time.'

'As you like,' she said shortly and went towards the door to the dining room. The idiotic words crowded in on her and demanded to be admitted. She felt tears of self-pity welling up, warm and tempting. They would rinse away those idiotic words like Kiel Canal, like curls, grown-up, last time.

The boy looked after her with raised eyebrows. Then he shrugged and walked over to the window and looked out. In such transparent spring light you suddenly became aware that there was another world on the other side of Bygdø.

7

The main event of the spring in those circles was Wilfred Sagen's end-of-year ball. Originally it had marked the end of classes at the dancing school; now it had become an end-of-season event, a faithful copy of the grown-up world.

For Little Lord himself these balls were full of duties, and lacked the irresponsible gaiety which grown-up parties filled him with. Besides, all his cousins, the two girls and three boys, were automatically invited, and that included Uncle Martin's and Aunt Valborg's twins Mikal and Fredrik, who at this time of year were home on an Easter visit from their English school, where they were to learn to become men of the world according to Uncle Martin's precepts. Wilfred always had the feeling that the older boys were paying their dues to provincialism every time they attended a children's ball at home. The gathering was a confusing mixture of outgrown

73

sailor suits and approximations to Eton uniform, which made the original group from the dancing school look like a left-over rump – if for no other reason than that they knew each other too well and were unmasked in advance, as it were, behind all the clean fingernails and polished patent leather shoes.

Little Lord had filled his ball card with an exemplary selection of cousin Frida and cousin Edle, plus the three overgrown diplomatic daughters from across the road. It was always difficult to find a market for them, partly because it was as if they became all knees and elbows when they danced and partly because they made no effort at all to learn Norwegian. Little Lord was completely immersed in his role then, he had no other outlet together with his contemporaries, who supplied him with no other loneliness than to feel that he was alien. But Mother's glance rested on him from the doorway to the sitting-room, and Aunt Kristine's warm velvet glance rested on him from somewhere in the vicinity of the buffet; by long-standing arrangement she was always there to lend a hand. And when he danced past between these vigilant glances in the dining-room with the table moved back, he felt it was a reward for all his efforts and struggles. Those glances said 'my clever boy', 'my little gentleman'!

It was a little embarrassing that Mother could never resist serving a hot supper before the cotillion, even though it was tacitly agreed between the families that they would restrict themselves to one table laid with open sandwiches and one with luxuriant cream cakes, with intermittent servings of hot grog and raspberry pop between the dances. ('If the intention is that the children are to eat half a grouse each now that they're no less than eighty øre apiece, then the whole point of holding a children's ball is undermined!') Yet a shiver of anticipation passed through the rooms when the gong announced that supper was served, with 'ladies' and 'gentlemen' alternately around the festively decorated table, just like in grown-up parties, with a glass of red wine standing ready at each place. All of Little Lord's end-of-season ball romances were woven together with the memory of grouse in sauce and a kind of jelly tasting of wine with a thick vanilla cream which he no longer liked. There was something artificial about all of it, about the romances he invented from year to year, about the affected playing-at-grownups tone which had little to do with his real desire to play a role, about the comical paper hats and all the shiny cardboard medals – all things which delighted his guests and which his 'English' cousins accepted with an enthusiasm he felt must be fake. *He* was amused by it as if from a distance, but with a pride on his mother's behalf which he never omitted to emphasize in his brief speech of welcome. That was almost unaltered from year to year.

The cotillion was over. The dances on the ball card were all finished. Young men emboldened by good food had forgotten their shyness before the last lawless half-hour when the dancing was wild. It was the unruly finale when anything could happen. ('At that Fru Sagen's they don't finish until midnight, what are they thinking of?')

Still wearing his cardboard medals, Little Lord stole into the farthest corner of the smoking room and listened wearily to the tumult in the dining-room. It sounded alien and childish to his ears. It was his first spring ball without curls. He knew now that it would be the last. There was the sense of an ending in everything around him, not only of his curls and of the 'season' but of everything which … he didn't know. He stood in the farthest corner of the room and did not know. His glance fell on the terracotta statuette of Leda and the swan, but he did not know. It was treacherous of him not to be in there with them now, not to be having fun, he hadn't had any fun all evening, just pretended. Suddenly he felt that he understood how Mother had felt that day when she was so anxious about everything. Uncle Martin had been there. There was something disturbing about Uncle Martin's visits. He knew about the world, he made Mother uncertain. He had wanted to get rid of his curls for many years … Uncle Martin was in alliance with all grown-up powers, but despite that he was no friend. Uncle Martin's little men had to pass through a kind of machine in

75

England, where they were formed for use in the city and in business, but without the loneliness within them for which he was longing …

Little Lord could hear the surge of noise from his boisterous guests as he crept out onto the balcony facing the sea and stood there looking out over Frognerkilen, which lay smooth and black beneath the stars. Far out in the fjord a motorboat was chugging on its way from darkness to darkness. Three lights were all he could see on land over at Bygdø, and then the dark silhouette of the hill by the king's forest. 'Ladegård Island' Aunt Kristine called it. It sounded so enticing. Because she said it, the name took on something mysterious which blanketed the whole landscape at night, something exciting and lawless which she had perhaps barely hinted at, something about the place being a kind of refuge for the lower classes on Saturdays. Perhaps it was one of those quick glances from Mother – those glances which could make the others stop in mid-sentence and which she thought he didn't see – perhaps it was just those which made certain sentences so exciting and made his throat feel dry …

He leant out over the railings of the balcony in order to tie up one of the dry rambling roses which had come loose in the wind. From there he could see that someone was sitting at the bottom of the stone steps down to the garden. Behind him, inside the house, the music had now changed to a riotous two-step; Fru Zimmermann at the piano was doing her utmost to bring the party to a noisy climax before the end. Distant chimes from the doorbell had long since begun to announce that the various servants had arrived and were now sitting sleepily along the walls in the hall, or peeping secretly in through the door at the dancers – all sent out into the night to bring home flushed little girls with pink bows, and gangling, sailor-suited boys who were ashamed of being called for. They were calling him from somewhere inside.

He registered the habitual ceremonies going on behind him as he leant out over the railings in order to see better. They increased his excitement at this unprecedented event in the night: a stranger on the bottom step down to the garden. At last something he had to himself – like a promise of transgression. Then he discovered two things simultaneously: that it was Aunt Kristine sitting there, and that she was crying.

His first impulse was to creep in again. With all his heart he hated the situations he always seemed to get caught in, finding out secrets people were trying to conceal. But at the same moment he was overcome by a tenderness which made him forget everything else, even the distant calls of his own name which he could hear from afar, behind the closed doors.

He scraped his foot along the balcony floor. She got up at once and came towards him up the low steps.

'Oh, is it Kristine?' he said in a surprised voice; for once he found it difficult to get the words out. 'I just came out to get some fresh air,' he added quickly. They met on the top step. A single ray of light caught one of her eyes; there were no tears, but it was dark from crying.

'You too, my dear?' she said and gave him a quick hug. He felt a hot wave pass over him, so different from the detached feeling he was used to from a thousand hugs from his aunts. His throat tightened.

'Aren't you cold?' he asked out into the darkness, towards where her face must be. He reached out his hand, without any other design than to make contact with something in this unfamiliar situation. His hand met a soft breast. It rested there for just a moment before it dropped back as if it were cut off at the wrist. His body left the balcony they were standing on, as if it was floating with its legs upwards out into a dizzying red room. And before he knew what he was doing he had put his arms around her neck and pulled her head down to his. He put his mouth on hers and floated off again in a moaning somersault into space.

'But my dear!' she said, pulling away. The scent of her was vanilla and cocoa, it enveloped them like a defence against the rest of the world. The last desperate notes of the two-step sounded piercing through the night, and the thumping sound of all the feet in a last mad leaping run across the floor.

'You're not angry with me, Kristine?' he whispered to her. 'Are you cold?' He could feel she was shaking. He could feel that he was shaking too. Now they could clearly hear the voices from inside. There were many of them shouting for Wilfred and Little Lord.

'Hurry up, go in!' she whispered. She stroked his head quickly and clasped his hands in her soft warm hands.

'I'm not angry. Not angry. On the contrary …'

He felt a quick push in his back and tiptoed in, stole behind the golden drapes and entered unseen, so that he was standing in the middle of the room before they could shout any more.

Where had he been? What had he been doing? The questions rained down on him; not aggressive, but curious. He summoned up all his presence of mind and answered that he'd been getting some fresh air, it was so warm. 'I've been flying!' he thought.

Most of the guests were already in the hall, where they were being helped into their coats in irritated haste by sleepy servants. Their outer clothes looked grey and workaday on top of all those festive sailor suits, over all the bright dresses and red ribbons. It was as if small bonfires of exuberance were extinguished by their everyday wear, a blaze of festivity and pleasure which now merely glowed in red cheeks and tired eyes as the farewells and thanks gradually died away in the stairwell, and two or three waiting carriages rolled away, whilst the scattered remnants of the gathering walked off, subdued, with their accompanying maids, and the most independent ones, those who had not been collected, set off in isolated groups of four or five through the silent night streets.

Mother and son came back from the hall. In the dining room the maids were moving the table and chairs back into their places. Aunt Kristine was there now as well, he caught a glimpse of her through the open door. The breeze from the open windows in the dining room blew in refreshingly under the billowing curtains and dispelled the perfumes of the children's hall.

'Well, was it a success, darling?'

'Fantastic, Mother – thank you so much for this evening!'

She looked searchingly at him: 'You were absent for a long time – ?'

'It was so warm in here; all these – children!'

It slipped out. He heard the words and was surprised himself. Mother kept looking at him. Then she went to the doorway and announced: 'I think we'll leave the rest of the clearing-up for this evening. Thank you for your help, all of you.' Then something occurred to her, and she went quickly over to the writing-desk and took out her purse. The extra help curtseyed deeply and the maids said thank you for the tip.

'And you, Kristine, a thousand thanks for helping me yet again, me and Little Lord.'

He was standing in the middle of the floor in the large living room and heard the name Kristine as if for the first time – so full of melody, of song and secrecy. At that moment Aunt Kristine came into the room. Suddenly they were standing face to face. He felt a flutter of unaccustomed embarrassment. But the next moment it was transformed into a dizzying feeling which overwhelmed him yet again, and filled him with a sweetness which almost lifted him off the ground. He took a step towards her, but she raised her hand almost imperceptibly. As she did so, Mother came in again.

'And now it's time you were in bed, my boy!' It sounded so unexpectedly brisk, like when Uncle Martin said humorously manly things to him. There was something unnatural about it. Instantly he adopted the behaviour of a well-brought-up child. He held out his hand without looking up at Aunt Kristine: 'Thank you for your help!' And he turned round in the doorway: 'Thank you, Mama!' For a moment his glance rested on both of them. It felt like a blow inside him as his glance met Kristine's. 'Good night,' he whispered to the door as he went out.

The two women stood together like strangers. Susanna said:

'I have a strange feeling that this was his last children's ball.' And when the other did not reply: 'And now we two will have a well-deserved glass of port before we go to bed.'

'Thank you, Susanna, but I don't think I will tonight,' was the unexpected reply. 'Besides, I feel rather tired; you know, I think I'll go back to my own place tonight.'

'But my dear. We've made up a bed in the guest room for you. You always … And then all on your own – the streets …'

Kristine shrugged: 'Really, you think we live in a town full of thieves and robbers … Seriously, Susanna, I would rather go home.'

Fru Sagen stood for a moment on the steps out to the street. She followed with her eyes the still youthful figure as it crossed over, turned and waved. Then she remained standing for a while longer. It was deserted everywhere, not a person in sight; it was night. It was as if the house behind her wanted nothing from her right now, as if something was over. She was so unused to thinking, she didn't know what it was and didn't even register that there was anything.

She was so unused to thinking. But instinct found its way in her, and told her that something was over and that everything which lay ahead was uncertain and different. And when she went back through the rooms it was as if there had never been any party here, as if all the young people had been ghosts – as if everything was being lost in something intangible and worrying, all this which was *hers.*

She went over to the fireplace and jabbed a poker anxiously at the last glowing log, to make sure it wouldn't send out any sparks. As she straightened up and replaced the poker on its stand her glance fell on the photographs there: one of her husband, Christian Fredrik Sagen, as a young man, wearing the uniform of a ship's captain; the other of Little Lord with his soft curls falling over his collar. And she stood there letting her eyes wander from one to the other; to and fro her eyes wandered, and when she really tried to focus on one, they slid over to the other. In a way both became one, and in a way they receded into the distance as well – both of them.

Then she quickly gathered up the train of her gown and walked alone through the hall and up the stairs.

8

Now things were closing in around him; now he began to know them. It was as if the spring shed its light over them and showed them separately, so that he could see everything clearly. He would defy them, or else he would surrender, surrender to everything. His own body became his dearest friend and his bitterest enemy, a source of delight and shame in unbroken succession. And in this tapestry of abruptly shifting happiness and unhappiness his awareness of the tensions around him was growing. He noticed the open watchfulness on Uncle Martin's face, and a certain reserve even in Uncle René, on the occasions when Wilfred visited him by arrangement so that the two of them could plunge into Uncle René's marvellous art books and together investigate 'The Lady in Blue' or one of those still lifes by Braque which sent cold shivers of joy through him when he arranged in his own mind all the disparate elements of the picture according to an inherent musical principle.

Watchfulness and reserve …

Even Mother was not in all things the friend he could always approach as a matter of course, and he realized in deep shame that it was his own fault, because he couldn't confide in her, because all his thoughts went to Aunt Kristine with the secret depths within her, deep between her round breasts, the deep abyss in her eyes, the depth of secrets in a sorrow that only he knew of and yet in the last analysis knew nothing of at all.

The whole world around him was a conspiracy of suspicions aimed at everything which was covert in his own mind and his own actions. The world around him was full of suspicion about his defeats and his desire for transgression; a lurking jungle where *discovery* lay in wait with yellow eyes, waiting to encircle him and creep carefully forwards, a little bit further forwards each day – so that finally one day or night it would attack him from all sides at once and capture him in a net of guilt.

During this time he was doing well at school. He always did when the summer holidays were approaching. He was possessed by an ambition to come top in exams every single year. It used to be in order to make Mother happy. But this year it was to spite her, because he suspected that she didn't think so highly of him now. In addition it was the last year he would be attending Frøknene Wollkwarts' school. From the autumn he would be moving to a 'proper' school, to Uncle Martin's relief.

It was important to have *something* in order in the midst of this cauldron of contradictions and guilt. He wanted to arrange his *sortie*, as Uncle René had put it. You should always make sure that your *sortie* was in order. At least when nothing else was in order.

But his success didn't make things any easier for him. The constant praise from Frøknene Wollkwarts made him think that they would be writing home again in order to reassure Mother. He became tired and hollow-eyed from all his nervous speculation. Every morning he loitered in the doorway, tense as to whether the postman might bring a letter which would reveal an earlier correspondence. But the maid Lilly also loitered in the doorway, and every single morning they had a silent and hostile race from their respective doors, over the hall floor, to get to the postman first. She hated him now, Lilly, he knew it deep inside. And he felt that she suspected or knew something. Neither did he have luck on his side in all his shady enterprises any longer, it was as if his luck and his insouciance had deserted him at the same time. All his gleeful dissimulation was clothed in a mask which undermined its effect, and that mask positively shouted to the world: I am false. No, things would not work in his favour any longer. One day when he came home from school she came towards him with a letter in her hand; it was crumpled; she must have read it several times; it must have tormented her.

'I don't understand, my dear, here is a letter from your teacher, she writes that she is pleased with you now, that you are doing well in all subjects and you'll perhaps come top in the exams after all.'

He tried the old carefree expression.

'Wonderful, Mama!' The exclamation sounded forced. 'Aren't

you proud of me, then?'

'But I don't understand,' she repeated. 'Haven't you worked hard and done well all the time? It's not many months since she wrote …'

He could have thrown himself into her arms then, he could have played the old trick with tears in his eyes and confessed everything, or nearly everything – all that seemed so overwhelming. But the impulse to surrender himself was met by an opposing impulse: to let the mystery remain open, to let her fear grow slowly. He said indifferently: 'Oh, there was a time when things were going really badly. Perhaps she thinks she's written to you about that.'

Mother stood there with the letter in her hand. He could see that her fingers were crumpling it nervously. He knew those hands, he had loved them as he had loved everything about her, and her hand informed him that she was greatly confused, halfway between wanting to believe and not being able to. And he knew that it would take only one more word on his part for her to believe the best with utter certainty, that she would repress and forget all doubt and all unpleasantness, as so often, yes, as she always did.

But he didn't give her that word. Something in him refused to give her it any longer. Something in him thought defiantly: you'll have to grow up some time, you too, just like your brother Uncle Martin, just like – Aunt Kristine. *She* has a sorrow to bear.

A sorrow to bear – he wanted that too. One single proper sorrow and not all these worries which just created unease and fear every time he went through a door. He wanted to be like Aunt Kristine: to have a sorrow. Or to share her sorrow, to comfort her, no, to bear it for her – all alone! – So that she could cease to have any sorrow and just waft her fragrance towards him with an abyss between her breasts.

'I shall come top in exams, Mama, don't think any more about it,' he said shortly and left her. He stopped for a moment outside the door, he stood behind the closed door and *saw* her standing quite still in the middle of the living room floor, with the mysterious letter in her hand. He knew that if there had been anything bad in that letter she would have defended him through thick and thin; nothing could have broken her resistance then. But there was something good which she couldn't understand. Soon everything would become clear to her; that he had become another, that he was his own person, full of desire and secret deeds. Best to let it come. Best to let his happy childhood come tumbling down with a crash.

He walked through the hall and up the stairs to his room. There he remained standing irresolutely between his bed and his desk. And at the same moment he saw everything in a new light. His little paradise, so different always from the messy dens of cluttered boys' rooms he had seen at his friends; so completely and absolutely his own it had been; so *present* … now it was a child's room, a room to grow out of.

And still he was aware that he could run downstairs, that he could slip in to Mother and lay his head on her lap and say … no, he wouldn't need to say anything. It was enough that he *was*.

But he didn't want to. His legs wanted to, but his thoughts didn't. His thoughts were a spiky globe, like the globe on top of the old night-watchman's staff in the hall at Uncle René's. A globe from which the spikes bristled in all directions, wanted to go their separate ways, out to do violence at night …

Then there was a knock on the door. Fru Susanna Sagen was standing there. It was the first time he thought of her with her full name, a lady. He didn't notice that she was different now. She wasn't holding the letter in her hand.

'I forgot to tell you that the Sagens have written to us from Copenhagen,' she said, 'to ask whether we – or you – would like to come down this summer and spend the holiday in Gilleleje.'

Straightaway he walked into the trap – if it was a trap: 'But aren't we going to Skovly – you and I?'

He watched as her eyes filled with tears at once. And it was only then he realized that she had been different when she entered.

'Do you want to, then – just like we used to?' she said quietly.

Now he was in her arms. Now he was where he had always

been. And yet not quite in the same way; because now he knew that he was there.

'Of course I want to!' he said out loud, and yet in a strangely expressionless tone; so expressionless that he wondered whether she would notice. But she didn't notice. She gave him a hug and said in a little-girl voice: 'I didn't know whether you would want to – this year. And it is very kind of them to ask us.'

He pulled away awkwardly, feeling cheated. But he couldn't show that now. The good childish dissimulation surfaced in him again like a duty, and he said: 'It's not a proper summer unless we're at home in Skovly.'

It worked. He rejoiced in the fact that he had convinced her, that everything was good, as it had been before. He was filled with the happiness of making her happy: 'You must remember that one summer we spent at Gilleleje, how we missed Skovly, both of us – because you missed it as well, didn't you, Mama?'

He had done it. He saw her become sensible, become the adult on behalf of both of them, because he was a child.

'Well, in that case I'll write back at once then, and say many thanks for inviting us, but … oh, I'll think of something.'

'I'm sure you will, Mama!' he exclaimed enthusiastically. 'You'll come up with the right sort of excuse …'

They stood facing each other, she only half a head taller now, so young again, so carefree. They were almost the same person for a moment, a moment of intoxicated abandon to everything that had been.

'That's settled, then!' she said abruptly and turned away.

She was gone. He knew that she had to conceal her emotion. He sat down on the edge of the bed and felt a great emptiness descend on him.

That one summer down in Denmark with Papa's distant relatives – they had been so kind to him, and so alien … That painful longing every single day and night for the dear old wooden house in Hurumlandet. *That* was the incarnation of summer, with the deep garden with the fruit trees which had grown far too high and cast shadows so that it was like being at the bottom of the sea when you walked on the grass beneath

85

them … That had been the real summer, the only one; and perhaps it would continue to be real summer throughout his life. Every gap in the carved pattern on the veranda, where he had stuck his head through and pretended he was a watchdog and barked, and where he suddenly couldn't get his head through any more! Every path made golden by glinting sun between the tiny mounds which had been Mount Sinai and the Cape of Good Hope, and the two narrow streams which had been Tigris and Euphrates, and the old rotten bridge where Joseph's brothers had cast Joseph down and where a terrifying animal called Kakaksaks lived at the bottom … the old arbour under the linden tree with the solemn soughing in its crown, day and night the same quiet whispering voices to which he gave names and characters. The chestnut tree on the grass outside the kitchen door – with the green table beneath it where they gutted fish and picked over berries in the autumn. The smell of green leaves in his nostrils when he climbed the trees and picked cherries, with a basket hanging on the nearest branch … and of apples, the smell of newly-picked apples spread out over unvarnished wooden floors which had been scrubbed shiny clean to receive the autumn's harvest … The beach with the scary waves when large boats had passed – waves that once upon a time had driven him far up the shore, frightened as he had been of the surges of the sea, before the sea had captivated all his thoughts and challenged him to heroic deeds … The old brown-stained swimming hut with the rotten railings which were patched up a little every single year and were never any better – the first time he had *dived* from the diving board, and come up to the surface again after the daring deed with his curls plastered to his neck – and had looked up into Mother's face shining with pride …

And the quiet walks beneath dim hanging foliage towards evening; the heavy scent of jasmine around midsummer; secretive shadows beneath the trees which grew enormous towards dusk and turned into living, muttering beings with a message to everything around them. Breakfast on the patio with small birds which came in and cheekily ate crumbs off the cloth. The tame hedgehog they called Jonas …

That was every summer. That was every summer in one summer; a memory and a state at the same time, a bliss which was real and yet invented, because nothing was simply what it was; not the flag which they hoisted on Sunday mornings – it was a ritual. Nothing was simply what it was in summer, because everything *meant* something, *was* something in a make-believe way which was truer and greater than trees, sea and falling shadows: a richness without form and without borders, all joys in one joy which came at random and did not ask why.

He sat on the edge of his bed, feeling a great emptiness. It was as if all those summers gathered together inside him and turned into nothing, yes, as if the sum of all the joy which flooded through him at the memories – as if it suddenly exploded with a dull flash and dissolved into nothing.

He was frightened, then angry. Now he knew: she had set a trap for him, and he had walked into it with his eyes shut. Why not go to Denmark for once and have fun with his kind Danish relatives? They could be as alien as they wished: that was just the point. It could be a splendid escape from everything which surrounded him so threateningly. He was on the point of jumping up and running down to Mother to ask her to change her mind. He knew she would do so if he asked.

But he didn't get up. Suddenly he didn't have the strength to meet that little smile which would conceal her disappointment. There was also the problem with Father's relatives – he didn't really know whether she liked them, or they liked her. It was like all the other things about Father, all the things he didn't know.

There was also the thought that at Skovly – no doubt Aunt Kristine would visit them this summer, just as she always did. The thought passed through him like a lightning bolt, scary and sweet. He had *not* thought about that. It had *not* been part of the calculation. Just for once there had been no calculation. He knew it with certainty as he sat there. He knew it with a kind of pride.

He knew it with a little less certainty as he sat there – a little less and less certainty, that it hadn't been part of a kind of calculation. That suspicion too came to him with an awful pride.

*

Suddenly he was invaded by the memory of all the times at Skovly when he was afraid of the dark. More than that: he was *there* again. All the intervening time disappeared and he could smell the very scent of the panelled timber house with its silken wallpaper: a composite atmosphere created by a huge timber hall transformed into a rococo room with fleur-de-lys on the wallpaper and sofas and chairs with curved legs; worn white and faded gold, but shining, shining – a complete contradiction of the whole artificial national-romantic farmhouse with wooden carvings like a gigantic cuckoo clock. Timber logs and silk! On the outside a troll castle, on the inside a chocolate box. And how matter-of-course this glaring contradiction had always been – a house which had to look like that, that too a fixed *state* – until Uncle René one time had let fall a remark about style, and everyone had laughed. From that same moment he could *see* the house, but he loved it more from then on, as a sort of enchanted monstrosity, a palace for the most preposterous of princes …

Those nights in late summer when dusk gathered thickly around the house and enclosed it in drapes of darkness. That was when his cousins had been visiting. They shared the large east-facing room with him, with its made-up beds along three walls. And *he* had to go to bed first because he was the youngest; they insisted on their rights. He would hide away in all the corners to try and escape notice. Right until a voice said: '*Now*, Little Lord!' And there was no way out.

The trip through the deserted hall where one lonely lamp shone dully, intensifying the darkness; the stairs themselves, where he kept right over to the side by the banisters so they didn't creak; the long chilly corridor upstairs – and then the bedroom … He stood in the middle of the room, tingling with terror. The windows were empty holes against the blackness, and outside the linden tree bower whispered its eternal song. With one bound he was over by the windows and rolled down the blinds, first one, then the other, shutting out the night. But the dull blue surfaces of the roller blinds exuded darkness. Again he was standing there, white with panic, not daring to move, or to undress, or to light the lamp, nothing at all.

The box of matches on the dresser! That comforting little flame which diminished at once and didn't *want* to give him light … The glass lampshade, a big white one, which he lifted off gingerly so that it didn't touch the chimney, setting it down carefully in the darkness; then he lit another match and replaced the chimney quickly so that the flame began to draw. Those warm, welcome moments when the flame grew and he got the white lampshade on it and the light spread. Then the dreadful discovery that it didn't spread far enough, not everywhere, that there were dark patches outside the glow of the lamp; in them the horror lurked more intensely than in all the other darkness.

He stood right up against the lamp then, staring into its faint light and feeling the pulse hammering in his temples. Surely his cousins would come soon. He would hear them on the stairs, on the third step from the bottom which creaked, because they walked in the middle of the steps and at the side by the banisters. Such an endless expanse of time, an endless wait full of terror without bounds. The crashing of a distant sea was like thunder inside his head. From the corners hands reached out, and even the closed veranda door was no protection against the dreadful *outside* which wanted to come in. Not a scent, not a murmur could reach him to help. His own enormous loneliness grew into a separate being, a being which took up residence in him, invaded him from inside, so that not even the tiniest spring of courage was still present within him. He was dissolved by fear from the inside, could feel his own contours being rubbed out and disappearing, and the awful thing was that he could not move and prove that he existed in this process of total dissolution.

Then he heard the creak of the stairs. They were coming! Jubilation shot through him. Saved! Saved once more, but at the very last moment this time. In less than a second he regained his own boundaries within the room, regained contours and existence; the corners withdrew into their own darkness and became what they were, the boundaries of a room; the door to the *outside* became a protection, and the room inside took on its safe reassurance against the great terror.

But then a new fear shot through him, the fear of being caught red-handed, afraid. There were fourteen steps on the stairs. They had passed the third one when it creaked. Now they must be halfway or even further. They were coming. They would laugh at him. He moved quick as lightning to save himself: kicked his shoes off and under the bed, jumped into bed with his clothes on and pulled the duvet right up to his chin, lay as still as a post and breathed deeply and regularly as if he were in a deep sleep, whilst his heart hammered.

But his cousins were not taken in. 'Little Lord,' they whispered to test him. He answered with deep breathing. 'You're not asleep, we know you're not.'

And then the dreaded footsteps towards the bed. The duvet which was pulled off in a sudden jerk: 'Ha! In bed with his clothes on! Mummy's boy is afraid of the dark!'

Humiliation. Humiliation again, God knows how many times. Humiliation in front of his older cousins. 'Mummy's boy is frightened of the waves! Mummy's boy bathes in the pool with his mother! Mummy's boy daren't go to the privy in the dark and shits under the willow tree!'

And it was true, all of it was true. He lay stretched out beneath his assailants' scorn and was flayed alive by it. All of it was true, he was a coward, afraid of the water, afraid of the dark, afraid. And Uncle Martin's vile, well-brought-up brood missed no opportunity to assert themselves. They knew he didn't dare take revenge, because any attack would be an admission. He really had squatted under the willow tree once because he didn't dare go any further along the path between the bushes to the outhouse with the communal toilet, with its little child's seat an extra step up beside the two holes for adults. Hedgehogs and rats had crossed the path that evening, and the bats flew so low over the lilac hedge that it was as if they had come to take him with them in their darting flight. In the end he had squatted under the tree, but it was almost in the middle of the path anyway. And the next day someone had trodden in the result and his cousins called him Littleshit as soon as the grownups were out of earshot, and they had told Erna and Alfhild from the white house just behind the hedge, and the little girls in their light blue dresses which always smelt freshly ironed and – blue … they held their noses when Little Lord came past, and grimaced as they silently mouthed 'shit'.

And it was true that he bathed in the pool with Mother inside the leaky bathing-house which smelt of wet wood inside. Fearfully he climbed down the steep wooden ladder to Mother who was standing in the pool with water up to her breast, in her striped red and white swimsuit, where the pattern was chequered by the patches of sunlight that entered through the vertical planks surrounding the pool – and she had enticed him down into this degrading dance for frightened children, on the slimy bottom of the pool: 'Hop said the goose, dance said the fox, so we hop so we dance so we sit dooooown …' And on this 'dooooown' his head went right down under water and the world was splintered by a deathly fear which just made him wish for obliteration. And then Mother's laughing face when he came up again and was still alive … What treachery in that laughter, what deceit to first tempt him under and then laugh. And then all at once: the gust of laughter from his cousins who had stolen in to watch, the two laughing faces high up above the pool's lifting tackle with the threatening chain above an iron track with scratched lead paint. And Mother's all-too-mild reproach to them for standing there laughing: 'Just wait you two, one day Little Lord will swim like a fish, much better than you can!'

But no. He would never swim. They could hold him in a

harness just next to the bathing jetty as they did before. And he would do the same thing as last time: let himself sink when they slackened the harness rope to see whether he was floating a little bit; let himself sink right down and cling on to the rotten stump which had once been a mooring post, but had since decayed and sunk. He had clung on to the stump in order to die then and there, and however much they pulled on the harness from up above he didn't let go. He was strongest. He could die. That would serve them right.

He couldn't remember how it had ended that time, but someone had jumped in and loosened his grip on the stump and got him ashore. He had cried with shame and anger when he came round.

No, he was not going to swim. He would let them believe he was going to, he would set off with the large swimming ring around him and push off strongly from land, he would swim a few strokes out to sea in the ring, and then he would slip out of it and let himself sink. Then they would find him in the autumn when he drifted ashore by the lighthouse and was blue and bloated. Then Mother could play 'Hop said the goose' with the corpse until it disintegrated, just like that blue corpse of a dog they had found on the beach once and which he could never forget … And it was true that he would run like a wild thing far up the shore from the crash of the breakers as they arrived, those ominous shadows on the sea which turned into foaming monsters as soon as they found land on the long sloping beach and rushed with their jaws gaping wide to reach and swallow him.

There was much more which was true that they did not know about, and that he had a permanent terror they might discover. He was so frightened of thunderstorms that he felt nervous and twitchy as soon as they started to gather and no-one else had noticed they were coming, except perhaps for Mother; she was also nervous in thunderstorms. He was so frightened that he was even frightened of sunshine in July. For someone had once said that the sun and the heat made the air heavy, and in that way even the good weather was the source of terrors to come, so he became frightened of the sun too.

Every time the sun declined and the air grew cool he sighed in relief, he had been given a reprieve, it had not built up yet, but it would come. Then there were only the long shadows to be afraid of before dusk arrived in earnest. The long shadows were like forerunners of the dusk, sombre messengers who stole metre by metre over the grass and the low hills and drew their fearful pattern between the trees and whispered everywhere: now we are coming, we are the stealthy knights, but after us comes the great prince. Where those words came from he didn't know, but he knew that they would surface in him and bring their own terror, which he hid inside a different terror, the terror of being discovered.

And when the thunder began to rumble after hours of threatening build-up he felt himself growing more and more still, until his whole body was hollowed out by a nauseating sucking feeling which turned into stomach cramps as the first lightning flashed. He had found a particular way of concealing that terror, because Mother too became nervous and always retreated into a corner, where she sat looking at the wall. Then he retreated into the corner with her and sat beside her on a stool, as if to comfort her. And there was no-one who suspected the real reason, except perhaps Mother, because both of them were so terribly afraid. And once when the air was electric they had seen sparks flying between them in the darkness in the corner. They were like chosen ones for the lightning's threats.

After the thunder – that was the only time there was peace. When the wet grass shone in the cool new sun which had not yet had time to store up dangers, when the birds began to sing and the air at all levels was fresh and new, then his joy was without bounds, and he wandered alone through the trees and out onto the hills and down to the sea and thanked God in solemn hymns which he composed and sang loudly and emphatically: Dear Lord Our God Thy Mercy Is Fair Dear Lord Our God Thou Showst Thy Worth Dear Lord Our God Who Clears The Air Dear Lord Our God We Praise Thy Earth. And he could throw himself down onto this earth and burrow into it with his hands and thank it because it had not devoured him, and he knelt down on the shore at low tide and placed the palms of his hands gently on the water which was now calm as a mirror, and thanked it because it had not devoured him. And he stood on tiptoe in the light and begged it to continue to be light and not to let the darkness come and devour him. And he walked around the flowers on the glistening meadows and asked them to forgive him if he had trodden on them, and ran back to the path so as not to tread on any more blades of grass. All were friends *after the thunder*. For all must rejoice in eternal friendship that this time they had avoided annihilation.

Yes, it was things like that they laughed at him for, and much more besides. There was no limit to his defeats. Like that time he was five and had boasted that he was so good at reading and Mother was proud and let him read aloud from the newspaper, when he had read in secret eighteen thrilling instalments of 'Nick Carter, king of detectives' and had got as far as episode 19: 'Morris Carruther, king of criminals.' And he was going to read aloud for Mother and both cousins and his uncles and aunts on the patio. There were two columns on each side of those instalments, with no line between them, just a narrow space of white paper. And when he had been reading for a long time Uncle Martin got up with his glass in his hand and said that was a peculiar hodgepodge the boy was reading, and came over, glass in hand, and looked over his shoulder. Then he'd discovered that he was reading straight across the page, both columns together, and that's how he had read all eighteen instalments, that remarkable boy … The laughter when it came; giggles, cascades, waterfalls which drowned everything; mocking howls from his cousins under cover of the grownups.

Then he had got up calmly, hot with shame, and walked out onto the rocks and picked up a stone in his right hand and put his left hand flat on the rock, and then he had lifted the stone and brought it down with all his strength on the end of his left-hand ring finger, so that the joint was crushed and the nail had to be removed.

It was pleasure he had felt – the pleasure of humiliation. That summer all the shame had brought out a good side in him, which turned its meaning upside down and made the terror and the shame bearable.

Just as his joy at the sunshine stored up fear in him, so there was created inside him that sweetness of defeat which made *two* of everything which from the beginning had been *one*, which made his joy sad and the next moment made the terror sweet. And with all the shame, a taste like honey could spread through his body. And this taste of honey could stay with him during his flight from the waves, and make him continue the flight past the safety zone by the barberry bush, which was never splashed by the sea. And even the lightning brought him a touch of that sweet power, which flashed through him with pleasure at the terror.

Only that creeping fear which lived in the darkness held no hint of pleasure. Only the solemn hymn *after the thunder* held neither terror nor pleasure: The Good Lord …

Humiliation with pleasure – he had always felt it, when he thought about it. He had stood on the high mountain by the sea, alone on a bright summer's day, and thrown big stones straight up in the air one after the other, to see whether they would fall down on his head. And he carried on throwing for so long, stone after stone, and waited with his eyes closed and in unbearable tension – until finally a stone did fall on his head and made the world explode. Bleeding and half conscious he lay on the mountainside afterwards and felt the good and the bad pain, streams of blue and red through his body, and the deadening pain which grew in his head with the gaping wound, and his hair which was slippery with blood.

And when he stole – always with sweetness and terror in him. He was always stealing something during those terrified years. There was one warm July day with thin mist over the sea when he travelled into town with Mother, who was going shopping. At two o'clock they were standing on Stortorvet watching the golden ball sink down on the spire at Christiania Glasmagasin; then everyone knew that it was two o'clock. After that they went into the shop and he stood there holding Mother's hand with his right hand whilst she talked to the assistant, but with his left hand he was stealing tiny salt-cellars of coloured glass with a star on the base from the counter on *that* side; yellow, green and red salt-cellars; first one, then two and three, until he was gripped by fever and stole fistful after fistful of salt-cellars and shoved them quick as lightning into the pocket of his wide blue jacket, holding Mother's hand all the time. And it was good, it was good. And it was good that time he took the thin spout out of the oilcan by Mikal's bike which was leaning on the fence, and stabbed it into the rubber tyre on the front wheel so that the air came hissing out. But when his cousin came out and discovered the bike he was about to set off on, then it was just shame and not good any longer, and he couldn't confess because they wouldn't believe him, but just ask why, why … And once he stole an Indian elephant in ivory from Uncle René's cabinet and trudged through the town with it all the way out to Vaterland to sell it to a junk shop, but the owner threatened to call the police, and then it was just fear and not good. All that autumn he had gone around with the elephant in his pocket and hidden it in a different place each day, until one day he wrote a note from 'Father' and went to a different junk shop in the same street and was given eight kroner for the elephant, and it was completely dizzying and horrifying, and now everything was over. But it was good. Everything dangerous was good. But not what followed after the danger. To sink down was good, and never surface again, to be lost was good. But it was not good to come up again despite everything and have to be in tune with everything around, with the really good people who felt good being good. That was not good.

They knew it. They knew about him; the cousins, perhaps everyone, perhaps the whole world had a system for knowing everything about him.

But not the secrets. Those no-one could know. The important thing was to keep the secrets. They didn't know about the thunder, and not about the stones he threw up into the air –

not until that time they found him bleeding and he told them about a stone from the air, a meteor, about an enormous bird, because they didn't believe him, about a strange boy, a giant with a stone in his hand, a monster …

They knew nothing about the secrets. They knew nothing of the girl with the orange.

*

That long deserted corridor with the dull gaslight at the far end. That was where they lived at that time – with the toilet at the end of the long corridor and half a flight down into the bitter cold. Along the wall on one side there was a row of bottles on the shelf with specimens of adders pickled in alcohol; they hung in graceful curves, each in its own bottle in the gloom, and he called them something or other: Father.

And it was almost bearable on his way out to the cold, because he had the gaslight in front of him then, on the way out; besides, he was going to 'the little room' as they said … But on the way back, when the gaslight was behind him and there was just one long shadow growing, falling in waves across the bottles of adders, and there was darkness ahead and *lots* of darkness, and he couldn't know for sure that there was a door at the end of it, and that everything would open out in joy and happiness as soon as he reached that door and opened it to the hallway's gleaming light of hanging lamps and light from open doorways within … then it was not to be borne. All the time the corridor was there and there was just the gaslight behind him and everything was growing darker and darker, then the fear was ahead of him and no longer behind him; everything which could devour him lay ahead, everything without hope – for what if the door was not there? And what did he know about a door in the darkness, perhaps it had been an illusion?

Then there was a crack of light on the left-hand side of the corridor. In the gap between the shelves of bottled adders in the fading gleam of the gaslight, there was a light; and he could hear the chatter of voices inside. *The maids* lived there. Emma and Marie – they lived there. And he had never really registered that they actually *lived* there; because during the day they were just 'the maids' who polished shoes and made meals and cleaned and had days off. Now suddenly they lived there and existed and emerged from the night and became reality. And all he knew was that they would rescue him, because there was light through the crack of the door.

It was Emma. He remembered it now. No, not remembered. Because it *was*. You don't remember. You are, you know; he knew it all at once. You experience once and for all or you pass by. It was Emma.

There were two beds when he stormed in. He'd never been in the maids' room before. There were two beds which stood on either side of the room, to the right and left of the door. Straight ahead was the window with the roller blind and a vase of flowers painted on it. And in front of it a chest of drawers with two plaster horses, their necks crossing.

The one in the bed on the left had already settled down; it was Marie, the kitchen maid. She muttered something grumpy and turned over; she was asleep. But Emma had not gone to bed. She was just about to. She was standing there in her corset and lacy bloomers, an unfamiliar and delightful revelation. Of safety, and – he was instantly aware of it – of danger.

It was Emma. And she had smiled and understood. 'Were you frightened?' she said. And she was unlacing her corset at the same time, just like Mother did. 'Were you frightened?' she said.

And Emma said: 'You shouldn't be frightened!' She said it as he lay with his head in her lap and almost forced her down onto the bed. She said: 'I'll go in with you and put you to bed; that miss who looks after you has already gone to bed.' And he knew now that he had known at the time that she said 'miss' with contempt and hostility.

And he had bored into her, to Emma, forced her down, in fear that she might leave him or take him away from there. For this was what was good, safety and fear mixed together. It was Emma who said: 'What *are* you doing!' in a voice he didn't

know, and 'What *are* you doing!' in a voice he knew less and
less – which said: 'What are you doing. What are you …' In a
voice he had never heard. Whilst he bored and bored into her
for fear that it might stop, for fear of the corridor out there, of
the gaslight and the bottled adders which might be called
Father, for fear that something would happen again which had
happened before and which was not part of the satisfied fear of
letting yourself sink underwater and biting fast to something
right down there, right inside, which never ceased and from
which no-one returned.

And the voice which had said: 'What *are* you doing!'

And he lay in the seaweed and bit fast, clung fast to the
innermost darkness which must not let go, which was death
which was life which was fear which was pleasure which was
drowning.

It was Emma, it was the voice, it was the depths, it was Emma,
it was the gaslight at the end of the long corridor and the smell
of the toilet, and good and bad and everything everything
everything.

Marie was snoring in the other bed. He knew that now,
always: Marie was snoring in the other bed. And that too was a
part of the pleasure: that it disturbed him, created secrets and
a special space, that everything expanded into infinity.

He died there. He smelt the scent of damp wallpaper and
died. He heard the hiss of the distant gaslight and knew
everything and died. And it was good to die. He wanted to die.
And if he lived on he would die again. Always.

It was Emma. She was faithless. She said to Marie, who woke
up: 'I think the boy is crazy, only five years old!' She stood with
the gardener under the carriage-shed roof one evening and
said: 'What *are* you doing …' in just the same way. He knew.
Always and now. The times flowed together.

But she was good to him that evening. She took him back
and put him to bed when the horrible moment came and he
came *up* again; when he knew that life would go on, that the
good obliteration was over and was not the end of everything
as it should have been.

Perhaps the world knew everything – was there a secret system which existed just in order to display his shame? But she had been good. She had put him to bed and tucked the duvet around him and said: 'When Mummy is away then …' And he had smelt it: the scent of oranges. He had smelt it, but he hadn't dreamt it, for Emma didn't smell of oranges. She smelt of honey. It was something else. It was the sight of Emma as he came in.

And suddenly he looked up from the edge of the bed where he was sitting, looked up at the wall, at the picture which hung there, a pathetic reproduction in oil: 'Girl with an Orange' … Time and space disappeared in layer after layer and flowed into one. *That* was it – the picture which had hung over Emma's bed, which had stayed with them in move after move through the years of upheaval …

It was *that* picture, that idiotic picture which had filled him with sweet horror every time his glance had fallen on it and which he could not bring himself to throw away. A mockery the whole thing, a brown-eyed lass with an orange in her hand, a cracked oilprint in his room, he who was familiar with Degas' ballet dancers, who had bathed his eyes in Bonnard's blue. 'Girl with an Orange' – that repulsive creature in a simple gold frame, that was Emma, all his shame and desire in terror of the long corridor of darkness.

He got up angrily and went over to the picture, wanted to seize it in both hands, tear it down from the wall, smash the frame over his knee, rip the picture to shreds and hurl it out of the window.

But as he stood there, shaking, in front of the girl with the orange, she changed expression before his eyes, *took on* an expression: it was Kristine, Aunt Kristine – could be; looked like …

Rubbish. It was a poor reproduction of some banal 'masterpiece', one of those rectangular horrors moved from maids' room to maids' room to cover up marks on the wallpaper.

And yet: it looked like Kristine. It had the secretive melody of her glance. Did Kristine have brown eyes? Of course she had brown eyes. Surely he had always known that? Her hands, a little lazy, resting in a loose grip around the fruit, just like Aunt Kristine's caressing hands which took hold of everything so gently; hands without decisiveness, but also without virtue, confectioner's hands …

He stood in unconscious revolt in front of the picture he hated; lowered his own thin hands which were also so full of shame. Recently – just a moment ago – he had wanted to use them to shatter that stupid picture, now he lifted them again to caress the cracked surface shyly. But the moment his fingers touched the hands holding the orange it was as if a cold fire of fear and desire shot through his whole body. The girl in the picture looked at him in imperturbable amazement, the girl in the picture from the maids' room. It had stayed with him through all the years since then; it had persecuted him. So there *was* a secret alliance of powers which wished him ill, which wanted to expose him through and through and destroy him with shame.

Yes, he had suspected it. His luck had deserted him, luck from the disguises and the lawless expeditions, from his guilt-ridden self-love. They could come and take him now: his cousins, Frøken Wollkwarts. For he was the only one who knew that pleasure and horror are the same thing and that desire carries with it regret, and regret carries desire. He wanted good for the sake of evil, and evil for the sake of good. He wanted to drown; to besmirch himself in order to become clean to besmirch himself to become clean … He wanted to fall to be able to rise, then to fall and to rise again.

He wanted to fall. He sank to his knees by his bed and buried his face in the crocheted pattern of the bedspread. And when the ecstasy of weeping overtook him it was as if he was carried on waves over land and sea, through kingdoms of sun which blackened in the light and slowly grew red: a dark sun. But the waves carried him onwards through water, through purifying blue and patches of light filtered through the branches of fruit trees to a land of green moonlight where light was shadow and shadow light and where it was good to shrink gradually to nothing: the cessation of everything.

'Kristine,' he sobbed.

9

He awoke on the floor where he had fallen asleep. He was aware at once of what had happened. It had happened to him before at moments of strong emotion, falling asleep without warning.

The moonlight fell in a broad stripe across the table and the floor with the velvety bedside rug which turned green in moonlight. He took out his pocket watch and turned its face to the light. It had stopped at one o'clock. Had anyone been in and seen him sleeping like this? The thought filled him with shivering distaste, like all exposure.

He went to the door. It was locked, thank God, he must have locked it in his agitation when Mother had gone. He must have slept through dinner, supper, everything. So no doubt they had come and knocked cautiously, but they never woke him when he slept like that during the day. They knew his sleeping fits.

With his shoes in his hand he crept downstairs, through the hall and into the living room. The room was bathed in moonlight. The clock on the mantelpiece under the glass dome showed five past one. He looked at his own watch. It said one o'clock. It must have stopped at the moment he woke. The thought immediately made him feel anxious. Shivering, he stood there in the cold light and thought: I was asleep, so I was alive – but now?

His own room upstairs suddenly seemed eerie to him; he didn't want to go back there. He looked out at the dark lid of Frognerkilen bay, pierced by a spear of moonlight. He would get his bike; he wanted to be out in the night, cycle until he felt free. He acted quickly so as not to change his mind. He took a box of matches from the shelf on the fireplace, hurried through the hall still carrying his shoes, grabbed his grey coat from its hook, dropped the latch quietly and tiptoed down to the outer hallway where the bike stood. The outside door was locked.

The door upstairs was latched. He was in a trap, in a stairway with eight steps which he couldn't see, but which he could feel around him with greater clarity than all those times he had stormed up them two steps at a time, or stolen down them deep in thought.

He was thinking sharply now, a trapped animal. He could feel pleasure at the unexpected pulsing joyfully through his veins. He picked out the thinnest key from his cycle kit and pushed it into the old lock on the outside door. He concentrated intensely on what a lock might look like inside, he would have to investigate that some time. Some day it might perhaps be fun to break in somewhere rather than out – some day or other.

A blessed feeling of triumph surged through him as the lock gave way. He hadn't expected it. It struck him that he was always amazed when something worked. He pushed his bike out and closed the outer door silently.

The carbide light wouldn't light. It didn't matter. It was moonlight and bright. He put the matches in his pocket and threw his leg over the bike. He was filled with a sense of glee. He cycled over the sharp shadows of the avenue's trees on the road, like a staircase with no bumps between the steps. It was easy; everything was easy. The glee danced inside him and made him sing out loud as he emerged onto Drammensveien. Where should he go? He would follow the moon!

I shall follow the moon, he sang, pleased with the impulse. He had to cycle uphill, he was so full of power. Not until he was up in Løvenskiolds gate did he feel that he had used his breath and his muscles sufficiently to be able to slow down and abandon himself to freedom.

Lille Frogner Farm lay bathed in moonlight. He decided to take the narrow path which led up the hill through the farm, between the main house and the outbuildings; the path was muddy there and it smelt of warm cow. It was so slippery that he had to get off his bike and wheel it through the houses. There it was completely dark, the moon didn't reach it. He went slower and slower on the treacherous path. He got out of breath, but he was possessed by a vague desire for all things.

He stopped to get his breath back between the houses, to inhale the smell of animals. Here was a piece of farmland between the villas and the yellow apartment blocks, just next to pastures where sheep grazed in spring and autumn. He felt the desire to *see* these houses, to see the crevice he was walking in deep in the darkness, he wanted to know everything. He struck a match and looked around quickly as it flared up. He struck another one, looking greedily around at the unfamiliar objects: a dark red outhouse wall which rose up into the moonlight and vanished there – and on the other side the corner of the main house, greyish-white and worn. He lit match after match in his urge to see, suddenly obsessed by the idea. He wanted to see it all, he wanted to have the good feeling of seeing, seeing it light up. He struck the matches two at a time.

But he couldn't see enough, he wanted to see more. He used a match to illuminate the ground to see whether there was anything he could set fire to which would provide light, so that he could see here between the houses where anything could happen and seeing was vital.

There were a few twigs a little way up the hill. He collected them together, his hand shaking. He had only three matches left now. He had to be careful if he was going to get the fire to light. He put down his bike and knelt down. The first match blew out as it was lit.

He was filled with a terror of not being able to *see*. The second match he carefully shaded with his hand, and lowered beneath the thin twigs; they glowed but did not catch fire.

He crouched down close to the fire. There was a faint glow in the long sticks. He wanted to have a light here between the houses in the good smell of animals and manure, he wanted to make it flame up in a great joyfulness he could only imagine. He wanted to hear the fire crackling, and see; yes, *see* how the flames brought everything around to life, made the houses come alive.

The third match made the fire catch. He lay down flat on his stomach and blew cautiously; the flame was born, it grew bigger, not big, but a little bigger. He was filled with glee, this was what he wanted.

He took his watchful gaze from the fire and saw that the flames were already throwing light over the red outhouse wall which had been a shadow in the night. It started to come alive in small patches, as if he were creating it out of the night so that it could be *seen*. Everything should be visible, should live and be alight around him. Delight was streaming though all his limbs. He was a part of the great lawlessness which was also in its way alight, full of joy and raised up above all small acts of lawlessness. It grew into a great flame inside him, it rushed up high into the air and sucked up other flames after it, sucked the small fire after it too. Suddenly it was growing rapidly.

Then he heard footsteps and a door creaking. He started up, jerked back into a reality which had become distant. He stamped out the fire and grabbed hold of the handlebars in the same movement. Now he could hear the outside door being opened behind him and detected a gleam of light from the back over his shoulder. But he was already in the saddle! He was in flight through the dark and thrilling void. The bike slid down the muddy path. Then he felt solid ground beneath his wheels and swung up Bondejord Hill; that would slow him down. But in a moment he would reach the crowded wooden buildings of Briskeby and be able to hide amongst the low houses there, where the trees gave shelter from the moonlight.

When he reached the passage between the low wooden houses it was quiet, nothing was happening. He lay down and listened for a moment, but couldn't take his time, he changed direction and went left again. Suddenly he couldn't think clearly any more – his head had been so clear! I'm doing something stupid now, he thought. But he had run out of ideas. The coast was clear in Briskebyveien. Uranienborg church was bathed in light. I should have stayed in there amongst the houses, he thought. The moonlight fell brightly over the old smithy at the end of Industrigaten. He could read the smith's sign. SMEDJE, it said. Then there was the whole crowd of old wooden houses along the right side of Industrigaten again, but he didn't take the time to swing in amongst them either, he had lost his calmness now. He felt he could hear people everywhere.

The street leading upwards was a muddy lane, but he kept to the edge where it was hard. No-one could have followed him on foot, but on horseback? Or in an automobile? The police had automobiles, he had read about it. He had read about bands of thieves with automobiles in France, who robbed banks and were pursued with guns across the whole country … He himself was a thief in an automobile being pursued by others. He leaned forwards on his bike and streaked through the night like the moon's evil friend, a creature who created fear. Fright and exultation hummed through him, creating a storm in his veins, of tension, of driving blood …

He stopped in an unknown street. No pursuers anywhere. He hadn't met a single person, he now realized. No-one had been after him. The man at Lille Frogner Farm had no doubt put out the fire and gone in again.

But what had he been thinking? Who had he thought it was? All pleasure left him at the thought. What remained was once again the gaping fear of the consequences. Of the consequences which he always forgot when he was excited; there were many of them now, they were as yet undiscovered, but if they were linked together: the *consequences,* all the consequences …

He got off his bike and went up close to a house in order to read the street name on it. *Sorgenfrigade.*

The word sank deep into him as he stood there with his bike. What a street name, what a word: *sorgenfri*. Free of cares. Free of sorrow. A dream, a hope …

But perhaps many people were free of cares? Free of sorrow? He had wanted to take upon himself *one* sorrow, but he was frittering it away in cares caused by sudden impulses, what was he doing? And in icy fear he asked himself there in the street what he had intended with that fire. He saw animals breaking out, on fire, heard cows screaming from the stalls where they were tied up. Was that what he had wanted? He stood there gripping the cold handlebars. The moon was low in the sky, it was almost dark in the streets, but the light of morning was lurking.

His saddle suddenly twisted as he got up on it again; it must have come loose when he dropped his bike on the ground by the fire. He dismounted again and got out the heavy wrench in order to tighten the nuts. At that moment a policeman emerged from the darkness and said: 'Are you cycling without lights, my lad?' He was a small, broad man with a short dark beard under the black helmet with its gleaming spike. 'What are you doing out at this time anyway?' he said.

Little Lord became instantaneously cold and clear. I am Wilfred now, it shot through him, this is dangerous. He threw himself on the bike and pressed the pedal. But the policeman was quicker and grabbed hold of the back of the carrier. The bike tilted over. He put one foot on the ground, turned round quick as a flash with the wrench in his hand and hit out with all his strength at the hand which held him fast.

It let go at once, then made another grab, but this time into thin air. The boy and the bike had a lead of five paces. The man ran, but the distance increased. The boy felt a strength within him which could conquer miles and manpower. He swung round the next corner and sped down another street with tramlines, turned again and found a long straight road. He could hear a whistle blowing behind him, lonely in the night.

The deep exultation welled up in him again. He was riding a fiery horse at a gallop and his pursuers were thundering behind him: many hooves, many hooves! But they couldn't catch him. He didn't turn round, the street he was riding along was bumpy and treacherous. He kept his eyes concentrated on a metre in front of his tyre, terrified of being thrown to the ground by something unexpected. But they couldn't catch him. All was lost, or all was won. It was all to play for. A marvellous peace descended on him as he flew, yes, he flew, like a Blériot over the Channel.* Him with his cap on backwards!

A thought struck him: what if another policeman appeared and stopped him for riding without a light! He was the wanted night cyclist, he was 'the bicycle thief' of Kristiania. Time and space dissolved. But his brain was working quickly and clearly.

He stopped and looked round. The street was empty. He pushed the bike in between the bushes in a park and locked it, putting the key in his pocket. He walked uphill on a steep slope with no path, like a low forest. Was he out in the country? No whistles behind him, no people. Just the low moon which gradually rose higher and came into view as he climbed upwards.

On the top of Blåsen he sat down and looked at the fjord in the fading moonlight, a new world. A world so alien, with the Fagerborg Church spire close by and the dome of Trefoldighets Church standing out in the picture in the middle of the town – it caught the moonlight; so alien and distant a world that everything floated back to the time when he had fallen asleep with his longing that afternoon. Kristine – he had forgotten her since then. The girl with the orange …

Dead tired and wet with sweat, he lay down on the hill. But the tiredness had gone at the same moment. Everything which had happened was almost obliterated, or hidden as if behind a veil. The connection with what he had experienced at home in his room returned. The past – it had overwhelmed him then, like a kind of fainting. Now it became present again, everything that had wanted to force its way in, that he had fallen asleep to get away from.

There was something similar between that time and this. He knew it now. That he was facing a decision. He sat up on the hill and let the night stream into him …

The autumn after that summer with all the defeats. He had become the clever boy then – that was how it was, he had become the boy who did what they expected him to. For within himself he was on the way to knowing that defeat carried a kind of victory deep within it, and that the fear and pain would turn to courage and something good.

That was how it was. His first day at school, when he arrived with Mother and Frøken Wollkwarts asked questions. Yes, it was true he was starting school a little late, but on the other hand he could already read and write, and knew a little French. They had had a governess. He was the talented and modest boy who bowed politely but without embarrassment. He knew it all now, because it began to take the form of a plan from the first moment.

And the first family party he had gone to: the little charmer, whom aunts made a fuss of and uncles regarded with raised eyebrows. He remembered his schedule; nothing was to be left to chance. And normal life at home – now he dared to meet his cousins from Skovly. When he was seven they had been able to frighten him with everything. Now he was eight! From now on he could be self-aware, but within limits. 'Thank you' was a good word. 'Thank you very much' and 'many thanks' – they were good words, they made an impression. He learnt to say: 'Is that a new dress? It's very pretty.'

It was worse to face the ski jump. It was worse to learn to swim.

The terrifying abyss of the ski jump before the tiny platform which would swallow you in your flight!

The ski jump at home, in the garden down towards the railway line … That miniscule jump which Dick from next door built under his direction, and which they imagined they would come rushing down … and Dick was from Holland and not used to hills, and he himself … and Mother – Mother was sitting in the bay window then, sitting sewing or something, watching him encouragingly from the window. But she couldn't see him when he was on the slope, and he took off standing and fell and brushed off the snow at the foot of the slope where she couldn't see him, and went quickly back up the slope under the jump and skied down in a rush, all the way down to the fence, so that Mother would believe – did she believe? – that he hadn't fallen.

And again and again. He fell and brushed himself off, ordered Dick to measure the length, clambered up and pretended and *rushed* down, proudly erect when Mother saw him. Waved from where Mother could see him, and she waved back. Up again. Up again. Jumped and fell. Fell. Fell. And laughed at Dick who was from Holland and fell before the jump and was not used to hills …

His cousins who took him up to Stasjonsbakken by Huseby and all the horrible hills where Mother couldn't see. Mitts and hat with earmuffs and packed lunch in his breast pocket. And the dreadful jump, an abyss of terror. The final abyss – annihilation.

His cousins at the foot of the slope after jumping. His cousins at the jump, scornful, exultant. 'Aren't you coming?' 'Don't you dare?'

The slide, the inexorable slide towards the abyss, towards the jump, towards 'the brink of the chasm' … And then – the great nothingness. Hovering, dying. 'Four metres, boo – o – o!'

The happiness of discovering that he was alive when he had slid on his back with skis spreadeagled all the way down to the bottom. The bitter, fast zigzag up to the top, past the jump, past the jump: upwards. Again. The terror. The shout from below: 'Ready!'

Jumped. Fell. Jumped. 'Lean forwards, Little Lord!' Leant forwards. Fell on his back. Up again. Jumped and fell. Up again. The dread. Jumped, hovered, died. Fell. Leant forwards. Fell backwards. Was afraid. Was afraid. Afraid. He had made up his mind to do it. Stayed on his feet.

Why? He had made up his mind to do it. Made up his mind to jump, to swim, to be the best. Best of whom? Of all. At school. On the ski-slope. In the water. Best.

A year of terror. A winter … A year of toil, of the urge to kill the next-best who threatened to be the best … And a break with everything earthly when he learnt to swim the following summer. A flight, an initiation, a victory …

To feel the water running freely between your legs, to be aware of the depths beneath you in the dark, to be alive in the sea, be alive independent of the land. And not to be afraid … That had been his greatest victory, the greatest experience of all. It had driven almost all other fears out of him that summer – until it became a habit to be able to swim, and old terrors hesitantly returned.

And Uncle Martin who had stated over his glass on the balcony: 'Well, that boy has the makings of a man!' He had said it as if he had had grave doubts, but nonetheless. And Mother had said: 'Yes, of course, I've always known that …'

But little Aunt Valborg was the only one who had looked concerned at all his success: 'I think Little Lord is forcing himself, he's wearing himself out for us.'

And that was right, he was wearing himself out; but not for them, for himself, to be big and not to be mocked, to be able to open himself out and get to do all the secret things which were waiting, all the base things which were calling to him. He avoided Aunt Valborg's searching smile that winter, because she was the only one who had discovered part of the truth; perhaps it was because she was so small that she didn't look down on him from so high up.

He avoided investigation, kept away from searching glances, was always ready with his eagerness to help. At school he demonstrated a determination to be best which was bound to succeed; and he knew it all the time, and he knew that Frøknene Wollkwarts did not like it, however much they praised him. He knew it because it was part of his schedule to dazzle them so that they couldn't see into him, so that he could keep his secrets to himself.

On the other hand he had deliberately created secrets. He made secrets out of everything, out of the most innocent things. Dutifully and without appetite he ate food he didn't like, so that they would believe he liked it. ('Oh yes, Little Lord is really fond of tomato soup …') – it gave him a secret thrill to deceive them and a further thrill to register how easy it was if you were on your guard all the time. ('The lad is rather nervous, ma'am, I'm afraid he's being driven too hard …' – 'On the contrary, doctor, he positively loves school, and competitions and ski-jumping!')

He hated it. He was petrified. It was as if his stomach was being sucked out of him as he was waiting to jump, and the first time he went skiing with his class on the homemade slope near Tryvannet, he actually soiled his trousers as he was waiting up in the forest for his turn. But afterwards he polished the tiny silver cup eagerly and cast admiring glances at it standing on the shelf as proof: fifth prize. He would never get higher than that, he knew that. He knew that when they were ten years old and had to jump at Lille Heggehullet he would be found out, because it was impossible to lean forwards far enough when you were so frightened.

But the cup was a proof, proof of a step further along the road to freedom from discovery and mockery, so that he would one day be able to live his proper life in the world of secrets without anyone having any idea where or who he was.

He collected proofs, grades, praise. In homework he was weeks ahead, he learnt columns of the encyclopaedia off by heart and unearthed foreign loanwords from Meyer's dictionary, so that he could say *exceptional* and *variable* and *retrospective* and *inferior* straight out without hesitating, and without a sideways glance at the grown-ups, like children when they do something daring.

Once he had crushed a finger-joint in rage because they had caught him out in a pretence; that was the last time. He talked with Uncle René about *the representatives of Neo-Impressionism* and knew who he was talking about. He had discovered that everything can be learnt by heart, a way of behaving, a temperament.

He jumped up, shivering with cold, from his stone on top of Blåsen. The moon had set, it was beginning to get light in the north-east. He had been day-dreaming again, just like at home by his bed. Or had he?

All at once the events of the night appeared to him in all their clarity. He was in danger now. He might have set fire to a farm. He had hit a policeman with a helmet and beard. He was being pursued. A word occurred to him: *wanted*.

No, he had not been day-dreaming. He had drawn strength, that was it, from the thought of all his defeats and how he had conquered them. Now just like the time when he was six and seven – and all the years of false achievements since then – he was confronting a choice, a new battle for his secret world.

He had all the advantages and the others had none, because he alone knew what he knew, and because he was clever and well-brought-up and obedient and well-dressed. He was no patched-together poor boy who avoided eye contact when he was questioned and for that reason alone seemed guilty. He was the only one who had taken no-one into his confidence and couldn't be reached by suspicion so long as he remained lonely and false and showed no weakness – nothing of all those bubbling contradictory feelings which boiled inside him and at times threatened to explode him …

He soon found the way towards home. The morning was light and cold. He walked along holding the key to the bike chain in his pocket. The bike would have to stay in the bushes where he had left it; he could collect it later. A boy with a bike could be a dangerous object in the empty streets this early. … Or even better, he could get someone else to collect it – Andreas. It was a dangerous bike to be seen on in the near future, it was the only Raleigh he knew of. In fact Andreas could borrow it for a while after the exams were over. It wasn't so important to have a bike in the time remaining before they left for the country. And Andreas would be pleased and grateful. He walked homewards shivering slightly, and felt little spurts of warmth at the thought of making Andreas glad.

But it wasn't safe for him to be wandering the streets. He must get home. Yes, Andreas should have the bike. But he must get home now. If he only had some reason for being out. Someone could appear – a bearded policeman …

He heard someone coming further down the street. He ducked into a gateway. The footsteps came closer: police footsteps. He slipped into the porch, there were three steps up to a door which was locked. But he shrank back into the corner and heard the footsteps coming closer, then going past. Quickly he ran to the gateway and peered out. The back of a woman delivering papers shuffling along the row of houses, the heavy bag on a strap over her shoulder pulling her sideways. He breathed out in relief. The woman stopped and put the bag down. Then she took out a bundle of papers and unlocked a front door. She left the bag where it was.

A new thought occurred to him. The woman had used her own key for the outer door, it was a big block of flats, she would be away for a long time if she was going to go upstairs and put all those newspapers in the letterboxes.

As quick as a cat he was standing by the newspaper bag, and snatched up a bundle. He saw that the key was still in the door – she was obviously going to lock it again after her. For a moment he contemplated locking her in, in order to win time. But that shouldn't be necessary, he must surely have ten minutes' head start. Besides, the woman wouldn't notice that the papers had gone until she neared the end of her round. He ran round the nearest corner and came out in Theresegaten; it lay before him, empty and gloomy in the growing light. He took a chance and ran the first bit, then swung into Josefinegate at Bislet. If he met anyone between here and home he could slow down at once and study the houses he was passing: whether this was the right house … He was the hard-working boy from modest circumstances who delivered papers before school. He sneered in shamefaced triumph, then looked round alertly. It was important to enter adequately into the part, not completely. Play the part adequately. It was as if he had read it somewhere. That was his strong point – and he knew it now – playing the part adequately.

He met no-one. He didn't need to play any part at all. There was no-one living in this district who had to get up before dawn. He sneered at that too. There were so many to make fools of: those who were different, those who were your own sort, and yourself. He could laugh at everything when he wasn't afraid.

And he wasn't afraid. For he'd made up his mind. This time just like the last; and all his thoughts that day and night had led him towards this: to awareness of the fact that that summer and this time were two very similar periods, in which the main thing was to assert yourself, to be bold and clever, so that no-one could get close to you with guesses and suspicions. In that way you kept yourself for yourself and you could do remarkable things behind everyone's backs and laugh at them in secret.

114

All at once he remembered the stupid criminals from the Nick Carter serials. They had waved revolvers around and made a rumpus in the darkness, they had drawn attention to themselves so that any old policeman with a beard could have detected them, and ultimately it made no difference whether you read a story like that a column at a time or straight across the page. That thought made him feel light. It relieved a weight, the remains of a weight from long ago. He moved the bundle of papers across to his right arm and held up his damaged left ring finger in the morning light. The tip was still slightly flat, and the nail was striped lengthways. But it wasn't deformed. No-one could see it if they didn't know.

He smiled tautly. That was precisely it: no-one could know anything unless they already knew or suspected. He had a secret finger, but he also had a secret soul. The whole of him was secret.

When he reached the avenue leading to the house he looked round quickly; then he pushed the bundle of newspapers under the little footbridge over the ditch in front of the house next door. No-one would find it there, and in any case he could move it later. He looked at the time: quarter past six. In fifteen minutes the maids would get up. Then he would ring the front door bell and Lilly would open it and he would say that he'd got up early and gone out for a bit, he couldn't sleep any more, he'd slept so long yesterday. He'd say the whole thing or just part of it, depending on how Lilly seemed. He would be friendly, perhaps winning – or merely stand-offish and arrogant – depending on how Lilly seemed. He was full of confidence in chance now, in pretence: he was no longer indecisive; it had been a weakness, but it was past.

He went in through the door with the lock he had picked. *Morgenbladet* was wedged into the handle. The paperwoman didn't have a key to this house. He sneered at that too. He sat down on the stairs to wait until it was half-past six. Then he would ring and make Lilly believe him. After that he would lie down on his bed for a bit and then wash and go down early and meet his mother, well rested and energetic. He would make her happy by talking about the summer. He would worm out of her whether Aunt Kristine was going to visit them at Skovly this year …

The thought jolted hotly through him. He would make sure that Mother invited Kristine as before, and why shouldn't she? But first and foremost he would make Mother happy, she deserved it. Previously he had made her uneasy. That wasn't necessary any longer. It was because he had vacillated and been somehow split. Now he could simply make her happy by behaving as she expected, and live with the secrets inside him without her or anyone else noticing.

He sat down on the stairs. There was five minutes to go until half-past six. He yawned and threw a glance at the newspaper he was holding. His glance fell at once on a small headline:

CYCLING PYROMANIAC AT LARGE

The hallway rocked for a few seconds. Then he gathered himself together; it was like the ski-jump. 'Lean forwards!'

The letters slowly settled down in front of his eyes. About the tenant farmer at Lille Frogner Farm who had been awoken by a raging fire. About the pyromaniac who was frightened off and jumped onto a bike. A young man, might well be around 17 … vagrants had been seen in the area …

There you had it. The crooked smile appeared on the boy's face again. It wouldn't occur to them that the arsonist was fourteen for example, it wouldn't occur to them that he was a schoolboy, a very permanent resident from Drammensveien. He was about to laugh out loud when his glance fell on the following report:

ATTACK ON POLICEMAN

Again the hallway began to rock, the letters danced and shrank into thin stripes. Once again he pulled himself together before the jump and let it happen: … knocked him down with a heavy weapon … fled in the night. Was it the pyromaniac from Frogner?

He tried to smile, thinking that they were certainly making a meal of it.

But the smile wouldn't come now. He had to learn it: had to learn to smile all the time, even when no-one was looking. Just to be prepared … He read: 'apparently well-dressed, around 16, but it was extremely dark in Sorgenfrigate …'

Now he managed a smile, now he could do it. It was dark in Sorgenfrigate – that was good – it was pitch black and murky in Sorgenfrigate. Perhaps there were vagrants in that area too. Vagrants in the darkness in Sorgenfrigate, Nick Carter in Kristiania. Dark men aged around 17 who fled in the night after violence and arson. Unbridled glee was bubbling inside him.

But the glee had to be reined in as well, everything had to be reined in, fenced in, as a protection around the secrets. He looked at the time. Twenty to seven. Yes, he would adopt the bold approach to Lilly, regardless of how she looked. He was a conqueror now, a bold lad who'd been out for a morning walk.

He got up lightly and ran up the stairs with the newspaper in his hand, and gave a short, loud ring. Footsteps approached.

'Good morning, Lilly dear, here's your newspaper boy!'

10

It was examination time at Frøknene Wollkwarts' private school.

The large corner room with windows out to the street and to the schoolyard had been cleared of the two tables. Instead there were chairs set out along the walls for parents and figures of authority who had been invited to attend the oral examinations. The two Frøknene Wollkwarts themselves sat side by side on two chairs at one end of the room with a small table in front of them covered in books and registers. Frøken Anette raised and lowered her lorgnette according to whether she was directing her glance down at the books or out into the room. And this movement contributed to giving the ceremony its rhythm of action and evaluation. The pupils were summoned from the side room two at a time, and took their place in the middle of the floor during the examination.

Little Lord enjoyed this ceremony. He enjoyed the fact that unfamiliar grown-ups were present, it gave it an aura of performance; he knew his subjects inside out. He enjoyed having Mother enthroned in the row of mothers and the odd stranded father with an umbrella between his feet. He enjoyed the awareness of Mother's discreet elegance amongst all these strangers who observed each other stealthily. With his back to the auditorium and his face towards the expectant faces of the two Wollkwarts ladies, he had a faint impression of Mother's perfume enfolding his own significant figure, giving it a particular, supple self-confidence.

But even more he enjoyed the ceremony which followed, when the results were announced to varying degrees of silence from the audience. Then all the pupils were gathered into the large corner room and stood muttering in a group by the window to the schoolyard. One after the other they came forward and read a poem they had chosen themselves – it could be from the set texts for that year or from their own further reading. Many of the boys had chosen a psalm, partly because their incomprehensibility made them easier to memorize, and partly with a vague feeling that they would win sympathy by declaring themselves on the side of the god-fearing.

Little Lord felt a strange floating calm as he walked into the centre of the floor – this time facing the whole circle of listeners – and announced the title of the poem he had chosen.

'At the Mercy of the Farmer's Daughter – an old Danish ballad,' he said in a firm voice.*

A shudder of anticipation passed through the classroom. Frøken Anette Wollkwarts nodded trustingly and glanced quickly at her sister, who also nodded, somewhat uncertainly. There was something about this boy, he always had to choose something singular. But the word ballad commanded respect and confidence in his educational attainment; he was one of the pupils who read around their subjects.

Little Lord began:

> One day I was riding out of town,
> to visit a farmer's place;
> the farmer's daughter gave me a bed,
> but it led to my disgrace.
> For I could not sleep in peace.

Someone in the room cleared their throat as Little Lord continued:

> I asked her where her father was,
> 'At the assembly,' she said.
> I asked her where her mother was,
> 'She is asleep in bed…'

A certain restlessness was apparent. He could feel it both in front of and behind him; he saw the Wollkwarts sisters exchange an uncertain glance, but carried on regardless:

> When I had drunk for a little while,
> not long she did me spare,
> the maiden went to her father's barn
> and a bed she made me there.

Now there were loud whispers in the schoolroom. One of the Wollkwarts sisters made as if to stand up, but Little Lord was looking straight at the wall in front of him. He felt a fiery sweetness in his veins as he persisted. It had never happened at an end-of-year celebration that a pupil had been stopped because of the poem he had chosen.

> 'Now you must hear, you handsome youth,
> now you shall do my pleasure;
> or with the strength of my own hand
> your young life I shall sever.'

'Little Lord!' It was Frøken Signe who had finally stood up

fully: 'How many verses are there in this poem?'

'Seventeen, Frøken Wollkwarts.'

Frøken Wollkwarts pursed her lips in confusion, incapable of making a snap decision. Members of the audience looked at the ground or glanced furtively at one another. Little Lord continued:

> With one hand she pulled my hair,
> the other was on her knife:
> 'This moment you must do my pleasure,
> or I shall take your life.'

'Little Lord! I think – I think we have heard enough of this!'

It was Frøken Signe's voice. It had a metallic timbre, but even so it was half smothered by the whispering from the room. He *could* have missed hearing it, over-excited as pupils often were during this part of the end-of-year formalities.

> Then I stripped off my tunic
> stripped off my red shirt too …

'Wilfred!'

This time no-one could avoid hearing. He came as it were out of his deep trance and looked straight at Frøken Signe Wollkwarts.

'Frøken Wollkwarts?'

'We have had enough of your Danish ballads. I don't think you quite understand … I mean: they are really not suitable …'

Her glance slid over the rest of the assembly, perplexed. There was the odd hidden smile here and there on the lowered faces. The birds were twittering in the old trees in the schoolyard. Wilfred went back to the half-circle of boys at the end of the room.

'Next!'

Andreas came forward, looking pale.

'Ole-the-Flower-Seller by Jørgen Moe,' he said in a low, thick voice.*

'Louder, Andreas.'

'Ole-the-Flower-Seller by Jørgen Moe.'

It was not much louder. The birds twittered volubly outside.

'Very well. Begin.'

Everyone knew about Andreas' peculiar passion for 'Ole the Flower Seller'. Otherwise it was the action poems which were most often chosen, 'The Devil's Tune', 'Koll and his Axe', or 'Dyre Vaa'.* But no-one had ever heard Andreas recite 'Ole the Flower Seller'. It was just something he muttered to himself at quiet moments.

'I remember so well ...' someone whispered, in order to get him started.

'No whispering, please!'

Frøknene Wollkwarts were once again in command of the situation. Something unheard-of had occurred. Now it was vital to make things go smoothly, so that the solemnity of the end-of-year celebrations would have its traditional effect. All eyes were turned hopefully towards Andreas as he stood there dumbly on the floor, and on many lips you could read the all-important first line. And all at once out it came, as if out of a machine:

> I remember so well from my childhood days
> a bear who came ...

Laughter burst out from the group by the window. Parents and dignitaries tittered in a restrained manner. Signe Wollkwarts drew herself up authoritatively and roared: 'Silence!' It had more effect on the audience than on the pupils.

'You said "bear" by mistake, Andreas. It's easily done, it's nothing to laugh about.' A severe glance reprimanded the room. 'Of course it should be ... well, go on – or rather: start again.'

> I remember so well from my childhood days
> a bear who came ...

This time the laughter was irrepressible. Even Frøken Anette couldn't help smiling. But her sister cut through the frivolity: 'Of course you mean *beggar*, Andreas, don't you? It's the one where the poet remembers this sad story about the thoughtless children who nailed Ole's wooden clogs to the stairs so that he fell and was killed, isn't it?'

Waves of blushes flooded over Andreas' face. His hands opened and closed, opened and closed.

'Isn't it, Andreas?' repeated with a gentleness which carried an undertone of threat.

'I always thought it was a bear,' said Andreas quietly. 'That's why I thought it was so good.'

The laughter erupted again from walls and corners like an explosion. Andreas, the maths genius, dedicated geographer, perhaps a poet too in his own way – stood there utterly at a loss, looking as if a world of mystery and beauty had come crashing down around him. *A bear* was already spreading from mouth to mouth with its bleating sound; a sound for mocking and deriding. Frøknene Wollkwarts realized that this pupil must really have been a victim of a curious misunderstanding with reference to Jørgen Moe's childhood memories.

'That is completely impossible,' said Frøken Signe coldly.

Little Lord stood there in the group, feeling that she was betraying them, betraying one of her pupils to the mockery of the other boys, and to the laughter of the grown-up visitors.

'Frøken Wollkwarts,' he said in a loud voice. 'I always believed it was a bear as well.'

Suddenly it went deathly quiet.

'Nonsense, Wilfred,' said Frøken Signe calmly.

'I'm sorry, but I did. I can't help it.'

Again the situation was unheard-of. The examination ceremony at Frøknene Wollkwarts' preparatory school had always been marked by harmony and praiseworthy achievement. What sort of spirit had suddenly invaded the gathering? Parents convulsed with laughter and pupils who were behaving either like idiots or like revolutionaries.

'Next!' said Frøken Anette. She did not say it loudly or sharply, but her tone had a decisive ring. There were to be no further scandals today …

Little Lord's thoughts were in a whirl during the rest of the ceremony. Dully he followed verse after verse, heard how they were declaimed monotonously or with that studied expressiveness which grated on his ears even more. He knew them all and had worked out his own way of saying each one of them. Behind the dullness his thoughts tumbled to and fro in expectation of catastrophe.

Why had he chosen to prepare that singular ballad? It was true enough that he loved those half-incomprehensible relics which filled that thick volume with its drawings, which were so appealing to his imagination; it stood on the top shelf of the bookcase, on the far right. He had made them his own, and yet they belonged in a place where it was not so easy for him to reach them.

He liked the racy poem 'At the Mercy of the Farmer's Daughter', but it was not in his interests to challenge Frøknene Wollkwarts today, his last day at this school where he had in essence had such a good time and learnt so much. For whole days and nights he had been floating – yes, actually floating – in terror that his teachers and Mother might come into contact in some way or other which would expose his pretences over the years with letters and messages and all those tricks which must now stop. He also had a vague presentiment that once the first stone in the avalanche rolled down the cliff, a lot of other things would follow, and he would be left exposed as a depraved youngster in the eyes of everyone he was fond of. He stood there in torment amongst the other pupils, and asked himself coldly whether he was longing for catastrophe? For an exposure which would finally put an end to all the misery …

But that wasn't how it was. He had made himself a daily life filled with necessary secrets, and perfected it in its modest way during this last winter and spring. And all of this was merely a preparation for the mixture of humiliation and liberation which he would meet in the near future. Not for any price did he want to challenge these people, at a time when everything depended on them if it weren't to go wrong.

And yet he had challenged them. For the first time in the whole of this lawless spring he was seized with fear of himself; fear that he was not in control of what he set in motion. He knew that silly joke with the ballad was carefully planned. The other, about the bear, that had happened on the spur of the moment. But both episodes were equally risky for him, and almost equally incomprehensible. What was he thinking about, choosing that ballad? And the other thing: was it not a part of his plan that no-one should catch him doing anything spontaneous – that everything should be calculated in advance …

He felt Andreas' eyes on him. For a moment he half turned towards him. His eyes were shining in gratitude and despair. He saw a pale smile cross the face of the condemned man – the one who is condemned to be stupid.

Little Lord thought: he's grateful to me. I can use him for something when the occasion arises.

He kept close to Mother as they made their farewells. With all the means in his power he wanted to prevent any conversation between her and the teachers. With uncharacteristic clumsiness he interrupted the goodbyes just as Mother was standing shaking hands with the ladies. He apologized, but would not be put off. He managed to make the ceremony as short as possible. 'But Little Lord, what's wrong with you,' said Mother, 'grown-ups are supposed to say goodbye first, you know that very well.'

But he persisted, and got her to leave with him. Frøknene Wollkwarts stood there with sweet-and-sour smiles, struggling to maintain their authority. 'Exam nerves,' muttered Frøken Anette with panicky affability.

Mother and son walked down the street in silence. Everything looked barren in the sunlight. That good day – that day which had always been so good – all of a sudden it was a day full of threat.

She stopped. 'Little Lord,' she said, 'now I want an explanation.'

'But Mama, Frøken Wollkwarts was so nasty to Andreas!'

'That's not what I mean. That at a pinch I can accept. You did it in order to help a friend. You know what I mean. The ballad.'

They were standing together on the gravel pavement. They had walked here so many times – and four times previously after a similar exam ceremony, always in a good mood and full of anticipation.

'Aren't we going to Rolfsen's to eat Danish pastries today?' he asked.

'I don't know,' she said, and began walking slowly. Two heavy, horse-drawn waggons rumbled loudly over the uneven cobbles. It gave him time to think until the noise died down.

'Mama,' he said, 'if I'd read that poem out at one of Uncle René's music soirées …'

'What then?' she said coldly.

'Then you would have laughed.'

'No we would not.'

Once again Fru Sagen had that impotent sense of her own inadequacy. She had felt it briefly amongst the serious parents in that stifling schoolroom. But always before she'd had reason to be proud of her clever boy during the exams. Now it stole over her again.

'Are you sure about that?' he returned quietly.

She looked down at him, worried. It wasn't so much *down* any more. When was it he had grown like that?

And yet again that painful feeling that everything was about to change.

And then all at once the opposite, pleasure that everything was the way it was after all.

'Of course we're going to Rolfsen's.'

His hand slipped in under her arm. That warm, confident grip; an escort's arm, bringing a sense of loss and a flash of contentment all at once.

'Four Danish pastries?' he said coaxingly.

'Four Danish pastries.'

'The largest ones, the eight-øre ones?'

'The biggest they've got.'

'And hot chocolate with cream?'

'In this heat?'

'Mama, it must be hot chocolate with cream.'

'Very well then.'

They fell into step on the way down into town; arm in arm like an engaged couple, leaning slightly towards each other. In Rolfsen's on Egertorvet they sat in the innermost room with the marble ceiling and the gold-framed mirrors. Flakes of Danish pastry clung to his lips as he said: 'You know, Mama, wherever I finish up in my life and whatever I have to eat and drink, I know that nothing will be as fine and as good as this.'

She looked at him, touched and yet uneasy. There was something obsessive about his need to enjoy the best, to have a good time, which could occasionally frighten her, something which brought to mind the thought: one day when it's not just a matter of hot chocolate. One day when it's not me any more …

But her thoughts were once again of the sort which came and went, and when they went they had never been there, just knocked at the door like tiresome relatives you were expecting to visit, and therefore you thought you heard someone at the door. Her mind was not trained in dealing with unpleasant matters, so when she opened the door a crack there was no-one there …

'And after this, Mama, we'll walk home along the quayside, we haven't done that for such a long time.'

They walked home around the quays, the whole stretch from east to west. Full-rigged ships with bristling crossbeams, redolent of adventure, were rocking at anchor by the enormous buoys at Bjørvika, and the old, dirty grey *Kongshavn I* was being spruced up with paint and canvas over the rear deck, preparing for the lively traffic to Kongshavn Baths with its theatre and park. Little Lord could see signs of summer everywhere, but mostly the coming summer was evident in the smells from the sea, hot and sweet with all its variants of tar and rope. And all those great iron hulks with threatening black funnels towering up and sooty men in sweaters and trousers on deck; the foreign tongues. He'd often sneaked down here at dusk and seen mysterious women being helped on board, and heard words which could mean all sorts of things, depending on the way they were spoken; he had played with the idea of stowing away on a boat and vanishing into the world. He'd met other boys roaming around the docks with the same hapless longing in their eyes; they recognised one another at a glance and bolstered themselves with words they had picked up, and stories about the sea. It may be that none of them believed what the others said, but it didn't matter. For they were at the borders of the same unknown country and didn't begrudge the presence of others.

Now and then they heard whispered stories of someone who had really done it. Now and then he had seen a report in the paper …

Now here he was walking along with Mother on his arm. The day was bright and full, just beginning to fade. And it struck him as he walked along guessing the names of ships before they could see the letters, that a quayside like this was two things depending on how you experienced it, a boat was two things, he himself was two completely different people. And Mother? He peered searchingly up at her face, elegantly poised above the slim velvet collar of her suit, covered by and yet fully visible behind a grey veil as thin as a whisper: was she two completely different people? Was everyone? Was everything? Two or three or an endless number? Was the yellow main mast on the *Bonn* yellow to his eyes only, and e.g. blue to someone else? Or if it was yellow in everyone's eyes, was that simply because they had agreed about it – about what it meant to be yellow? Was the definition of Fru Sagen a stylish lady in bluish-grey with a youthful curve to her cheeks and mild, grey-blue eyes which matched her suit? Were her characteristics 'amusing', 'kind-hearted', 'easily swayed', 'lovable' … *Were* those her characteristics? Was *that* her? And why, if that was so – when he himself was walking along in this delightful moment and had hardly any features in common with the boy who roamed around the streets and along the quays on those darkening afternoons with his throat dry with desire and his eyes shining with lust for everything, things known and as yet unknown, which drew together into a fiery focus …

'Little Lord, you're forgetting to guess!'

'*Bonn*.'

'I can see that as well.' She was every bit as eager at playing the game as he was: 'But what about that one right out on Vippetangen?'

'Boo, that's the new *Kristianiafjord*, that is, everyone knows that.' Tall and straight and elegant, the nation's pride loomed over all the others with its two yellow funnels. Until quite recently the Danish boats bound for America had dominated this area. *Kong Frederik af Danmark* and whatever those great black boats with a red ring around the funnel were called.

'But the one behind it?' he asked, 'the one where you can only see the top of the funnel?'

'No, you can only see the top of the funnel, as you said.'

'*Kong Ring*,' he said triumphantly.

This time she thought he was bluffing. She wanted to catch him out now. They walked more quickly, and she was filled with an excited *Schadenfreude* she couldn't explain to herself; it must be the remains of a bad conscience because she had not been stricter earlier on.

But it was *Kong Ring*. The name shone out with yellow letters on a black background when they got close enough.

'Little Lord!' she said, disappointed and relieved at the same time. 'How have you managed to learn all these ships' names?'

'The boy is very quick to learn,' he imitated Frøken Signe's slightly fluting voice. Mother and son exchanged a quick glance. She shook her head gently, let her glance rest on all the summer activity, everything which was reminiscent of carefree days and the way things had been … Without daring to admit it to herself, she was imbued with a fear of everything which was not this, which was different, inexorable.

'Mama,' he said, 'let's go home along Ruseløkkveien and see where little Gudrun disappeared!'*

'But my dear, that's so unpleasant.'

'Do let's do it though, Mama. Shall we walk through Vika?'

His mother looked indignantly at him: 'You know very well that we can't walk through Vika, I can't.'

The low wooden buildings lay in front of them, with strange people crowded into narrow passages: the *others*, those who were not like them. They walked along Søgaten, past Vestbane railway station and up into Ruseløkkveien. There they peered into the channel between the market stalls, and he talked in a low voice about the sinister door which led down into the sewers, that door which had not been locked on that fateful afternoon when little Gudrun had run in there to hide, and they found her later half eaten by rats …

'How do you know so much about it?' she asked, worried, as they shuddered and walked on. 'We've talked about it as little as possible.'

He was bubbling over with a sensation which he couldn't explain to himself. It was as if his two beings were beginning to flow together, as if he was taking his mother to illicit places.

'Oh Mama, how about the two of us going to Tivoli Theatre?' he said breathlessly.

She looked at him, horrified. 'Tivoli Theatre? After you've been with me to the National Theatre to hear *Lohengrin*. How many of your friends have done that, do you think?'

'I know, Mama, but can't we? Go and see "Divertissement Exotique" with Life in a Moorish Harem and a teahouse in Nagasaki and genuine geishas, five of them?'

'Have you gone mad, my dear?'

'Let's do it, Mama. Then you can tell Uncle Martin about it afterwards. About the mystical secrets of Indian fakirs …'

'Are you making all this up?'

'Cross my heart, Mama, that's what they're showing.'

Again she was seized by the desire to catch him out. This was fabrication and fantasy, a brazen attempt at pulling the wool over her eyes. She turned on her heels and said: 'Fine, let's go over there and see what they're showing.'

The silence hung heavy between them. There was no sun between the houses here. When they emerged into Stortingsgaten and turned in towards the illuminated entrance to Tivoli, the gas lamps along the balustrade of the open-air restaurant were already emitting a weak light. A lower-class crowd in a fug of beer fumes was flocking round the posters.

'There you are, Mama,' said Little Lord, hurt. It was the first thing that either of them had said for some time. And before her astonished eyes the posters shone out in their intricately carved frames:

DIVERTISSEMENT EXOTIQUE

INDIAN FAKIRS' MYSTICAL SECRETS

LIFE IN A MOORISH HAREM. SPECIAL FEATURE!

A TEAHOUSE IN NAGASAKI. FIRST TIME IN EUROPE

GENUINE GEISHAS

She had a vague impulse to apologize; then she was bewildered: 'But Little Lord, how can you know about this?'

'It's in the newspaper, Mama, every day, on page 4 of *Morgenbladet*. Do you know what they're showing at Bio Cinema?* *Broken Hearts*.'

At last the laughter came. Mother's laughter, that trilling childish laughter which was not aware of anything in the world but having a good time. It was as if a lid had been lifted, and what remained was inexpressible relief – that all these secret things were printed every day in her own trusty *Morgenbladet* and that her talented, omnivorous boy had read it. And at that moment it was as if she had found the explanation for that improper ballad which had scandalized the virtuous Frøknene Wollkvarts. Yes, yes, they did their best, peace be with them. It was as if she had to forgive a whole world now that she was forced to forgive her beloved son, who had only used his two healthy eyes: on ships' names, advertisements, poems and posters. What in all the world was she worrying about?

She squeezed his thin arm in hers, and was immediately filled with a desire to do something unusual, like in the old days, like so often out in the world; in those good and dreadfully painful old days when her life had been a froth of days and nights, a torrent … compared to the quiet flowing of the river in this Kristiania, the quiet approach of an old age she seldom gave any thought to.

'Well after all, why should we two not go to Tivoli Theatre?' she said experimentally. But then she stopped herself: 'It's such a long time until eight o'clock.'

'But Mama, you can see there are two performances. It's Saturday, so there are two performances, it says so on the poster.'

She hadn't seen that either. All the things she didn't see. And all the things those boy's eyes saw and those ears heard.

'Of course, it's Saturday,' she said, in order not to appear stupid to this quick-witted young escort. They queued up at the window together with all those strangers with the strange smells. They were like two children bent on mischief as they passed through the entrance and turned up the steps to the theatre. A doorman in an admiral's hat tore off the ticket stubs. In front of them lay the auditorium, with tables painted silver and chairs with curved legs. A waiter in a dazzling white knee-length apron came over and conjured up a pad from his apron pocket and a pencil from behind his ear.

'Have a glass of sherry, Mama,' whispered Little Lord.

'A glass of sherry, please,' she said automatically.

'And for the young gentleman?' The waiter leaned over the table and smiled jovially.

'A glass of sherry for me too!' whispered Little Lord.

She had already ordered it. The waiter had raised an eyebrow at that – or had she imagined it? 'You're mad!' she said happily.

'You can easily drink two glasses of sherry,' he said. She looked around furtively at the unfamiliar surroundings. The air in the room was thick with smoke and smells. A stout figure with a bowler hat and beery expression stepped over her feet with its back to her. She felt a delicious shiver as she sat there; for some reason or other she started to think of Aunt Klara and her grammatical correctness. Little Lord was sitting singing *sotto voce* in the din as the room filled up and the tobacco smoke began to form a veil over the tables, linking them in a good-humoured solidarity.

'Little Lord, you're singing!'

He sang louder. He was singing *Die Angst, die Axt* – to a made-up tune with a singular compelling rhythm.*

'I was thinking of Aunt Klara!' he called over to her.

She felt a jolt like lightning: 'What made you think of Aunt Klara?'

'Die Zusammenkunft, die Feuersbrunst!'

'I don't know, I don't know …' He sang this phrase too. He was possessed by a feverish anticipation which increased with the surrounding noise; shouted orders for beer and herrings, for shots of aquavit and beef patties and herrings and beer, for toddy and coffee and herrings and beer.

There was a sudden buzz in the room. He could see the conductor's baton between two thick necks with bowler hats on top. It was as if that thin stick pierced the blanket of fog in order to demand silence. And the next moment the wind instruments sounded shrilly. The noise and the shouts rose again at the same moment and blended with the music as if in a battle for survival. Arms were raised, waving at waiters who threaded their way continuously between the tables, swinging their shining trays on flat raised hands. They all knew that it was vital to get supplied with refreshments before the curtain rose. Shouts and music came together in a celestial harmony. The noise made any attempt at conversation impossible. Mother and son received their large schooners of sherry, elegantly placed on the silver table in front of them. They looked at each other, filled with delight at the whole thing.

Then all at once it fell silent as if in church. The red curtain parted and revealed a stage on which stood four demonic fakirs in shining gold silk, lit by Bengal lights.* There was a burst of applause and shouting. Then there was silence again. Only the sound of men sucking beer from their moustaches passed through the room like a prearranged signal. One of the fakirs raised his hand. The performance could begin.

Each act was received with shuddering fascination. Little Lord stared entranced at the eerie movements, and when the fakirs retreated backwards into the wings his hands were wet and numb. He couldn't applaud, couldn't say a word. The pierced cheeks, the dancing snakes, human bodies floating, weightless in the air just as in everyone's secret dreams, his included – it filled him with a horror and an ecstasy which were more bewitching than even Peter Cornelius singing *Lohengrin* at the National Theatre. Now and then he could glimpse Mother's face through the fog of tobacco; she leant forwards over the table in front of them when the performance became too vivid. She whispered close to his ear through the applause: 'How do you like it, dear?'

'Super, Mama. Super!' He was frightened to death that she would want to go.

But when *Life in a Moorish harem* manifested itself on stage with five skinny girls of obvious Germanic origin, dressed up in orange silk trousers, she suddenly burst out in hysterical laughter. People turned round indignantly. The flaming red lighting on stage and the Moorish walls of cutout cardboard behind the ladies had a thrilling effect on the spectators. Mother and son looked down at the table in torment, and did not dare exchange the smallest glance. Not for one moment did they want to provoke all that folksiness they had ventured into. Then Little Lord slipped his hand cautiously into Mother's and squeezed it. And that was enough. At the same moment they both collapsed in giggles again. But fortunately the ladies of the harem had started singing a monotonous Eastern song, solidly supported by the woodwind players in the orchestra. The vision and the melody cast a spell on the company around them.

The jubilation reached its climax with the genuine geishas. The audience surrendered unconditionally. With tiny Japanese steps they performed such graceful manoeuvres on stage that the backs of the two necks in front of Little Lord became shiny. Mesmerized, he stared at those two necks each time they twitched so close together in their ecstasy that his view of the geishas was cut off. It was like looking into a landscape of rivers and mountains and moist valleys, and deep craters with forest all around. He felt the same euphoric horror as the time he was at Kunio's menagerie and was allowed to hold the four-week-old lion cub: frightening and entrancing …

'Little Lord, what are you looking at?'

He pointed discreetly. He saw Mother's eyes narrow in disgust. She picked up her sherry glass, but it was empty. He quickly pushed the other glass over to her. But now he could see that she was pale.

'Do you want to go, Mama?'

She nodded. As carefully as possible they wove their way out through feet which didn't move an inch, and feet which moved reluctantly as little as possible.

But as they were walking together down Drammensveien on that half-light late spring evening with the red sky of sunset in front of them, they were overtaken again by the same uncontrollable mirth. They walked along laughing towards the light; people turned round and looked, but they didn't care. They were walking arm in arm, laughing into the sunset, on their way home *from* an excursion to a thrilling foreign country, *to* a world which was theirs, which was safe. They turned into their own avenue with the old trees and the old wheelruts, dried at the edges now, towards their own house.

'I shall never forget this evening with you, Mama!' said Little Lord.

II
_____

THE GLASS EGG

11

He recognised her as soon as the boat rounded the point. She was standing on the foredeck amongst cases and barrels, the only woman amongst men in blue overalls. Her straw hat with its narrow brim was shielded by a veil which was fastened at her neck, and she was wearing a cape with a gold lining over her green dress. He saw it all like an image he had been expecting, and thought there was always something of the indoors about Aunt Kristine, no matter how much she affected an English style when travelling.

But as the small fjord boat drew closer he suddenly couldn't recognise her, and began to believe he'd been imagining it because he had thought of her standing there. The lady on the deck suddenly seemed smaller and perhaps a little older …

Then she waved. Disappointment swept over him. It struck him as surprising that his perception at a distance had been correct.

But as he stretched out his hands to her at the moment the small gangway was put ashore, it was after all Aunt Kristine, no it was Kristine, not 'Aunt'. He had stopped thinking of her as an aunt in these weeks of longing and dreams which had transformed everything.

The boatman passed him two large cases – so perhaps she intended to stay for a long time. His sunburnt face sought hers for a kiss that she returned.

He glanced up and noticed that people on the benches on

the foredeck were watching them.

'Yes, I travelled second class all the way, actually. The fresh air …' He was startled. Was it true that Aunt Kristine was poor? The very word seemed alien to him when it was applied to someone in their own circle. It was not possible that someone could be poor without being – well, different.

Together they went up the steep path towards the house – she light and graceful from the very fact of being in unfamiliar surroundings, he an escort burdened with cases.

And it was as if she went through a series of transformations before his eyes as they ate their late breakfast of small lobsters caught illegally in pots, followed by tea and marmalade on the veranda, where they sat opposite each other at the white slatted table covered by a grey linen cloth.

Aunt Kristine got up to fetch her handbag, which she had left in the hall. Mother looked at him, irritated, when they were alone: 'What are you staring at Kristine for? You look as if you're going to eat her!'

He looked away when she came back. He looked anywhere else, over the sea, in the other direction entirely, towards the garden where the birds were growing quieter as the day advanced; it was going to be a warm day.

He felt hurt and ashamed, caught unawares. He had relaxed his feverish exercises in self-defence during this holiday time with just Mother and the few friends from the nearby houses on both sides. Nothing had confronted him with the dangerous reality he had escaped from – all the unexplained events. Out here at Skovly everything was different, a safe haven. And what did Mother mean by saying Kristine and not 'Aunt'?

Mother showed Kristine up to her room as the maid came in and cleared the table. Alone and more lonely than he had expected to be on this day he wandered out into the garden and took the path down past the old well which rose up like a weathered brown pyramid behind the greyish-white clump of tall aspens.

And now he realised what it was he had felt at breakfast: Kristine changed the whole time! From the moment she had taken Mother's outstretched hands by the white gate – then she was 'Aunt' Kristine, a lady, the same as she had been when the boat was pulling in. But then – when he passed her the marmalade and the toast and they looked into each other's eyes for a second, then she was not a lady any longer, but 'the woman', the creature from all his daring dreams, ever since that moment he had sat and steeled himself at Blåsen one cold morning, up until all the lonely hours at Skovly as he strolled around collecting plants, in order to avoid joining in the boisterous games with the children and young people on those first giddy days of the holidays. Those were the days when life was renewed for many of them; they didn't see one another all year otherwise, but out here they knew one another from all the summers, and it was as if there had been no winter, no school and no lies. *That* at least was something they all had in common.

But now and then – when they confided a few things to one another about what had happened during the year since last autumn – he was seized by a feeling of being a stranger to those of his own age, and even to the older ones. He was a stranger to their innocence, to their childish school stories and their petty transgressions. He had not realized it properly before. And it dawned on him that it was because for him this was the summer of decisions, the one which would change him once and for all and set the seal on his *otherness* – everything which would horrify them if it was put into words.

He could see them from the garden now; they were standing by the large window upstairs, Mother and Kristine. He could make out his *aunt* from more than a hundred yards away. From the other side of the tall hedge he could hear the voices of his friends, with Erna's lively and serious voice the loudest. He felt a jolt; he always felt a jolt at the thought of Erna. There had been 'something' between them from one summer to the next, ever since they were tiny, something which was present but never developed, a childish devotion he liked knowing about, but that had suddenly become more insistent during these past weeks. He crawled cautiously forwards and pushed aside the leaves to make a gap in the elm hedge. He saw Erna standing in the midst of the group, eager and flushed, in her faded blue dress which reached only down to her knees. Child, he thought. But at the same moment, and for the first time – even though he had seen her every day these last two weeks – he saw that she was not as much of a child as he had believed. He remembered too the glance she had sent *him* the first time they met this year, a calculating glance from top to toe, the same kind of glance that Mother had been giving him this last spring …

They were going out to the islands, two boatloads of them; taking a picnic, they were going to collect feathers and swim, they were going to *occupy* the islands – a game from all their summers, a game full of artificial drama, as if there was anyone who would prevent them from conquering those two bare rocks out in the fjord, with their white, innocent boats, with their picnic baskets and bottles of lemonade.

A new jolt. He felt a desire to call out to them, to reveal himself to them all as they stood there on the gravel path with the white seashells neatly arranged along the grass on both sides; he wanted to call that he was coming too.

'We ought to get hold of Wilfred,' one of the boys said.

But Erna pouted and said curtly: 'He was expecting a visit from this aunt …'

And she said 'aunt' in just the same way as … But was it possible that he had given himself away like that? And could it be possible that these 'women', his mother and now this little girl Erna, that they were so sharp, so suspicious or so sure in their instincts – whatever they called it … Could it be possible that they suspected a connection which was such a deep secret dream that it had hardly reached the level of consciousness – at least not that level where things happened in reality! Not even he had linked those things together, not to himself: the determination and the painful desire on one side, and on the other, he himself as he was. He had not acknowledged that it was he who was involved, that it was he who wanted to experience such joyful and depraved things. When his thoughts toyed with them day and night it was as if it involved someone else.

Tenderness and irritation welled up in him. He let the foliage fall back into place. He looked back at the house. There was no one in the window now. At the same time the young voices moved away on the other side, down towards the sea and the boats.

Well, so what? He stood up from his kneeling position on the grass: was this not exactly what he had wanted – to be alone, someone they didn't know? He noticed that it was painful to be less of a child, and he knew that he didn't belong amongst the adults, but so what? Did he want to belong at all? He wanted just to *be* …

And feeling sure of himself all at once, he went back towards the house in order to make himself useful and appear composed. It was when he was cool and thinking quickly that things fell into place for him; it was in moments of weakness that everything got into a tangle … And as he walked – at a new, relaxed pace, with his head held unnaturally high – the thought of everything that had happened this spring came into his mind: the reports in the papers after the 'arson', the worried letters to *Morgenbladet* about young delinquents, even from respectable homes, who indulged in criminal activities, about a new spirit that was abroad. And that the police were *following a lead.*

He laughed with his head held high: it wouldn't lead them to him, at any rate. It was tracks left by the childish braggarts who told each other secrets on street corners at dusk. Not *his* tracks; they were covered by circumstances. No little bearded constable with a black helmet would find him, not with all their leads. It was the poor boys who were collared, junior schoolboys and dim-witted adventurers from his own background who committed petty crimes for fun and couldn't keep quiet about it.

He searched quickly over the unkempt lawn, which was always allowed to remain a wilderness for games and sports. He gathered up the flowers he could find, pansies and red clover and daisies and buttercups; bladder campions and toadflax completed the profusion, creating a clashingly childish bouquet. 'Hello!' he called happily as they came out onto the porch. He ran up the steps – and he could tell that he was wearing his 'shining' expression as he reached them, breathless: 'A little welcome bouquet for Aunt!' He held out the flowers respectfully. He could feel that Mother was looking at him; all her irritation had evaporated, and now all her glance said was 'what a good boy you are'. And he saw Kristine's glance which said something quite different. Now she was Kristine again, not an aunt – despite that fact that she was standing right next to mother accepting his homage, with a flaming face. He saw that she had a dark red swimsuit over her arm.

The bathing hut was the place where everything could happen in this summer full of harsh desire. The bathing hut with its sultry smell, a mixture of sun-warmed wood and salt water in the bottom of the tank. Here there was something secretive about the whole thing: the very walls, with their patterns of peeling paint and knots in the wood that could be formed into something sweetly indecent; the comically flickering oval mirror in its green cardboard frame with *Pellerin's Margarine* written on it; even the poor-quality rough mirror surface which reflected crooked and distorted faces – in everything there was something threatening and tempting that he hadn't noticed before. And the tank with its heavy mechanism of steel beams and chains and the restless, glittering green light down there where his defeat had been played out … even the memory of those undignified scenes became somehow alluring precisely because the memory involved disgrace. And the seaweed which peeped in through the slats, sucking and beckoning, always in motion – everything spoke the same arousing language; the narrow wooden couch, covered with ice-cold waxed cloth, where you could rest after bathing with a fluffy towel to lie on. Everything contained possibilities; memories and possibilities flowed together into a sweet depravity which possessed him constantly. And those coloured panes of glass with green, red, blue and agitating yellow colours! So marvellous and frightening to look at the beach and the hills and the willow trees through them, to move from patch to patch, from the fiery red to the distancing blue, the calming green … and then in a sudden leap over to the dark yellow, which created a mood of thunderstorm and a terror which filled every fibre of his body. Then finally to disappoint your eyes with the normal clear glass, where all of nature suddenly became unthreatening and stupid; everyday life …

He circled around the bathing hut when Kristine was down there bathing. He didn't watch. There was nothing to look at, because Kristine set off swimming from the opening in the tank, and even her shoulders were covered by the dark red material of her swimming costume; even her hair … There was less of her to see than at any other time. But to stand behind the knoll when she was in there, and know that she was there. To get up confidently and go over there, pull the door open and see her standing there, white, soft and naked, and then … His fantasy had explored all the possible variations of the situation: a smile, open arms, two breasts and a dark bush; a horrified scream, two arms crossing, trying to cover up; or some other form of horror which he could pretend was put on: anger, anger and indignation that were there to be overcome … And from his own side: fake timidity, or even astonishment, as if he had not known that she was there; surprise and delight that she was *so* beautiful – an attitude which could cover a great deal; or blind determination, aggression, force!

Everything could be possible, everything *should* be possible. But in the end, in the end! – just one thing, the one unheard-of thing that would consummate everything and transform everything.

She was always alone in the bathing hut. Mother complained of rheumatism; but it was no doubt because she couldn't swim. He felt sorry for her because of that, she always bathed otherwise. But his sympathy was overshadowed by the dark pleasure of his thought experiments …

145

… Or *he* might be there. He could be standing there when she arrived, in the middle of the floor and plain for her to see in his aroused state which was almost permanent. He could be standing there as an unexpected and grotesque obscenity which would scare her out of the door, or even better make her swoon a little. Then he would storm over to her and tear the clothes off her, that loose summer dress with covered buttons down the back; he had touched them and knew how to deal with them … Or even better: she would stop, stiffen, let her glance take in all of him for a moment; understand, and be powerless in the face of his childish desire, which would appal her and put paid to any thoughts of childishness.

All ways and possibilities had been thought through, raged through in a fever with a dry mouth, in visions, in anguish and in joy, and at times drained dry in moments followed by shame and disappointment – like looking through the clear pane of glass at the end. All possibilities had been exhausted with an aching groin and a sore throat. It was her, and sometimes him. But just as often it was not him, not anyone definite, just someone filled with his bitter sweetness; or it was not precisely him, but neither was it anyone else! Someone in him. *That* in him. That *on* him which was greater and more powerful than him, the stiff animal on him; and his stomach and thighs and chest … things which boys joked about in veiled terms on the street corners in the growing dark and exchanged shy stories about, but which he wanted to feel, to know, to use as it should be used – the only thing that could make his painful spring season complete and make him really alone.

But there was another Kristine as well, not only the white fantasy in the sultry shade of the bathing hut. There was the one who had cried, the little girl Kristine who had stood at the bottom of the steps to the garden and cried. And her he could love with tender innocence, with a devotion which was full of comfort and manly advice about life's trials. He had words for her. He had masses of borrowed and lived words, words he had read and words that had come, full of comfort and wisdom and courtly tenderness towards the weaker one, who had suffered.

146

Such a Kristine lived in him at times, and she lived with her full strength as well, but she was not his 'aunt' either, she was a woman, defenceless, someone life had been hard to and whom he could take under his wing, friendly and strong. And there were Kristines who were somewhere in between, just as there were parts of him that were mixtures of all his creatures, rapist, lover, protective brother, even uncle or husband. There was an infinity of transitions which corresponded to the transitions in them both, and to situations so rich in their possibilities that not all the days and nights in the world would be enough to dream them all through. And he created all the variations and served them to himself in consciously measured portions, made according to the secret recipes which were his, which were his life.

And everything was filled with words, just not words he could say to her.

He could pass the bowl of salad across the table to her, and even the little 'Help yourself' stuck in his throat. He went out after dinner under the trees and let the incomprehensible folk ballads overwhelm him again, the ones he only half understood, dark and thrilling:

> Skammel he lives in Thy*
> both rich and lustful was he;
> he had five courtly sons,
> of them two came to a bad end …

There was something great about this, about the mysterious 'lustful' and the sombrely dramatic 'two came to a bad end.' But in his morbid circling when he knew she was in the bathing hut it was another verse of 'Ebbe Skammelsøn' which came to him, and it came with obsessive force:

> Out there in the courtyard
> he girds up his loins;
> and then he climbs up to the loft
> in to the maiden Lucielille …

And it rang out for him with a seductive tone, that Lucielille, who was Kristine, both the one he would protect and the one he would seduce by force in the loft or the bathing house.

> 'Arise, maiden Lucielille,
> And plight me your troth' …

That was when Kristine rose up, horrified, naked, with outstretched arms …

> So they drank the betrothal cup …

The words came without his will, they surged in him *against* his will, words he loved to intoxicate himself with and words which were indifferent or came with harsh, disappointing warnings:

> Then answered Ebbe Skammelsøn
> as tears ran down his cheeks:
> 'I had intended you as my wife
> and not as my mother.'

He couldn't stop them coming, the verses; not that verse either, even though it left an unpleasant taste. He was young, but he was a lover – and Kristine in many ways a child, with her soft hands and the scent of cocoa in darkened rooms.

She was his Lucielille! He sang the name as he walked. It tasted of honey and vanilla, it tasted like looking out through the red pane! He could swing to and fro in it, fall asleep in the name like a sweet melody of woven creepers, and he awoke to it; then it was a fanfare. He dramatized it and used the name to transform her presence into something bloody and threatening. Tragic.

Yes, it had to be tragic! It had to end dreadfully. There had to be steel at the end, and tears, tears …

It was Ebbe Skammelsøn
he drew his sword;
it was Lucielille
he consigned to the earth.

— —

He met Erna in the pine forest. She was in her pale blue dress, cool as oats, smelling of washing and young skin. He was immediately enchanted by the contrast. From the hot redness he plunged into a blue bath. She said: 'You never come over to see us any more.' They were standing quite close to each other in the bright wood with the paths to the sea dropping steeply down. She filled him with longing to escape from the prison of desire and wild dreams. She said: 'That aunt of yours …'

They stood kicking at roots and brushwood. She filled him with shame. Why had she said 'that aunt'? What was it with women, both Mother and Erna, a woman approaching old age and a young girl, what was it that made them guess things he somehow did not admit to himself, even though he lived in it? He was struck again by that word: instinct.

She said: 'We could have rowed out to the islands together …'

'We?' he said vaguely. 'All of us?'

'We,' she said. They stood there, getting no further. Suddenly she began to cry.

'What is it, Erna? What are you upset about?'

She turned away and walked off. He followed up the steep path through the pines. Many summers of cool infatuation came together in him all at once and built up to a wave of sympathy, of shame and amazement and guilt. This was not a part of his pattern, it had taken him completely unawares. But the bright wood around him became what it had been before, and the glitter of sea between the trunks, and the smell of pine needles and ants and resin. Nothing was bewitched any more.

They arrived at the old stone table. They were in no-man's-land between the properties.

She sat down on the wooden bench on one side. He didn't

dare sit beside her, so he went round to the log which stood on end to make a chair just opposite. Small sharp stones lay on the dark table surface. They had used them as markers when they were playing hopscotch round the table; the table itself was the best slate of all.

She didn't look at him, just sat drawing with a sharp stone on the surface. He picked up a small stone as a marker as well. It was like an agreement between them. He wrote, half unconscious of it: *I love*. He didn't know what he meant by it. He sat staring at the table top with the words.

Finally she looked up with moist eyes. 'I've written three words,' she said, covering what she had written with her left hand.

'Me too!' he said, and quickly wrote *Erna*, whilst pretending he was just making something clearer.

'Can I see what you've written?'

'If I can see yours …'

Slowly they got up and changed places. They walked round opposite sides of the stone table and held each other's glance the whole time. They arrived at exactly the same moment and bent over the words at precisely the same time.

'Wilfred!' she wailed, and ran round the table as he came to meet her. They sank into an embrace which was unexpected by both, clinging to each other. He ran his lips over her young girl's hair, fresh as flax, which filled him with its blue fragrance. Neither of them dared to pull their head away the tiniest bit, so their mouths brushed slowly over each other's cheeks until they met. Her mouth was hard and a little rough, salty with sea. It was a kiss that didn't grow or change, a state something in them had been longing for through their childhood summers. They had neither bodies nor hands, just mouths which were one single mouth.

Just as suddenly they released each other and stood there, embarrassed. But then their glances fell on the stone table again; they could just make out the words on each side. With an awkward jump they came together again, but not embracing this time; they just stood close, close, the top of her head by his chin.

'Is it true?' she stuttered, 'is it true that it's me you love?'

And he stuttered back: 'Is it true – that you love me!'

And 'It's true, it's true', they kept repeating – so long that the words became meaningless for them and they had to laugh with bashful happiness. She said, standing by the table: 'Are we engaged now?'

The word danced inside him, so unexpected and ticklish. 'Yes, now we're engaged,' he said decidedly. He wanted to move close to her again, but she moved away from him and solemnly folded her sunburnt, salt-encrusted little girl's hands. 'Thank you, God,' she said quietly.

'Thank you God? Why do you say that?'

She turned fully to him and said: 'Because I've asked God for this since the first summer we were here.'

Terrible innocence – ! Hand in hand they walked silently around the little clearing round the stone table. They hardly looked at each other, they looked out over the sea which was glittering through the crowns of the low-growing pines on the slope below them; they looked at the short rough grass they were walking on, at each other's feet in the grass. Their happiness was so full they didn't dare use it to form words about this happiness, just small words about other things; their situation was so complete that only tiny caresses could intrude and confirm it, two foreheads touching, a gentle hand on hair. And everything was expectation; they were rich enough for everything, could expect everything from a life which stretched out in front of them and would never come to an end.

Compelling innocence – ! There was a song of all the summers in them. It was a song of childhood; it coloured their light blue love and ensnared their senses in an imprisonment full of sweetness. Here they had played hopscotch and drawn thick lines with the edges of their shoes in the rough grass; here paradise had been recreated. And if there was a snake in their paradise, it kept at a distance, afraid, outside the circle of light they wandered through, child's hand in child's hand, mind in

151

mind. Yes, the sky over their innocence was a sky of childhood and vanished summers which returned to life and made their hour of bliss into a game, like all the games had been – and yet a game which carried a threat within it, because they were *not* children, but played a little and were not grownups, but had played a fragment of the grownups' game and had played it with grownup words scratched on a stone surface, words which had been unheard of until then. The biggest word – was it already too big?

Quickening innocence … as if drawn by a magnet they circled close around the stone table and stopped – at precisely the same moment – and *looked* at what they had written. Together they felt ashamed and proud of what they had dared. And when their glances met again over the table top a warm blush overcame them both: not until this moment was it really true; the knowledge became complete, it became dangerous …

Deceitful innocence!

They walked stealthily towards each other now, not with the open, bodiless embrace like the first time, but in a closed, burning hot one. And now they had arms and legs and their mouths met without clumsy fumbling, and they who had been bodiless became nothing but body, which possessed them so that everything spun and they tumbled over in the hard grass. 'No, no!' he whispered in the prolonged embrace. 'Yes, yes!' she moaned and pressed him to her thin girl's body. All the frightened snakes peeped greedily into paradise and their tongues flickered.

One moment – and they freed themselves again, at precisely the same moment and by common consent. And this time as they stood panting together it was eye to eye and without shame, but not without fear, fear of a new knowledge which changed everything. And when they began to walk again they were not holding hands. Now the words *Danger – Do Not Touch* were painted in enormous letters all over them, every inch of their trembling bodies. And when hands or elbows touched as they walked down the narrow path, breathless, sparks flew which could ignite the whole forest around them.

They parted at her gate. The summer day had grown opaque, with a thin mist rising from the sea. Pale dusk began to sneak in between fruit trees and berry bushes. They parted with a shy glance, heavy with affirmation.

On the way home he remembered the words which would give them away up there on the stone table; they would give away their miraculous new secret to the whole world. He took the path up through the forest in order to wipe them out. It was growing dark quickly between the pine trees now, and the sea was no longer glittering so cheerfully through the treetops. When he had almost got to the top someone came walking down towards him. He lowered his head in order to slip past, but something about the sound of the footsteps made him look up.

'Aunt Kristine!'

The words were meant to come easily. But they came as a husky gulp in his throat. 'Good evening, dear boy,' said Aunt Kristine calmly. And as they stood there, she a little higher up than he so that he suddenly felt like a child again facing her: 'Well, aren't you going to walk home with me?'

He looked at her in panic, unable to find himself.

'I just have to go up into the forest and fetch something,' he said absurdly. He walked on quickly without waiting to see the effect of his words. He heard her start walking again slowly, humming, as if she had a secret, he thought.

When he got as far as the stone table the three words had been wiped away on both sides of the table. There were still two damp patches.

12

White flowers of panic opened up in him. He was discovered. His secret was no longer his. And more than that, what had been discovered was something he wasn't sure was completely true.

It had been true until a few moments ago, joyfully, painfully true, brimming with truth. But discovered by *her* eyes, his love for Erna appeared dimly as a misunderstanding – in *his* eyes.

It couldn't have been anyone else. She was coming straight from there, guided up to the stone table by – oh, that word he had heard but never understood the implications of. Instinct, an impulse towards the truth, towards debasement of everything which was secretly golden.

For the words had been there?

He stood leaning blindly over the stone table and didn't know for sure. He bent right down over one of the damp patches and could make out his own writing in the finest of outlines, those three impossible words; at that moment they meant nothing to him, she didn't really exist any more. A silver-grey dusk lay over the transparent wood, and the sea wasn't sparkling cheerfully at him any longer, it shone like dull slate.

He stood there, moaning aloud in small gasps of pain. Then he ran downhill in long leaps, filled with a desperate hope of catching up with her before she reached the fence where the wide path started. From that it was a short distance home, too short to be able to explain anything. But moments later he could see the back of her light dress in front of him on the path. What now? Had he been up there such a short time? Or had she walked *so* slowly? And what was there to explain anyway – to her, when she couldn't even know about the secret he had with *her*!

Then he saw that the back ahead of him knew he was there. He had run soundlessly in his light gymshoes. She couldn't have heard him. She had *known* him all the time, known him with her back.

And suddenly he was aware of the smile on his own face, and was seized by a wonderful certainty.

'I say, Aunt,' he said, threading his arm confidingly through hers. She didn't give a start. She couldn't even be bothered to pretend. 'What do you say to going that lovely long way round along the beach before supper?'

Did he really feel it – her arm trembling in his? He didn't

care to think it through; he didn't want to risk the great feeling of invincibility which had just possessed him. Obediently she followed the gentle pressure of his arm and let herself be led down through the thicket of aspen and alder, which grew so close that they formed a tunnel down to the sea. Did they *have* to walk so close here, because the path was so narrow? The questions could be felt just as shadows; they were not allowed to take over and ruffle his new calm. There was dynamite in every step. Lightly and slowly they walked in step down towards the sea which beckoned with a gentle evening sigh.

There were worlds inside worlds, but now he and she were in one of them. And all the worlds swung in a kind of interdependence. But this was the only one, the one here and now.

Was it she who stopped – or did he stop her? They were nearly down by the sea, and then it would be too late. Suddenly they were standing still together, equally tall, eye to eye. He took her head between his hands and felt the strength in his body melting away beneath him.

'You are a bad boy,' she said in a low voice.

'Yes,' he whispered.

'A really bad boy.'

'Yes!'

Their faces did not touch at any point. Only their mouths sank tenderly into each other's and held each other softly. Then it was as if they both withered away, sank together as one and dissolved.

'A really bad boy,' she kept saying when they had broken away and stood there breathless.

'Yes!' he whispered again. And she kissed him on this 'yes' with his open mouth against hers, which then slowly opened.

'Really, really bad!'

'Yes! Yes – '

'Bad!'

'Yes!'

'Bad, bad boy!'

He met her mouth as she said 'boy' with pursed lips. He laid his open 'e' over her inviting 'o'.

'Bad …'

And he finished it with his 'o' whilst her mouth was wide open with 'a'. It was like driving a dagger of rebellion into a smile. Every cell in his body was alive in that kiss which spread through them until it made them powerless. But his numbed hands were clumsy instruments for finding their way in that carapace of garments beneath his fingers. Soon it would be too late for his untrained organism, which was reaching its limit in frightened spasms. And she didn't help him, merely continued half-whispering words without meaning, in a last explosive embrace which dissolved everything and shattered his world into dull splinters.

And just then she pushed him away from her and stood facing him, quivering. Her glance was suddenly strangely cold, and her mouth loose and wet. She looked so lonely and irresolute at that moment that he recovered from his trembling confusion and took a step towards her, with a new intention. A caress, of atonement – he was unsure: sympathy with her or with himself, and already a hint of new, awakening desire …? But she raised her hand and gave him a tap on the cheek, quite hard, almost a box on the ears. Then she went quickly up the path again, quicker and quicker under the thick greenery, until she was almost running. She did not turn around.

All at once he felt no numbness any more, just childish amazement. He walked slowly down the path to the sea, over the rocks and the seaweed at its edge, out into the water which rose up him, cooling him, until it was deep enough for him to swim with his clothes on. He crawled ashore on one of the rocky islands and lay down on the sun-warmed rock on the side furthest from land. No-one could see him there. He couldn't bear the thought that someone might see him. He was open, transparent. But even out there it was as if eyes were watching him. He kicked his shoes off and hung them by the laces round his neck and slipped into the water again, away from everything which was staring in that open space without secrets.

Later he was lying on the headland beneath the lighthouse, his clothes beside him, in the last rays of the evening sun, waiting for them to dry and for something to change, outside and inside. But nothing changed, and his clothes wouldn't dry properly. The sun had lost its power, as he had lost his.

He was sitting on a hill in a world which seemed to ebb away and turn into a kind of shapeless jelly. No shame, and no consolation which sank slowly over him with tiny excuses, preparing to be victorious in the long run. Nothing to be apprehensive about, but also nothing to look forward to – just a defenceless openness which made him empty, with no secrets which must be protected and concealed for inner enjoyment.

'Could that be Wilfred sitting there?'

He leapt up in panic. The voice came from the sea. It was Madam Frisaksen, rowing her fishing boat. She inspected the three lighthouse lamps several times a week. She always rowed with what looked like woollen cuffs over the oars. People called them Fru Frisaksen's fingerless gloves; they said she couldn't stand the sound of the oars in the rowlocks ever since her husband was lost at sea. The brown face with its spider's web of wrinkles glowed in the red evening sun as she turned towards him. 'Did I startle you?' she asked mildly.

At once he felt he was ready to be master of the situation, naked as he stood. 'You must excuse me, Fru Frisaksen,' he said politely with a small bow, 'I'm not wearing any clothes, I got wet.' He made no move to pick his clothes up.

'You don't need to worry on my account,' said Fru Frisaksen warmly. She glanced up at the lamp which was making its pale progress behind the six glass windows. She didn't moor the boat, just let it float there and drift a little. He saw that she had her fishing gear lying in the stern. All of a sudden Fru Frisaksen became the very incarnation of homeliness, sitting there in the white boat with the sun's reflections glinting off it; of homeliness and security and everything which was without fear and without desire.

'Well, I'd better try my luck with the whiting as the sun sets,' she said in her unmistakable dry voice. 'My regards to your mother.'

'Good evening, Fru Frisaksen,' he said politely, and this time he did reach down for his clothes, so that he wasn't standing completely naked in front of her, lit up by the sinking sun. He had a feeling that it would seem demonstrative, like hooliganism.

Silently she rowed out towards the fishing grounds which cut across the headland with the lighthouse on the one side and the skerries on the other. That was the point where the whiting were to be found. She had an unshakable conviction about it. In rainy weather towards evening the fish were everywhere, and would take any bait. But in the golden summer evenings, they were only to be found there. He stood watching her take her bearings and ship the oars, let down the anchor and bait the line and throw it out. There was something positive and confident in every movement, an assurance of a world order. He had never thought about any of this before, just that she was part of the picture: a woman in a boat.

Was it the case that something was changed about him, after all?

Had Aunt Kristine - - had she felt the same as him after all? Or something similar – however it was *they* felt it - - something like how it should be, how it should have been? Was it true that something was changed, after all? That she was neither angry nor sad nor shameful – that they had a deep secret together, so close together that it was almost like having it all alone – or that it was more than having it alone? For when the great mystery happened, he had to share it with someone, with one other. That was what was so great, that there were two of them. Two! Two! The word became a song for him, an incantation, an obscene conjunction of three letters placed in mysterious proximity to one another. He hadn't thought of that before either, that there were three linked letters in 'two'. A hard, steely 't' which was linked by the bridge of the 'w' to the open 'o' and melted into it. But in 'three' there were too many letters, with an 'r' in the middle, as if peeping in between the others. – Erna!

The closed sound in that word 'two' was like the mysterious meeting between two people of the opposite sex, a glaring obscenity of a word which he had to repeat and repeat to the peak of excitement: 'Two, two!' And he could only say it twice each time, 'Two, two!' The magic of letters, which he had only sensed in incomprehensible poetry, now opened the way into a world. He would conjure words into deeds, and deeds into words, and in that way give both word and deed their full value. Equal value: to say was to do. 'Two, two!'

His vision of Fru Frisaksen shifted on the spot. He saw her sitting in the dying gleam of light. A little woman in a golden bowl. Now he could see that she was hauling a shining whiting over the gunwale. She was one and only one, a secure but lonely exile in a boat. He pulled on the damp clothes he had been apprehensive about, but now he felt a special thrill at that too. When he was dressed and had forced his feet into the wet gymshoes, he stood up and waved exaggeratedly to the lonely woman in the boat. She waved back and held aloft a fish, also with an exaggerated movement. He clapped his hands silently with sweeping arm movements, so that she could *see* that he was applauding. She nodded her thanks out there in the boat. He turned and walked inland with that remarkable word inside him that excited him so that his body was filled with a new pulsating sweetness.

Two. Two.

'So you're flirting with Fru Frisaksen, are you?'

This time he didn't jump. It was Mother's voice. It came from the top of the rocks near the sea, from 'the bastion', where she often walked alone. He smiled up at her with assumed assurance.

'Where have you been, my dear?'

The summer evening and the voice were one. The sunset – Mother … He ran round the gloomy hollow where he had played as a child (as a child, 'as a child'!) – in wide-eyed happiness at being able to comfort someone who was out on her own, a woman he loved.

'But your clothes are wet. Did you fall into the water? … And the whole evening – where have you been?'

'And you!' he said. He pitched his voice to match the gentle peace of the evening, a question, noncommital, a caring question, a caress she had to fall for: 'What have *you* been doing all day?'

He knew she would fall for it: 'What, all day!' she said. 'It's only since dinner time …'

He knew it. He knew he could lure her onto the defensive. But it wasn't meant as deceit; he didn't want to let her find him out. And at the same moment he knew that she didn't really want to find him out either. She could have asked out of habit, and because she had missed him. He put his arms round her and was aware that he was rehearsing sounding unrehearsed: 'I love you, Mama!'

'It's been a long time,' she said quietly.

'Since when?'

'Since everything, since you said that.'

Together they walked up the gravel path, inland towards the house, away from the sunset and Fru Frisaksen. 'Aunt Kristine has gone to bed,' she said lightly.

Too lightly? Where did this suspiciousness come from the whole time? The answer resounded joyfully through him: from his own bad conscience. He was a victor, and a deceiver. He loved her, loved her as a mother, as a lady, as a father. 'I'm still a bit taller than you,' she said, laughing. 'Shall we measure – properly?'

They stood back to back in the faint light of approaching night, and pressed their flat hands on the top of their heads. But they couldn't agree about who was the taller, they argued about it and pretended to mind. He said: 'We could ask Kristine to be the judge.'

He registered that she seemed deflated for a moment. 'Your aunt has gone to bed!' she said in a low voice. 'We mustn't wake people.'

They walked towards the house with their arms around each other's necks, and again he felt a new happiness. It was physical, but without the disturbing sweetness which otherwise possessed him constantly. Her hair brushed him with each step. They felt the gentle peace of two old lovers in a settled life, *wanting* to be without passion. He saw her in his mind as they walked towards the house, he saw her walking restlessly towards the Bastion, as she had done on a hundred occasions when he was a little boy and always in danger because he couldn't swim yet and because she overestimated the dangers of the beach, being a landlubber herself. 'It's *her* I love!' it sang in him. And Erna appeared to him – her hard kisses. And the town appeared to him for a moment: fires behind gloomy outhouses at night, lonely forays at dusk – it all appeared and reminded him that all these things were uncomfortably simultaneous. He saw the light in Aunt Kristine's room, shaded by the dark blue roller blind. All worlds were one, and he knew that it was vital to keep them separate. For each world had to be a secret in order to count. It had to be genuine and his alone. 'Mama!' he said. 'Mama!' She said: 'What's all this fuss about?' He shifted abruptly: 'Shall we have a little of the cold fish from dinner, just you and me?'

She looked happily at him – a mother's look to a son who is on his way away from her, a last anchor: 'Are you hungry?'

'I am hungry, yes! – And you could take a glass of Liebfraumilch!' He said it on the spur of the moment, inspired.

'What about you?'

'Milk. I'll fetch both.'

'Oh, but opening a bottle just for me … !'

Now he had her. He knew it without triumph, he knew it with love.

'You know I can decant it. And then you can give me a tiny drop as an excuse.'

Yes, he had her now. And as he dived down into the ice-box with its mingled smell of new ice-blocks and old zinc and cold meat on planks like bridges over the ice – and he saw the one golden bottle which had been laid down as an extra temptation just for this evening – an extra temptation for every single evening he could remember – he thought of Kristine, quick and hard. – Come down, he thought – come down and ruin everything in a single second, that's why you exist, my love.

'Come here, I'll open that bottle then, if that's what you want.'

'Go in and sit down, Mama!' He patted her gently on the bottom. 'What sort of son do you think you have? Perhaps you're afraid I'll screw the corkscrew right through the cork?'

In his eagerness he had spoken loudly. She had to shush him. It turned into a conspiracy over the old ice-box. He whispered, 'All right, if you go in and sit down!'

'Do it quietly!' she whispered. 'Aunt could hear us!'

He got it ready quietly. He was freezing in his damp clothes. He arranged things on the tray, remembered the vinegar, forgot the milk glass.

'No, not there!' he whispered dramatically, as he came in with the tray.

He indicated with his head that she was to sit on the white rococo sofa. Then he set it out on the table, everything, the small titbits; he poured wine into the glasses, just a little in his own, Mother didn't like him drinking. He refilled her glass and held out the dish of cold trout. And as she was helping herself he reached his hand over the table and stroked her golden brown hair with a pleasure which remained in his hand instead of transferring itself brutally to his body.

Mother ate. All at once she ate so greedily that he was alarmed. She didn't take the time to chew. She ate like someone starving. She dropped small pieces of the delicate fish. 'I think you were hungry!' he said. The sighing of the summer night could be heard outside. At last it was almost dark. It was only now he noticed the two candles she had lit on the festive table they were sitting by, their festive table.

'It feels as if I haven't had a bite all day!' she said happily. 'As if I've been afraid of something.'

'Afraid?'

She raised her glass. 'That cursed instinct!' she said lightly.

He was frightened: 'Instinct?'

'You don't know,' she said. 'You're a child, you can't know, but it's like fear that something is over, that everything is over … But now you must taste the wine too, just a drop.'

He tasted it. They looked into each other's eyes across the table.

'Skål, my dear,' she said. And her eyes were warm in the soft glow from the candles.

'I'll tell you something, Mama,' he said seriously: 'You are the prettiest.'

'Of whom?' she said surprised.

'Of them all.'

She said: 'Little Lord!'

He heard that she meant to say it lightly. He pretended she had said it lightly. He raised his glass and held it gently to his mouth, felt the cooling peace from the yellow liquid, a desire for more. – Erna! he thought suddenly.

She said: 'What were you thinking of?'

'I don't know, Mama. That it's so good to be out here.'

'Erna's a nice girl,' she said.

He was startled, but he could see she hadn't noticed. That cursed instinct, or – was it just chance. He wanted to know now, whether it was so that everything was examined at the same moment it happened, or earlier; whether people whose shifts of mind were related shifted in such similar ways that nothing was hidden from the one who was guessing.

'Why are you saying that now?' he asked. He could hear that his voice was strained.

'Yes, I wonder.' She looked at the clock, horrified: 'Really, my dear, it's high time you were in bed!'

He knew that was just something she said, and she knew that he knew. It was like an agreement that all words and sentences were a code between the two of them. *Two. Two.* That exciting word. It brought everything back.

'By the way, she dropped in to ask for you.'

'Who?' He tumbled back through worlds.

'Who? Erna! We were talking about her … '

'When? When, Mama?'

'Oh – a while ago, an hour or so. Actually she didn't ask.'

'What did she do, then?'

That cursed instinct. That cursed, cursed instinct. What had that shy girl been guessing about him – she could never be persuaded to drop in otherwise …

'What did she do? I suppose she came to see – me. She brought some beautiful anemones.'

He followed her glance to the bunch of flowers in a green vase on the white baby grand. He hadn't seen the anemones before. So Erna had left a reminder. In a way she was with them now in the sitting room.

Mother emptied her glass and began to gather the things together. There was no enchantment between them any longer, just open suspicion – or was there? He couldn't believe that she believed or knew or even suspected anything.

'Actually they were planning a trip out to the island, now I remember she mentioned it. Tomorrow, I think.'

'Will you come, Mama?' he asked suddenly.

'I - - '

'Don't answer now!' he said quickly.

'What do you mean?'

'You know.'

'All right, I know. But I think I'm too old for playing pirates, you know. So we'll stay at home – Aunt Kristine and I.'

'So will I, then,' he said.

'Why?'

She had expected that. 'Perhaps we'll come after all,' she added. 'Kristine, at least. She wasn't here when Erna popped in …'

As if she had said: you and she weren't here …

'All the better, Mama, then we two can stay at home!'

But there was no consciousness of victory in him, and he didn't win this time. He had to believe in the deceit if it was to work.

She said it was late. Her voice was small and decided now, there was no code any more. Silently they sat by the remains of the meal, incapable of pulling themselves together and going upstairs.

'No …' was all she said as she got up. Together they went upstairs. He saw a light from Kristine's room through the crack of the door. In the cool darkness their hands touched weakly. 'Good night,' they whispered together.

'Like a prisoner!' he thought when he was in his room. Like a prisoner under investigation whom everyone knows a little about – or suspects, or guesses. They all knew something, but he didn't really know anything other than that his inner urges tumbled him rudderless between those he was fond of, and made him the only open one, the one without secrets.

Even his body ached because of his knowledge of it all, of being the property of others in a little world where mighty things happened without him being able to control them. He went out onto the curved balcony over the arbour under the linden tree; there was a ceaseless sighing – that fragile play of humming voices which must live in the very trees, since they sighed even when the weather was still.

The sea lay pale in the dim night. Seagulls were mewing out by a seine net. A narrow shining stripe in the pale water showed where Fru Frisaksen had rowed her soundless course from the whiting grounds.

13

Wilfred woke up. He didn't want to go to the island with the children. That was the first thing he knew. He called them children now. Yesterday had given him experiences in the night, and new possibilities for today. Exhausted, he was staggering on a frontier where he had to be alone for the opening skirmishes. On the other side was the loneliness he craved.

He looked over the books on his shelf and sat down with the French art history he had been given by Uncle René. They had nothing to say to him right now, neither the pictures nor the subtle explanations he only half understood, but he dived into them absent-mindedly and dutifully, just waiting for something to happen. Outside the morning arrived fresh and clear, but he didn't want to let it have anything to do with him. The time for play had to be over.

But just as he was searching through shelves and cupboards, he came across the old toys which were left behind from many previous summers, and picked them up, filled with a pleasant melancholy. There was the battleship 'Akasa' which he'd made out of wood, with large nails down through the funnels and a complicated system of companionways and bridges, with a Japanese admiral on top, carved out of a root that looked like a head with slanting eyes. And there were boats of wood and celluloid, shop-bought boats with sails and propellers and seats and rigging – all of them things other boys had envied him and which he had generously allowed them to ruin over time. They had never appealed to him.

Then he heard the clamour from the children and youngsters below. They were coming up the path from the sea, laughing and shouting; now he could hear the sound of oars from below. It was him they were after, they wanted him to go along. At once he felt terrified – of meeting Erna, but not just her, everything she stood for, what he was sick of, simply sick of. Excuses built up inside him, one after the other: headache, need to study, simply prefer to stay at home … He peeped out of the window and saw them coming, girls and boys, a few bigger ones too, much older than him, with red and blue and green clothes and towels and shawls and scarves and fishing rods, and one with a trumpet which he kept on blowing. Now Mother called up. Now he heard her talking to them. Now she said he was upstairs in his room, that she would fetch him. She called again.

He felt like a trapped animal. Nowhere to hide from this avalanche of goodwill. Aunt Kristine – where was she now? Was she in bed with a headache? He felt ill at the thought, he couldn't stand meeting her in the house, but he had to meet her – somewhere else, an imagined place beyond the frontiers of what was possible, in a casino … Fantasies coursed through him as he stood there irresolute between the table and the window and didn't dare look out, or hear Mother calling.

For she was calling. Talking to the youngsters outside, and calling.

'Little Lord! Wilfred!'

Suddenly he felt he couldn't leave her to face them alone either. He couldn't bear to shout, or hear anyone else shouting. He went down with the art history in his hand and met the whole flock by the veranda steps. Mother was standing amongst them. He searched feverishly for excuses, but here in the sunshine, amongst all his friends, no excuses seemed valid any longer.

'There's Wilfred. Just a moment, I'll get the picnic ready!'

He looked quickly at his mother, but she looked away and let the children buzz around her. Then she went inside quickly to get his things. He felt a cold anger at her for that. She had made a promise on his behalf, sold him in order to make things easy and push him back amongst the children, all just so that she could stifle the great anxiety she had revealed last night.

'Erna's down by the boats,' someone said.

Why? Was there someone who knew something? Was there anything to know?

Again he felt that dull rage inside at the suspiciousness which was taking him over. He was tarnished by it, lost his good, indefinable loneliness.

'So what?' he said coldly. 'I'm going to stay at home and read art history.'

Those closest to him stood there open-mouthed. It just sounded incredible and affected in the sunshine. There was Mother, already out of the house again, with a picnic basket and a thermos flask of cold lemonade, everything which signalled to him that she wanted to force him back to childhood.

'Hurry up then, Little Lord … no, we'll stay at home, your aunt isn't up yet, she had breakfast in bed, she had a headache.'

'But Mother, I asked you - - '

She pushed the picnic basket into his hand and turned at once to the youngsters; a young, lively mother amongst young people. 'Why don't you come too, Fru Sagen!' someone called. Others joined in. But she pushed the idea away with both hands. She had no difficulty finding words and excuses: she was expecting visitors the next day, she had to do some weeding, she had a guest who was ill in bed, Wilfred's aunt, yes … And now they really must be careful, that old paraffin engine of Jørgensen's, was there anyone who knew how to handle it? She was deafened by crowing shouts – exactly what she wanted. Everything must drown in noise and exuberant farewells. There mustn't be a moment's peace, and in a way she became the organiser of the whole thing, even though it was planned in detail and they had only come to collect Wilfred, because Erna had called by and let them know?

Yes – of course she had, they'd hardly had the chance to talk. But here was Wilfred, anyway. He had started poring over his books and studying first thing in the morning, have you ever heard anything like it! Ha ha. Ha ha ha! Together with her they suddenly found it tremendously amusing. The eternally young Fru Sagen was holding her worried son up to ridicule, and liberating them by doing so.

She walked with them down the path, the centre of the crowd, and as far as possible from Wilfred. She drew them, she drove them with her merry laughter, her delight in everything, which gave *them* delight. A young visitor of the Jørgensens with cream-coloured linen trousers and the first wisps of a beard fell head over heels in those few minutes, and chatted her up boldly all the way down to the jetty where the boats were waiting; Jørgensen's old tub was to tow two fishing boats, whilst three of the lads were determined to sail a small boat with a spritsail, and were forecasting the weather from the almost invisible shadow they could see way out in the fjord: it heralded wind.

Like a merry bridal procession they set out to sea,* as it were duty bound to be jubilant so long as the invincible Fru Sagen was standing on the wooden planks with the cheery sunbeams lighting up the piles. They joked about the engine, it started up with angry explosions and sent clouds of blue smoke out into the summer's day which grew brighter as they got further out. Now they saw her walking alone up the path from the jetty. One last shout from the sea – but it didn't reach her.

Then the voices suddenly died away on board the boats. The heavy chugging of the engine made the summer air dense. The last Wilfed saw of Mother was a narrow back going up the path, and there was no joy in it.

'She's game, your mum!' called one of the boys through the noise of the engine, looking cheerfully at Wilfred. He was startled. His bitterness at Mother's betrayal was replaced by an urge to defend her. But when he looked into the freckled face of the gardener's boy Tom he could read only admiration and childish reverence behind the bold expression. He could feel Erna's hand against his on the gunwale. Her hand was cool. He had hardly looked at her. Now he looked into a shy little girl's face, stained the greyish-brown of the permanent residents, so different from the sudden mulatto brown which visitors acquired over a weekend. There was something deeply healthy about this girl which fired him up in a different way. Flaxen hair, flaxen dress. Flaxen through and through. Something cool and guiltless but enticing nonetheless, with those calm blue eyes which revealed all.

'Didn't you want to come?' she asked.

'Well, you weren't there!' he said eagerly. Yet again he felt that happy falseness overwhelm him, leading him on to play and play again. Or *was* it falseness? Was he not bound to fall headlong in love with her right here in this frame of blue and silver. She was created for this – she was good weather herself, summer from top to toe, the whole of her. He bent his head confidentially towards her and talked through the noise of the engine.

She put her mouth close against his ear. It didn't look conspicuous, since they were sitting so close to the roaring engine.

'I've been thinking about you all the time,' she said seriously.

Why did that irritate him? Because he hadn't been the first to say it – or simply because it was a challenge he couldn't leave unanswered – ?

'Me too!' he whispered back, shamefaced. 'All night!' he added. It didn't sound any more convincing. But her eyes became dark and moist. She stroked his hand on the edge of the boat. Hers was hard with dried salt …

'All night long!' he stressed, hoarsely.

'Haven't you slept at all?' she asked, worried. It sounded to his ears like blatant irony. But he knew it was concern and naiveté and nothing else at all. He tore out the short silk lace from the neck of his sports shirt and knotted it around her wrist. To reward her, to console her? He didn't know, but he knotted it painstakingly with a sort of fisherman's knot he had learnt.

'There!' he said. 'Now you'll never be able to undo it!'

She looked at the cream-coloured silk lace, silently moved. She stroked it with her other hand, she held it against her cheek and looked at him, dreamily and sincerely. And he returned her gaze steadily. Now he had convinced himself that he loved her.

They invaded the island with loud battle cries. In front marched the boy from town with the trumpet, and then came the gardener's boy Tom with a flag painted with a skull and crossbones. They planted it on the cairn in the middle of the island. They held hands and sang a low mystic song as a sign that they were the lords of the island. Childishness through and through. The older boys were drawn in, embarrassed, and soon became the most eager. Wilfred let himself be drawn in. He suggested they should play treasure trail. One team had to leave written clues and the other had to find them. But they had to use stones to hold the clues down so that they didn't blow away in the light breeze, and anyway it was almost impossible to be unobserved on the low island. Only in two places was it cut through by a kind of gorge with water at the bottom, full of driftwood and glass floats from the nets. The team with the clues was so easy to find that they had to change to different games, with no other aim than to release an excess of energy which had collected over a long winter full of studies and the stale air of school.

Erna called to him in a low voice. She was bending over the

rocks right down by the beach, and signalled to him to walk quietly. In a silent bound he was with her, staring down into a seagulls' nest with an egg which was moving on its own. It was clear that the egg was in the last stages: the baby bird was about to hatch.

Soon a group had collected, standing staring at the mystery in the small dishevelled nest. Filled with awe, they watched the miracle happen, as the wet, sticky baby bird, far too big, struggled out of the egg; all at once it was twice as big as the egg it had been in, kicking and crawling and trying to stand up in the nest. Erna had taken Wilfred's hand, she was weak with emotion. In some obscure way it became a ceremony which was meant for them, as if they were looking at their firstborn, watching it crawling helplessly and touchingly out into an existence full of grown-ups and dangers.

At that moment a frightful clamour erupted in the air above their heads. Before they could react they had a canopy of white birds above them, screeching angrily; a few of the birds plunged down in desperate dives, threatening to hack them with their beaks. Some of the boys picked up stones and sticks to keep the angry birds away. But Erna intervened, indignant at the violence.

'Let's move away,' she said, still moved and deeply serious. 'They only want to protect the youngster. It must be the last one this year. We must leave it in peace.'

The flock of birds followed them with furious shrieks until they were a good distance from the nest. She sat down on the rocks and looked out over the sea, filled with a calm he had not seen in her before.

'Have you ever seen anything so moving?' she said. 'Those poor birds went crazy with courage, just to defend one single helpless baby. Do you think it's just instinct?'

He jumped. That word again. 'Where does that come from,' he said, 'instinct?'

'Isn't that what you'd call it? They way they behave, the way *we* behave too – without knowing why? Things we guess … '

'What do you mean, guess? The seagulls are only defending

their young, isn't that simple enough?'

'Yes, it's simple. But in some way they knew that baby was in danger.'

'But that's just what they didn't know. Because it wasn't in danger. None of us would have harmed it.'

'Yes, but if we'd wanted to – ?'

'But we didn't want to. I don't think all that guesswork is anything special,' he said. 'Besides, you all guess wrong.'

'All of us?' she said – 'Wilfred, you're not cross with me?'

He took her head between his hands. They looked round quickly, then met in a quick kiss. They heard cries nearby; the others had started looking for baby seagulls in the crevices, and it was clear they had found some.

'Why did you say *all*, Wilfred?'

He stroked her hand.

'I just think everyone does so much guessing. It's not a good idea,' he said.

He thought at the same moment: how strange, we're sitting here quarrelling like old people, about something we daren't talk about, but which is really important.

But now the others had found several baby birds and were obsessed with the idea of protecting and defending them, to such an extent that the poor babies were scurrying on their long legs from crevice to crevice, scared out of their wits by all that protection.

'Food!' someone yelled.

'No, no! Swim first!' called others. There was a hubbub with swimsuits and swimming trunks. Previously the children hadn't used that sort of thing much when they were alone. Now they suddenly became aware that they were bigger. There were also a lot of strangers all at once.

'That's how it is with people too, I think,' said Wilfred tentatively, 'I don't think they want to be protected so much.'

'Don't they want to be guessed or protected, then?' she asked. And he was moved by her trusting face. She said exactly what was most important to him. She stood there fiddling with her yellow swimming costume. A mother too young, who had already become superfluous. But now the first ones were already in the sea, they had to hurry, it was a disgrace to be the last one in – a disgrace which obviously had to fall on someone, just not on themselves.

The big boys from town did something they called Indian swimming, which consisted of splashing much more than the others without moving forward any faster. Soon everyone had to do Indian swimming, and there was a commotion and a splashing that made the water spray up in rainbow drops over a bubbling cauldron of bodies and panting heads. Then they had to find out who could swim furthest under water, then they played tag. Snorting and exhausted, they hauled themselves ashore one by one; gleaming and spitting, they made their way to the steep hollow where some of the girls were already busy mixing everything from the packed lunches together, so that no-one would know who had brought what and no-one should eat their own food.

'Tom,' someone said. 'Where's Tom?'

It was down on the beach someone said it first. Those who were up by the food conferred and called out. Cries of 'What's happened to Tom?' came from up on the hill where four of them were sunbathing. Suddenly all fell silent. Someone said: 'His clothes are up here.' Then they all started calling urgently: 'Tom! Tom!' And then with long-drawn-out shouts: 'T-o-o-o-m!' And finally in a single bellow from throats choked by panic: 'To-o-m! T-o-m!'

Then silence fell over the whole island. Some ran soundlessly on bare feet up to the summit to look, others to the beach or out on the rocks. No-one was shouting any longer, all were *looking*. But no-one could see Tom, not anywhere.

Wilfred felt an ice-cold hand around his wrist. He looked into Erna's eyes, full of despair. But also something more. Challenge?

He was also frightened, but not panicky. Now he could hear the random shouts again, some tearful, some commanding, as if they wanted to conjure forth the vanished Tom from the rocks they were searching.

He gathered his thoughts with an effort of will which

was almost painful. His clothes? They had found them some distance away from the scattered boys' and girls' clothes behind the boulders on the south side.

Then he realised something with complete certainty, something he just thought his way to: Tom didn't have any swimming trunks. He could see the living room in the gardener's cottage: that tiny space. They didn't have swimsuits and that sort of thing at the gardener's. Tom had no doubt been too embarrassed to go swimming with the others …

Wilfred realised he had been squeezing Erna's arm. Now he let go of it abruptly and set off at a run without a word. He ran towards the northern end of the island, which ended in a narrow headland with rocks sloping out into the sea. He ran quickly and softly over the little hill, taking care where he put his feet. He ran with a gleeful conviction that he was right in working things out whilst the others were just fumbling blindly. The whole time he could see that little gardener's cottage on the plateau. He ran as fast as he could, yet conserving some energy so that he was not quite out of breath when he got to the headland. There he stopped abruptly and looked down into the water. It was clear as glass and unmoving here on the lee side. He could clearly see the bottom falling away; brown seaweed swayed gently in the current beneath him. He walked seawards from rock to rock, staring down, searching systematically, sector after sector of glistening rock beneath water and seaweed.

Then he saw Tom. He was lying face down, white and naked. His thin legs were distorted in the refracted light, appearing long and wavering.

Wilfred turned round to summon help. But he could barely hear the distant shouts from the other side of the island. He waded out, taking care not to fall with each step. It was deeper than he had thought. He was out of his depth before he reached Tom. He dived down quickly and put his arm around his neck, bending his body upwards so that Tom was kneeling on the sea floor. He thought in sharp bursts of everything he had heard about life-saving, about getting the victim onto your back and swimming under him.

Tom was heavier than he had thought. He just sank. But as he was about to change his grip, he felt solid rock beneath one foot. A moment later he was standing with Tom half out of the sea, on a small rock just next to the headland. He just had to wade ashore with the cold body, heavy and limp in his tired arms.

At that moment he saw Erna appear over the top of the hill. Her yellow swimsuit was flaming against the blue of the sky. At once the whole of his tired body was suffused with a joy that would let him conquer everything.

Then Erna turned round up there and waved. Wilfred hauled at the lifeless body, breathless and exhausted, but with his thoughts constantly fixed on what he had read in *The Boys' Own Manual* about resuscitation.

When the first of the group came pelting down the hill he had Tom beneath him, lying on his stomach with his head lowest on the dry strip of hillside behind the headland. He was on his knees, straddling the naked body. The boys reached the headland. The shouts died away. The girls came storming on their heels, he could feel them forming a group behind and around him, a half circle, row upon row of tense, expectant, helpless children, who were just waiting for him to perform a miracle. He worked on the boy rhythmically and purposefully. Was it right, what he was doing? Was this what it said in the book?

He was so tired now that he was on the point of sinking down over the wet body. But he daren't let anyone else take over, daren't stop or ask if anyone knew any better. A deep voice from somewhere gave him some good advice – but it was unsure. It was as if it wasn't a matter of Tom's life any more, but his own. If he could manage it, if *he* could manage it …

Then water began to run out of the mouth of the figure beneath him. He couldn't remember who it was any longer. It was a body with a head on that rock, he turned the head to move it away from the rock. And now the water came out in great spurts. The boy was retching.

175

Wilfred turned him around. He had help now, they laid him on his back, his head lolling over to one side. Wilfred leaned across him and listened to his heart. He couldn't hear it beating, but could feel from the body that it was alive. A red mist appeared before his eyes. He wanted to look up and ask for help, but he slipped away into something unknown. He felt himself throwing up.

'But Mama, I didn't even dive, I did none of the things you're talking about, I walked into the water and pulled him out!'

He was weary of it now. Mother and Aunt Kristine and he were drinking coffee after dinner. The children were still running around telling their parents and anyone who would listen in excited voices that Wilfred had saved Tom from drowning. The gardener and his wife had dropped by briefly, they couldn't be away from home more than half an hour. Both had wept with gratitude. The doctor had said it was in the nick of time. If a brave fellow hadn't come along in time out there, they wouldn't have had any Tom now – the only thing they had in the world.

Even the journey home – such a contrast with those terror-filled moments which had been succeeded by muted jubilation – had been a triumphal procession, where everyone had suddenly been seized by a solemn desire to pay homage to the one and only. He had said it as soon as he came round on the rocks, that he hadn't done anything special, he hadn't even swum out, just pulled him out. The more he protested, the surer they were that it had been an act of heroism. That glorious day required even more glory. They *wanted* to raise him into the company of heroes. He could still see Erna in the boat on the way home; she sat with her blue eyes drinking him in, without a word, blind and deaf with admiration and happiness because he had done it.

He felt like walking along the light path over the fields to the gardener's, to visit Tom and *see* that he was alive. But he didn't dare because of all this gratitude. He knew that the gardener and his wife would receive him like a compulsory gift, someone they were obliged to share all their love for Tom with. Tom himself was in bed, not allowed to get up, although he claimed he was as right as rain and just wanted to go out and have fun.

But his parents had been full of concern: he would have to stay in bed for a few days. It was as if they wanted to bind him to them and couldn't bear him to be out of their sight, even though they had not known what it was to lose him until after there was no fear of losing him any longer.

And Mother glowed. Not that she talked a lot or boasted, but she kept saying to Kristine how proud she was of him. Kristine had listened to the story with a shy smile. It was as if she felt she had no right to join in the admiration. She was only an onlooker, and not even that so much as all the youngsters; they had experienced the accident. She couldn't join in the conversation, neither about cramp nor about resuscitation. And yet it was as if there was a gladness radiating from her too, from her to him as he sat there knowing how she felt.

'So in other words, you did absolutely nothing?' said Kristine ironically. 'You just wandered by chance out into the sea and picked him up, and then brought him back to life?'

'Not by chance. I *thought*. That was the difference. I thought he was embarrassed about bathing naked. And I thought he didn't have any swimming trunks.'

'So then it was just a matter of going and finding him!' said Mother.

'That's right.'

'But how did you guess he didn't have any swimming trunks?'

'I didn't guess. I saw it in my mind.'

Mother and Aunt Kristine exchanged glances over the liqueur glasses. What was it they suspected from each side of the wide arc of their speculations?

'That's something you always say,' said Mother, a little troubled: 'that you *saw,* that you can *see* …'

Wilfred felt wary at once. He realised that they were guessing about him. He had a deep conviction that this joy in *seeing* was one of the paths into the land of secrets. That was how it worked for him. It was probably different for others. To *see* and to *know* – those were good words to hold fast. See with something other than your eyes. Know more than just what you were sure of.

'I just wish everyone would stop talking about it all,' he said. 'I'm glad Tom's alive, I'm sure he's a good chap, I hardly know him.'

He got up and went out into the garden. He knew that they were looking at each other in silence now, they were sitting there thinking they knew. And what they thought they knew was that he was a modest boy who didn't want praise for something any other boy would have done – and could have done, if he had just thought enough about it. But as he *saw* them sitting there, surrendering to their need to admire something, he knew also that they were so painfully wrong; painfully for him. For that kind of deceit wasn't a part of the strategy he had drawn up for himself. A word occurred to him: *banal.* He grimaced …

But there was something in him which was the complete opposite as well, if he could just think about it on his own. Something of what had flooded through him during those precious seconds when he had been concentrating most keenly out there on the rocks, and which he had still not worked out. Something about *not* destroying! And there was something else again, something which plagued him as he was walking down in the fading daylight – down to the shore again, to the jetty where the brief adventure had begun. – Yes, that was it: had he wished for someone to come and help him when he waded knowingly out into the sea to search? And why did he *know* that the boy was exactly there?

He hadn't wanted to have any help.

But if he hadn't managed to get him out alone – would he rather that Tom had died than get him out with the help of others?

He didn't know. But he knew that he was glad that no-one was there.

And after that? Then – when he was leaning over the 'corpse' and working on it according to instructions he remembered only vaguely, and which he had definitely never practised before, did he wish for more knowledgeable help then, for guidance – ?

He did not wish for it. When that older, unknown boy with a deep voice had given him good advice, he had listened to it with irritation, as if through layers of resistance.

In any case, the boy hadn't known anything for sure either – he was just saying something for the sake of it.

But if someone else really *had* been better, surer, more trained and strong …

There wasn't anyone.

But if – ?

Would he rather Tom had died than accept help?

Did he just want to show off?

And once more he had to take those small moaning steps along the path; they kindled an inner disquiet which could not be stifled. For was it not the case that he had practically been prepared to kill Tom – he who had saved him so heroically? Was not that the innermost truth, which tormented him so that he couldn't stand being praised for quick thinking and resolute action?

The fact was that Tom in some strange way had become dear to him – now after the event, even though he had never bothered much about that freckled lad with the white body when they bathed. When he knelt astride the half-dead body and as it were rode him back to life – was it not that he was sitting on the dead Tom as if he were his property, the horse of his courage, riding him directly to death, for all he knew?

He walked along the path, moaning softly. For even if he was still not quite sure that was how it had been, yet – he was on the point of being certain. And he knew it more and more surely as he gradually had to peel off layer after layer of excuse and self-praise. For it came to him with the others' words, with all the hearty claps on the shoulder he had been given on the way home, with Erna's admiring glance and Mother's understanding reaction to his modesty. He had to reject it all as something nauseating and absurd; it was alien to him.

Because of a need for absolute honesty?

He kicked at a stone with all the force of disgust; the stone flew in a wide arc out into the sea.

That was just the problem: when he tormented himself like that it was not in order to be honest 'through and through'. It was in order to destroy something which had grown large and misshapen enough to become an accepted truth. It was to make it small and pitiful enough to be alone with it somewhere no-one could reach to share it with him – the innermost core of his solitude, where nothing could shine except with the lustre he himself gave it. Then *that* could be as 'false' as it wanted.

He had walked all the way out onto the headland where the lighthouse was. He felt a cool satisfaction at having got through to a layer which seemed to be the last. All gladness had disappeared in him now. In its place there was a good hard stone in him, sharp-edged and painful, a place to stand, to be for always. A stone as hard as the rock he was standing on, but not long and indistinct like the headland, caressed by the sea towards sunset. A small hard stone with sharp edges, to hold within himself, a place to be, and at the same time a weapon.

The soft wash of a fishing-boat reached him from the other side of the headland. At the same moment he saw Madam Frisaksen's white boat darting swiftly forward from behind the lighthouse. Madam Frisaksen herself was sitting there, brown and dry, with her back half turned to him on her silent way to the whiting grounds. When she crossed the end of the headland she could see him in the red evening light. She rested on her oars.

'Well, isn't it that lad who's been saving folk from drowning?' she said mildly – or was it ironically?

He felt a wave of redness surge through him. What was it about that excluded woman which gave him such pleasure?

'Good evening, Fru Frisaksen!' he shouted, bowing politely from the knoll he was standing on. 'Are you off to try your luck with the whiting again, Fru Frisaksen?'

He knew she was flattered when you called her 'Fru'. The

grown-ups always said 'Madam' about Fru Frisaksen.*

'Is that right, what I hear about you pulling young Tom out of the sea?' she asked over the top of her oars.

'Yes, Fru Frisaksen. I pulled him up on land, he must have slipped.'

'Right,' she said quietly. Sounds carried far across the water. 'Right,' she repeated, pulling on the soundless oars again. She kept the boat steady in the current so as to steer clear of the headland. 'I suppose Tom was a lucky chap then,' she said.

'Bad luck with the fishing, Fru Frisaksen!' he shouted happily. 'I hope you don't get a bite all evening!'

She nodded sagely. She understood. It was not done to wish people good luck with fishing – it was tempting fate.

'Pfui!' he called, spitting into the sea in her direction.

Fru Frisaksen's face opened up in a smile, so unusual that it looked as if her face would crack. Then she nodded once more and rowed silently out towards the fishing grounds, which were sparkling with red reflections.

And again he was left staring at this lonely creature in a boat who belonged to a different world – not the noisy world of the holiday-makers, hardly any world at all. It was as if she was floating into a land of shimmering renunciation, of something which rested in itself, with no relationship to any other thing or person. She was rowing silently into a cold sun.

'*I suppose*,' she had said. '*I suppose* Tom was a lucky chap then.'

Besides, she hadn't praised him at all, just seen it from Tom's side, perhaps from the gardeners'. They were the only ones who knew her here.

But when it came down to it, what did she think about the day's great event, the one which would would dominate the summer gossip for the rest of the week and perhaps longer?

No doubt she didn't think anything.

And all at once it passed through him exultantly, as he stood there hypnotized by the tiny vessel like a drop of gold in the blue of the evening: *Fru Frisaksen was the one who didn't give a damn about anything.* Who didn't give a damn, a damn, a damn! Who had enough in her own tiny universe.

That was how it was. She exuded that mysterious contentment of absolute indifference, of calm. It was like that with his own Uncle Martin too, just in a different way. *His* circle was large, was stock exchanges and foreign businesses and a whole edifice of concerns and triumphs on his own behalf and that of others. But deep down it was just something he surrounded himself with in order to be left in peace and because that was the sort of thing that was expected. In reality he didn't give a tinker's cuss – that was exactly the way he put it. Music, those small delicate works of art which gave rise to such violent emotions in others, which affected Uncle René so that you could see him go white as the impressions vibrated through him … even all the poverty, and the danger of something in the offing – everything which Uncle Martin talked about in so many worried words … he couldn't give a damn about it, that was the truth. He knew it now, Wilfred, standing there on the beach, empty and yet full of an inexplicable inner jubilation, that was how some people were. Were they not the true egoists in this world?

The grown-ups had so often talked about egoism. It was as if they were holding a rotten apple when they said the word.

And yet they didn't know what it was! They thought it meant looking out for your own advantage above all. They didn't know about that passion he would feel as he barricaded himself behind layers of solitude, where only he existed deep inside and turned into a hard stone, shining with polished politeness and all the consideration they demanded of him. When he had made himself independent, when he had become a stone without any thought of other stones, then no-one would be able to see anything other than goodness and warmth and courage. He would be rich like Uncle Martin – because he was actually really rich – with simple habits, so that they all said: look how modest he is, he does a lot of good on the quiet. Rich and assured and without asking for a moment whether things were right or wrong. Why else had they let him learn so much – so much that others didn't, music, that spring in France with Mother – before school … if it wasn't that he was to use all that early promise they talked so much about to become as hard as stone?

So stupid all those people were – ! So easy to see through with their guessing. They always looked for what they *wanted* to guess. And when they were wrong, they modified the result so that they had almost guessed right after all! And then they went around knowing nothing about one another, less than nothing, because what they knew was wrong from the start, misled as they were by hazy suspicions, by wishes which suited them in all their littleness.

But they thought they knew! Mother about him. Aunt Kristine about him. Uncle René who had been given a young aesthete to foster.

Fru Frisaksen was the one who knew. No doubt she had arrived at it through bitterness and other people's contempt. They said that husband of hers could drown without it making any great difference. He didn't know *exactly* what they meant by that. They said that Kristine was not really one of them. He didn't know precisely what they meant by that either. But he was sure he knew as much as the people who said those things. He knew – because on this intoxicating evening he had grasped Fru Frisaksen's secret – that people just talked about things, talked and talked. And the more they said the more fuzzy the meaning became. Only when something was really upsetting or threatening did they become different. Then they made people into heroes – everything they longed for …

He walked up onto the path again, and was summoned over the garden hedge by Erna's parents, who were eating their evening meal at a plain wooden table beneath the large chestnut tree, where things were always dropping into the food. They were eating something called Health Food, a sort of cereal with milk on. Wilfred was forced to dip into a small portion of Health Food, it stuck in his throat like a cork. Erna's father was the principal of a children's home and knew almost everything about education; the small amount he didn't know he learnt about in England on a grant-funded visit to an institution every year, where you could find out even more about education every 15-30 June.

He talked about character and training and something he called purity of mind. He was the only one in the place who went about with a bare torso and scrubbed himself with sand and never ate cooked food. He praised Wilfred's deed in pedagogic terms; it turned out to be a manifestation of Baden-Powell's positive sporting philosophy, which never left anyone in doubt as to what he should do.

Erna's nine-year-old little brother listened with sly ears from the radish bed where he had been sent to weed.

Wilfred glanced surreptitiously at Erna. For the first time he could remember he saw an expression on her face which wasn't entirely open. Surely she wasn't sitting there feeling ashamed of this phonograph of a soothsayer, whom they laughed at so heartily when they were sitting on the veranda with their whiskies, his uncles and all those smug gentlemen who knew everything in their own way? Even Erna's mother, who humoured her husband by wearing a kind of national costume when they had guests – she was stirring her healthy dish absent-mindedly. Was it so certain that what he said was stupid, just because everyone thought it was? If it hadn't been for the grating voice Wilfred would be inclined to give him at least as much credence as he gave all the soothsayers back home.

'I agree with you completely that you shouldn't make a song and dance about the most self-evident assistance to a friend,' said Wilfred. He felt a secret thrill at using Uncle Martin's expression 'make a song and dance'. When he used grown-ups' words to other grown-ups, they always looked uncertainly at him. Erna sent him a swift glance. Was it gratitude, or anxiety that he was poking fun …

Erna's father chuckled appreciatively and conveyed a spoonful of milk and cereal to his mouth. He looked like a cow chewing the cud. Wilfred seized the opportunity:

'But I'm not so enthusiastic about this scout movement from England,' he said thoughtfully.*

Erna's father adopted the indulgent smile which pedagogues

assume when ignorant people express doubt about their ideas.

'So – our young friend doesn't like the scout movement?' He looked round his family and waved the little brother over from the vegetable garden, so that he could benefit from the instruction as well. He was a little scamp with wiry hair who only had eyes for the bowl of blackcurrant jam. 'May I be allowed to ask whether our young hero is entirely familiar with Baden-Powell's principles?' Now he had a firm but friendly grasp of the little one's wiry head.

'I've read them thoroughly,' said Little Lord lightly. 'I think everything they say about honesty and cleanliness is pretty similar to what everyone else says. But I think it's too simple for ordinary boys. It just seems like an echo of school rules.'

The principal actually sat bolt upright in his chair. It was entertaining to tease him a little, not too much.

'I believe that people – perhaps particularly the very young ones – are rather more complicated and have a range of motives for their actions; they will be pretty much indifferent to all the self-evident do-gooding of that Baden-Powell chap.'

Erna was staring down at her plate, her little brother was fidgeting about – in amusement or impatience? Their father was about to say something sharp. But at that moment it was as if a thought occurred to him. He said simply: 'Maybe you hear contrary thoughts at home. Environment plays an extraordinarily large role in forming young people's opinions.'

'I'm sure,' said Wilfred, conciliatory.

It was time to take his leave. He knew well that children and young people were only invited in by Erna's parents to be given a lecture. A little devil nudged him as he got up. 'We children are no doubt most influenced by what we hear at home – perhaps most often in the opposite direction.'

He shook hands politely with Erna's mother and said thanks for the delicious food. The father looked at him benignly. Wilfred felt like a butterfly on a pin. If he had stayed another ten minutes he would no doubt have become one of the pedagogue's 'case studies', which were so frequently described in the monthly magazine for physical and spiritual health. It was delivered to their house on Drammensveien all year round. He had never thought before that it was probably Erna's father who sent it.

He strolled home between the two elm hedges, bubbling over with glee at Erna's wholesome father, who garnered patent wisdom from a course in Kent every June. At that moment there was a rustling in the foliage; Erna pushed straight through the hedge and was standing on the path in front of him.

'It was mean of you to poke fun at my father!' she said. Her cheeks were flaming with indignation. She looked delicious.

'I wasn't poking fun at him. I just disagreed a bit.' He became irritated in return.

'That's the same thing where Father's concerned. You must remember that no-one ever disagrees with him.'

'Then it's about time,' said Wilfred indifferently. 'You all think this health obsession is pretty boring as well.'

They were standing close to each other now. She softened, looking dejected. Her sudden anger had evaporated. 'Do you think he's really stupid?' she asked.

He looked at her, disarmed. All this devotion didn't do any good. She obviously wanted everyone to be right.

'No more stupid than others who set themselves up as authorities,' he said. 'Do you know Fru Frisaksen?'

'That dreadful woman?' She looked up at him, horrified.

'She doesn't put on an act,' he said. 'You don't either, actually, but you're not grown-up yet.'

Now she was both happy and puzzled. 'What about you then, Wilfred?' she said, 'do you put on an act?'

'Yes!' he said and quickly put his hand round her hard neck. For a moment they stood with their heads against each other. Someone called her from the house on the other side. Erna was already half-way into the hedge. It was obviously not just theory which demanded obedience in that house.

'Say hello to your little rascal of a brother,' whispered Wilfred, 'I don't think you'll make a scout out of him.'

She turned around in the hedge. She was like a part of everything which surrounded her.

'I say, Wilfred,' she said quietly, 'can't you lend me one of those art history books – ?'

He was struck dumb for a moment, then he felt moved. 'Pooh, don't read things like that, it's just showing off when I do it,' he whispered. The calls from the house were coming closer.

She stood there shaking her head, helpless. Then she shot into the hedge.

'I was just looking for puss!' he heard her calling back.

Honesty! he thought merrily. And being in such a good mood now, he dared to pursue the thought:

I was putting on an act when I pulled Tom out of the sea as well. I knew she had to be close behind me.

14

Aunt Kristine had a migraine.

Her migraines appeared out of the blue. Mother would smile a little as Kristine drifted sideways through the rooms, looking for the nearest place where she could sink down into a horizontal position. Kristine maintained in a resigned voice that it was bitter to suffer from precisely the two afflictions which everyone suspected you of faking, insomnia and migraine. There was always someone who had heard you snoring at five in the morning.

For Wilfred it meant relief. His insistent desire abated for a while as soon as sickness came into the picture. On the other hand her condition was not so pitiful that it called upon the chivalrous side of his feelings. Besides, his aunt's description of her symptoms was so vivid. He could never understand why people had to go into so much detail about their illnesses.

But his summertime world at Skovly was split – after he had been looking forward to it as a way of forgetting past sins and as a prelude to the great transformation. Kristine was a disappointment because it reflected on his failed attempt at conquest when she withdrew from him now. Erna was a disappointment because her touching devotion drained all his driving energy – he had visions of vice and was given a butterfly to play with. Mother was a disappointment because she was going around guessing at things he was not even properly guilty of. But he had grown out of that summer game they had both looked forward to.

It was all because he himself was a disappointment. His visions were supplanted by half-hearted initiatives. The treasure chest of his childhood had lost its shine. Even that old game with things that had washed up on the shore had taken a different twist. Those fantastical things from the sea, from boats and distant lands – as they reached the shore they had always taken on a fairy-tale aura, even if it was just an old mattress. There was always expectation around everything which came from the sea. It was as if he expected everything from the sea now, as if childhood might return in the form of all the things he used to come running home with, glass balls, household utensils. He knew it was contradictory, looking for the gleam of all that was lost when it was a new world he wanted to force into being. It was no good. The things he found were simply what they were, a dull protest against the dream he was defiantly trying to enjoy.

Once when he had come home with a float from a net, someone had asked whether that was worth picking up. A world threatened to come crashing down. But at the same moment he had registered his certainty as a victory: only dull, grown-up stupidity could meet such phenomena with shabbiness. Now it was as if things from the beach were on the point of acquiring a meaning, being transformed according to his expectations, but he could hear a whispering of alien voices which were *also* his own: is that worth picking up? … Treachery was at work within him, two forces which betrayed each other. He sided with each in turn, with the gleam and with what killed it.

Only one thing was worth striving for, and it created havoc within him with a dry, dark red taste which possessed his body and thoughts; that could not be gathered up, could not take form in the glow of expectation. It had to be acted upon.

Aunt Kristine had a migraine and Erna was a butterfly.

Nothing had helped him to flee from anything. Those idiotic episodes from last spring had popped up again in the newspapers, after the visit of the British fleet had invested *them* with a gleam for three weeks.* Now letter-writers were crowding the columns with comments on the criminalisation of youth, alternating with those on Elias Tønnesen's latest escape from the penitentiary.* They maintained that the arch-thief was every boy's hero; even the sons of good parents were suspected of getting involved in robberies, and even worse than that. Kristiania was more or less invaded by young people who copied the gangs from France, to whom it was all a sport …

Sport!

And Uncle Martin had announced from his own *Social-Demokraten* that the public would not tolerate any protection of upper-class children. Poor boys, his mother had sighed then.

He knew that the worried glances conveyed nothing other than concern, but it tormented him because that concern made him into a child again. Only last summer he had loved that concern, as recently as last spring he had needed it, as a distraction. Now that he was just on holiday, doing things he was praised for, it became burdensome that she was protecting him. Those skinny boys from Grünerløkken, he thought, they would have been suspected; not him. He could do what he wanted. He *would* do … but he didn't want her concern.

One day there is a letter for Little Lord. He finds it in the yellow wooden box on the jetty. It smells of shut-in sunshine when you open that box, almost like in the bathing hut.

The letter is lying at the bottom, on its own apart from some scraps of that issue of *The Missionary* which made its way out here by mistake weeks ago. He reads the writing on the envelope several times before he dares to pick up the letter. A hand grips his heart. A letter means something wrong. The large, round, slightly irregular letters reveal that it is from a child, a boy in his class – all the possibilities whirl through him.

Deep inside he knows who it is from.

He doesn't open the letter at once, he picks it up gingerly and looks around. The south wind ruffles his hair gently, everything is as it was before on this jetty where he knows every stone and where he can see the deep grooves cut into the posts by the hawsers. Everything is as before, and everything is different because of a letter: he has entered a new state which completely transforms the previous contradictory 'state'. This new state shifts everything in time. It takes him back to all the alarming things from last spring; all the undiscovered things resurface and give him a hollow feeling in his diaphragm.

He walks along a path at random with the letter, up between two garden fences which need painting. At the top there is a kind of viewing point where there is never anyone except on Sundays. It's like a small, trodden-down crater, with dust beneath trampled grass. Suddenly he takes the letter out of his pocket, drops it on the ground and walks away. He gets the idea that maybe nothing *exists* if you don't let it; that when he turns round some way away there won't be any letter, just the brown, dusty crater with thin grass growing on it. But when he turns, the letter is lying there, and he runs quickly over and picks it up so that no-one else can get there first. He suddenly knows that no-one must get there before him and discover that there was a letter for him. Letters are an event in summer. Everyone will demand to have at least a hint as to what it is about.

Then he opens the letter and sees at once that it is from Andreas, and instantly he knows that it is about the bike Andreas could borrow if he went to pick it up at Blåsen after that ill-fated night of arson and 'violence against the police' as it said in the paper. Andreas writes that the police have been round to see them twice to ask about the bike. The first time was long ago, a couple of weeks after the end-of-term exams at Frøknene Wollkwarts', the second time when the family came back from their short visit to the aunts in the country at Toten. It transpires that someone from the police has noticed that smart English bike and recognised it. He admits he has used it regularly.

And at first Andreas simply denied it, but then he admitted that he borrowed the bike up at Blåsen, but he put it back again the first evenings. They knew the bike was an English model and a bit different from the bikes here at home. And now Andreas' father has demanded that he tell the police the truth, or at least tell him. But he's not going to tell the truth, not to anyone. Because he thought perhaps it was something Wilfred had done, and he, Andreas, was not the sort to betray a friend …

Signed: *your friend Andreas.*

Wilfred stands there with his stomach churning. But his hands are steady, they're not shaking. Friend, he thinks and feels a wave of shame and guilt. The next moment he is hard again, hard and alert. A friend. What are friends for? He lent Andreas the bike for an indefinite period. It was an experience for Andreas, who has no bike. By chance Andreas has got involved in something in connection with that bike. It's not his problem. Was it his intention back then to transfer anything to Andreas in the event that the constable had taken note of the bike? Was it his intention to hurt Andreas?

It was not his intention. He is quite sure of that as he stands there in the small crater on top of the lookout point. He knows at the same time that he had thought it would be good if Andreas went up to collect that bike – for various reasons. He had so much on just then. He's not the sort to betray a friend …

Who's not the sort? He, Wilfred. He's not that sort. Andreas isn't that sort either. They are friends, stand shoulder to shoulder. Andreas stands shoulder to shoulder. Now it's his turn. Or perhaps it's Andreas' turn for a bit longer? Andreas hasn't finished with the matter yet. He'll have to work it out himself. After that it will be *his,* Wilfred's turn. Then *he* will have to work it out. They stand shoulder to shoulder.

He tears the letter into small pieces to demonstrate that he's finished with it. What is it Andreas actually expects from him? Nothing. There's not a word in the letter about him expecting anything. Or was there something? Anyway, it's too late to check now. And what can he do, really? Soon, very soon, they will stop digging into that episode. There wasn't actually any fire, and that stupid constable has been involved in a number of incidents since then, of course. In fact no-one is interested in it. It's just something the newspapers are writing about. As for him, he's finished with it. He's involved in something quite different and more important …

And suddenly it all rises up to confront him. It washes over him like a mighty wave you can't see the end of in any direction: Erna, Kristine, Mother, the police … Feelings, words, everything he has said and done, as if it was someone else who had spoken and acted for him and led him deeper into a thicket of absurdity. He stands there with the pieces of the letter in both hands and clenches his fists: 'What's wrong with me?'

The next moment terror struck him. He knelt down in the brown dust and bored his fingers down through the gravel, through the grass; wanted to bury the remains of that ill-treated letter, bury himself with all his cares and his conscience: 'What's wrong, what's wrong with me?'

He stood up, suddenly triumphant, filled with impotent anger at them all. He would kill them, yes kill them, one after the other, in a cunning and unheard-of way, kill all that consideration they were stifling him with, and all temptations – until he emerged alone and clarified, with no family or self-sacrificing friends who were shaking in their shoes because of his misdeeds. He would exterminate all devotion in himself and around him and stand alone in a world which was stupid, stupid, and which he would torment just as he desired.

He had an amazing sensation of floating as he stood there alone in the shallow crater. Fragments of tunes from music he had heard washed over him and turned into a different, new music which arose within him; words he had read came floating along and broke away from their context and created new sentences with threatening import. The cool summer wind became a storm which surged around his ears and made

192

the benevolent day violent. He was possessed by a desire to annihilate; it filled him completely and inflated him into someone he didn't know. He felt an amazing surge of growth happening to him, and it did not release him. It made him bigger, really big; it was no longer a matter of being grown-up, but of being *big*. He was powerful. He could do everything. He could hover, condemn to life or death. He could avenge himself to the thousandth generation on all who wanted to violate his right to expand and be big.

He saw the small white steamer setting out across the fjord. It rounded the pole in the middle of the fjord and the sun blazed suddenly in all the windows on board; then it turned in again on the other side and went out of sight. All at once he felt tired and abandoned. All swelling thoughts of revenge vanished with that peaceful boat. Andreas, he thought, he's there in town now, up in Frognerveien, and he's at his wits' end. And he saw again that timid face as he was reciting 'Ole the Flower Seller'. He saw Andreas' father under the fan palm in the dining room with the unpolished silver plate in the sideboard, as he had sat there once with a newspaper over his head, like a buffer against the world.

And now it was precisely this world against which that man was tying to defend himself that would descend on him like an avalanche, and all because a boy in a different street, in an entirely different world, had loosened a stone – out of a need to unsettle, to disturb the balance of all that surrounding security which found no echo in him? No wonder that Andreas' father demanded an explanation. No doubt he had enough from before, with all his worries underneath the palm.

Despite that, it seemed to Wilfred deeply unfair that he, who felt the stirrings of a conqueror's knowledge, should plunge himself into misfortune for the sake of keeping the peace in a dining room on Frognerveien. What was it about his friend Andreas that was so special? He couldn't even remember exactly what he looked like.

Betray. Betray a friend …

Just words – perhaps? Wasn't that precisely one of those words they surrounded everything with, so that people like Andreas' father could sleep in their rocking chairs with a newspaper as a protection against flies? People have to learn to cope, said Uncle Martin. People have to stand on their own two feet. He looked down for a moment at his own long legs, sunburnt and sockless. Was he really standing on them? – and were they his?

Yes. Because this was all just temporary, something he had to get out of – to reach his great independence where he could be alone. That cursed letter. It was as if he couldn't get rid of even the torn remains. Suddenly he couldn't think of a single place where he could get rid of them. He threw them up into the air. But they blew back like a cloud, almost all together, and fell around him, all those white scraps with stupid blue ink on them. Strange wind which blew in circles …

Yet again he gathered up the scraps of letter and stood there clutching them in his hands. Then he pushed the scraps into his pocket. He would take them home and burn them, of course. Nothing could be simpler. Just hold a match to them – somewhere or other, and the whole letter would cease to exist.

Cease to exist, cease to exist. But not in Andreas' world. That perhaps consisted entirely of fear and bad omens right now. That anguished letter was not a warning, but a final cry for help from someone who needed rescuing. It wasn't a question of lying face down in the water, white and silent. And it wasn't a question of heroic deeds, but of decency.

Decency – ? Who was it who had used that word? What a torment. What a torment to have words always humming just beneath the surface; other people's words that wanted to get out and be used and in a way create the ideas themselves. How could he know what everything was when there were so many words around them, grown-ups' words that he had taken over before he got his own words, because he had always been amongst grown-ups.

Uncle Martin. Uncle Martin again. He was the one who talked about decency. But he was rich, he was secure, he was fat …

Perhaps you needed to be fat?

Fat like Uncle Martin, or poor like Fru Frisaksen, or both. Invincible. He felt as if the sun was shining straight through him, as he stood there unable to make his mind up. A lobster casting its shell – he had read about them. They hid away under rocks and overhangs, with no protection even against soft fish. And he who had believed he was …

Yes, but he was! He was not transparent. God sees everything, Frøken Wollkwarts had said, without any real conviction. So if this God, whom not even Mother believed in, could see straight through him as he stood there – and took no notice of him and his letter … He was the only one who knew anything, after all. That little scaredy-cat in town, and that weak father of his – what did he, Wilfred, know about those two that wasn't in a letter that hardly existed? It wasn't *his* palms and soup smells, merely a conglomeration of mess and poverty that he had gone exploring for fun. Besides, Andreas had warts on his hands. If it had been Andreas lying there face down in the sea, he would have taken care not to touch his hands. He could always have saved him a bit from dying, but he didn't want to touch his warts.

The bear – ! He could picture Andreas' helpless face at the exam festivities, he felt yet again how the bottom dropped out of his world as he stood there with his treasure, 'Ole the Flower Seller'; and suddenly there was no treasure - - just like he himself with Nick Carter once long ago. Yes – he *had* saved him from dying a bit, warts or no warts.

That confounded bear. That confounded, damned, infernal desire to get involved in other people's affairs. What was the point of that for someone who wanted to be alone? He could have let that fool stand there with his bear. Wouldn't Uncle Martin have done just that? Fat and good-humoured, he could no doubt betray the whole world and afterwards sit in a comfortable chair and smoke his cigar and talk with concern about poverty and threats to the social order; about this war he was so preoccupied by. Perhaps it would be a great idea to have a war – something which swept away everything people had got mixed up in, so that they could get out and save their country …

But suddenly it was as if that letter meant something quite different to him. He knew he had to choose now, between all the things: Mother, Erna, Kristine, school - - The music academy, which Uncle René had written to Mother about; there was a place for him there. But he didn't want to meet that Mozart again, that young genius they had made him read all about, who was pushed and pushed by the sort of father who was going to make something extraordinary of him. The letter – he had torn it to pieces. Like everything else. It was all in pieces. Every time he had to choose between things, he had torn them to pieces instead, so as to escape from having it all around him, escape from choosing. Perhaps that was what they were all doing, and that was why they went from one thing to another, just *pretending* at everything.

Not Fru Frisaksen. Not Andreas' father. They were what they were.

But when some people were what they were, that meant they were failures. All the others pretended and pretended, so long as they could keep it up. But perhaps the problem was that they didn't make enough of it! That they couldn't keep it up, not all the time. And that must be when they suddenly got a sad look on their faces and answered absent-mindedly, or became unreasonable. Like Mother. Like Kristine. Like Frøken Wollkwarts when she was mild and understanding, and then suddenly was not mild any longer, but abrupt and determined and with repressed anger behind her mildness, so that the boys froze in anticipation of something unreasonable …

He had reached the other side of the narrow isthmus as he walked along pondering. There was an overhang of the hill here which made it dark even at midday. There were no houses here on this edge, which was marshy and stony, marshy and stony, right until you got over onto the other side of the plateau with a long, shallow inlet of the fjord where the water smelt and bubbled over a muddy bottom. Right in there was where Fru Frisaksen lived; but in the middle of the plateau was the gardener's house in the midst of a patch of cleared land, drained by years of toil.

He walked round the gardener's house in a wide arc. He couldn't bear the sight of Tom any longer, and especially not of his industrious and grateful parents. He heard the gardener's dog barking between the buildings. But when he stood outside Fru Frisaksen's red house, he was seized by a kind of lethargy. He had no idea what he had been thinking, going out there where no summer visitors ever went. Now he could see that the house wasn't red at all, but grey, with just a few red patches on the end wall to the north, where the sun had least effect. So she must be so poor she couldn't afford any red paint. Or perhaps she didn't care? The house would see her out, she must have thought. She was the type who didn't *pretend* …

Of course, that was what he wanted. He wanted to see the house. It was grey. It was happy with its grey colour, which actually was quite pretty, almost silvery grey. One of the windows had sawn-off planks nailed over it; in another there were rags and newspaper. Far out where there was just enough water he could see Fru Frisaksen's white boat; although that was grey as well. It was no golden bowl, lying there in the shadow of the hills. It must be a long way to row each day, round the three lights and right out to the fishing grounds.

All right, so it was a long way. The house was crumbling and the boat shabby and the distance long. Those were her problems. He knew that now. It was no more remarkable than that. Out here she had found her solitude. If she couldn't become mistress of her fate in competition with other people, she would become so without them. It was just a matter of conquering what was there, of retreating until what you had to conquer was small enough and easy enough to conquer. In that way everyone could come to be a ruler.

So now he knew *that*. He turned and was about to walk back in an arc across the plateau. The bog cotton nodded at him from all the small clumps, the redshank flew up from the pool in the middle, peeping. In his pocket he could feel the scraps of

197

letter. At the same moment he sensed someone watching him.

He turned round just quickly enough to see Fru Frisaksen pull her wrinkled face away from the one window with glass in it. He made up his mind quickly, went straight over to the door on the south side and knocked hard. Fru Frisaksen came to the door at once. 'So it's you now!' she said. She didn't seem surprised.

'Yes indeed, it's me now!' he said cheerfully, copying her intonation.

'Does your mother need help with something? Doing the laundry perhaps?'

He thought for a moment. 'I came to visit you, Fru Frisaksen.'

Was she suspicious, or maybe she was touched? It wasn't possible to tell. 'Come in then,' she said.

He went in with a feeling of uncertainty. He was so used to guessing what people meant. They said the friendliest of things when they were full of enmity, or they masked pleasure with indifference, but Fru Frisaksen didn't even ask him to sit down. It wasn't so easy either. The table was covered in a tangled fishing net which spilled out over the attached bench and across the floor. Otherwise it was neat and tidy, but there was nothing to sit on. The brass rail on the stove was gleaming. There was a sweet smell of something – like at Andreas' place on Frognerveien.

'That's what it's like here,' she said. 'I suppose you were curious to see what Madam Frisaksen's place looked like?'

'Yes,' he said.

'Your mother doesn't know you're here?'

'No.'

He stood in the middle of the roomy kitchen floor and enjoyed just being honest.

'Well, that's that,' said Fru Frisaksen. 'Now you've seen what it looks like.'

Was there a hint of unfriendliness in her tone after all? The door to the small bedroom was ajar. He stole a glance in there and could just make out a bunk bed with a dark grey counterpane.

'It's just the bedroom in there. There isn't anything more,' she said.

'I know,' he said.

'You know?'

'I could work it out.'

A gleam came into her eyes now, a stern friendliness which was reminiscent of the expression he imagined in them when the sun was slanting and she was on her way to the fishing grounds. 'I see,' she said, 'you go around working things out!'

'Yes.'

All his glibness had disappeared. He couldn't be bothered to invent anything, or feign anything. He stood there as if in a trance.

'Fru Frisaksen,' he said finally, 'is this what it's really like?'

'Really like?' She stood looking at him for a moment. 'You mean, is this all? Yes, my boy, this is all – since Frisaksen died.'

He thought: now she could allow herself the luxury of a sigh. That's what my people would have done.

'How long ago was that?' he asked.

'Fifteen years this autumn.'

He felt intoxicated by her uncompromising hardness. 'And no-one comes to visit you here – what would happen if you were ill, Fru Frisaksen?'

'You mean if I took to dying? It might be four or five weeks before anyone noticed that.'

He thought: she *will* ask me to sit down. I shall get the better of her.

'I would notice,' he said, 'when I didn't see you rowing past in your boat.'

'I wonder?' said Fru Frisaksen quickly. 'There's a great difference between noticing that you're there and *not* noticing that you're *not* there.'

He got cross because it was true. 'I *would* notice!' he said.

'Right, let's say that.'

It occurred to him that they were discussing a painful topic. Why had he forced himself upon that poor woman?

'I'm sorry,' he said. He turned towards the door to go. On

the wall just beside the window a photo was pinned up by a drawing pin. It was a young man in seaman's clothes, almost a boy, photographed against a café sign, with three woman and a man walking along the pavement in the background. He stopped demonstratively; perhaps now he would get an explanation.

'From Portugal,' he said.

She went over and took down the photo, then looked at the back.

'How could you know that?' Now her eyes really were twinkling with a sort of kindliness.

'I didn't know, I guessed. Women who wear that kind of thing on their heads – I've seen pictures of Oporto.'

'O-p-o-r-t-o,' she spelt out slowly, with the photo held out at arm's length, as far from her eyes as possible. 'You guessed right. It's my son, Birger. Yes, it's a long time ago.'

'I can see that.'

'You can see that?' Now she seemed genuinely surprised. 'How can you see that too then?'

'It says 1910 next to Oporto, that's two years ago.'

'Just think, is it two years …' she said. She dropped her arm and just stood there holding the photograph. 'Is it so long ago?' she said.

'Where is he now?'

'That's the last I heard from him. He was a ship's boy then.'

The two steps to the door were an infinite distance. He had no idea how he was to manage them.

'It must be sad for you, Fru Frisaksen!' he said. Those cursed tears, now they came into his eyes from force of habit, his habit of dissimulating when he knew that tears would be effective.

She stood there, looking straight at him. Her thin lips suddenly moved – a faint trembling, which drew her lips inwards – like a seam that's stitched on the inside, he thought, in order to check his tears. 'Well, goodbye then, Fru Frisaksen,' he said, holding out his hand. She took it quickly. Her hand felt like a hard root. He went out quickly and closed the door quietly behind him. Then he walked slowly away from the house, half dazed. The low gardener's house swam in a mist before his eyes, and the greenhouses floated over the plateau like mirages. Now he needed to find somewhere to go with his tears. Suddenly he could see no way out, just wandered slowly inland. Sea birds were flying in from the fjord, low over the land. There'll be rain, he thought.

Then he heard someone behind him; he turned quickly and it was Fru Frisaksen. She was holding something in her hand, a glass egg. 'I thought perhaps you could have this,' she said breathlessly, holding out the egg. 'He had such fun with it, Birger did.'

Those damned tears – it was too late to hide them now. He stood there with the glass egg in his hand and let his tears flow. She was standing right in front of him in the stiff grass, and it was only now he saw that she was smaller than him. And at that moment he no longer minded about those tears that no-one in the world should have seen. Suddenly it didn't matter with Fru Frisaksen.

It was just for a moment, then she turned away again, dry-eyed and dry through and through. She muttered something as she trotted off again – not running, not walking, just trotting with small regular steps. He saw that she wasn't wearing shoes, just thick oversocks fastened with string.

'Thank you!' he called. But it was as if he was dreaming. His voice stuck in his throat, couldn't get out. He walked a few steps after her. But then she was inside, behind a closed door. As if she had never been there.

He stood clutching the glass egg in his hand. Didn't dare look at it yet. For now it was as if beings all around him could see straight through him again. Lobster without a shell. Fru Frisaksen's cold glance had been replaced by a glance coming from everywhere, a mighty eye he was shut inside, so that it could examine him from all sides. He raised his hands above his head to defend himself against it. But it was there. He walked along with his hands raised, but the eye was around him on all sides. He walked quicker and quicker, started to run, holding his hands up the whole time with the good, smooth glass egg in his right hand, he ran quicker and quicker over the plateau, past the low greenhouses, over the marsh, towards the cliff where it was dark and cold. The whole time with his arms raised, his plimsolls dripping wet after a while. The seagulls flew up from the plateau as he ran, circling low over him and around him, following him like a hostile cloud, but not attacking, just something hanging over him and after him, they too a part of that enquiring eye, with their sharp shrieks and their cawing – until it seemed that the whole of space was a white eye turned on him.

When he reached the shelter of the cliff he threw himself down, panting. He lay like that for a long time. It was like a den in here where the eye couldn't reach. Then he stole the glass egg out from beneath him, where he had hidden it from the eye. He held it up to the grey light outside the den. There was a little white house inside the egg, a fairytale house. When he turned the egg over, it filled with snow. The little house lay inside the egg in a whirl of snow, a whole world to itself, protected by the snow and the form of the egg itself. A world of snow. He let the snow settle over the house. Then he turned the egg gently again, and it started snowing again. He stared at the glass egg, hypnotized, and was slowly filled with delight and horror, which was one and the same feeling and encapsulated everything: the dead ship's boy Birger – or was he sailing the seas and couldn't spare a postcard? Had he too hidden in a world which was to be his alone, just as the glass egg with its miracle of snow had no doubt been his whole world on many dark autumn evenings under the paraffin lamp in the house by the bay, whilst the lighthouse keeper sat straightening out nets which had got tangled and which he had finally been caught in. Hadn't they said they had found him in a net at the end, stuck fast like a fish? From the far distance in his soul perhaps he heard his mother's voice – the voices of all mothers, calling and calling with a longing which just pushed you further and further away. Could he himself not hear those voices now? Or was it music: humming Mozart, humming, humming, an endless filigree of notes … No, it was rain. It was the rain rushing outside the den he was lying in. Finally it had arrived, that redeeming summer rain – the crying of that enormous eye which surrounded him.

He felt in his pocket and touched the damp fragments of the letter from Andreas.

The world of the egg – that was what brought everything together. He saw the opening of a different den, into the darkness between planks of wood where he had played at tempting little boys into violence. The letter from Andreas. Fru Frisaksen's husband who had got trapped in a net. Birger, who had moved further and further into his own lonely world, where he was no doubt caught so fast that he didn't have an innocent thought to spare for his wrinkled mother in the grey house which had once been red. Andreas' father, lonely under the palm. Yet again he held up the egg and let the snow sprinkle the little house. There was a bewitching loneliness over this enclosed space full of falling snow. Perhaps the ship's boy Birger was sitting in a deserted bar in Pensacola now, remembering the egg and feeling he was in such a world, hypnotized by his misdeeds and incapable of even the slightest communication. He had got trapped in his own net.

Now he himself felt the net around him. It was as if it was pulling tighter and tighter, and soon it would block off the opening of the den under the cliff. He got to his feet with the egg in his hand and ran out from under the cliff, bent double. The rain was pouring down. It had washed away the whole of the staring eye which had surrounded him. The seagulls were flying low over the land and took no notice of him as he headed back to the isthmus which led out to the island.

Back home he knew something had happened as soon as he entered the house. There was no-one in the hall, no-one in the sitting-room or dining-room, no-one out on the covered veranda. Mother came quickly downstairs. She looked serious.

'Why didn't you come home for dinner?' she asked.

'Is it so late? I didn't know …'

'So late, it was four hours ago. Where have you been?'

'At Fru Frisaksen's.' It just popped out.

'At Madam Frisaksen's – why?'

'I don't know. She gave me this.'

Mother took the egg in her hand without looking at it. 'Aunt Kristine is leaving tomorrow,' she said.

He knew he had to ask why. But it was as if he couldn't be bothered. He felt as if he was still in Fru Frisaksen's sitting room, he could smell the sweetish smell of thyme. *That* was it. That was how it smelt at Andreas's as well. They put thyme in the pea soup.

'I was going to go to town tomorrow as well,' he said.

'To town, why?'

'I've had a letter from Andreas. There's something I have to help him with.'

He could see that she would demand to see the letter. He pulled out his pocket, and some of the pieces fell out. The rest he dug out of his trouser pocket. 'He's asked me to come. It's to do with school.'

'Nonsense,' she said shortly. 'Not tomorrow, at least. Later perhaps. Kristine is taking a trip to the mountains, to Aunt Valborg and Uncle Martin.'

He thought quickly: what has she said – since I'm allowed to go to town another day, after she's gone? He would have to take the bull by the horns.

'Why is Kristine leaving?' he said.

Mother seemed to exhale the words: 'Your aunt thinks it's a bit boring here with us, she has such a short holiday.'

Could she have said that? So direct – or perhaps it wasn't direct? Had she actually been rude in order to disguise the fact that she felt troubled by what had happened, but had not led to anything further – she had kept away from him since that afternoon.

'Well, I have to go into town some day,' he said coldly. He was still clutching the shreds of the letter.

'That suits me fine,' she said. 'I have to go to town one day, so we can travel together, and you can go and visit Andreas while I have my hair done.'

She was still holding that strange egg in her hand. He couldn't understand why he had let her keep hold of it. He held out his hand. But now she held the glass egg up and looked at it in the fading light. She turned it in her hand so that it started to snow. 'But for all the world,' she said, 'an egg like that…'

'I'd like it back, Mother,' he said, 'it's mine. It was Birger's once.'

'Birger's?' she said, staring at him. Now he could see that she was examining the egg. Her finger followed a thin line which was etched on the egg. He hadn't seen it before. It formed an S.

'It was Birger's!' he said again. He was cross now. She wanted to take away everything which belonged just to him.

'Your father was holding that egg in his hand when he died,' she said.

15

From the moment mother and son separated on Egertorvet Wilfred knew that everything was going to go well. The actual ceremony in the café had not gone so well. Despite their struggles to find the old tone, it really just become more and more distant. But it made it easier that they were both aware of it and stopped trying.

Now she watched him crossing the street, so straight and free – a young man!

Those three days since that evening at Skovly had been less difficult than she had imagined beforehand – if she had ever faced up to the fact that her little boy would one day have to know about his father. The boy had shown a maturity which would have horrified her six months ago. Now his first question was not about his father's death, but about Birger and Fru Frisaksen. It was as if he was obsessed by this woman whom she had forced herself to forget over the years. He had simply asked how old she was. And when she had answered truthfully that the woman who lived in the bay was about her own age, it was as if he had known the rest at once: 'Is Birger Father's son?'

She couldn't understand it afterwards, but it was as if that story only became completely true for her at the moment he asked. A story was exactly what it was. Ever since she had thought of it as a 'story' – not that there was someone living, six years older than her own beloved boy, who was his half-brother, if you thought about it the way people did nowadays … And now, after all these years, when it appeared to her as a far more urgent reality than it had done at the time, not to mention all the years since then as a vague memory, it was suddenly not painful any more. That injury which had been sealed up inside her was transformed into a mild curiosity: these people had carried on living a sort of life just as before. The despised Madam Frisaksen was suddenly not a figure in a boat, an image you had to accept as a slight blot on the landscape in the evenings with an extremely vague connection to something in the past. She was the same person who had once done domestic duties in the country houses, and who had attracted improper glances from some of the gentlemen on account of a kind of wild gypsy beauty of the sort that other women hate, and which as a consolation to them soon fades. She was lighthouse-keeper Frisaksen's life sentence for a youthful indiscretion and – so it was said – the real reason for that gruff faun's growing melancholy; until one day he was *found* – that expression was always used that autumn. The details were glossed over as too unpleasant. But the fact was that this creature was still Madam Frisaksen and counted as a sort of widow of a well-regarded servant of the state. And her son …

But when Little Lord had said: 'But then he should really be called Sagen? Why shouldn't he have just as much as I have …' – that was too much for Fru Susanna, for goodness sake! What kind of ideas did he have about the way the world functioned? Ideas, it was true, which had scandalously enough been aired in the country's parliament,* but which were rejected by all decent people and which he at least, boy that he was, could not have grasped

Although how much had he grasped, really … Later that

evening, when she asked him how he had come to think so much about that kind of thing, he had answered: 'I didn't think, Mother, but I guessed inside myself without being aware of it, I think, because we always guess, because we'd rather guess and hint than ask and explain, because it's a part of being well brought up.'

She hadn't had much to say to that. Six months ago, she knew, she would have been crushed by those words, not by sorrow, but by disappointment that the boy lived in a world beside the one they shared; a world full of guessing and God knows what else. Perhaps a completely different world, for all she knew.

Now she suspected that was indeed the case, but at the same time she knew that it wasn't true to the extent she would have believed if it had come as a shock to her. So she for her part must have guessed – also without really knowing it – that many things had changed, between them and in general. She was reminded of her brother Martin, as they were sitting there in the living room and had calmed down a little. Was it something like this he had tried to prepare her for with his constant reminders that the boy was growing, that he was even an unusually early developer? It was true that she had thought of him as a little Mozart at the spinette. Early developer, yes – but in his own way, or rather in her way: a dream …

How mature she had only realized when, thankfully, she had been brought up against the question she had always imagined would be the worst of all; it didn't even come as a question. He had said, and clearly meant it to be the end of the conversation: 'Mother, I believe that Father's death was a surprise. Don't tell me any more about it this evening.'

All those tears – she would rather forget them now. All the questions which were not asked. She would rather remember that he came over to her chair, sat on the arm and took her hand, and said: 'Poor Mother, it can't have been easy for you either.'

Although that 'either' continued to pain her. Who was he thinking of? That madam in the boat or her bastard son at sea?

Or was he thinking of himself? Was her Little Lord not happy? Was everything they lived an illusion, an existence on the sidelines of real life which only counted occasionally, just as she sometimes had the feeling that all of her own existence only had the authenticity she herself granted it in her indolent rejection of anything unpleasant?

She stood watching him walk across Egertorvet in the dusty August sunshine. She saw how straight and slight he looked, how tall and supple he was. She cast a furtive glance around to see whether other people had noticed. But they were preoccupied with keeping an eye out for automobiles and horse-drawn carriages which came into constant conflict because of their different speeds on the corner of Akersgaten and Carl Johan.

When he reached the parliament building he turned and waved. She felt a wave of pride wash over her, the pride of a mother and a young girl at the same time, and straight after one of abandonment. She saw him set off walking quickly towards Atheneum, where he was going to take the Frogner tram up to this friend he suddenly had such an urge to see.

As Wilfred got off the tram in Frognerveien, he saw Andreas and his father coming out of the house where they lived. He stood across the street, not knowing what to do. He'd had the feeling that his plans would work out somehow or other. He had a sensation of victory, of all the convincing childishness he knew he could assume to conceal his far from childish thoughts. But he had counted on finding Andreas at home alone. So idiotic. The two hours he had before he was to meet Mother at home on Drammensveien were no more than precisely the time he suspected they would need in order to reach some kind of result.

What kind? He had no idea. No thought of sacrificing himself or being noble. Just to visit his friend and let fate decide. Now it looked as if fate was deciding things for him in a quite different way.

Father and son walked up towards Frogner plass. He crossed

the street and followed them at some distance. It was the middle of the day and Frogner was deserted for the holidays. No-one to hide behind if one of them decided to turn round.

But neither of them did. They walked along slowly, slightly stooping, as if with a definite goal in mind. They certainly weren't just out for a stroll. Now they were turning down Nobels gate, and he ran as fast as he could so as not to lose them round the corner.

They were right in front of him as he rounded the corner, so close that he pulled back and waited for a moment. Then he fell into step behind them again, just ten to fifteen metres back. A little way down the street they swung in to the left between the small houses. He followed quickly. When he got there, they were nowhere to be seen. There was a small house with a modest sign on it: Police Station.

He felt icy cold. So that was it. He had arrived at the last moment, or perhaps already too late? The most important thing was that he had arrived. This was different from all the times before; not for a moment did he play the game that he could change his mind. He knew that this was how it had to be. And all the time he could see Fru Frisaksen's face in front of him.

He came in to a hallway with three coathooks and a spitoon. He knocked on a door. A tall policeman in uniform opened it. He looked quickly into the room behind him. There sat Andreas and his father on two straight-backed chairs. They looked lost. 'Those two,' he said to the policeman, 'I saw them come in here. I'm the one who owns that bike. That's my classmate Andreas, he wrote to me, I lent it to him.'

Soon after he was in the middle of it, just as he had imagined. The small bearded constable was there as well. He was in plain clothes now, and looked like an abandoned little troll. Little Lord stood straight as a taper and answered all the questions, his name, why he had left his bike there, what he was doing in that part of town. He answered politely and quickly that he had cycled over to have a look round, but had strained a tendon in his leg and had left the bike there and locked it. Then he'd taken the tram from Bislet down into town and the Bygdø tram home. It was for the same reason he'd asked his friend to collect the bike, and let him borrow it for a while. The little troll of a constable was asked whether he thought this was the boy he had seen that night. The constable squinted up at Wilfred under bushy eyebrows and tried to look fierce. Wilfred had shot up since the spring. The constable looked into that open, honest face, so different from everything he thought he remembered from that night in Sorgenfrigaten long ago. Then he shook his head. 'It wasn't him,' he said.

Andreas' father treated the boys to cakes and pop in the pavilion in Frogner Park. He took out a brown leather purse of the sort where you shake coins out into the lid, and paid as soon as their order arrived. 'You can have more than that, you know,' he said to Wilfred, when he didn't want a whole bottle of red pop. It was the first spontaneous thing Wilfred had heard him say. The invitation itself was transmitted by means of a dig in his son's ribs. Andreas gleamed behind his glasses, bursting with the need to confide. He drank so much pop that almost straight away he had to visit the toilet, which was in a little shed right over by the main courtyard. Wilfred was left with his father, who wiped his white forehead with a tired gesture.

'You're the one they call Little Lord?' he said. And suddenly his face opened up in an angular smile, which looked unnatural, as if it was years since the whole smiling mechanism had been used.

'My mother called me that. Well, she still does quite often.'

'Andreas talks a lot about you. It's good he has a friend like you.'

Wilfred felt uncomfortable, as if he was sitting on nails. Just that word 'friend' made his insides churn. His triumphant lie at the police station had succeeded above all expectations, or rather precisely according to the vague expectations he always fostered on lucky days. But this he had not calculated, that he should be bogged down in intimacy with this pathetic man he felt so little sympathy for.

'Andreas is a good chap,' he said thickly. He wasn't looking forward to good old Andreas coming back, relieved, and energetically setting about fraternizing together with his father.

'Is – is Andreas' mother better now?' he asked cautiously.

A shadow passed over the face of the grown-up.

'She'll never get better,' he said. 'But don't say anything to Andreas.'

So these two were pretending as well, playing the same game as they played in Little Lord's family. But the game came to seem so poor and mean when he thought about that brown dining room on Frognerveien. Could they not have been like Fru Frisaksen – straightforward and unpleasant?

'Oh well – ' the man sighed, narrowing his eyes against the August sun which shone through the trees in the park. 'It's fine for us with this lovely park just next door,' he said. Instantly the boy reconstructed the chain of thoughts which had led to this: everyone was in the country, they had just been at Toten for a while, it didn't sound much fun. Now they were back in their nice flat in town – it was just fine for them, right next door to that lovely park, tram to the front door, dairy in the same building …

'No, when you live here it's no hardship being in town in summer,' said Wilfred.

The face of the man opposite lit up. 'Yes, isn't that so, that's what I say as well – that lovely park and …' he made an uncertain gesture. 'Besides, we went to Toten for a while,' he added. 'Andreas loves being at Toten.'

Did he really believe that? Wilfred stole a glance at him. Toten was the worst thing Andreas knew and his mother's sister was a 'fat madam' who spent most of her time in the barn with the cows and asked them to fetch water all day long. And the house was full of flies …

'And then you don't have the flies in town,' said Wilfred.

'That's right. The flies!' Andreas' father became more and more cheerful. Andreas came back at that moment, ready for cake and more pop. 'Your friend and I were just talking about how pleasant it is to be in town,' said his father, 'just think of all the flies!'

Andreas threw a quick glance at his friend. Had he let slip that Toten was infested with flies and unbearable on a summer holiday? Wilfred could see his anxiety like an extra layer over his face. So he wanted to spare his father that truth as well.

'… so I mean, even if you like being at Toten …'

Again that grateful gleam in his eyes. Would he never escape getting entangled in saving people from their own falseness? Why could these two losers not be open and honest with each other – why should Andreas not know that his mother was mortally ill, why should they play let's pretend day in and day out when they didn't even get so much out of it that they could stop worrying about upsetting each other for a single minute?

Andreas' father looked at his watch. Wilfred thought: you know exactly what time it is, you old office fixture, you have a watch in your head buzzing away like a fly; you *always* know what time it is. Now you're going to say goodness me is that the time …

'Goodness me, is that the time …'

Wilfred had looked at his own watch: 'Half-past twelve!' he said, sounding amazed. Was there another grateful little glance from that transparent man?

'I'm sure your father has to get back to the office … And I have to meet my mother,' said Wilfred. He thought it was best to rescue them from all the words and at the same time help himself to get away. But it was easy to see the disappointment on Andreas' face. They were so easy to read, these people, that you felt you were cheating them.

'So that matter's all done and dusted!' said Andreas' father, getting up.

Wilfred thought: that was clever of him, he rounded it all off with the requisite comment, and at the same time cut short any explanations which could be uncomfortable both for him and for us.

'It must be awful to be guilty of something,' said Wilfred,

looking boldly into the man's eyes – 'I mean, when you see how easy it is to give the wrong impression.'

'You're a sensible lad all right,' said Andreas' father calmly, holding out his hand. Wilfred took it. It was a flabby hand, flabby and slightly damp.

The boys sat there for a bit longer. Wasps were paddling in the spilt pop on the table. There was a faint rustle in the old trees. The intrusive August sun hurt their eyes. Andreas smiled conspiratorially behind his round steel glasses.

'You tackled that police chap fine!' he said.

Wilfred looked at him coldly. 'It's not difficult when you're telling the truth,' he said. Andreas looked as if he'd had a bucket of cold water thrown over him. He started to say something, then stopped. Now he looked just like when he was standing in the middle of the floor at Frøknene Wollkwarts', reciting the poem about the bear.

'I'm going to earn money to get my own bike,' he said instead. 'I'm going to start work at the warehouse where Dad works.'

At last a straightforward comment. Wilfred felt a warm glow of pleasure. 'I think that's just great,' he said. 'What a good idea. It's decent of your father as well.'

'Decent?' Clearly Andreas hadn't seen it from that aspect.

'Yes, it's decent of him. Instead of letting you just hang around and live off your family, like …' Wilfred pulled a face. He realised he was making too much of it, but now he'd got started: 'My uncle Martin says that times are changing, that the working classes … I mean, there's going to be a different order now, people like us who own something from before will have a terribly difficult time, people will demand their rights. He says there'll be war between England and Germany. England has 66 battleships and Germany only 37. He says England ought to attack now, before Germany grows even stronger, and before this Kiel Canal is opened.'

'War? Is there going to be a war?' The boys regarded each other tensely, fired up by what they imagined of war and violence.

'Yes, not in this country of course, but between England and Germany, and then it might well happen that others join in, he says. Russia has fifteen battleships and Austria-Hungary thirteen …'

'How do you know all that?'

'Don't they talk about things like that at your place? Uncle Martin …'

'They don't talk about war. Father says that politics …'

'And art …'

'They don't talk about art.'

'What do you talk about then?'

Andreas thought for a long time. 'We don't talk so much,' he said. 'You know Father … there's so much. And then Mother.'

'But she's better now?'

'That's what Father believes. My brother heard the doctor … it's hopeless … but you mustn't tell Dad that!'

Wilfred sat looking into that open face which was struggling to keep its secrets. The dislike he had felt towards the father had evaporated. Andreas was playing his little game as well as he could behind his glasses. It wasn't up to much. But it was obviously sufficient in a family where they accepted the pretence, however simple it was.

Afterwards the boys walked down Thomas Heftyes gate, talking about the war which was to come. Wilfred's eagerness had disappeared now. He didn't believe so firmly in Uncle Martin any more, and to be honest he wasn't so bothered about it; it had been a passing sensation. But Andreas couldn't stop imagining things, it was as if he was wallowing in the word war, as if it was something that would put everything right in the world and in Frogner. When they got to Elisenberg torv, Wilfred slapped him on the shoulder; he didn't want to walk any further with him, he needed to be alone for a while and work out whether what had happened was something good, or whether it just made everything worse.

'Now you mustn't rush off and tell your father there'll be war tomorrow!' he said cheerfully.

'Oh no – Dad,' said Andreas, 'he's so afraid of everything.

We never tell him anything …' He stood there clinging to their togetherness, sentimental and curious.

'Didn't you dare pick your bike up?' he said suddenly.

A while ago Wilfred had been ready. Not now. 'Dare?' he said, 'what do you mean?'

'Well, since you wanted me …'

Annoyance welled up in Wilfred. Best to attack at once, then he'd get rid of him. 'Good thing you're getting your own bike,' he said, 'then you won't have to borrow other people's!'

He hadn't taken the outstretched hand, he didn't want to touch the warts. When he turned round, Andreas was standing on the same spot, still holding out his hand. Wilfred waved quickly, Andreas looked at his hand and waved back, manly and absent-minded. Wilfred didn't turn again. He walked slowly down the hill towards Drammensveien. As on a previous occasion when he had walked away from Andreas, he could feel the hostility through his back – hostility and admiration, curiosity and self-sacrifice …

'To Hell with him!' he said to himself in Uncle Martin's voice.

16

That autumn was full of affirmation for Little Lord. He had found it strange that things turned out to be connected when they couldn't have anything to do with one another. So he made haste to prepare himself so that the unexpected connection between things wouldn't take him by surprise and tear everything to pieces, as people were always complaining. 'If only *that* hadn't happened,' they would say …

It felt as if people in town were waiting anxiously for something after the summer, and at the new school in Skovveien boys from different areas met and sniffed at each other warily.

The French aeronaut Pégoud was to perform at Etterstad and turn his aeroplane on its back so that he was flying upside down.* It was going to happen one Sunday in September. The boys in the new class didn't get to know one another in the usual way, circuitously and with sudden advances, it was just a question of whether they were going to Etterstad to see Pégoud. Everyone asked and no-one had any answers, because grown-ups are slow to decide about important matters. The newspapers wrote that it could be risky for the public, but the organizers answered that pilots like that knew exactly where they were when they were up in the air, and the French aeronaut would stay out over the fjord and uninhabited areas, and the arena would be fenced off, so there was no danger in going up there to watch.

Little Lord said nothing at school about his family's plans. Late in the summer Uncle Martin had had a visit from a French lawyer who was doing some business for him in Marseilles. He looked exactly how everyone wanted a Frenchman to look: he had a dark, thin moustache and pointed shoes and wore a morning coat before lunch. Little Lord was sent into town with him to look at the Viking ships which were kept under a corrugated iron roof in the grounds of the University, and M. Maillard was delighted to be shown around by a courteous young man who spoke passable French and knew the difference between two or three red wines. It caused a revolution in the expectations his countrymen had filled him with when he embarked on a journey to that icebound country where people wore untreated skins all year round and lived on raw sheep's bones and brandy.

The French lawyer had promised Little Lord that he would be able to meet the aeronaut Pégoud and get close to his aeroplane on the great day in Etterstad. So when they asked him at school, he just answered: 'An aeroplane – is that worth looking at?'

'Yes, but just think, he's going to fly upside down – ?'

Wilfred was terrified at the thought that he might be invited to go along for the flight. He admitted vaguely that it might perhaps be a bit exciting to fly upside down. Nowadays he was used to being driven in Uncle Martin's open automobile at Bygdø on Sundays, and only a few of the boys had ridden in a private automobile. But they did recognise all the different taxis, those with numbers which went from 200 upwards.* Some said there were over thirty of them, but there weren't many who had ridden in one of those either.

The second time M. Maillard and Wilfred were in town together they met Aunt Kristine in Halvorsen's café. 'Well, if it isn't Little Lord!' she squealed, clapping her hands together. He registered that the meeting was not accidental; she hadn't called him Little Lord for many years and was not normally so amazed by a chance meeting. Besides, she made a lot of fuss about the fact that she and the lawyer were to have a glass of sherry and he a portion of vanilla ice-cream for 30 øre and two 10-øre cakes, a custard tart and a cream roll – for 'aren't those your favourite cakes'?

The three times the Frenchman had been at a dinner with them – once at each uncle's and once at their home on Drammensveien – Aunt Kristine had sat beside the lawyer over coffee, and each time she had let him be amused by her awkward French, which she made more childish than necessary; Uncle René himself had said that she spoke it extremely well. Now here she was at Halvorsen's, pouting over her sherry glass and pretending she couldn't form the clear French vowels they always placed such stress on at home when they had 'French days'. And the lawyer held up his fingers, slightly stained with nicotine, as if he were forming the vowels in mid-air. A couple of times he touched her mouth with his fingers as well, as if to urge the sounds into place. Everyone in the café had turned round to watch them. Wilfred felt uncomfortable. He stared silently over at the Masonic Lodge in order to think of something else. But all the dark passion welled up in him again. Kristine was no longer Aunt, not for a moment, and all the helpless little-girl behaviour was swept away as she sat there with the severe veil pulled up over the tip of her nose and nipped at a sherry glass which looked as if it would last forever.

The whole of Sunday Kristiania streamed up towards Etterstad around 11 o'clock on that sunlit September day.

Wilfred and his mother and Aunt Kristine went with the French lawyer in Uncle Martin's automobile. But when they arrived on the hill over Vålerengen, there were policemen in shiny helmets who directed them to drive round; there was such a crowd of people on the muddy road that it was difficult enough to make your way forward without automobiles getting in the way.

The whole Etterstad plateau was roped off, and people pushed impatiently forwards as far as they could get, without stopping to think that what they were going to see would take place up in the air, so that it made no difference whether you were in front or at the back. But up by the topmost entrance round the back the French lawyer produced a card, and then they were all directed in through a special opening, and Wilfred was standing beside the aeroplane even before he had glanced across and down the sloping plateau with those thousands of chattering, expectant people.

Inside a wooden hut stood a little man encased in leather from top to toe, barking out orders to the three French mechanics who were running to and fro between the hut and the aeroplane. But when Wilfred was pushed forward to be introduced to the aeronaut, a brown sinewy hand was extended from the leather and the stern face opened in a flashing smile. He and the lawyer knew each other already, and M. Maillard presented Wilfred as his French-speaking friend from the North Pole who would so dearly love to be taken up for a flight.

Wilfred felt an icy shiver of fright. But fortunately the aeronaut held out both hands and raised his eyebrows in a kind of wordless gasp, then said something incomprehensible which made all the French people laugh. Soon after they heard a rustle of movement and elated voices from down below the plateau. The mechanics had pushed the aeroplane forward into position and had started to rotate the propellers, whilst the motor produced some subdued hiccoughs. Someone pushed a bag of warm peanuts into Wilfred's hand; he'd never seen nuts like that before, but his mouth was so dry from excitement that they just turned into a cloying paste as he chewed. The next thing he knew, the aeronaut had left the hut, and when they themselves came out and saw all the people behind ropes a few hundred metres down the slope, the leather-clad god was already wearing gloves and goggles, buckled into a seat between the four wings of that fragile machine; it was so surrounded by bars and struts that it looked as if the man was sitting in a cage. Together man and machine resembled a giant grasshopper.

The aeroplane taxied across the slope in the sunshine. It hopped from hillock to hillock as the speed increased. It was only now they could see that the whole terrain was full of hillocks and clumps; the fragile machine could capsize at any moment at that high speed. But then it bounced a couple of times and was almost airborne. One final time it touched down again and the thin wheels got a hard jolt. Then it was lifting over the downward slope towards the north and was free. A roar of enthusiasm rose from the plateau, and Wilfred felt more than he heard his own shout of joy and happiness as the grasshopper climbed. For a moment it was as if he were lifting off himself; he realised he was standing on tiptoe and pushing up, as if to help the aeroplane upwards. But there was no need for any further help. It circled in a long victory loop out over Bjørviken and the fjord. When it flew in front of the sun, all hands were raised as if by command and shaded people's eyes. Some pointed out *there, there* … But others just laughed: the aeroplane had already arrived *there,* over Nesodden. Now it was flying this way again. A man said: 'It's doing 150 kilometres an hour, just think what that means …' The lady right next to him said: 'Don't say anything, just pray that he comes out of it alive.'

Then Wilfred noticed that his right hand was being grasped firmly, it must have been like that for some time. He looked down at Aunt Kristine's blue-flowered hat – a whole sea of tulle and flowers over pale yellow straw. Her hand was squeezing his, and their arms came into close contact at that moment.

'Are you frightened, Kristine?' he asked, in a moment of overwhelming tenderness.

The face she turned up towards him had a gleam of something – something transfigured he had never seen there before. Her mouth was slightly open and moist. She was breathing quickly and irregularly, so that he could hear it in the solemn silence as the flying machine flew towards land, so fragile up there under the heavens. Someone looked at a watch. The man who had spoken earlier said: 'He's been up in the air for ten minutes now.' 'Ten minutes!' said the anxious lady. 'How do you think he's going to get down again?'

A buzz of rapturous terror arose from the slopes as the machine turned in over land again. Everyone bent their heads at the moment it passed. Then they craned upwards again and all heads turned the other way. The machine was passing over the farms in Østre Aker. The man he didn't know said: 'He's going to fly upside down now.'

The machine made a short swing north, so that it was easy to see as it approached them again from the Grefsen side. Now it was flying towards them against the sun, with the September sunshine playing on the pale yellow wings; they seemed as thin and delicate as gauze, as if they might split with the intense pressure. People howled and whimpered with glee and fright as the machine approached the area where they were standing for a second time. Now nobody bowed their head any more. They knew it could happen at any moment, the miracle which was even more tremendous than what they were already experiencing. Wilfred glanced quickly at the group around him and at the flattened faces out there in the crowd. Insatiable with greed for sensation they were turned towards the unbelievable, whilst their howls changed into a deep roar across the plateau.

And suddenly all was still. He looked up quickly, just in time to see the aeroplane bank and fall sideways. It was right over the plateau now, and a wave of emotion passed through the people, who stood in frozen flight from the terrible thing they couldn't look away from. The next moment the machine stopped falling and was flying upside down over them, gliding out over the hills towards Ekeberg. They could clearly see the pilot with his head down between the struts of the plane. Then it turned into the sun again, and the next thing he knew was that the aeroplane was coming towards them again, but this time the right way up. The cheers from the plateau came towards them like a curtain of sound and echoed back over them as if from a roof.

The next thing he knew was that his hand was in pieces – it felt crushed. He could feel Kristine's arm like a strong serpent coiling around his arm. They had fallen a little behind the others, who had pressed forward a few paces in their excitement. Now they were standing almost face to face, hers turned upwards, searching and bewildered with delight and neediness.

He didn't know how it happened, and it lasted perhaps only a moment. But the meeting of her body with his in those few seconds was so intense that it was as if no time at all had passed between now and that painful time among the alder trees. It was as if he himself was flying through the air – and landing safely. Not burnt out and confused, but full of blessed arousal, a state which was fulfilled in itself and yet contained the promise of sweet catastrophe.

And somehow he knew now that she was feeling the same as him – like the promise of consummation between equals. She too was standing there as if she had landed temporarily in a place which was secure only in one thing: that it offered the possibility of continuation.

The machine must have landed during those seconds. Soon after, the pilot was standing amongst them in the doorway to the shed with flowers in his hands, whilst his countrymen, both men and women, hung on him and kissed his cheeks and anywhere they could reach. Wilfred and Kristine went forward too, but she didn't kiss the pilot, just shook his hand in a comradely way and muttered a kind of thank you for the show.

Wilfred walked over to the machine, which was now being checked over by the three mechanics. At that moment there was a roar of triumph from down in the multitude. They had broken through the ropes and were surging in a wave across the plateau. Wilfred stood by the plane, watching them coming;

they were like a huge dark animal, possessed by the desire to get closer. But now the police and wardens with braid on their caps emerged from all sides and blocked their path with long arms and solid fists. Wilfred stood leaning lightly on the plane, watching the incident, and at that moment it occurred to him that it was as if he was always on the side where the few were, those who were permitted, who were smiled at and not shut out.

Was this what it meant to be a loner – what he was longing for?

Some boys' voices called from down in the crowd. He saw a little group from his class who were trying with desperate boldness to find a way around the solid police backs and through to the paradise of the moored ship of the heavens. It looked as if they were pinning their hopes on Wilfred, as he hung around there like a Saint Peter at the gate, with a godlike gleam around him in the view of all those hungry boys' eyes.

Now the policeman caught sight of them, and back they went behind a chain of uniformed arms, which shoved the condemned souls brutally backwards at such a speed that some stumbled and others fell over the stumblers – until the enthusiastic crowd was suddenly transformed into an angry, howling mob which felt it was being shut out from the good things.

Then the leather-clad pilot walked forward from the shed he had retreated to. He threw a tired glance over the masses of people and made an intimation of an ironic bow. That changed the mood of the crowd. The next moment new cheers could be heard; ecstatic whistling and gleeful laughter flew like doves towards the clear September sky.

No, no! thought Wilfred, mentally distancing himself from the turbulent sensations: this was not how I wanted to be alone, not to be elevated above others. He felt an impulse to go over to his comrades outside the ropes and surrender his preferential position. His triumph was enormous as it was. But he was indifferent to it.

And because he was indifferent, he didn't act on his impulse either. They would regard him as something approaching a god for the first few minutes; he had touched the machine and talked to the miraculous Frenchman who flew through the air upside down. But what benefit was it to him to have become a loner in this situation, as he had so many times before? It wasn't important to him to be above anyone, not above his comrades – it could just as well be beneath or far to one side, far, far away. Just not *amongst* them. Not amongst anyone. Not *a part* of. Not a part which was governed by other parts. Better or worse was a matter of complete indifference to him.

His body was still burning after that intimate contact with Kristine. It was all so different from that time last summer, because he was no longer a boy half-stifled by desire, striking sparks off an unwilling adult. It was a situation which had matured in the very atmosphere around them, a situation which was unavoidable and which they were a part of *together* – driven towards each other by forces they had set in motion long ago and which neither of them controlled or wished to control. And to be in *that* way a part of a machinery which he wanted to be his destiny – that was something other than being one of many who were acting and feeling. It was to be the one selected by destiny who was to perish or be raised to the heights, where everything glittered, and from where the world must appear cloudy and dull grey.

The invited guests on the plateau chatted away unaffected, but beyond it the police and wardens had fastened the ropes again in front of the expectant crowd, who slowly subsided after the stormy breakthrough. Everything was full of suspense on this blessed September day, with high sun and miracles under the heavens. Small boys with coloured trays of nuts and chocolate round their necks shouted their wares and were greeted by cheerful shouts from all sides. Three drunken tramps caused a riot with bold oaths beneath heavy moustaches, and children in sailor suits stood with their legs crossed and needed to pee, to the despair of the grown-ups, avid for new experiences; they were so keen not to miss anything. It was 17 May in September.*

223

It was said that the Frenchman was going to go up again, and this time with a passenger. Just then the lawyer and the pilot walked back over to the plane. A feverish murmuring broke out behind the ropes. The French lawyer led the little group which was making right for Wilfred as he stood just next to the amazing machine. He was about to move politely out of the way when the lawyer spotted him.

'Here we have our young friend I was telling you about,' he said, gesticulating animatedly. Pégoud came over to him and asked in French: 'Are you the young man who is so keen to come up in the air with me?'

Wilfred felt dizzy. He saw his mother and Kristine over at the shed behind the group. They had glasses in their hands, champagne was being poured for the diplomats and guests. He saw that Kristine was watching him between the heads of the men who had walked over. The lawyer smiled: 'Wasn't that what you wanted?'

'Oui, monsieur,' said Wilfred groggily. He knew he had said something of the sort in an unguarded moment down in town one time, when they were talking about the forthcoming events. The adults nodded to one another and glanced across at Mother and the other ladies. Wilfred felt Kristine's burning glance. Had she an inkling of what they were talking about, these incredible men who had, it seemed, accepted him into their circle and spoke to him as if to an adult? And at that moment he felt a shiver of real anticipation, not simply fright and the hope of escape.

'My mother …' he said in a low voice.

'Of course – we must ask your mother!' The lawyer was about to walk back over. But Wilfred stopped him: 'I was going to say that my mother – perhaps it's just as well …'

The gentlemen looked at one another and smiled enigmatically. Then they nodded and murmured to one another. And from now on it all happened so quickly that he wasn't really aware of what was going on until he was led up the low step over the struts and into the machine itself, to a seat half beside and half behind the pilot's. They had wrapped him up in an over-large leather coat of the same kind as the pilot's and put a helmet on his head. Now he was looking at the world through a pair of enormous goggles, which already shut him out from his surroundings and made them unreal and distant. When he turned round in his seat as far as he could within the straps they had fastened round him, he could still see his mother surrounded by men in top hats and ladies carrying parasols, and far off behind the ropes he could see the crowd as something thick and dark which was irrelevant to him, did not belong in his world.

The mechanics were fussing around the machine; one of them was already at the front by the propeller, which he turned hard the wrong way. The motor coughed and began running regularly.

Wilfred sat with his eyes tightly closed as the machine bounced over the bumpy plateau. Once he peeped up and saw the brooding trees on the edge of Etterstad rushing towards him at breakneck speed, but he quickly closed his eyes again and only registered that they had taken off when the bumping stopped. His hands in their stiff gauntlets were clinging to something or other in front of him. He was wedged tight in more than one way: between frozen panic and an alien feeling of senseless joy, which was not strong enough to release the cramps in his body. He noticed with a flash of pride that he had not prayed to God, but with an equal flash of awareness admitted that it was only because he had forgotten to. And now it was too late. For now they were flying in the air. He knew it without being able to tell in any other way than that the wind pressure was so fierce. In any case, no power on earth or in heaven would make him open his eyes. That would be the end of everything.

Then he heard a voice from somewhere. It was a human voice, shouting through the roar of the wind. It was merely a reflex of well-brought-up politeness, but he opened his eyes for a fleeting second and *saw* the earth below him and ahead. It must have been the green dome of Trefoldighets Church which had appeared clearly in his line of vision before he closed his eyes again tightly. But then he heard the voice again, and this time it was just next to him; he opened his eyes again and saw a blur of dark green treetops.

But this time his eyes did not close automatically. They remained open for several seconds, and he saw the fjord swinging towards him as if on a turntable. And now he caught sight of some streaks down below and some red dots in the blue sea. It must be the sailing ships moored to their red buoys at Bjørviken. Now he could also see a steamer by the quayside, like the model of a steamship that he had often admired in the window of Bennetts on Carl Johans gate. And now he could see the town itself, the streets, they outlined themselves as if in a drawing beneath him. He could see the palace. He saw it swing round the turntable and disappear. Hovedøya with the red roof of the munitions store was almost right beneath them!

But at that he suddenly found himself looking *down*. And this time his eyes shut firmly. He had seen something quite other than that distant unreal panorama. He had seen the thin floor beneath him and the struts which held the wings of the biplane together. And at that moment he realised for the first time that he was airborne and that only a few sticks separated him from empty space.

Then the voice called him for a third time, and when he opened his eyes again a marvellous happiness stole over him and released him from his cramped position. His hands loosened their grip on the bar in front of him, he let his body relax back in the seat and *saw* – saw with insatiable eagerness how the town was coming towards him again, that the blue, blue fjord with its islands was swallowed up by the speed and succeeded by brown and green forest which came rushing straight at them. And this time he didn't shut his eyes. The earth came towards him, and he couldn't take his eyes from it. It grew into something more than a hill with lots of houses on it, singly and in clusters. It became something gleefully irrelevant, something tiny and insignificant which suddenly made *this* a vivid reality – the fact that he was up in the air, in the sky itself, that everything had changed places and was now in order, and that *he* – alone – was floating over all this irrelevance which formed itself into a comical little pattern beneath him, precisely as he had known it must be; a pattern of tiny little things without power, with an order he was raised above. Raised above and separate from, shut out of in a way which was subject to *his* will and not that of the things. It was no longer the things and all the pettiness that controlled him and put him in his place amongst them and made him a part of something, it was his organizing power that put all this distant pettiness in its place *beneath* him and made him the floating ruler over all things, alone and apart.

He leant forwards in his seat in order to catch the pilot's attention: that he was *seeing* now, he was there. He shrieked several times with a mixture of joy and terror, in a jubilation that burst all the boundaries of what had been experienced or could be lived by human beings.

But the pilot took no notice of him. He was hunched over a handle on a lever, with his other hand sort of thrust into a small piece of machinery which was further down on the other side. At that moment the Etterstad plateau opened beneath them, and Wilfred understood that Pégoud was tense because he was preparing for landing.

A new terror shot through him. This was the most dangerous part, he had read that. Flying up in the air suddenly seemed to him to be something safe and jubilant which should have gone on forever. Now the hill down there was hurtling towards them, but as he prepared to close his eyes again he caught sight of the people in a three-quarter circle around the plateau, kept back behind the ropes, he saw the raised faces, white ovals in a dark mass, and they rushed towards him like something threatening and hateful: the inescapable. Death.

But this anguish was shorter than he had expected. After the first three sharp bumps had made the machine shake, he felt the speed dropping suddenly as they bounced over firm ground. He must have closed his eyes again, because when he looked around, everything looked just as it had when they led him up into the plane wearing the large leather coat. Now he flopped out of the same plane, the sleeves flopped right down over his hands, everything flopped and swung around him, the very ground he stood on gave way, and he sank to his knees in a kind of numb gladness. But now he could also hear the cheers from down the hill, behind the ropes where all the people were. He pushed himself up to stand up crookedly. His mother came running towards him, and Kristine and the lawyer … He straightened up and was released from the leather coat. The next thing he knew was that Mother was hugging him to her and pouring out words in Norwegian and French over those standing closest, over Kristine and the lawyer and the pilot. Her eyes were shining with anger and pride and champagne. 'My little boy!' she sobbed hysterically. 'My own little boy …'

Wilfred freed himself manfully and reached out a hand to Pégoud, who shook it. 'Merci!' he groaned. 'Merci beaucoup!'

At the same moment he realized that his groin was cold and wet. It must have happened on the way up since it was already cold.

'Do you think we can go back home soon, Mother?' he asked unhappily. He had a bad feeling that he was going to be humiliated, right now when everyone was looking at him. 'How does it feel?' 'Were you frightened?' … The questions danced in the September air. A little French lady drowned him for a moment in an upholstered embrace and called him 'Mon petit héros', even though she was almost a head shorter than him.

'Yes, I was frightened!' he said suddenly in answer to all the questions. The answer was translated and hummed in the air. It gave rise to little screams of happiness from the ladies. But Pégoud pushed forward and shook his hand again. 'He's the bravest débutant I've ever had,' he said calmly. 'He had his eyes open nearly all the time!'

Again the mood dissolved into happy laughter. It was as if everyone had done a heroic deed. The only one who didn't accept the general plaudits was the pilot himself. His role was practically over once everyone had assured those close to them that their dearest wish was to be taken for a flight. As this was going on, the mechanics had pushed the plane into the provisional hangar, so everyone could feel safe from being taken at their word. The crowd of people was on its surging way back to town.

Fru Sagen and Wilfred were invited to the Consulate, where there was going to be a reception for the pilot. 'Do you think I could get out of it?' he whispered to Mother.

'Get out of it?'

'Yes, I just feel so …' He grimaced. 'It's just near our house, so I could just disappear when we arrive.'

She studied him for a moment, curious and concerned. Again and again she had seen that dark expression passing over the young face like a cloud – over a face which more and more came to resemble a face which had been heavy with clouds.

'Would you rather be alone, then?' she said.

'Yes, I want to be – alone.' He saw her disappointment. She was like a child, she had wanted to enjoy her triumph, to show herself off with her heroic son who had flown through the air. If she had known it in advance, she would have fainted if necessary in order to prevent it; now she couldn't help giving in to the temptation to shine.

'I'm really sorry about it, Mother. For your sake.'

'For mine? Is anything wrong?'

Again that searching look of concern which was an attempt to invade his being. It was only now he realised that the little accident in his trousers was not the real reason why he wanted to get away from the party. Something had happened to him up there under the sky, something which provided an explanation, or an initiation.

So much easier then to confide in Mother the shameful little secret, since that was not what *was* the secret.

'I want to whisper something,' he said, pulling her head down towards him.

Fru Sagen collapsed in happy laughter and looked around furtively. This delightful honesty thrilled her so much that she was on the point of relaying it to someone. But she pulled herself together and looked into his eyes with the same stealthy seriousness as the time they had visited Tivoli together and kicked over the traces one spring evening.

'Just make yourself scarce then, when we get back!' she said happily and gave him a little tap. He stood there watching her, full of surprised distrust. Could this grown woman he was so fond of be *so* easy to deceive? Was it possible that everyone *always* let themselves be persuaded to believe what they really wanted to?

Yes, it was possible. That had always been his experience. It was his deceitful triumph as a child to have discovered it early enough so that he never said a completely true word, never gave himself away. That discovery was one of the stones in his edifice, which was called solitude, with no interference from people and circumstances. He smiled back a secret smile and put a finger to his lips, and Mother drew a cross on her throat in return. The game was under way between them, yet again, always renewed – as it always had been. That wonderful game which made everything different from how it really was and strengthened his certainty that it was possible to live a lie, so long as you were careful enough.

'The only thing is that both the maids had time off to come and see the show,' said Fru Sagen. That little remark struck him as something incredibly comical in the midst of his train of thought. 'You're right, Mother,' he said, intensely serious, 'it would be a shame if a hero like me were to perish for want of being looked after while his mother is at the Consulate being fêted.'

Again she tapped him lightly on the cheek, pleased and relieved that this last objection had been overcome. It was so rarely that she went out amongst complete strangers, she had been worried about so many things – how they were changing as she stood idly by … Today she was possessed by a strong desire to join in again, as she had been wont to at the time when Kristiania's hundreds of small happenings were a part of her life.

*

Wilfred let himself in to the empty house, revelling in the joyous liberty of exploring his own restlessness. He took a long bath and went down into the living room, naked under his bathrobe, which swung around him in a way he found grown-up and devil-may-care. He felt the temptation of his own body like a mild pleasure, because he knew that he would overcome it now. With a feeling of mature superiority he stood by the large window looking over Frognerkilen and stared out at the sky which was clouding over with blue-grey clouds. The September day had been warm until now. Suddenly the water out there was ruffled with black ripples. He watched it as if from another world, raised up above it. He was reliving the gleeful panic of the moment when he had seen the fragile machine beneath him and around him. Again he raised himself up and stood on tiptoe, as if to stimulate the longing in himself to float, to cut loose from all that bound him, to crash and perish all alone, without the boundaries the presence of others always imposed. Yes, this was what he had been aiming for. Once he was sitting in Frognerpark, drinking fizzy pop with some ridiculous people. They were content with that; they had talked of war, they had shuddered at the word, as you were supposed to. But he – now he realized it – he had felt the word as an enormous release, as a possibility, a flight, a catastrophe. All his daring little adventures with fire and violence had been childish steps towards this state of terror and autonomy.

He went over to the cupboard and helped himself to a glass of sherry from the carafe, drinking it with disgust and pleasure. It helped him at once to float a little more, to let his nerves remain in that unreal state he was so afraid would cease. He wanted to drive the restlessness of his body up to a swinging which was so violent that he himself would have to follow like a – like an aeroplane which was thrust out into empty space by its thundering engines.

The doorbell rang. He swore mildly, in adult fashion. He went to open the door, not caring that he was still in his bathrobe. He was playing some sort of role now, he knew that, but he hadn't decided what. Because of what he *was* he would be able to master any situation.

'Kristine!'

He heard himself that there was something exaggerated in his intonation – not surprise, but rather something affirming, as if she were determined by his willpower. Breathlessly, she walked into the hall with all the wall hangings which muffled the sounds.

'You sound as if you were expecting me?'

'In a way. There's no-one home.'

'I know.'

Now everything had been said. Nothing could be changed. All the old doubts and fears lay like memories in the warm air. But no longer as barriers. He drew her to him.

'We're mad,' she said in childish protest.

'Are we?'

He led her inside with assurance. She was wearing the hat with blue flowers on it from Etterstad and a pale beige cape over her shoulders. He didn't help her off with either, he led her gently and confidently towards the stairs. But when they had reached his room, he tore her hat off and threw her cape onto a chair.

'Not so roughly!' she said sharply, attempting to take the lead.

'Really?' he said ironically. He could feel the stranger's power in himself. Who could this stranger be, who gave him the authority to be outside himself?

They kissed each other passionately. At once all age difference had vanished. It was not like that time by the alder trees, no unacknowledged desire he should be ashamed of.

'What are you doing, boy?' she moaned tentatively. It occurred to him that she was perhaps even now not aware of what it was she wanted – even now, she really just wanted to play a game.

'What am I doing?' he said harshly. He was full of determination and knowledge. 'You know what I'm doing, Kristine!' he whispered against clothes and skin. 'I'm doing everything!'

Then she was not playing any longer. Not helpless, not surprised. She helped his over-eager hands with almost maternal slowness. The slanting sun shone in through the curtains and lay like a shaft of holy light across the white body in which he began to drown systematically. Once she whispered that someone might come. He knew coldly then that all resistance was defeated, if there had been any resistance. 'No-one can come!' he breathed back. It was words with no meaning – a ritual: he could just as well have said something else – anything at all – they were not his own words, and the actions were not his own. Slowly and with a mounting awareness which surprised himself, he knew what had to be done, as if generations of certainty about the decisive step became clear to him at a measured pace, so different from in those hot, agitated dreams where the stages in the action all came in a rush and with no clear order. There was within him a stranger's desire to perform the act perfectly, without the haste and destructive uncertainty of a beginner. All at once he was no longer an adolescent fumbling with unaccustomed feminine delights. The stranger was within him, whispering wise advice to him about control and slowness, about giving and not just taking. He felt the ecstasy with *her* body and with his own – borne through widening circles of sweetness of mind and body, where he could take note of the journey and keep their common body under blessed control.

Their embrace was dissolved in slow delight, they floated back together through the spheres, with no sudden switch from sweetness to shame. The experience was so much greater than he had imagined that the reaction too became a surge of joy which completely took him over. She lay there, letting him discover all her body's secrets with no false modesty. The transition to gentle intimacy without excitement became an initiation between equals. And he knew it. He knew the whole time that he had been good for her, with no shame on her side. The strangeness was still in him – no, the stranger: for it was as if there were a real unknown being within him, another who had guided his actions and still inhabited him with the

233

erotic wisdom of generations. It filled him with the new, happy certainty of being the victor …

Over whom? His thoughts returned in fits and starts – but slowly as well, without any sudden exposure or anything oppressive. They returned in mild amazement that the greatest thing of all really was so great and yet no more difficult than that. There was no catastrophe, no plunge downwards from barren heights. The very stages of ecstasy were engraved in his memory, as if it had been a mountain climb towards an attainable goal with fixed resting places and securely fastened ropes.

But as his erotic activity was about to resume, she pulled gently away and sat up beside him in the bed, examining him. 'Wilfred,' she said, 'this was terribly wrong – of me. But the way you have acted, it doesn't feel like that!'

He knelt by her then in gratitude, he bathed her body in tender caresses, not aggressive and harshly demanding as they had been, but worshipful and full of gratitude. He felt impelled to this, to show her gratitude, but there was also some calculation involved: that this was right, this was how it should be done. It was the stranger within him who told him how he should act as a lover. It was a stranger's power giving him gentle commands. But not a commanding power which threatened his own independence – a being who wished him well.

'You have initiated me to life,' he said seriously. And when she was about to smile, to stop things becoming too solemn: 'No, I mean it, it's not a childish outburst, you know that. You have initiated me.'

She took his head tenderly between her hands and looked at him for a long moment.

'I almost believe that's true,' she said quietly. 'I almost believe you have released me from regret and bad conscience.'

'But you mustn't regret it!' he said with unexpected forcefulness. 'You have made what is nearly always shameful and scary for young men into the loveliest experience for me – don't you think I'm aware of that?'

'Wilfred,' she said, 'you are the dearest person I know, and you must never say that you love me, because you don't. But you are the most grown-up child I know, and the most childish adult.'

And *she* said this in return in a way which meant he didn't feel hurt, even though she called him a child.

'You remind me of *him*,' she said, holding his face away from hers and smiling.

'Of whom?'

And again she had to smile, this time at his comical jealousy which really made him childish, but in a different way.

'No, it's not anyone I've known in that way,' she said quickly. 'But there was a man … I shouldn't have said it.'

She had a frightened look in her eyes now. She was staring out into the room, which was filled with autumnal dusk from the last rays of the sun through the windows. He turned round involuntarily to follow her gaze; it was as if she could see another person in the room, one he couldn't see and didn't know.

The slanting rays of sunshine were falling on the portrait of his father which was standing on a chair against the wall. The red light was playing in his short beard, and endowed the brush strokes with a life which went beyond that of the oils or the colour. It was as if that face – so weak and so authoritative at the same time – emerged out of the frame, out of the pattern the artist had constructed, as if it could suddenly address them, as if it were saying something to them both with its melancholy eyes so full of burgeoning life.

And at that moment he knew him. For the first time he knew him. For the first time in his life Wilfred felt a dark current of kinship with this painted being which had once frightened him – as if all age was wiped out, all time and distance. And he knew that this was the wise stranger who had imbued him with skill in what he had not known, a lover amongst men, a man who had brought shame and happiness to his fellow human beings and was present in them as a mystery every time his name was mentioned.

Slowly he got out of bed. She followed him, gathering up some clothes on the way. With the suppleness of a cat she had donned her complicated garments before he had attempted the slightest concealment. Naked as God had created him, Wilfred stood before the portrait of his father, watching his sinful eyes examining him knowingly. But without the irony which always threatened with adults. Possibly with appreciation. At least without reproach and half-spoken words about guilt.

He turned happily towards Kristine, filled with a devotion which for the first time effaced his own bitter drive towards self-assertion. There was the sound of a door opening downstairs. It was the maid Lilly returning. He recognised the footsteps at once and wasn't alarmed; as he started to reassure her she raised her hand to indicate that she too had understood.

'Your mother could be here at any time,' she said without expression.

He looked at the clock. An hour had passed. For the first time he registered that dazed certainty about the mystery of time – that it existed in their own blood and only there.

'I don't think so,' he said lightly. 'Mother was really in the mood for a party today, it was lovely to see her like that.'

He was throwing on his own clothes casually whilst they talked in low voices. He felt all the calm of experience, not needing to be ashamed of the secrets of his dress. They kissed quickly in front of the picture of his father and turned as one to face it one last time. The ray of sunshine had moved away from it now. It was in shade, looking quite dark against the cheerful splashes of sunshine further up the wall. It was as if the man had said what he had to say and shared his experience as long as it was necessary. Wilfred picked up the painting and hung it back on the hook where it had always hung, without him seeing it.

'I'm going now,' she whispered, 'I want to go alone.'

'I'll meet you on the corner, at Skarpsno café.'

'No. I want to go for a walk, a long walk alone.'

'A long walk with me.'

'Alone, I insist. Goodbye Wilfred – my dear.'

He stood in the narrow window in the hall, watching her walking up the avenue. She did not look lonely now. She walked quickly and easily. Then she was up by the main road. He felt a heavy sweetness surging through him. He stayed there for a long time, looking up along the empty road and imagining her in the picture exactly as he had just seen her, her cornflower-blue hat, the cape over her shoulders, those light footsteps which carried his secret in their very rhythm. He stood by the narrow window watching the dusk falling and the dim lights of the gaslamps as they were lit up the road. He was still standing there when Mother came walking down the road.

'Has something happened?' she asked, as he helped her off with her coat.

'What could have happened? I've been here all the time. Did you have a good time with all those Frenchmen?'

'I was worried. Yes, I had a good time, I suppose. But I'm getting too old for gadding about like this.'

'Nonsense, Mama! You're only saying that so that I can say you're not too old.'

'Well say it then, hurry up and say it!'

They stood face to face, mother and son, as so often before, as they always did, playing an old game, the game of a woman of the world and her ersatz cavalier, as Uncle Martin said.

'You were the prettiest of all the women up at Etterstad,' he said, putting his arm around her waist as they went into the living room. 'Did you drink champagne the whole time?'

'Rubbish!' she said. 'Kristine was prettier, they were all prettier. No, they don't drink a lot. The pilot was a teetotaler. They talked and talked so my tongue feels quite sore; my French has got a bit rusty over the years.'

They stood facing each other, happy and forgetful. All those quickfire words, so easily spoken and so quickly forgotten, all that goodness and fragile security – it had tormented him for a long time now, when he had to become part of it again. Suddenly he realized that it didn't bother him any longer. He could act it quite naturally, as before. Or it wasn't an act at all. There was no lonely barricade he had to defend against a mother, or against uncles and teachers who wanted to invade him and take charge of him and what was his.

'Aunt Kristine wasn't at the reception,' she said. 'They'd forgotten to ask her, they were quite upset about it, they tried to telephone her twice.'

He glanced briefly at her. Was it that damned instinct again, asserting itself? She had said she was worried …

'Kristine doesn't have a telephone,' he said challengingly.

'They rang the confectioner's. She's often down there on Sundays to get the place ready.'

'Well, she wasn't there today then,' he said. He could hear himself that his tone was a little sharper than he'd intended.

'Obviously not,' said Mother mildly.

But he wanted to know it now, to know whether there were secret forces at work which could pass information from one person to another about what everyone was up to.

'You could have sent someone to find her – I mean, if it was so important!'

But she didn't react. 'We could have,' she said wearily, – 'why didn't I think of that.'

Was that irony? His suspicions flared up again.

'But she may not have been at home either!' he said.

'But Little Lord,' she said – and he noticed she was using that name again – 'why are you making such a fuss about it?'

Steady now, steady, he thought. Don't make it obvious, don't tempt fate when you don't want to give things away. Because you don't want to, surely? No, surely not!

'Sorry,' he said, 'I don't think I've quite come down to earth again yet!'

Did she glance at him to see whether there was any hidden meaning? Oh, if only nobody had mentioned that word instinct, if only they hadn't said it so often. It was as if there was always guessing going on, something cloudy which made situations unclear. If only people were straightforward and taciturn, like Fru Frisaksen, like – like Erna …

'By the way, do you know who was at Etterstad today? Erna! I saw her in the crowd behind the rope. The whole family was there.'

'No doubt her father said that it was the high speed of the aeroplane which defied the law of gravity.'

'Really, Wilfred,' she said, 'I'm sure Erna was frightfully proud of you.'

'And were you, Mother?'

'Frightfully proud. But you haven't said a word about what it felt like …'

There was no danger any more. They weren't talking about Kristine any more. Again he felt a temptation to play with taking risks.

'Felt like?' he asked.

'Yes, felt like – flying!'

'Oh, that – !'

It was as if his thoughts were once more driving him towards the inevitable, as if events were suspended and had to be brought to life again in the darkening room. He could see the last reflections of light from the water outside caught in the mirror with the dull gold frame.

'It felt – marvellous …'

'Marvellous? But you must have been afraid!'

He looked in the mirror. The soft glow of silver from the water was changing the whole time.

'Afraid? Yes, I was. Of course I was afraid. The take-off …'

'The take-off – didn't it make you dizzy?'

The water in the mirror changed to grey. So the sun must have deserted it with its final rays.

'Yes, I was dizzy. I was – floating. It was blue.'

'What was blue? The sea?'

'Blue! Everything was blue. It was like enormous – circles … they grew inside me and outside at the same time.'

'Your stomach,' said Fru Sagen, 'it must have been your stomach.'

'St - - yes, of course …' But again it was as if the picture in the mirror was calling him, as if it had more to say. He saw another picture in the dark mirror, the picture of the man up there on the wall, the one he had once taken down.

'Mama,' he said, 'please don't get upset at me asking, but Father – was he a handsome man?'

She got up at once and went over to the window.

'What do you mean – handsome?'

'I mean, was he the sort of man – well, they must have liked him?'

'Who?' Her voice was dry and abrupt. She looked over towards Frognerkilen.

'Well, people. Women and such.'

She turned round, but remained standing by the tall window. She seemed small and white against the darkness outside. He couldn't see her face properly.

'Why are you asking?' she asked.

He tried to make out her face. He hadn't meant to hurt her. But he felt a surge of defiance.

'Is it so strange that I ask? You've never told me anything.'

It was as if she wanted to come over to him now, but she paused. It looked as if she were seeking an ally out there in the darkness. 'Did I frighten you, Mama?' he said, going over to her instead.

'Why should you frighten me? Of course you didn't frighten me. No – it's perhaps not so strange that you should ask … Listen, darling …' Suddenly she put her arm around his neck, so that they were both standing turned towards the window: 'Has someone been talking to you about your father?'

'No, that's just it. You, for example – you never do.'

They were standing together facing the dark water with the fading gleam of the waning daylight. It was as if they were talking to a mirror together and so felt less alone.

'Your father was extremely popular,' she said, 'with people – women – and such.'

She was making fun of what he had said. He felt offended. She was talking to him as if he were a child, but at the same time with a kind of concealed anger.

'You don't have to tell me anything,' he said peevishly and walked away again. The clock on the mantelpiece ticked sadly, filling the room with silence. He knew that he was upsetting her now, but also that it was unfair for him not to know about it.

'It was only because you said that about the egg,' he said impulsively. He wanted to go now. He didn't want to descend from the heights where his body and soul were still circling. He wanted to be alone and savour it.

'That episode with Madam Frisaksen, you've heard all that,' she said.

'You're right, Mama,' he said. 'It was silly of me, and anyway I'm really not that curious.'

He wanted to get away from the whole thing. His fine indifference had returned. 'Besides, I've forgotten to do my homework for tomorrow,' he said.

He had given her an excuse, she could say well for heaven's sake, you'd better get on with it; she could find an outlet for her irritation and say that you mustn't let fun and games distract you from your work.

'Oh, homework!' she said dismissively. It was as if she was ready for a fight. He just wanted to smooth it over and be alone. She followed him away from the window, went over to the mantelpiece, lit a cigarette; that was a rare event …

'That episode was not the only one,' she said. 'And it wasn't just an "episode" either, it was the norm.'

He sat down, feeling suddenly tired and despondent, and a little curious. She sat down as well, staring at the glow from her cigarette: 'They liked him all too well, people – and he liked them in a way. I mean, he may have despised them, I'm not sure, perhaps he didn't care about them at all, or about himself either. In a way it became a part of him. In another way it wasn't that at all. But you can't understand that.'

He moved closer, shifted the ashtray over to her politely.

'Perhaps *you* didn't understand it,' he said carefully.

'No. I didn't understand it. I don't understand it now. I never think about it any more – hardly ever.'

'And now I come along and shatter your peace?'

'Yes!' she smiled. 'You've shattered my peace. There's always someone who shatters your peace when you want to run away.'

'But Mama, it's so long ago!'

'Yes, it's a long time ago. It's something which doesn't exist. Not any longer. But yet – sometimes it's there anyway.'

'I do understand that, Mama. The problem is that you think I'm a bit stupid.'

'No, darling, I don't think you're stupid – on the contrary!' she sighed despondently. 'It's just that – you're a child, you're all I've got … no, I know what you're going to say, you're not a child, and perhaps that's right, I don't know, I don't know anything, that's what's wrong with me, I don't know anything!'

He moved close to her as she sat there on the sofa. He knew she was almost crying now, that she would cry if he asked – and that she didn't want to cry.

'I don't give a damn about Father!' he said – 'as Uncle Martin says!' he added, to smooth it over.

'Yes, Uncle Martin,' she said, clutching at the excuse. 'He's told me so often that I ought to talk to you.'

He said: 'Mama, please do me the favour not to talk to me about the kind of thing grown-ups feel duty bound to talk to children about when they're not children any longer.'

Was she laughing? Was it possible that there was a frivolous giggle coming from the semi-darkness next to him? He had spoken in genuine anger. And he had made her laugh! What a mother – she was the loveliest thing in the world …

'That was the thing about your father,' she said with a burst of energy, 'they wouldn't leave him in peace.'

'Who wouldn't leave him in peace?'

'People.'

'Female people?'

'Yes, female people,' she said, as if enjoying the vulgar sound. 'You know he was a ship's officer,' she said, as if it was an explanation.

'The portrait upstairs is in uniform.'

'Yes, of course … But he wasn't one for very long. He – left.'

'Didn't he want to do it any longer?'

'No. I mean no, he didn't want to do it any longer. So he started in shipping and made lots of money. To everyone's amazement. He was so clever.'

'Did you get rich then?'

'We spent a great deal as well. A great deal. It was just as much my fault. We were never alone.'

He was on tenterhooks now. There was so much he had suspected previously. Later it was all forgotten for something more important.

'We were always on the go, you see, darling. I don't know why it was like that, but it was. We wanted to be a part of it all, I suppose we had to, in a way – we travelled a great deal as well. Those modern paintings – no-one else round here has things like that … Did you know that your father played in public? He gave concerts.'

He didn't answer. He knew that, but it had never been something that concerned him.

'Could he do so much?' he asked weakly.

'He could do anything. Or rather, he had a kind of talent for everything. He succeeded at everything.'

She stopped again – each time as if to get her breath back. He was afraid she wasn't going to continue.

'Wasn't that great, Mama?' he asked.

'No, it wasn't great.'

Her confidences came in short bursts. He thought: she's been waiting for this for a long time. And even so, she's sitting here holding things back.

'So now you know everything about your father,' she said childishly, and full of childish satisfaction she said: 'It's a good thing you asked.'

'I don't know anything,' he said. 'The glass egg …'

She got up at once and went over to the window again:

'We've talked about that.'

'Not about the connection between that and – and all the rest!'

'We've talked about everything. Someone must have taken that egg – stolen it …'

He walked over and stood beside her. The good feeling of floating was still with him. He didn't know himself why he was asking right now. It could be for her sake – so that she could unburden herself; it could also be because the wise man on the wall in his room had advised him.

'Did you lose all that money again then, Mama?' he asked.

'Lose it? No! Not all. What do you think we're living on?'

Together they looked out into the night. A solitary light on the Bygdø side threw a bright spear of light out over the velvet of the water. He looked straight into the darkness as he asked: 'Why did Father shoot himself?'

'He didn't shoot himself.' The lie came automatically. They didn't look at each other, just out into the darkness with the quivering spear of light across the bay. A train thundered past on its way from town. The sparks from it came to rest like stars, and died.

'Good night, Mama. It must be late. I still feel as if I'm floating.'

He had almost reached the door when he heard her say:

'It wasn't my fault.'

Again she was outlined white against the window when he turned. She came slowly towards him and took both his hands in the darkness. 'We had such a good time together, you and I. You were a child.'

'Yes, but Mama, I'm not a child any longer.'

She examined his face in the darkness; it felt as if fingers were moving over his face.

'Aren't you?' she said.

'No, Mama. You know I'm not. But we can have a good time just like before – you and I …'

'No,' she said.

'But Mama! What are you saying?'

'We can't have a good time like – before. You must understand, darling, that the thing that's wrong with me is that I don't keep up with the times. That's what my brother Martin always says. I don't take – the consequences, he says.'

'Of Father's death?'

'No. For me he continued to live. I couldn't believe it. Until I'd forgotten him Almost forgotten him. Then in a way he had never lived.'

'I think I understand you, Mama. You can only acknowledge what's in front of you. The rest you don't want to know about. If anything changes, you won't go along with it.'

'How long have you known that?'

'I don't know. On the other hand you go around guessing about a whole lot of things which may exist. But you don't really know about that either. Until you're forced to know about it. Then you either reject it or feel offended.'

He was on shaky ground now. He was guessing as he had always guessed, and as she had guessed – the family disease. He was guessing that it had to be like that. But if that was right, she would deny it.

'Now I think you're being just a little too sharp!' she said, with something of the old lightness.

'Why did you say that about Erna – that she was at Etterstad?'

'But darling – it's just that I saw her.'

They had arrived where they had to, where he didn't want to arrive right now, because he still felt the sensation of floating and it was the biggest day of all. Whatever she says now, I'll agree, I won't oppose her with further questions …

'Actually there was something quite different I wanted to talk to you about,' she said suddenly. 'Confirmation.'

'Mama!'

'What's the matter, darling?' she said, irritated. 'We've spoken about it before.'

'I don't want to upset you, Mama, I would do anything not to upset you. But as you say, we have already spoken about it.'

'Yes, but why, darling – why don't you want to?'

'If you really must know, I don't believe in God.'

It sounded too solemn, he hadn't meant it like that. He just didn't want to hurt her. Now it sounded like a declaration in front of the altar. She just waved it away:

'What sort of nonsense is that, who does believe?'

'I don't know, I've no idea, Mama, but I don't.'

'It's not a question of believing or not. Your Uncle Martin, my brother, what do you think he believes in?'

'The stock market, I suppose. What's he got to do with this?'

'He's your guardian – in your father's place. And he thinks …'

She sat for a little, then got up agitatedly and moved to the fireplace. 'There's something else, it's just as well you know now. You weren't christened.'

He had to laugh. And when she didn't join in, he had to laugh a little for her as well: 'You say it as if it was a calamity?'

'It is a calamity. It was your father. He was very stubborn on certain matters. I …'

'Yes, Mama – what about *you*?' He followed her, to comfort her.

'I had much less strength of will, I forgot it. – But don't you understand that you can't be confirmed without being christened?'

She was wringing her hands. Yes, she was literally wringing her hands as she stood there with her back to the mirror. He just wanted to help her when he said: 'And now you had thought of getting me christened surreptitiously, I suppose?' And when she didn't answer: 'Mama, have you already spoken to the vicar about it?'

'What was I to do?' she said crossly. 'It wasn't at all unusual, the vicar said.'

But now he, too, felt his irritation rise:

'So you agreed to push me to church in a pram, wearing nappies and everything? – Honestly, Mama, I agree to a lot of what you ask …'

'*You* agree to what *I* ask! Isn't it me who lets *you* have everything? That silent keyboard to practise on because you can't bear to hear all the music, I've ordered that for you.'

Something touched him – a feeling of tenderness, of calculation.

'It was just a bit sudden, Mama. There's no great rush …'

He was floating. Yes, he was aware that he had the upper hand, he could afford to make concessions. Something had happened to him which placed him above all children. 'There's no great rush,' he said, 'we could put it off a bit, I mean so that it happens a little more gradually.'

She was a little persuaded. He could see that. A little.

'Then I'll promise you something in return,' he said. 'I shall be best in everything I do. At school, when I go to the conservatory – I'll be best there too. In everything.'

She shivered a little, as if she were gathering an invisible shawl around herself.

He saw that she was afraid. But he had made a decision in that moment.

17

Wilfred was top of the class at his new school.

He divided the day up in a new way now. He did his homework for half an hour before dinner and an hour after it. Then he went for a short walk and after that practised for two hours, partly downstairs on the grand piano, partly upstairs on his silent keyboard. Just the one day a week when he went to the conservatory he dropped his practice, on the advice of his teacher. In the evening he read French and art history in turn, apart from the one day a week when he went to the gymnasium. There it was a struggle to be best, because he retained a certain fear of the trampoline and the horse.

At the conservatory he met a girl called Miriam, she was in the violin class and was the daughter of a knitwear wholesaler. On the way home he carried her light violin case for her to her home in Oscarsgate, and they would often walk a few times round Meltzers gate and Riddervolds gate, or right round Uranienborg Church on those dark autumn evenings. It was already frosty in October. Some evenings they stood on the wall in front of the church looking at the Northern Lights playing over the Tryvann ridge. They always discussed music on these walks home, but when the Northern Lights rolled up over the ridges to the north and east it was as if they both felt the influence of mysterious waves. Then they could hold hands and feel as if a current of cold light was passing from one to the other. And at that moment neither of them found anything to say.

Kristine had left for Copenhagen shortly after the day of his initiation in September. She had been up to see them for one brief visit, without mentioning anything about leaving. It was Mother who had told him later, one evening when he was reading his French. It was said casually, along with other small matters she interrupted him with. It struck him that it was a little too casual. It didn't bother him too much that Kristine had gone away. The one time she called she had seemed tired and a little old. He thanked her silently, but he didn't love her.

He thanked her a little every time he thought about it, and he thought about it often. The new boys at school were always talking about 'doing it', and there were those who believed you could go on having children all your life when you had done it just once. They drew sexual organs on little scraps of paper and sent them round the classroom. He smiled the first time he got hold of such a paper, then he folded it in two and deliberately tore it in half and dropped it into the desk in front of him. After that no-one sent him any more drawings.

He thanked her as well because it helped him to preserve the wall around himself which he had decided to build that evening they had talked about confirmation. He was excused lessons with the vicar now, and had managed to postpone the christening. He knew from experience that postponement could be indefinite in a family which avoided any unpleasantness.

He thanked her too for his physical wellbeing, that she had helped him to become someone that everyone was completely satisfied with. In the evenings Mother would occasionally glance over at him suspiciously – as if all that industry and good behaviour was a bit too good to be true. Several times he noticed that she broke off a telephone conversation when she realised he was nearby. Then it was Uncle Martin who had been reminded of his responsibility and wanted to hear about his great progress, or perhaps Aunt Valborg; she was less enthusiastic, and said that young people ought to get involved in a judicious mix of right and wrong … When Mother looked at him like that he knew that such thoughts were bothering her as well. She could say: 'Do you really have to spend *so* much time on your French?' She could tempt him with a trip to the Kosmorama cinema. He didn't always say no to that either. He didn't make so much of it that she was bound to see through him. He went along with her in everything, even in frivolous trifles. He told her about Miriam and about their short evening walks. He made a point of keeping no secrets. At the same time there was nothing which was not pretence from start to finish. At last he had succeeded: she knew not the slightest thing about him. Not her, not anyone else.

One day he met Erna on his way home from school. She was at the Berle school in Professor Dahls gate and lived in Lyder Sagens gate.* What was she doing between Vestheim and Drammensveien straight after school was out? He was on the alert the moment she appeared in Skovveien.

'I thought I'd go a different way,' she said. It sounded like an excuse.

She was still tanned after the summer. She was always tanned, with a dull healthy colour that reminded him of her father. They walked on together, on his way home. That was just the way she was headed today. She had to go to the dressmaker's. Actually, he was supposed to be at the dentist's over in Observatoriegaten, he suddenly remembered.

That was just the way she was going too, when she thought about it.

They walked down towards Lapsetorvet, slower and slower. That dentist – it wasn't so important after all. He had to hurry home. They were expecting visitors.

They stopped, facing each other. She was wearing a medium blue coat edged with a narrow strip of fur, it all looked very sensible. She pulled up the sleeve on her left wrist and held up her hand.

The silken lace from last summer. White and faded from frequent washing, it was still in place round her wrist. He felt a stab of anger like a rain of arrows. He quickly seized her hand in his own, and with a single tug he released the fisherman's knot he had tied that time in the boat, and put the thin braided lace in his pocket. Tears welled up in her eyes, tears of anger and hurt.

'Give it to me,' she said. He threw the lace out into the street, where it fell onto the tramline. A tram came along at that moment and ran over it.

'You can't wear that,' he said harshly. He walked on for three steps, then turned and laughed. 'I'll give you a diamond ring one day!' he called, and turned on his heel. Then he walked quickly away. But he had seen in that brief second that she was bewildered. A little gleam of light was dawning in her eyes after what he said. He laughed out loud as he walked on. He stopped and laughed, aware that she was still standing there, looking after him.

The musical evenings at Uncle René's had started up again every third Thursday. It was rare for there to be professional musicians there now, and Uncle René was not so nervous about performing his small compositions any longer. One day, one of his pieces had even been played at a concert – as an encore. He was more and more inclined to regard himself as an artist, and lost something of his reverential attitude towards recognised professionals. Wilfred was also required to play. He played Chopin and Debussy at the conservatory in October. In November he was given Bach's preludes, and small études. He never played Mozart any more, and when they asked him to, he said he had forgotten it all. He had been given projects on Buxtehude and gave spontaneous little talks about polyphonic music on the musical evenings. It irritated Uncle René, but Mother sat there with her eyes shining, stealing glances at all those sitting around.

At family gatherings he was attentive with all his little duties. He explained to Uncle Martin how much all of Uncle René's teaching had meant for him – just loud enough for Uncle René to have an inkling of what they were talking about. He fished out little things from the newspapers about the stock exchange and business deals, and served them up for Aunt Valborg, who clapped her hands and called over to her husband: 'Martin, can you hear all the things Wilfred knows about? There are a thousand things I have no notion of at all!' Wilfred hushed her at once, and whilst it was still perfectly quiet he said: 'It must be awfully interesting to spend all your time on such matters, like Uncle does. I don't know anything, but I've picked up one or two things from him.'

To Aunt Charlotte he said: 'I don't think you should have changed your perfume – oh yes, I like that one too, it's lovely, but somehow it's not really you …'

When Lilly came in with the tray he quickly collected together the cups and saucers and helped her with the ashtrays. He had won an ally in Lilly, but it had been a hard battle for a while. That was last autumn, when Mother had been very irritable and nothing was good enough. There were still quite a few articles at the time about youngsters getting into trouble, and he knew that Lilly had the keen awareness of the lower classes, you couldn't pull the wool over her eyes. He knew that it was only *his* glance that had saved the situation a couple of times when she was about to answer back and say something about certain goody-goodies.

He had made an ally of her now, he had nothing but allies. At school he had no friends, he didn't let them get close to him. But he was always friendly and straightforward, and was often used as an arbitrator in the playground because he would never take sides. It was only Andreas who went around looking as if he knew something. But Andreas was struggling like a drowning dog to keep his head above water. Besides, he couldn't get rid of his warts. He used acetic acid on them, which made them go black.

It did happen when he was walking home on those dark evenings with Miriam from the conservatory in Nordahl Bruns gate that he was on the point of opening up a little, saying something real. That little brown-eyed girl with the soft eyelashes had a remarkable stillness which communicated itself to him; she told him little things from home, about her father who was orthodox and attended the synagogue. She was so brimming over with music that it was as if it overflowed in her voice and filled her being. She played at concerts for the poor in the East End. She told him how eyes would shine then. And she told about the solemn rituals of a Sabbath at home and how peace descended between her parents and her brothers. Then a feeling of solemnity descended on them too as they walked along. He was filled with a desire to join in, to belong to someone, let them give him something and give back. But then he thought quickly of how things were, how he had decided they should be. He could look around at the dusty streets in order to break the atmosphere. He could say: 'What is the point of all that music anyway?' Things like that! But it was as if that gentle little girl knew about that too, about why he said it. She didn't fix him with tearful blue eyes, wounded to the depths of her soul. She might laugh quietly. She could laugh quietly about anything. And when she said something, she didn't insist on it as he was used to. She said it because it occurred to her. If he maintained the opposite, it was as if she hadn't said anything, as if her whole being was full of certainty about many things. Once, in the sparse woodland behind Uranienborg, he threw his arms around her and kissed her for a long time. She let it happen, she kissed him back. They stood there embracing in the bitter cold of evening, violin case and all. After a while he put the violin case down on the ground. Then she laughed quietly, but didn't make any objections when he wanted to hold her again. She met him in open and unembarrassed joy, and he felt a tender desire which encompassed everything that had occurred. Then she moved her face away from his and stroked his cheek. She took off her glove and stroked him again. When he bent down to pick up the violin case the ground was covered with snow, it was already deep. They had snow on their heads and everywhere their hands hadn't been. Then she laughed. 'I think winter has come,' she said.

He told his mother about Miriam. Not that he was in love with her. He talked about her in order not to fall in love. He told her about school, exactly how it all was, about the fat teacher at the gymnasium who wanted to be the most agile of all, about all the music which streamed out of the conservatory and met him from the windows there, and that was how they played music everywhere, everywhere … And he was aware the whole time that he could say everything exactly as it was without saying anything as it was. He could feel the urge to lie a little, as he did before, just so that there should be something which was true. He knew she would be filled with gratitude then, with happiness: he gave himself away!

But he didn't lie about anything. He stopped himself because he wanted to. She would not tempt him into a cosy little lie which would become their code.

Snow arrived in driving force early this winter. Some evenings when they had arranged to go to the theatre they could suddenly look at each other, agreeing that it was more enjoyable to stay in. They said nothing then, but on one occasion Wilfred added: 'Besides, I have some maths to do.' She said: 'What do you mean, besides?'

'We agreed we wouldn't go to the theatre. It's snowing and windy.'

'Did we agree?' she said. 'We didn't say a word about it!'

They looked at each other. Then he laughed. 'Didn't we say it?' It was a matter of indifference to him. He'd wanted to make her pleased about their closeness to each other.

'Wilfred,' she said, 'I think it's uncanny.'

It was good. Everything was good. Everything worked out. He could make her think they were close to each other, that they were in touch. It made her glad, so glad that she could enjoy what was uncanny.

'You're right,' he said, 'it is strange!'

Would she take the bait? She took the bait. She always did. People took the bait when they wanted to. The fish swimming in ceaseless search of something to eat – didn't it have the same suspicion when it saw an idiotic hook bobbing about in the water? It took the bait. It wanted to believe the best, and perhaps its tiny little fish brain registered a sting of regret just as it felt the hook piercing its mouth: I thought there was something odd about that …

She said: 'Aunt Kristine – no doubt I should have mentioned it before …'

It flashed through him. Was he the one who was the fish, not her?

'What about her?' he said, opening his instrument case to find his compasses.

'You know she went to Copenhagen – ?'

He drew a circle. His hand wasn't shaking.

'She's back home again now …'

He got out his thin ruler. There was something about the hypotenuse. He was thinking about the hypotenuse now.

'Those two ladies of hers were looking after the shop,' she said. 'Would you like some coffee?'

'Thank you.' He held out his cup. He was normally the one who poured the coffee. He got up to help, but she waved him down. 'So what happened to the "homemade" sweets?' he asked.

'Oh, you know very well that most of the "homemade" stuff is bought from a factory,' she said. 'Cheating. That's cheating as well.'

He was using his ruler now. Carefully he drew a thin line, with his tongue in his cheek. He knew she was watching him.

'What else is cheating?' he asked.

'She went away with that French lawyer.'

The hypotenuse now. The radius. Diameter, circumference …

'She went … when did she go?'

'Darling, I told you that – it was just after that pilot had been here. Then she and Maillard, the lawyer, went to Copenhagen – together.'

The ruler. The compasses. A circle is a round ring. No, it's a line which joins up. And a line is the extension of a point. And a point is nothing.

'What about it?' he said.

'You perhaps don't understand, you're a ch- - you're young. It's – difficult.'

'Mama …' He looked up from his geometry. 'What's difficult?'

'You don't understand. I mean, we'll still invite her as we used to, talk to her as we used to. But – well, can't you see? It is a bit difficult.'

'Well, you didn't need to tell me about it,' he said, 'then I wouldn't have known anything.'

He looked down at his geometry homework. Not the whole time. He knew it instinctively. It was important not to be *too* unaffected.

'I never met your brother, her husband,' he said, getting up. 'Don't you think you're making too much of it, Mama?'

He had won now. Somewhere inside he must be bleeding. He could feel warm moisture leaking out through tissue. In a while perhaps something would run out of him. But for now he had won. It was the easiest thing in the world to smother a volcano.

He put his hand on her arm, pushed her down into the armchair and held out the sugar bowl. He went over to the mantelpiece and brought over the Egyptian cigarettes. He had won now. She thought *she* was the patient. He lit her cigarette for her. He went over to the window and said: 'It's snowing hard. You can't even see Oscarshall.' He came back at once, so as not to make too much of it. He lit the lamp over his geometry exercise so that he could clearly see the circle joining up.

'Copenhagen – ' he said, looking up, as if lost in thought. 'So they must have walked in Hyskenstræde …'

'Why do you say that?'

'Don't you remember Hyskenstræde? Don't you remember Overgaden oven Vandet? Or Fiolstræde – where you bought the Baudelaire – ?'

Yes, yes. Now he had won. He had almost overdone it. Now he had her back in childhood again.

'I really can't make you out!' she said, sipping her coffee.

A net again. A net to catch him in. 'Sorry,' he said. 'There's this geometry …'

'That Miriam – ?' she said. 'They say she spends a lot of time with her violin teacher …'

The hypotenuse. The radius. The circle. His hand reached

out for the compasses, but they slipped. She said: 'By the way, Erna's mother rang. They were going to have a dinner, the adults – she asked whether you would like to …'

The net. It was everywhere. A circle – you drew a circle with the compasses. But inside that cool circle there were a thousand loops of mesh. You thought it was empty, a mathematical possibility. But there was mesh everywhere. So she must have thought she'd filled his little circle with netting now, that she had caught him.

'I don't see why you're telling me all this,' he said.

She said: 'I just can't make you out!'

As if it was his fault. As if it was his fault that she was trying to poke and pry into all that little world which belonged to him, that she could never stop trying to smoke him out so that she could catch him in some trap or other where he would have to stay – just like the others – everyone in their private little trap which they couldn't escape from, just as all people were caught each in their own little trap, signalling impotently to each other that they were doing exactly as they wanted.

'Do you mean that everything is cheating?'

'Are you mad?' she said quickly. 'On the contrary, I mean that you have to see things as they are … tell me, are you really so busy with that maths?'

He got up. He could tell her 'everything as it was'. He could let a world fall apart, which he had been building up systematically through a long autumn, a whole world of pretence. He could make her see a few things as they were, so that she would be left sitting there open-mouthed and empty-handed. It was in his power to make her old with a few sentences.

He said: 'I think it's essential I do some maths. I'd better take it up to my room.'

But even as he was walking up the carpeted stairs, he knew that every step could betray him. Not too quickly. She was listening without being aware of it to hear if he'd gone all the way up, listening for the door closing. Even in his room it was as if she were there watching him; or someone was. They wanted to catch him, and perhaps something in himself wanted that too. He was under observation by the force inside him which was responsible for everything happening in an orderly and false way. He sat down at his desk, dead tired, but kept himself under control whilst he let his thoughts come one by one. Kristine … a few days later, perhaps just a day, or perhaps she was already planning it that day … Miriam – he could deal with it all if he just let it reach him gradually. A violinist. Adult … Erna, whom they were desperate to link him to, in order to link his childhood to something they thought *would* happen, which they didn't know *had* happened. They wished him well, they wanted to catch him. That's what it meant to wish someone well: to catch them, until they were struggling in the net and they could say: look how well off you are, you're in the net too, just like us …

He went out to the medicine cupboard in the bathroom and took two of his mother's sleeping pills; it was the first time, and after the first false exhileration, tiredness fell like a shadow across all his thoughts. He didn't even manage to get undressed properly. He woke up a moment later and looked at the clock. Ten hours had passed.

He emptied his piggy bank and went to school, but after the first lessons he said he felt ill and was allowed to go home. He walked down to Vestbanen and waited for a train for an hour in the station hall. There was no boat to Hurumlandet in the winter. There was brown slushy snow on the tiles in the waiting-room and in the corridors of the train. Outside the little country station the snow was piled high around the flagpole, but the road leading from it had been cleared that morning. He had cycled along it once, one summer evening when he had missed the boat. It wasn't the same road now. It was difficult to believe that it led towards Skovly.

Tracks led off to both sides as he walked, to farms and little villages by the coast. His own track became narrower and narrower, until it was just a faint path in the snow made by human feet. It had started to snow again, and for considerable distances the path was obscured. When he reached the place where it led off to the right towards the summer houses, there would probably be no tracks at all. In the winter the district belonged to the people who lived there all year.

He didn't even notice where the summer path started. He realised it a little later, that it must have been by the old stooping pine tree. It had been difficult to recognise it with its crown of snow. But it was too late to turn off now. That wasn't where he was headed anyway. It was just that he had thought of going to Skovly first in order to make sure of his way, and perhaps in order to see how the house looked during the winter; he had never been there then, hardly even thought about the fact that it existed in the winter too. It was snowing more heavily now, but he knew that he was walking in the direction of the isthmus between the houses and the peninsula. He was quite clear the whole time about where he was going. To Fru Frisaksen's, to see how things were there. He would walk into her living room and say here I am. He would paint the house for her, he would go fishing for her, and besides he had some money, quite a bit. He could go and break in to Skovly, there was masses of tinned food and other things, so they would have plenty to live on. She would no doubt be pleased that he had come, she was not one of those who surround themselves with astonishment.

It made no difference whether it was true about Miriam, it was enough that it had been said to him. It made no difference whether Kristine had planned her little escapade the day she initiated him. Should he begrudge her a little adventure? It made no difference if they couldn't stop pushing him and his little world into a trap where it had to stay put and behave according to the rules they had made, because they were caught. That's how they were, that's how *it* was. Even if he built all the walls in the world around himself, they would continue to bombard them with their tiny little guns in order to force their way into his world and make it one with theirs, in the centre of all the mesh they had spun around themselves.

He would knock on Fru Frisaksen's door. That was right, she wasn't old after all, it was just that they had called her Madam. He had seen her little boat in the sunset, a bowl floating in gold. He had seen her red cottage which was grey, he knew what it looked like inside, he had seen the photograph of Birger; through that low door his father had stepped, he must have had to bend down quite a lot in that stiff collar. But perhaps he wasn't wearing his collar then, perhaps he had nothing much left of all his dignity.

When he reached the isthmus the snow was blowing right in his face. He'd been in the shelter of the knolls until then, but now he felt the full force of the weather. He sank in so deeply that he had to pull his feet up out of deep snow before he could move them. He was taking ridiculously small steps, hardly moving forward at all.

He stopped to get his breath. It must be the sleeping pills from yesterday which made him so breathless, and made his head spin too, now that his blood was pumping with the effort. His thoughts couldn't escape from the ring they had been enclosed in since last night. The point had become a circle around him, he was walking round the edge of the circle, aiming at something or other. He couldn't find the path across the isthmus, but he was in no doubt of the way. Soon he could see the low buildings of the gardener's place in the middle of the plateau. There was no smoke from the chimney and no track led to the door. The dog wasn't barking. Perhaps gardeners were the sort of people who hibernated during the winter? Perhaps the family collected in a dark huddle in the big bed and spent the winter fast asleep. Perhaps they were a kind of flower, which opened in the spring and closed in the autumn together with other flowers, and lay breathing quietly beneath the snow, oblivious to night and day.

He walked around the house in a large arc, to be on the safe side. Those people might have long antennae with their gratitude. They might open their eyes wide and invite him to coffee. He wrinkled his nose. Then he noticed that his whole face was covered in a layer of wet snow, the whole of him was covered, he was only just separate from the countryside around. If he stopped, he would become a part of it.

He didn't stop. He went on. He hadn't deviated many metres. A little later the cottage appeared just slightly to the left. No-one had shovelled a path to the door here either. The snow had blown up around it so that it was covering the lower half. There was plenty to do here for a lad who was ready to help.

He knocked. He knocked again. Then he hammered on the door. He kicked away the snow and brushed some off the doorstep with his hands, then he tried the door handle cautiously. The door wasn't locked. He knocked again and listened for a while. Then he pushed the door right open and went in. It was empty. The fishing net was hanging tidily on a forked branch which had been pushed into a crevice in the wall. The brass rail on the stove was a little duller than when he was last here. The door to the bedroom was ajar. He opened it a bit more and could see Fru Frisaksen. She was lying on the bed with a grey woollen blanket over her. He recognised her by the hand which hung down over the edge of the bed rather than by her face which was visible above the blanket. She must have died some time ago.

He backed out into the kitchen and pulled the door to behind him. When he turned towards the front door he saw the photograph of Birger on the street in Oporto. He looked a bit like Father, perhaps; there was something about the forehead.

Outside it was snowing more thickly now. He couldn't see the gardener's house. But he went in the direction where he knew it lay and came directly upon it. He was filled with an astonished rage against these people. Could they sit here all alone in the world and let their neighbour die only a few hundred metres away? Without noticing that there was no smoke from the chimney, without asking …

But when he was standing in front of the house with the low mounds of snow-covered greenhouses around it, he remembered that the gardener's family didn't live out here in the winter. The gardener was a caretaker at a hospital on the mainland, where Tom went to school. He'd forgotten that until now. He never thought about the country around here except as a memory and anticipation of summer.

He didn't allow terror to take over. He would make his way to Skovly and ring someone from there, the sheriff. He passed close to the gardener's house and set a course towards the isthmus where it was at its narrowest. Once he had reached there, it was just a matter of cutting across all the knolls and then the summerhouses would appear, one in each little valley.

He had walked quickly to the gardener's house. The snow was not so deep on that side of the marsh. On the other side he sank in so deep that he was getting nowhere. He struck out backwards a little way to find his own tracks in the fallen snow, but not in such a wide curve that he would arrive back at Fru Frisaksen's house. Just a little short cut, so that he didn't see the house right then.

But he couldn't find the tracks, the snow must have drifted over them. It wasn't snowing so hard any more, but on the other hand the wind was blowing more strongly. It had got colder, his cheeks were burning but he could feel in his hands and feet that it had got colder. A dank fog was drifting in clumps from the sea. If he kept going with the wind on his left he must reach the isthmus, and then it was just a matter of cutting across all the knolls.

The after-effects of the sleeping pills made themselves felt in small pulses of drowsiness. It was as if the poison was being pumped round his body by all the movement. He walked a little more slowly for a while in order to calm down, but then he made almost no progress; then he ran in short bursts, but the snow was too deep, he simply stumbled. The best thing was to walk steadily, as if everything was all right. After all, he knew every inch of this land from the summer.

Yes, he had wanted to visit Fru Frisaksen. It had been a vague idea that occurred to him last night, when the net had tightened around him. It had been so relentless – all his mother's probing, one thing after the other, he hadn't been far from giving himself away. Instead he had made a sudden decision. He had known there had to be a way out somewhere, even if not for long, some time to take stock, perhaps until he managed to get on board a ship. The boys on the quayside had whispered on evenings flooded with light about those who had gone on board. So they must have been caught in a kind of net as well, they must have got up to some mischief which was on the point of being found out, they were the kind who were under suspicion.

He wasn't the kind who was under suspicion. Others could suffer for his exploits, it was all the same to him. But he lived in a world where there was no peace from everything that wanted to catch you, he had musician's hands which were held up to the light. And when he had won his world in peace with falseness, they would see to it that that too was a crime, it would become a crime to be good and kind and thoughtful, that would be the greatest crime of all. He had created a torture chamber for himself by being so dutiful, they weren't happy until they could find cracks in his mask.

He had just wanted to see Fru Frisaksen, he was longing for her, for her face which was both old and young depending on how you looked at it, for Birger's mother. In a way he loved her. She had rowed past as he stood naked on the headland. She wasn't surprised. She was rough, perhaps mean. But that was how she *was*. Then he had opened the door to her bedroom. He had never seen a dead person before. But she must have been dead for a long time.

The isthmus was not where he had thought. There was open water with a thin veil of ice over it which was consuming the snow with its wetness. He couldn't get across there. So he walked along the water in one direction, but then it opened out to the dank mist drifting in from the sea. It must be the other way.

He walked along the water in the other direction. He would find the cave under the cliff. There he could rest for a while, and perhaps wring out his socks. If the gardener's family had been at home he would have asked for a cup of coffee, they would surely have given him one – perhaps even a couple of slices of bread. But they weren't at home, they didn't live there in the winter. He would find that cave and perhaps wring out his socks there.

The cave wasn't there. There was no way across to the other side either. It was as if his whole summer land on that side didn't exist. It was like something he had dreamt. The whole of Skovly. There were no knolls to cut across, it was just the same flat land with its deep snow, and all the time water on one side with a biting wind from the sea.

He must have gone in completely the wrong direction. He tried to turn the map around inside his head, but he couldn't do it. He would just have to act as if he had turned it round. He needed to concentrate, that was what he had read in *The Pocket Book for Boys*, it was important to stay calm. Once he had brought a boy back to life like that – by staying calm, and thinking intensely. But that time someone had been watching. There had been people around him.

There was no-one around him now. He called softly into the falling snow, but didn't stop to hear whether anyone answered. He couldn't remember the contours of this promontory; it projected into the sea on three sides, but branched out at one point to form a long shallow bay. That was where Fru Frisaksen's boat lay when she was not fishing for whiting. But inland from there lay the knolls, on the other side of the isthmus which formed the border between his summer land and theirs.

He couldn't find the knolls. He walked towards where he thought they must be, but he couldn't find them. It began to snow a little more heavily again. He couldn't feel his feet, however hard he strove to make progress. He chose a different direction and was sure he would strike a steep hillside, that's where the cave must be. But it wasn't there. It was snowing so heavily that perhaps he couldn't see it. He walked more quickly, heaving his feet up out of the wet tracks, but the cave wasn't there.

It was a good thing he was fit from his gymnastics. He was extremely tired now, but he thought it was a good thing he was fit. He walked a little in all directions, but couldn't find the knolls, and not the sea either now. He had the feeling that he was inside something enclosed. And suddenly it was clear to him what it was: the glass egg, he was walking inside the glass egg, that's why he was so drowsy the whole time, he couldn't get any air. And now he knew he was walking inside the glass egg it explained everything, you couldn't get out of an egg like that. The more he moved around, the more it snowed. It was snowing and snowing inside the egg. There was only one difference: there was no little house in this egg, that house on which the snow fell ceaselessly.

But there was the house after all! It all fitted. He saw it just ahead of him in a clearing in the fog. Then it disappeared into the snowstorm again, then showed itself once more. There was the house, and the snow was falling and falling inside the egg.

It was Fru Frisaksen's cottage. He knew that too. At least he knew it straight after he had realised he was in the egg. It had grown darker now, he must have been walking for a long time. The train had left at half-past one. He pushed up his cuff and looked at the Swiss wristwatch Uncle Martin had brought with him from Berlin. He had to wipe the snow away from the thick leather strap. It was six o'clock. He had been walking for quite a long time, it wasn't surprising it was beginning to get dark.

Should he try knocking again? The door was shut. It wasn't certain that what he remembered was true. He had been a little vague after those sleeping pills; he had just dreamt it. Step by step he trudged towards the grey door. It was almost cleared of frozen snow now. He was the one who had brushed it away. Straight away he felt so sick that he had to fall to his knees by the front step and let something come up. Afterwards he felt heavy and exhausted. He wanted to creep away from there a bit – just so that he didn't have to see the house any more. But it was getting much darker around him now. So he crawled back. He was so tired. He had to get into the cottage, whether he had dreamt it or not.

It wasn't so easy to get to the latch. Suddenly it was so high up. He supported one arm with the other so as to be able to hold on to the latch when he reached it. Then he managed to open the door and crawled in onto the floor of Fru Frisaksen's cottage. It occurred to him that he ought to have walked in confidently and offered to paint the house for her, to go fishing. He crawled in over the doorstep. The snow was blowing in through the doorway behind him. He turned round on his knees and tried to sweep the snow away with his hands so that he could close the door, but more just came in. He lay down on his back on the floor and looked up at the ceiling.

It was dark when he woke up. He was shivering so much that he couldn't get his hands working to shut the door. Then he remembered the snow which had blown in, and now he managed it. There wasn't a lot more. It must have stopped snowing. Soon he had the door shut. He was standing up now, but his clothes were clinging to his body. He let his teeth chatter loudly, as if he was doing it on purpose to keep warm. Then he fumbled around the tiny room, inch by inch in the darkness, until he found the matches on the shelf over the stove. Next he knelt down again and crept around feeling for wood. He found dry wood almost at once in the little alcove beside the stove. He didn't dare use the matches to make some light to search by. He could feel with his fingers that there were only a couple left in the box. He had never lit a stove before.

He had never lit a stove. But he had lit a fire. It dawned on him as he was laying the thinnest sticks crosswise in the stove, it dawned on him that he was good at making a fire. He prepared the firewood meticulously before he lit it. It caught at the first match. It began to crackle and roar. Fru Frisaksen had dry wood in the cottage, she was well organised, of course she had to be.

As the warmth began to spread from the stove he realised that he would never get the cold out of his wet clothes. He stripped them off one by one, and hung them up on the line over the stove, which he felt for in the darkness. Fru Frisaksen was well organised. She lived all on her own in the world and had to be ready to cope with the unexpected. He fumbled his way to everything. He whimpered slightly as he was feeling around, that little noise kept his thoughts at bay. The whole time his teeth were chattering, he made them follow a regular pattern, it became a melody, da-da-da-*dum*, da-da-da-*dum*, Beethoven's Fifth … He saved the last match. He took a burning stick out of the oven and held it up to see whether there were any candles anywhere, but his hand was shaking too much, and he couldn't see any candles. He caught a glimpse of the grey net on the wall as the stick flared up. Then he pushed it back into the stove.

His body felt warmer now that he was naked. The wet clothes were dripping down onto the stove. The hissing sound made him feel more cheerful. In Paris they had roasted meat on a spit. The fire had hissed. It was one of his best memories …

But he couldn't stay warm in the darkness. Now that he was dry, long shudders of frost reached him from the walls, together with an overpowering drowsiness which paralysed his thoughts. He strained his eyes to see whether he could make out anything to wrap himself in. He concentrated all his senses in order to stay alert in these moments, he knew they were decisive. The glow from the fire caught the net on the wall, it looked thick and compact as it hung there on the stick, it almost looked warm. And there was nothing else, not a single little cloth, apart from the one he knew was stuffed into the broken window in the bedroom. But his thoughts dismissed it, they forced him to focus on what was nearby.

He got hold of the net, jerked the stick it was hanging on out of the wall, and tried to spread it out to make something he could wrap himself in. But it turned into a tangled mesh in his hands. Now they were shaking again so that he couldn't keep track of anything. He pulled and tore at the dense mesh to try to make something useful of it. He found an opening and wriggled into the netting. It really did provide some warmth, at least it was something more than just his skin.

Afterwards the drowsiness overwhelmed him again, so that he had to use all his concentration to remember the fire. He got to his knees and fumbled for wood. The net obstructed him, he couldn't get his hands free, but had to pick up log after log with his hands inside it, and lift them the long way from the woodpile to the stove.

Some time later he awoke in a grey light. He was lying on the floor in front of the stove. It was bitterly cold, but there was still a glow in the fire. When he rolled over to the woodpile in the netting, he noticed that he was lying in his own filth. But there was nothing he could do about that. Log by log he built up the fire again, until the warmth returned and he slipped back into the comfortable state of fatigue.

The second time he woke it was dark again. The stove had gone out. He was shivering so violently that the mere thought of building a fire again was too much to bear. He crept around in the thick netting, searching for something to wrap himself in. He held his hands together in front of him. They were stiff and couldn't grasp anything individually. Then beneath layers of memory he remembered the bedroom. He crept in there and tugged at a corner of the blanket which was hanging down. But it was caught fast. He tugged, feeling a heavy weight as if someone was holding on to the other end. But he couldn't see who it was – something resisting him.

He crept round to the end of the bunk and tumbled into it with all his remaining strength. It was dark in here; with his two interlaced hands he could feel the hard blanket which would not give way. But on this side there was a bigger piece which was loose. He hauled on it, gaining a few inches, and hauled again. Soon he had commandeered a bit more from whatever was holding on to it. He was grunting with the effort of the struggle. Despite the shivering cold he could feel that his forehead was wet with sweat, and the whole time the Beethoven motif was pounding through him, running out together with his breath, da-da-da-*dum* - - da-da-da-*dum* …

Once he heard an intense twittering of sparrows or something like that; it was lighter then, and he was not so frozen. Another time mice were squeaking nearby, then it was dark. A few times he was asleep but clearly aware, at other times he was awake without being lucid. He knew a little about many things, and more each time he slept with the pressure of the racing streams of images which washed through him in hot surges. But he never knew everything all at once, it was like pieces of a puzzle, and when some pieces were in place others had shifted outside the frame of the picture and refused to be a part of it. At times he felt his legs clamped to something stiff, like sticks in empty space, it seemed to him that he had pushed his feet into the stove, but the fire had gone out and the sticks were cold.

Once he heard a dog barking too. It was barking and barking. It occurred to him that it must be Cora, who had barked like that when he was a child, and come and pushed her cold snout against his. But she wasn't allowed to do that. He wasn't to kiss Cora. Cora was dead – that was a long time ago. He was meeting her again now, and no-one could forbid him from kissing Cora on her cold snout.

He could hear the dog barking, far away and then closer – far away and then much closer. Close by. That's how it was inside the egg he was in – a snowstorm which went on the whole time, from all sides. And a little house, a tiny little house in the snow, with a woman inside it, so cozy.

III

WILFRED

18

It was not true that he was mad.

Not that they said that, but why had everyone at that hospital worn shoes that made no noise?

They asked too many questions as well. Things he could understand had been answered by the grown-ups already, by Mother, by Uncle Martin. They just wanted to hear his version.

But they couldn't hear it, because he didn't answer. Not them, not anyone. He was dumb.

The day Mother had come to visit him – he'd had a fit then. That was genuine enough, surely? It was the morning of Christmas Eve, he knew that very well. It was supposed to be extra moving. He had shaken his head. Then and later. That was genuine enough.

Genuine? What was there at that hospital which had not been genuine? – And afterwards – he didn't answer. He was dumb. It was a calamity.

They thought he was faking it. Especially Dr Danielsen, who had an unpleasant stare and strong convex glasses which made his eyes appear abnormally large. He positively *tempted* him to talk, laid traps for him. He had to smile about it now, afterwards. That man didn't know who he was dealing with …

Besides, he *was* dumb. He was shut in, in a glass egg. You couldn't speak there.

Andreas – he was an unexpected chap. He came to visit at

that hospital. Then Wilfred didn't shake his head. He felt like knowing about things then. Andreas talked, and he himself wrote on slips of paper, questions and answers. Andreas was attending a business course in the evenings, he was going to be someone. He had new glasses, he didn't look so stupid in them. He was having surgical treatment for his warts. He had bandages on his hands, they were clean. That was better than warts.

Later, Andreas came round to his house too. He talked. He had got better at explaining things coherently. It was his turn to speak now. Wilfred was dumb. Andreas thrived on it. He thrived on everything this winter. It was all thanks to Andreas that they had found him.

It turned out that Andreas knew the gardener's son Tom. He was attending a course as well. He was learning book-keeping and was going to be someone. Him too. He'd been calling at Frognerveien when Fru Sagen rang. The last hope … And Tom had puzzled his grateful head, that loyal head which never stopped being grateful for something or other. It must have been way back. Some time last summer. It must have been way back. He'd noticed a lot of things that summer, had Tom. He'd noticed Wilfred's lonely walks on the 'wrong' side of the summer land. From the windows of the gardener's cottage he'd seen how Wilfred walked in a wide arc around their house.

The two lads had talked a lot about Wilfred.

And when they heard that the family had tried all avenues except the police (Police! Police …) it struck him that perhaps out there – there was something out there …

They had joined forces with Tom's father. They had taken with them Fatt, the little hunting dog which was always barking out at the gardener's in the marsh. Tom's father was going to check on their house, but the dog grew restless. Besides, it looked so strange and shut up over at Fru Frisaksen's …

When Andreas mentioned that name, Wilfred's mouth started to twitch. A word wanted to come out. He opened his mouth to say it. He could do it, he didn't want to. For a moment he had wanted to, but he was sitting in an egg. He couldn't do it.

Outside it was bright sunshine and frost now. It wasn't snowing. – *That hospital?*

That hospital had been genuine enough. A proper hospital. Andreas could swear to it. Quite a small one – somewhere out in Asker. Perhaps because it was so close – so close to out there. A proper hospital. But not as big as the one his mother had been in.

Andreas talked. They were sitting in Wilfred's room. Wilfred wrote on slips of paper, wanted to know.

Your mother? – Wilfred wrote to ask.

Thanks. His mother was at home now, not recovered though – but he mustn't say anything to - - oh no, that was true …

An embarrassed smile passed over Andreas' open face. He didn't look so stupid any more. Wilfred didn't feel like tormenting him any longer.

And your father?

A grimace crossed Andreas' face: why was Wilfred so obsessed by his father? His father was no worse than most fathers. He'd been a bit unlucky. Quite unlucky a couple of times.

What was it like, having him there every day?

Huh! What a notion. People had their fathers there every day. That's how fathers were. That's what they did. They were there every day. Worked most of the time. Otherwise they were there, every day.

Wilfred thought about it. He hadn't seen it so simply. He sat in the large chair in his room on Drammensveien, with Andreas visiting him. He thought about what it must be like to have a father like that, who was there every day.

They sat there talking. Outside it was sunny and a hard frost. A new year.

Andreas talked and Wilfred wrote. Andreas thought that his friend had never said so much as now he was dumb. Not that it felt as if he was allowing him to get close now either. But it looked as if he liked his visits. He came once a week.

Not to mention Fru Sagen. Wilfred's mother was not alarming

any longer, not the sort of lady he had to swallow twice before he dared speak to. Not that she hadn't always been friendly and such, but so different.

She was different now, but in another way. Andreas struggled to find the words, both for Wilfred and for himself. It was good that Wilfred wasn't there to find all the words for him.

Would Wilfred like to hear more about his mother?

Wilfred shook his head. But Andreas made his own mind up now. He was attending a course, he was going to be someone.

It was hard of Wilfred not to let his mother come up to his room. It was hard of him to refuse to go down. It wasn't right, sitting there shaking your head about your own mother. At his house it was his mother who shook her head. But she didn't mean anything by it. It was part of her illness.

Would Wilfred let him ask her to come up?

Wilfred shook his head violently.

Andreas bought cigarettes for Wilfred. He was given money and bought Sossidis at 2 øre each. The boys puffed away valiantly as they sat there, though Andreas never smoked otherwise.

But he thrived on these visits. He was a confidant. Did Wilfred want Tom to come? Wilfred shook his head violently. Anyone else? Anyone from school? Wilfred shook his head.

Andreas was the only one. He was curious now. They sat for a long time without communicating, just blowing out smoke in thick clouds.

Was it really true that Wilfred *couldn't* speak?

Wilfred was on his guard at once. He must have let the lad go too far, like that time he asked about the bicycle – whether he hadn't *dared* collect it. Wilfred shrugged and smiled scornfully. Then he went over to the silent keyboard and played Bach with supple fingers.

Andreas watched the silent keystrokes. He suddenly felt it was uncanny.

It was Andreas who brought him the news about the foreign doctor. He'd picked it up one day as he was passing through the hall. Uncle Martin had been there, and Dr. Monsen, their house doctor – he was on his way out. Dr. Monsen didn't have much faith in this miracle doctor Uncle Martin had mentioned. He had called it smoke and mirrors. He had talked about a good thrashing.

Wilfred smiled appreciatively.

But Wilfred's uncle had gone on about this doctor, he was all the way down in Vienna in Austria, he wasn't sure what he was called, it was a strange name. It wasn't easy for him to catch it either, they said so many strange things in that house, things he didn't understand.

Wilfred nodded distractedly. It was all the same to him what the doctor was called. Dr. Monsen had been rather brusque with him a couple of times. He had spoken to him as if he was a naughty child. So the notion of a beating sounded quite likely. Once he had said: 'You can't do this to your mother. Have you *seen* her?'

He had seen her. It was the most difficult thing that had happened to him when old Housemonsen, as they used to call him, said that. He had a little grey moustache and an English look. He had large pores around his nostrils, and when he said that about Mother it looked as if the pores were expanding. 'Have you seen her?' he asked.

He had seen his mother as a kind of embryonic woman, she had a woollen shawl around her and looked as if she were freezing. The curving cheeks were taut now, the whole of the curvaceous lady who was his mother was taut and angular. This was not the lady who had drunk champagne at Etterstad, not the one he had played the game of pretence with from morning to evening. He was not her little cavalier. He was no-one's cavalier, he was dumb.

Erna had been there, it was on his birthday. He had shaken his head violently then. Miriam was announced once. He shook his head. At one point he began to shake his head in the morning and carried on doing it the whole day, not just when they went in to see him. He thought: I can easily stop shaking my head.

But then he couldn't stop.

He wrote on the paper to Andreas: *Do you think I can speak?*

Andreas held up his hands as if in self-defence. Now he was shaking his head too. Perhaps everyone was doing it, perhaps it was a new epoch.

It had never been Andreas' intention to say anything like that. He was just asking, he thought it was so sad.

Wilfred looked satisfied with that, but his glance became quizzical – he wanted to hear more …

It was just that it was so strange. Wilfred of all people. He had talked so easily, knew all the words that other people had to search for. It was so strange to believe, to know that he was sitting there unable to form those words which had come so easily. He would so much like to do something to help.

Really? Wilfred wrote a question: wasn't it actually just fine for Andreas to be able to say everything he wanted?

Andreas shrank back. Here was Wilfred again, the one he had to be on his guard against. He had felt great until a few moments ago, as if he was spying for a friend, bringing secret messages. But with a slight shift in expression it seemed that the silent master could put him in his place once more.

Father thought there would be war soon as well, he said.

So he was trying to assert himself! Him and that father of his! He was going to evening school and learning correspondence and foreign words, he could say CIF and FOB and invoice,* he had even tried out some simple terminology which he thought was a kind of freemasonry for those in the know.

Wilfred laughed soundlessly. He no longer had any desire to mock this boy, he was such easy game. But he didn't have much more use for him now. He had a good stock of cigarettes. Andreas was home and dry. He was going on courses, working his way up. Andreas was the future!

Next time he came round, he would shake his head.

When Andreas had gone he sat there for a long time with that ironic smile. It felt good to smile like that again. He went over to the mirror and watched himself smiling. Then he moved his lips softly, forming words with them. If he forced air through his larynx at the same time sounds would come out, words. Then he could just open the door and shout down over the banister and a whole world would change.

But he couldn't make any air come up through his larynx. Not in such a way that it became words, became sounds. It was no longer snowing in the egg that enclosed him, but he was still there. It had happened the moment he saw them all around him, it must have been at the hospital – if it was a hospital. It had just occurred to him that he could simply not answer. Then it had occurred to him a little more each time. If they had pressured him more, right then, then perhaps – he didn't know. But after a few days had passed, perhaps a few weeks, and he registered the silent questions from one glance and then another every time Mother or one of the doctors sat down on the side of the bed to find things out – then it had become more and more the case that he was completely unable to answer anything, to get a sound out. Because as long as he didn't answer, it kept the world at bay. What wasn't said didn't exist. It didn't exist.

It prevented the pictures coming too. There was that stove. The net. It had surrounded him, it had continued to surround him in all the chains of dreams that passed for sleep …

Dr. Danielsen had asked whether he knew that Fru Frisaksen was dead. Yes, he knew. He nodded. Had the doctor expected tears? He could easily cry, but not when the doctor was there.

Had he been fond of Fru Frisaksen?

He pulled a face. These people were asking from their world and hoping for an answer from his. Was it possible to answer that, for example? Or answer why he had gone out there that day. He could answer in Arabic – perhaps. He could do what boys did when they were small and felt isolated from the circle of grown-ups. They invented a language with masses of consonants, and gradually, as they chattered to one another in that language, it acquired a meaning beyond that of the words it could be translated into. It became a language for outsiders, a secret language without the normal meaning of the words, but taken together an expression of the fact that those who knew it were united in everything, against – well, against anything at all …

He could have answered in such a language. In its simplest form the name Danielsen would have become Dodanonielolsosenon. Pirates' code it was called, it was for the youngest. But bigger boys invented bigger languages which were so difficult they didn't understand each other. And best of all was when you made up your own language that you didn't even understand yourself. Then it was perfect as the expression of feeling encapsulated, distanced from the world outside, which was meant as a demonstration, but could be genuine for long periods. Once he had amused himself by talking such a language in the playground at Frøknene Wollkwarts. He used it until all the other boys were in despair, their thin faces going green as they tried to guess what he was saying.

He was saying nothing. And yet the language itself was full of resistance.

He could have answered this Danielsen in a language like that. Besides, he had a slight cast in his left eye behind the thick glasses. He simply squinted. God knows when he was actually looking at you. He was a traitor.

They were all traitors. In Mother's pay. Perhaps they didn't know it, but she had managed to spin them into her web – them too. Into that web she wanted them all to be struggling in. Not because she wanted to rule over them, but because everyone should be caught in a trap. They all did it. So you had them where you wanted them.

But when Uncle René had arrived with the new portfolio of reproductions in colour, made in France according to a new method – then he no longer had any desire to resist. Then he cried. And Uncle René with his magician's hands had not known what to do. He had held out a handkerchief towards him, perfumed with Aunt Charlotte's light eau de cologne. He had sat there fanning himself with the thin hanky in the hope that Wilfred would wipe his tears with it. He swallowed them and wiped his nose on the edge of the sheet, then he bowed to say 'Excuse me'. After that they sat for the whole afternoon looking at those marvellous reproductions.

He was a good man, Uncle René. When he'd been sitting there a while interpreting the silent signs, he became silent too. He probably didn't notice it himself. But he nodded and gestured and mouthed his questions, just like deaf-and-dumb people. He was so full of empathy. And when he was going he had held out the portfolio of reproductions, asking in that way if Wilfred would like it?

It moved him so much that he had pretended not to understand, he found it most fitting not to be able to imagine such a large gift. Then Uncle René had asked him directly, and then he had formed his mouth into a thanks which was almost like speech. And Uncle René had had tears in his eyes and waved his transparent hands in the air, as if he were forming it into a thousand bright hopes and possibilities – so different from the crass words of comfort everyone came out with, words divided between reproach and private magic: if only *they* desired it strongly enough, the cure would surely arrive. Each one had such a belief. Not Uncle René.

*

He heard footsteps in the corridor. It was Mother. He wouldn't shake his head at her now. He would come down, he'd quite like to go out for a bit. Outside in the street he could hear the creaking cold of the February morning as people and carriages went past.

She knocked. She put her head in just a little, prepared to be refused. He felt a wave of disgust. He nodded violently.

She was just about to withdraw. Instead she came in a little more, opened the door a bit more, astonished.

He nodded and nodded. It felt as if his throat was filling with loathing. He smiled and nodded, he was Lucky Little Lord. He made a sign with his hands that she should come over, he got up, he wanted to hug her, but the 'pirates' code' held him back.

She shut the door behind her and colour suffused her cheeks. All at once there was something of Fru Susanna Sagen again, her cheeks and her body began to fill out. He showed her to his own comfy chair. He walked nervously up and down between the mirror and the window. The desire to play became stronger and stronger in him, to the extent that he interrupted her when she began to talk.

He took a sheet from the pad and wrote: *I've read about a doctor in Vienna, perhaps he can cure me.*

She looked as if she was going to faint. She gasped several times, now she was dumb. Then out came the little hanky with lace edging, the annual Christmas present from Aunt Klara …

'But how on earth!' she gasped. 'That was what I was coming to tell you, to ask if you were interested. It's Uncle Martin who's heard about him, they say he's wonderful – Wilfred, where *did* you hear about this doctor?'

He shrugged. They had said so many silent things to each other over the years. Really he didn't need to write anything. Since this had happened, she had understood more clearly how skilfully they had tiptoed around each other in this house …

Read somewhere, he wrote on the pad. He held it out.

She read again. It struck her that everything could be sorted out in a world where everyone just wanted to smooth things over and forget.

He was about to suggest that they should go down together, he was going to write it down. Instead he gestured – that was enough. They might just as well be dumb, the two of them.

She followed him happily. In the doorway she said: 'Your uncle is downstairs.'

He stepped backwards, and made a gesture with his hands, a round shape.

'Yes, Martin,' she said. 'He's the one who found this Austrian doctor for you, they say he's a miracle-worker.'

She took his arm now. He shuddered and went along with her. Uncle Martin stood up as they came into the room. That was just it. No-one could act naturally. Uncle Martin got up as rarely as possible. He was courteous in his way, but he didn't normally get up. He said: 'Well, here's our big chap!' Wilfred pulled a face, he did so in order to warn him. Uncle Martin had spoken with exaggerated clarity. Did they think he was deaf? He was dumb. *That,* on the other hand, they didn't really believe. They acted in accordance with something they didn't accept. Peculiar.

'What do you know – our Wilfred knows that doctor in Vienna, *he* was actually the one who suggested it!'

She wasn't being natural either. Uncle Martin looked offended. 'We'll do that then,' he said, 'though his name isn't really known over here. Out there …' He made one of those expansive gestures which was the substitute for speech. Wilfred went over to him and made a guttural sound. Mother brought the pad over. He wrote: *I'm very grateful, Uncle.* Martin looked up, surprised. They smiled at each other. What an attractive smile. Could you smile like that in an office – weren't they trying to out-manoeuvre each other there, and what was an invoice?

He went over to the bookcase to find Salmonsen's Encyclopedia, and looked up invoice. Perhaps Andreas had misunderstood it somewhat, he misunderstood most things. Wilfred wrote on the pad and passed it to his mother: *Do you remember the bear?*

The story was told. Uncle Martin had heard it. He laughed too much, as if he hadn't heard it. Wilfred mimed a laugh. The patient ought to feel good, to be in a positive mood. They were easy to read now, they were a little afraid of him. This was not a pinching shoe. He could be mad.

Can't you come with me, Uncle?

That was just what they had planned. He knew it. Andreas had told him. Now it looked like a spontaneous declaration of confidence. Uncle Martin relaxed. He drank his whisky. Mother and he always made such a performance of that whisky. Uncle Martin shouted as if he was talking to a deaf person: 'I have to go there anyway. We two will have a good time together in Vienna!'

He could have blocked his ears. At least Andreas spoke quietly. Uncle René spoke deaf-and-dumb language with his lips. He was in sympathy with him. Martin yelled.

He didn't block his ears. He listened gratefully.

When?

Uncle Martin took out a little pocket diary and showed it to him as if he was half blind. His finger showed February 17. In three days. Wilfred nodded several times as a sign that he understood, the idiot understood. He carried on nodding, until that became too much as well. He carried on nodding anyway. The two grown-ups exchanged a look. He nodded for a while. He thought: am I putting it on? He didn't know. He couldn't stop nodding now.

He made one of his explanatory gestures to Mother: I think perhaps I'll go upstairs again after all … A glance at them both, full of apology, a little affirmative nod to Uncle Martin as a sign that the idiot had not forgotten about Vienna.

Suddenly he was longing indescribably for his silent keyboard upstairs. It had become his compatriot in his secret languages. Slowly and with careful fingering he played the beginning of one of Bach's fugues. He didn't know it very well. When he played a wrong note he pulled a face. He couldn't stop thinking about those two sitting down there worrying. That rational and deeply simple Uncle Martin – in the goodness of his heart he no doubt imagined a strained mind to be a chaos of impulses. For him, a nervous temperament must be surrounded by mystical horror. His striped suits were designed to keep things in their place, as everything was in place for this admirable stupid man who knew everything about progress and that the world was facing an upheaval. In great secrecy he had been busy for a year or so rearranging the family's investments. Mother had hinted at it with an awed expression. The mere phrase 'at par' made her dizzy with incomprehension, as if it had been a Chinese term.

Bach died away beneath his fingers as he sat there at the silent keyboard, knowing everything about these people. Why did he know everything? They had never told him anything properly.

Perhaps that was why. Perhaps you never knew anything about people except what you had guessed. Perhaps it was too easy otherwise – it wasn't reliable. But the things you guessed, those you knew. The dumb person had all the chances. You didn't expect anything from him. He could *see*.

He could see the world they concealed from him with careful consideration. They had always concealed as much as possible of this world, by instinct. Because there was *something* he mustn't find out. For that reason it had become a habit to let him know as little as possible about everything, and for that reason – precisely for that reason – it had been so easy for him to know more about those close to him than was shared with children in those families where everything was above board and as a result nothing was exciting.

That was it. He had always known it, but not so clearly. A silent keyboard like that one, so full of unspoken communication, it sharpened his talent for guessing, because its song was secret. It spoke the forbidden language, that language which couldn't be heard by all those who heard only what was audible. Between him and this silent keyboard there was an affinity which made them brothers, sworn conspirators in a world incommunicable to others. Never, never again would he touch a normal piano with all its noise, fitted only to disturb the secret sources of notes which sprang up for the initiated. Never more would he let his enclosed world be confused by expressions of general information. He knew it now, that he was in the process of becoming an inhabitant of a kingdom peopled by creatures and things which did not do violence to the senses.

The portrait of Father on the wall – how it changed!

That severity he had once read into it, where was that? He must have added it himself – in his naïve fear of fathers. So there must be something wrong in a family when there was no father. You needed a corrective. You ought to have *someone* you disliked in a family like that. A father was convenient for that. Without him it could easily be the mother who suffered. He had looked into these living rooms with fathers in his walks through the West End. It was as if they had a judgement over them, a weight which they silently transferred to their sons as guilt. In return they were surrounded with respect – in order to make the burden of guilt easier to bear. Wasn't Andreas' father such a man? In stubborn innocence he went around demonstrating his misfortune, so that everyone could know how he was suffering and what guilt they bore. And these men chose sick wives, or they made them sick with the pressure of their failure to succeed. Some of them took to alcohol in delighted misery, so that they could sit and mope in corner cafés where white waiters passed soundlessly by, pouring oil on the fires of their self-pity.

He had seen them through the curtains in those rooms, he had peered into the cafés. There they sat, dumb, with a devilish gleam of joy at degrading themselves, so that others could slowly perish beneath the weight of their debasement. He knew them. He knew them. They were the good men, those who didn't put on a show, who suffered.

Father had not been one of them. They wouldn't leave him in peace, she had said. Well, no – and he hadn't been able to leave *them* in peace. He hadn't loved them. Had he? No, he hadn't loved them, but he didn't despise them either – she was wrong there. She didn't know that. She said herself that she didn't know. He had put on a show out of defencelessness, been captivating – the one who took them in. Why? Because there was nothing else to do with them, they were so easy to conquer. So he must have been a polite man. Too polite to assert himself in the long run. And how young he must have remained the whole time, since he believed that he could get out of it by dying with an egg in his hand, a glass egg, where the snowstorm died away when the hand holding it stopped moving …

Yes, he knew him now. Was it not likely that they had said to him if he only *wanted* to? Was it not likely that he had said it to himself – as Dr Housemonsen had said it to him, Wilfred, and fired a glance at him which no doubt was meant to be hypnotic, to get him to speak   So he must have answered them, or he had answered himself, I don't want to want, I don't want to want so dreadfully much! *You* can want! Want as much as you like! Hadn't he said something like that?

Mustn't his goal-oriented brother-in-law Martin have irritated him to bursting point with his efficiency, with his exemplary behaviour in all ways? Mustn't their perfection in their specialities have got on his nerves so much that he had been forced to glimpse a wholeness which was fateful to the one who saw it? Hadn't he then fled into his egg, to Fru Frisaksen, to an uncomplicated love which was more dangerous than the whole cultivated pasture of his marriage with its associated deception and brothers-in-law.

He knew him now! A man who had seen roads divide and was incapable of choosing possibilities, a man who saw no way out, who had shut his eyes, just as he himself had done up in the air with Pégoud, because it made you dizzy to see more than you ought to see at one time: a future for you and yours …

Yes, he began to know him now, to guess. Once they had lived under the same roof. Then he had been the smoke from a cigar which disappeared in the morning, a pleasant veil which was pleasant for the one reason that he left behind him a scent of something departing.

What if he had remained there – ?

Then he'd be a father like all fathers. A man with his eyes shut. A blind man who saw exactly what should be seen and said the necessary words. A dumb man. And a deaf man, who heard and did not hear what was said and meant to be heard, but who in unchanging wonder listened out for the whispering of something unspoken beneath the stars. Until the whispering of the unspoken became too heavy to bear and he had closed his ears and become a father in shirt sleeves in a living room under the picture of a father in a living room. Blind. Deaf. Dumb.

A father like that in a family – who had asked him to come and go? Who had allowed some random Andreas to regard him as something taken for granted under the palm, a slightly uncomfortable apparition who felt duty bound to have had higher ambitions once upon a time, without noticing that he had never striven to attain them? Who had given an Andreas permission to let himself be treated to fizzy drinks in a park, whilst waiting for the person they couldn't avoid to leave – dependent as he was on people and things which weighed him down, weighed and weighed according to the law about bearing your burden to the threshold, to the grave.

And because he knew him he went over to this portrait which was more him than he had been himself and caressed it slowly, many times, stroked the face with its short beard, which had been painted in oil by an unknown man who was definitely not a master apart from in one thing: in wresting from the oils a look which must have lived somewhere in the artist's inner being, a look which had glittered like a – yes, like a glass egg, but where all the crackling flames had fallen silent in calmness, like snow which *had* fallen.

As he stood there by the portrait he knew many things. In this boy's room this face had lived and seen. It had seen all that a face can see in a boy's room. It had seen it with an enigmatic smile, which perhaps grew gentler and gentler. It had recognised it with horror and looked into a future with concern. But also with cheerfulness. For there was a concealed merriment in this glance which the artist could have put there inadvertently, in unconscious genius. There was a certainty of the inevitable in the tilt of this head, halfway between merriment and resignation.

A father like that, a human being. Who was he in relation to his nearest? They weren't his. He was theirs. Caught. But then he had not let himself be caught, not like a lighthouse-keeper in a net in a green sea in October. On the contrary, he had inspected his nets. With no ill intent. For it was not his intention to catch anyone. He had just watched them get caught. And smiled. Cheerful and resigned. That's the kind of man he was. And it couldn't go on. No, it couldn't go on. Not when the world had become an egg with a snowstorm.

Of course he knew him. A little more with each depraved excursion to the fringes of the permissible. Why had he never confided in him? A picture on the wall – simply a picture. Yes, but more than a person, because this picture was created with secret knowledge of the hidden things that people place a mask over, a mask which becomes natural and puts more and more distance between this person and the person it conceals. That's why a picture is truer, if it knows the secret, or suspects it, or reveals it without suspecting it. That's why this picture became more intimately known than a father like that, with all his phrases under the hanging lamp.

But did *he* know *him*? Did he have a father's ever-watchful concern for every unsteady step he took in this world where concealment was vital? He didn't know. He could read a great deal in pictures, he had learnt that, but not this. As a little boy he had drawn his father. They had exclaimed in amazement. It was his mother!

Was it? He was so sure he had drawn his father. The cigar – what about that? Did Mother smoke cigars?

That was just what was so comical. The things that boy thought of. Susanna in Hades, Uncle Martin called it. The smoke curled into so many spooky shapes around her head.

He stood in front of his father's picture and moved his lips as if in prayer. He had given in to Mother now, had behaved in friendly fashion, had been so good as to be friendly. He grimaced. And Father grimaced too. Not much. Slightly. That's how all his gestures must have been: suggestions, irony.

He asked her forgiveness for this. Not for his attitude, because she had determined that. She had disturbed his world with a fellow-feeling which was not in agreement with his. Like in mathematics where two figures were supposed to match and didn't, they just pretended to resemble each other. They were wrong. One was wrong with reference to the other. So the other one became wrong too.

Could two figures like that rub against each other and become the same? Pretend that they were alike for so long that they were? They couldn't fit together. They had to stand separate, and that was much more painful than if they had never been a bit alike …

He asked forgiveness for this, he stood there asking *him* for forgiveness, a man who deserted a ship that wasn't sinking, who said to a world: keep floating, because you can do that, I'll just sink a little.

So it must have happened that the snow stopped falling in the egg. The shine had gone off it, however much he shook and struggled. There was an S scratched on that egg – by chance. It had been scratched with a diamond. An S which begins and ends the same, a figure you can stand on its head. No-one would see the difference. The odd thing was that when you played Bach, there came a moment when you couldn't say whether it was going to stop. You were obeying the law of infinity, where one section was linked to the next and only the rhythmic development could make one section the last – unless you used violence.

He must have scratched his S in distraction, a sign of boredom. Susanna was a name. When he was little and amused himself spelling words backwards he had called his mother Annasus. It was so sweet. They laugh a lot at an only child. But *this* S didn't stand for Susanna, either forwards or backwards. It stood for the unfinished nature of his mind, for its fatal lack of limits. He knew him now.

And it was because he knew him that he had given in to his mother. She had no talent for practical matters. But she got her own way! And to Uncle Martin, her brother. He had talent. He didn't know that. They were going to travel together – a short trip, camouflaged as business, because if it didn't go well … Uncle Martin didn't know that, he was in good faith. *In loco parentis*.

He grimaced. But this time the picture didn't answer. Once again it was severe with its short beard and stiff collar. So no doubt he didn't like such thoughts.

That Uncle Martin was *in loco parentis*? He didn't give a fig for that, as Uncle Martin would say. No, but that he, Wilfred, was making fun of it.

He wasn't making fun. He was fond of them in his way. They wished him well. He would do as they said. He had a world they

290

couldn't reach. There had not been any choice, because they forced their way into all that was his from all sides and wanted to share what could not be shared. Love of the forbidden, and of those who were forbidden. He wanted to be dumb.

19

It was winter in Vienna. There was a thin layer of snow in the streets when they came out of the hotel on Ringstrasse. Uncle Martin was disappointed and quietly indignant. He could never get out of the habit of overestimating the arrival of spring in Central Europe. In the sleeping compartment on the way down he had described what they would find with a lack of imagination which became more and more panicky as it became clear to him that he was on an unusual assignment. His own sons had – thank God – never required his intimate intervention in any area, to the twins' and Aunt Valborg's unceasing relief.

The concept of being a guardian had never weighed on him so much as it did on this morning as he went out into the town he knew so well with a ward he knew less about than he could have guessed about the shoe-shine boy on the corner. With him you had at least the certainty that he shone shoes and smoked the stubs of small cigars of which other people had enjoyed the beginnings.

In pure distraction he was about to take his nephew's hand as they were going to cross the street just outside the hotel. He stopped himself at the last minute, but he had the feeling the whole time that he was a kind of shepherd, and that the sheep could at any moment be expected to slip away between the clanging trams or fall into a fire-trough.

At the little place in the corner by St. Stephan's Cathedral where he loved to eat his hearty breakfast, there were music stands placed on a podium which was squashed between the serving counter and a group of plush chairs with turned legs and a kind of imperial crown on the back-rest, carefully draped with a crocheted piece of material with holes in it so that the crown and the eagle could look out in astonishment at the golden morning.

Wilfred gave a start when he saw the music stands; he plucked involuntarily at Uncle Martin's sleeve in order to hold him back, but Uncle Martin, who thought it was the beginning of an attempt at escape, took a firm grip of his nephew's hand and led him mercilessly into the depths of the café, where mild men with small moustaches were already sitting fortified behind enormous newspapers on stands and tiny cups they were not drinking from.

'Uncle – do you think they're going to play?' he formed with his lips.

A smile passed over Uncle Martin's face. 'Not before twelve, my boy,' he said reassuringly. And was reassured himself. But he found it extremely unreasonable, this sensitivity about music in one who himself had such an eminent gift for music. He was not particularly musical himself, but enough so, at least, that he was not upset when they played. To tell the truth he didn't always notice.

For the tenth time he instructed Wilfred not to be nervous about his visit to this doctor they were going to see. It was true that he was a famous man in certain circles, but Uncle Martin had written to him personally and received a favourable answer. Martin himself had come to feel that he was something of a miracle-worker after he had learnt to lip-read when there was something particularly pressing the boy wanted. It occurred to him that that kind of trick was perhaps not so mysterious after all, if you just made an effort. In his experience that applied to nearly all areas of life. Someone who was alert could learn the most incredible things. It was just a matter of keeping your eyes peeled.

Wilfred had come to feel affection for his uncle the moment they set off on this trip. By agreement his mother had not gone with them to the station. So they felt there was a bond between them, something new and strange for both of them.

Uncle Martin had made it a principle to let others make his own sons into the men of the world their careers would demand of them. With his young ward in tow, therefore, it was as if he were discovering new and uncharted territory. Besides, his fluent knowledge of languages always made it a pleasure for him to give assistance to other people.

Uncle Martin looked at the clock repeatedly. The consultation was set for ten o'clock, and the doctor's consulting-room was no more than a quarter of an hour's walk away. It seemed impossible to make the various time-pieces in his pocket and on the walls move appreciably past the nine-thirty point.

When at length they walked slowly down the street the snow was already beginning to melt, and the town centre took on the shape he recognised from so many visits on business and other agreeable errands. Uncle Martin had reassured his nephew so earnestly that he had become nervous himself. Therefore he persevered with his reassurance to such an extent that Wilfred had to shut out his talking in order not to break into hysterics. He did not intend to begin to nod or shake his head when he was standing face to face with this miracle-worker. In general he wanted to make the most of his chances on this trip, if for no other reason than to give Uncle Martin the triumph that the trip had not been in vain. In any case he had no anxieties about his personal integrity in such unsophisticated company.

The house was a standard *fin-de-siècle* house with narrow stairs. The stairwell had brown panels with a golden stripe which attempted to follow the ascending stairs hopefully, but had to give up for long stretches at a time, worn away by washing and the ravages of time. Wilfred liked this stairwell, it was devoid of pomp, there was something anonymous about the house and the district which inspired confidence from the first moment. He had none of the run-of-the-mill patient's sense of importance at being the centre of interest; on the other hand he was not shy or nervous. In general he had no interest in the whole enterprise, except for Uncle Martin's sake.

They were shown into a small hallway by a friendly woman who didn't make too much of it. On the door was a modest sign. Nothing miraculous about that. But the woman was not dressed like a nurse. Neither did she have that professionally preoccupied expression which conveyed that she had to protect her master from intruders. She read Uncle Martin's card carefully, dropped it into her apron pocket and requested that the gentlemen be seated. On the wall there was no picture of the emperor Franz Josef. It was the first room Wilfred had entered where there was no such picture. There were two reproductions of Frans Hals, to which Wilfred drew Uncle Martin's attention. He for his part nodded energetically, as if to fend off any further embarrassing outbursts. He wiped his forehead with his handkerchief several times in that cool room. Visits to the doctor caused unpleasant ructions in his robustly healthy constitution.

Neither of them had noticed the door being opened when the doctor stood in front of them. The first thing Wilfred noticed was that he was extremely thin. The second was his handshake. It was quick and firm, completely without that secret reassurance, meant to inspire confidence, which he had got so used to from doctors whose whole being conveyed: now then, my young friend, we two are going to get along.

Then they were sitting in that spacious consulting room where there were no shiny instruments laid out or displayed behind glass doors in order to inform the patient that the doctor was quite capable if he so desired. It was a brown room, panelled like the stairwell, with dark leather furniture and two narrow windows with starched curtains which looked as if they had been hung up that very day. The doctor pulled his chair out a little way from his desk so that he was not barricaded behind a fortress wall; then he sat and listened calmly to Uncle Martin's stumbling account of some external features of the illness. Wilfred sat looking at the doctor's neatly trimmed beard the whole time. It was streaked with grey – he could be something over fifty – but mostly brown … and at his hands. He would have thought a miracle doctor like this one would have transparent restless hands, a bit like Uncle René's, hands which could make things disappear or reappear with nervous

294

movements. But this doctor's hands were small and firm and still, not even strikingly long. And his eyes were completely without that hypnotic gleam which might be thought to take over the minds of patients. Wilfred was a little disappointed. He was always aware of a latent urge for sensation. For a moment he felt overwhelmed with desire for something shocking to happen. He was disappointed at this thin man who listened so politely to his uncle's rather misleading account.

When Uncle Martin had finished, the doctor stood up and asked him to leave. He was not impolite, but a little peremptory. Uncle Martin gasped and protested. He had come all this long way …

Could Wilfred not find his way back to the hotel on his own? If not, they could order a taxi. The doctor was already holding out his hand. Uncle Martin looked around perplexed, but was given a nod by Wilfred, who was silently enjoying himself. As Uncle Martin left the room he sent him a glance which suggested that there was little hope they would meet again in this life.

Was that a smile which passed over the stranger's face? In that case it was the shadow of a smile, yet enough of a smile that it said: he meant well, let us two adults sort this out. Wilfred wanted to say something in thanks and his lips worked. But the doctor stopped him with a gesture and went over to the window. Then he turned round and said:

'Do you sing?'

Wilfred shook his head energetically. He made movements to show that he played. The other picked up on it at once: 'Yes, I know. You are also very interested in painting …' He reached quickly up into the bookcase, where works of all sizes and degrees of wear were fighting for space. He opened a huge book which had been lying on its side and which Wilfred had immediately guessed must contain reproductions. The doctor opened the book at random and held it out: 'Austria has also had its great artists,' he said. The picture showed a reclining woman surrounded by trees next to a stream – from the

Romantic school. The doctor pulled his chair across. They sat leafing through the picture book together. It was a kind of cross section through the ages: Spanish cave paintings, closed expressionless faces of Egyptian kings, Nordic rock carvings with their big-bellied reindeer marching on the spot. The doctor opened the pages at random. There was no calculated carelessness about his movements, no intention to reassure. You could see that this book was much used; in some places there were pencilled notes in the text. It occurred to Wilfred that the man was playing at being uncle.

At that precise moment the doctor got up and closed the book. He put it down and went over to the window again, where he stood looking out for a minute.

The muffled sound of carriages with rubber wheels could be heard faintly from the street. Then he turned and walked a few steps towards him, saying:

'Sie sprechen ja deutsch?'

'Aber natürlich, Herr Professor!' Wilfred answered instantly.

Did a smile cross the doctor's face? Not this time. Not a smile. Not so much. A tremor of understanding. Wilfred sat there with his lips twitching. They were the first words he had said for three months. He was not so much surprised as he was shamefaced.

A great indifference had fallen away, or was in the process of lifting. He began to talk, it was vital to him to explain to this unknown Austrian that he had not been pretending these last months, that in a way he had been able to talk, but when he tried … He mixed his perfect grammatical German, which even Aunt Klara was pleased with, with colloquial expressions, he insisted again and again that he had nothing against deceiving and lying in many things, but in this matter – !

Now the doctor did smile – an open smile, not broad and jovial, a smile which was more in his eyes than in his lips, and yet not that omniscient doctor's smile which said: Save your breath, young man, we wise men know everything … It was a smile of – yes, of contentment rather than encouragement, of wisdom, not knowledge.

Wilfred told him about many things, surprising things. This man was a stranger. And besides, a great deal was dammed up in him.

They sat there for a long time talking together. Wilfred watched the sun travelling across the window. Twice the phone rang, and the doctor took it, but his gaze held Wilfred's all the time. Then Wilfred thought he resembled someone he knew – Father perhaps? Something about the eyes. No, it was Fru Frisaksen he resembled … something free of all let's pretend, an honesty *behind* the pretence, *beneath* it, not set up in front as a façade, as a new pretence under the sign of honesty! The couple of times the doctor was on the phone were almost the greatest moments during the interview, because then *he* could study *him*, then he could feel his whole being set free. Because this man didn't bind you, like Dr Danielsen at the hospital, or like Monsen at home; he liberated, he was without that mask of insistent interest which finished up by conveying such a sense of obligation that he had felt under an obligation himself.

'Why did you ask if I sing, sir?' asked Wilfred after a pause.

The other man looked kindly at him and shrugged. 'Why? You have to ask about something. You see, music …'

'Does it happen that dumb people suddenly start to sing?'

'It happens – Have you read Hans Christian Andersen's "The Nightingale"?'

'The Nighting …' Wilfred understood almost at once. And he could read in the doctor's face the moment that *he* understood that he understood.

'It's true,' he said, looking down, 'that I felt like the artificial nightingale which has been wound up.' He could feel the tears coming now.

'Or like the real one,' said the doctor. 'The real nightingale which is banished by the plotters.'

Wilfred said, embarrassed: 'I was dumb towards those closest to me, I was made dumb by them. They made me dumb. They made me make myself dumb!'

He had said it. He had got worked up. It was vital for him to defend himself to this man who knew 'The Nightingale'.

The doctor nodded once. Not that excessively affirmative movement which said: I understand, I understand so well, I understand everything. Just once. That was precisely enough.

'And don't you find it would be rather inconsiderate towards those close to you to carry on with this acting after this?' he asked.

He was unexpectedly severe now. Wilfred wanted to protest, but the doctor interrupted: 'By acting I don't mean something false, I'm referring to the dissimulation that you set up in self-defence – do you understand?'

Wilfred nodded, he nodded several times. He sat there nodding and nodding.

'All right, that's enough nodding!' said the doctor with a smile. 'It's easy to carry on with that sort of thing. You imitate. You imitate yourself.'

Wilfred had never believed that it was possible to put your finger on it like that. He asked: 'Are you a hypnotist?'

The other smiled. 'There's nothing wrong with hypnotism, young man. It's just not appropriate in this case. You needn't be frightened.'

'I'm not frightened,' said Wilfred firmly. The doctor got up. He went over to the window again, and again a calm which was almost tangible descended on the room.

'Is that right?' said the doctor, turning at the window.

'Is what? – Sorry …'

'That you're not frightened? You said you weren't frightened …'

'I meant of hypnosis …'

'Or should we say you meant it generally?'

Wilfred looked down, ashamed. 'Of course I'm frightened,' he said.

'Of course you're frightened. Everyone's frightened.' – The doctor was silent for a moment, walked over to the table and sat down. 'You are a very mature young man,' he said. 'You have lived in what we call a sheltered environment. I would like to ask you whether you would be interested in undertaking a course of treatment here with me?'

Wilfred said: 'But I can speak now …' He registered at once

how naïve it sounded. But the other man got up and came over. Only now did Wilfred see that they were the same height, in fact he was possibly a shade taller!

'You're right,' said the doctor. 'And you must promise me – but no, you mustn't put yourself under an obligation to me, a stranger … But don't you yourself find that it would be best to speak from now on?'

Those tears, those damned tears. He didn't want to acknowledge them now. He had used them, as an expedient. He had made himself appealing with them – as he had made himself cheerful by smiling. But they came, they were there, something warm and repellent.

'Oh yes,' said the doctor, 'if we could just cry – cry and laugh – !'

He said it as if with a personal sense of loss, as someone would speak when they acknowledge their insignificance, but can't do anything about it. Wilfred felt it was best to say goodbye. He had heard that this miracle-worker was a busy man. He got up. The doctor came over quickly.

'I would like to hear you play!' he said.

Wilfred looked round the room. But the doctor walked over to the drapes opposite the desk and pushed open the sliding door. A small room was revealed, with golden plush furnishings, an overcrowded room with a balcony over the street and a shiny brown piano in the corner; it reminded him of the dining room at Andreas'.

'What do you like playing best?' asked the doctor, and went over to the pile of music on the small table with tassels. Wilfred answered automatically: 'Beethoven.'

'Really?'

'Why not?' He felt a small surge of defiance against this man's inspired guesses. 'Perhaps you prefer Debussy?' he asked.

The doctor smiled. 'I asked what *you* prefer!'

'Right now, Bach,' said Wilfred casually. And once again he wondered at the faint smile which passed over that careworn little face; there was something nutlike and concerned about it, at the same time healthy and ravaged; that was what reminded him of Fru Frisaksen.

He played one of the small preludes, then he played a fugue. He didn't realise it himself as he started, but it was the first time he had heard himself play for some months. It was a good clear instrument, a little fragile in tone, but so pure – like the man himself.

Then his conscious thought returned. It was like that time with an 'orchestra' at Uncle René's; he was not leading, and he didn't have the feeling that he was being led, but what was happening was an absorption into powers which resided in him without being his, and for which he was providing a channel.

When his thoughts returned, the feeling ebbed away. He brought the music to a conclusion. He stood up, embarrassed.

'Excuse me,' he said. 'And thank you.'

'I should thank you!' said the doctor, springing to his feet. 'Why are you apologizing?'

He stood there, feeling helpless. 'I don't know. I'd better go now.'

The other hesitated. Then he led him into the consulting room again and closed the sliding doors. How strange: it felt almost like home to him now, this room … He was about to go over to the door.

'Just a moment,' said the doctor. 'You know we agreed about your – what shall we call it – your strategy - - when it comes to speaking …' He smiled: 'How about ringing your uncle and telling him you're coming?'

For a moment Wilfred felt himself stiffening, as if his lips were tightening, and his mouth trembled.

'We don't know where he is,' he said thickly.

The doctor answered at once: 'We could try the hotel – although wait a bit …' He considered: 'I would guess that your uncle is at this moment sitting in Café Mozart drinking a glass of beer.'

Wilfred stiffened immediately: 'Mozart – why Mozart?'

'Because it's a well-known restaurant where tourists think they are experiencing Vienna. It may well be that that's true,

I don't know.'

'Forgive me, Herr Professor,' said Wilfred – he felt there was something comic in his own seriousness, but he persevered anyway: 'Is this something you two have agreed on?'

The famous doctor laughed, a hearty laughter this time, absolutely convincing.

'You are an astute young man,' he said lightly. 'It would have been a pleasure to cross swords with you for a little while – so we're agreed that we'll ring Café Mozart?' He lifted the receiver.

20

As soon as they were eating their soup there were two versions of Uncle Martin's experiences at Café Mozart. One of them, which was Aunt Valborg's, maintained that Martin had been close to fainting when he heard Wilfred's voice on the telephone. The other had emerged on maturer reflection and was proposed by Uncle Martin himself: when it came to it, he hadn't been so surprised. From the first he'd had a firm belief in this miracle doctor, and when the result was clear he had taken it calmly and instantly concluded his urgent business matters, at the same time as sending a telegram to his sister.

Uncle Martin was telling the truth, as far as could be determined. He had been waiting at the Mozart, and when the phone call came he had been preoccupied with other thoughts and his glass of Austrian beer. He had been extremely concerned about Wilfred, and had felt a strong urge to tear him out of the claws of this sinister individual he didn't really know anything about.

In the meantime his thoughts had wandered, there was plenty to observe as well, so that when he heard Wilfred's 'Hello, Uncle,' down the telephone it is true that he hadn't been surprised in the slightest. For a moment he had forgotten the whole thing. Later – yes, later he had made up for his omission and worked up a becoming swoon. So as far as that goes, both sides were right.

As little as possible was said about this Austrian doctor. The fact was that the family had been suffering, and now it was over. True enough, Martin could relate that the Viennese doctor had suggested keeping the boy for further treatment. He had used words like trauma, he had said neurosis. But Uncle Martin had dismissed the idea wittily, saying that the boy had recovered the power of speech and they had roses at home in Norway too. Aunt Valborg didn't look so pleased when he said that sort of thing.

It was over now. It was not the done thing to talk about what was past. It was the done thing to hold fast to the present. And it really had been an unpleasant time. Susanna Sagen had recovered amazingly quickly. She was no longer wearing a woollen shawl, and there was nothing of the little old woman in her elegant bearing or the curvaceous smile with which she greeted her guests.

Wilfred was not there, unfortunately. He was looking forward to seeing them all, but he was not there. He had thrown himself energetically into his schoolwork and music again. He was at the Conservatory and would come later.

Wilfred was not at the Conservatory. He had popped in to a restaurant in Stortingsgaten. Now he was sitting on a bench in Frogner Park with Miriam, talking about music. He said: 'But can't you see how he contorts himself, this Mozart, how he contorts himself and puffs himself up in order to please? Can't you just hear how he primps and poses for that proud father of his, all his life? He was unhappy in love too. He indulged himself in that. Everything was just as it should be with him.'

Miriam smiled.

She was surprised at this passion, at the obvious injustice in nearly everything he said. It was as if he was determined to be in the wrong, whatever he was talking about. When she smiled it was her way of disagreeing with him, he knew that, this boy who was so different from her own kind.

'And all this talk of grace, of harmony …' Wilfred lit his tenth cigarette on the bench and glared with hostility at the dark spring evening with a light mist over the ponds. 'Just look at these swans we humans put everywhere where there's any water, what do we want with them? Harmony, movement, they're put there in order to please us, more than that: to create a fantasy in us about happiness – about the swans' happiness. But look at them, how are they behaving? Yes, they're gliding along in majestic peace, there's something elevated about them, that's because they swim like that and have such long necks they have to hold their heads high. They have to do something with necks like that. But you can see how they're chasing each other, tormenting each other. Their eyes are in the wrong place too, probably so that they have too narrow a view and to sharpen their suspicions.'

She had to laugh. But it wasn't always a happy laughter. She felt a warmth for this boy which she would only half acknowledge.

'I don't understand,' she said, 'it's as if you all want so much to pick holes in everything, to find mistakes.'

'You all?' he said.

'Yes, you all. Remember, I've lived almost entirely amongst my own kind, we're Jews. We don't spend our time finding fault with one another in our family, not in general. We argue a bit, but we don't spend our time nursing grievances.'

He became serious at once. 'Your father – I know he had a difficult time … '

'Father? Yes, of course, Father too, why do you always ask about Father? The others, my uncles, my mother's brother – they've all had a terrible time. All Jews had a bad time in Galicia, all those who didn't own anything.'

'And those who did own something?'

'They no doubt suffered in their own way. But many of them bought their way out. Many helped others as well. We were helped. We're in a good place now.'

He sat there tasting the word. She used expressions like good, that people were good. It must be the ability to smooth over and conceal – which he knew better than most, to show the opposite of everything you knew.

'What do you mean, you're in a good place?'

She looked at him, surprised: 'What do I mean? Financially – yes, that of course. And we like being together as well. My brother is a well-known lawyer, you know that.'

'I have a friend who goes to evening classes,' he said.

She sat there for a while watching the swans. He was right, they did look vicious. There was more than just majestic calm in their movements, which always seemed to her to be 'queenly'.

'I know what you mean,' she said. 'You can't understand that there is so much to be gained by striving for something. Evening classes, the Conservatory … But it makes people happier!' she said, pleased to have found an explanation.

'Are they pleased – that they're happier?'

He had spoken in a low voice. It was not a question. She said: 'Why do you take such a dark view?'

'I don't know why everyone has to be so happy,' he said sullenly.

'No, I'm sure – your Mozart wasn't happy, was he?'

'Don't you think? I think he was just putting on a show.'

'Like you!' she said crossly. 'Just like you. Going around licking your wounds. That's what you're doing.'

He said defiantly: 'I know. But it doesn't make me any happier.'

'No, but you don't want to be either. Self-pitying people don't become happy. They would have to sacrifice too much. That's just what you're saying.'

'Miriam,' he said, 'I think I love you.'

She was sitting completely still now. She had a way of sitting still which was more than a pause between two movements. There was a thin rim of snow left along the edge of the dusty gravel square. It looked as if she was hypnotized by it.

'I would never marry anyone other than a Jew,' she said. 'I would never allow myself to fall in love with anyone other than the one I marry.'

He thought, and it was like a dampened fire in him the

whole time: it's right that she's good. That's how you ought to be. It made him hateful.

'Menkowitz from your violin classes is a Jew all right.'

'Yes,' she said. And a little after: 'He's a good teacher as well.'

Well, so what? he thought, irritated. There's no need for that. We've been good friends, we've walked home together, perhaps I love her. Northern Lights.

'I feel close to you when it's the Northern Lights,' she said with a little laugh. 'On the wall at Uranienborg. I feel close to you then.'

That damned instinct. Had he said Northern Lights? She'd been sitting guessing, hadn't she. Like Mother, like Erna, like Kristine. Were his thoughts always so easy to follow?

'When you wouldn't see me, when you were ill …' she said.

He didn't help her. He looked at the swans. They were swimming according to a system, closing in on one another. When *he* wanted to, she didn't. When *she* was perhaps willing, a third came along. Then the first attacked the third whilst *she* swam away, paddling calmly. Majestic.

'I'd been waiting outside for three-quarters of an hour before I dared to ring.'

Well, so what, so what … Once he had rung the bell at Andreas', and run and hidden on the stairs to trick an old servant. That's how he was, that's how they were, those who weren't good.

'Do you think it's any fun, being dumb? Sitting struggling with your larynx while people watch?'

'Perhaps I could have got you to speak,' she said. 'I believed I could.'

She believed she could have got him to. So that was what she believed. So she had presented herself humbly, like a servant of the temple.

'And why you exactly?'

She gave a small resigned shrug. 'My lesson's finished now,' she said.

The lesson was finished. Her music lesson was over. She had played truant as well, in order to be with him – lied as well, she who never lied. She had missed the chance to see her Menkowitz …

'I should be touched,' he said. 'We'd better go. I've got family at home as well, by the way. They've killed a calf.'

'That's more than you deserve,' she said, getting up.

He got up too, looking crossly out at the swans: 'It was more than that good-for-nothing in the Bible deserved as well. But they did it. They always kill a calf.'

They separated by the low wooden gate into Kirkeveien. He watched her walking quickly towards Munthes gate. The deep wheel-tracks were full of golden water reflected from the red sky.

'Your fiddle!' he shouted suddenly. He was still holding her violin case. At that moment a huge beer-cart came past, pulled by two spirited horses. He had to duck blindly to get out of the way of the hooves. He was drenched with water from the wheel-tracks.

'Did you see that it was golden?' he said, laughing at her. She was horrified, she'd seen the cart coming. The driver turned around furiously on his seat and asked if he was blind.

'Dumb!' he answered, pointing to his mouth and drawing a circle on his forehead with his index finger. She laughed. 'You *are* mad,' she said. 'What do you mean, the water was golden?'

'The same water,' he said, pointing to his trousers – 'this muddy water, which our maid Lilly will have the privilege of removing, it was golden in the sunset, didn't you notice?'

Together they looked up Kirkeveien, all the way up to where the birch trees began by Majorstuen. The salmon-pink sky made two golden stripes of the wheel-tracks leading upwards.

'Like with the swans?' she said, laughing gently. 'Well then, let it be golden. Let the swans hold their heads high. Let that be what you remember about them. Then you can clean your trousers yourself and remember that it was golden!'

Her eyes were golden too. Two suns setting – or rising. He didn't know.

'I suppose they're setting for me,' he said, handing her the violin.

'What's setting?' She didn't understand. He stepped towards her quickly and kissed both her eyes. 'Those two,' he said.

He stood and waved. She turned round and waved. Then he stopped waving, but did not move. She turned round right at the end of the street. She waved. He waved back. He ran a few steps, then stopped. Then he went back to the park. He threw a stone at the swans. It missed. A park attendant appeared, asking angrily whether he was throwing stones at the swans!

'Yes,' said Wilfred. 'Do you want my name?'

The attendant stepped back, appalled. He stood beneath a tree watching him. He didn't leave until the young man was walking towards the way out.

'Those eyes,' he murmured.

But when he got home to Drammensveien, he too stopped outside the house and didn't dare go in. He saw them sitting there, as he had always seen them and always guessed their words before they said anything. So they must be waiting for him to come in. Oh – they would be so unaffected, they wouldn't pause for a moment in what they were doing, on the contrary, they would carry on talking, Aunt Valborg and Aunt Klara would be absorbed in their game of Go-Bang* – until someone happened to catch sight of him: well, if it isn't Wilfred, how are you getting on with the music?

And all because they wished him well, too well. He could give them something in return – love. But not from him. Not his love. He could give them a love; Mother – he could give her a son's love, some son or other.

Could he also ask to look at Aunt Klara's brooch? In all decency, he couldn't do that, they couldn't expect him to return to a second childhood. But he *could* do it! On an impulse he might. Ask to see what was inside it, and inside that again. If he was lucky, he could carry it off.

To Uncle Martin he could show his gratitude. Not directly. Not Vienna. They were through that, it was past. You got through things, then they didn't exist any longer.

But what if you didn't get through things – what if they

weren't past? If every moment of experience was a world in itself with no preconditions in what went before, and no consequences as a result? If every moment was an organism, the beginning and end of all things – could you kill it then? That would be to use violence. And what did they do with the things they had got *through* – did they use a kind of eraser on them? That magic eraser which wipes out everything, hey presto …

This was how Miriam had stood outside the door, not daring to ring. So he should be moved? Well, he was moved. If she didn't understand that, then so much the better. She had her violinist, her brother was a lawyer.

Besides, he hadn't talked about getting married. You didn't do that until you were twenty-five. By then, someone like Miriam should have been a mother for ten years. She ought to become one now. He should have thought of that.

No, he didn't dare go in. Or rather, he did … He could go round by the veranda. Then they would be spared pretending to be surprised. He would come on them from behind if he went that way. On the other hand he might really hear someone saying something. That would be embarrassing.

He went round the house to the side which looked out over Frognerkilen. Oscarshall lay white and shadowless, like a piece of chalk beneath the dead sky. A train thundered past. He leapt up the steps under cover of the noise and stopped.

That was where she had been sitting that time, Kristine, down on the steps. So she was probably crying about a life which wouldn't amount to any more. Or perhaps about something to do with sweets, for all he knew. She was sitting in there now. He hadn't seen her since that brief time when she had popped in and not said goodbye. The story was forgotten. Stories changed. You got through them. Hey presto.

He stood listening for a while. It was Uncle René who was speaking. In that case there was nothing to listen out for. In that case it was better to hear it. He entered quickly through the little door at the side and said out loud, as soon as he had reached the raised step: 'Hello Mama, hello everyone!' And he went round to one after the other, eager, measured, glad …

exactly as they wanted him. Aunt Kristine's hair was streaked with grey. It was the first thing he saw. He didn't pretend not to see it, that would have upset her. So she no longer has anyone to colour it for, he thought.

They were happy to see him. Why should he not accept them and be happy too? He didn't ask to see Aunt Klara's brooch, but he made just enough of it for her to understand that he hadn't forgotten. He ran his fingers quickly over it and said: 'That brooch – you know, I remembered my grammar really well in Vienna …'

So now it was said. No-one would have mentioned it otherwise. Now they didn't have to keep silent about it, now it was as if they had been saying something about it all the time. It was always like that with things that weren't mentioned. The important thing was to say it first and not last – just hint at it. The important thing was that everyone was content, then they felt good. At Miriam's house they felt good. They were good. She played her violin for the poor.

He'd gone round them all. He was going in to get something to eat. He screwed up his face violently when he finally got away from them. Mother went in with him, so he covered his face with his hand so that she didn't see it. He had to be able to pull these faces so that he could speak. They mustn't take everything from him. One day he would discard them. Then he could do something else. In the end he could do nothing. That was what Father had done.

But Mother was not to sit with him. He might have an attack of honesty in order to please her: he hadn't been to the Conservatory, he had been sitting on a bench in the park with a girl. She would have been gleeful then, about how irresponsible it was – and because it was their shared secret. That's why he couldn't have her there. He would have to eat quickly. He would like to please her with something or other. But not with the little he could keep to himself. It was so little, it had crumbled away. He drank a glass of red wine and then another. He thought: there could be more of it, of what he had to himself, it could acquire dimensions!

He drank a few glasses of good wine with his grouse. He drank a glass of sherry with his cheese as well, and a small glass of port. As he was about to leave the table he looked round quickly and drank another couple of glasses of what was open. He had got into that habit now and then. Everything was so much easier then. Oh yes, it could take on dimensions! He didn't know exactly what, but there had to be a great deal of it. Once he had amused himself with robberies and little attacks, he had played with boys who got into trouble. There could be a great deal of that, it could become something. He folded his serviette and drank a hasty glass of port and went back to the others.

But he stopped in the doorway. Someone had mentioned the name of a vicar. It could have been chance, but it reminded him of confirmation. He stood there, it was too late not to have heard it. The vicar was called Stub, or something like that. They were all swooning over him; people had their children confirmed in Garnisons Church just in order to have Stub officiating.* He was unique, so kindly, almost as if he were not a vicar at all. That was the highest praise for a vicar. Now they had spoken his name. Wilfred said: 'He might just as well baptize me while he's about it!'

It went deathly quiet. Then Kristine laughed, a little barking laugh, and then Uncle René, silently. Then Mother and Aunt Valborg laughed too. Aunt Klara went as far as to hold her handkerchief to her nose.

'Well, I was thinking about this confirmation,' he said confidingly, going towards them. 'Mama is not especially Christian. It would have to be Uncle Martin – I have so much to thank you for, Uncle …'

It worked. It *was* confirmation they'd been talking about. They didn't give two hoots for it, any of them. It was actually Uncle Martin who maintained that it was practical to have a certificate of baptism, when you needed a passport – and in general …

It worked. Could it be possible that you could say things straight out and sort them out, instead of getting through and covering up and forgetting …

It looked as if it was going to work. If you were just bold enough. If you just had a glass under your belt. But they didn't know that.

It worked. Thoughts churned through him, but not in a mess, in perfect order. Perhaps that's how they behaved at Miriam's house. Just said what they thought? It couldn't be true. It had to be a one-off.

Uncle Martin said: 'I rather think the boy's right, Sussi – that is, if it doesn't mean a great deal to you, this – affirmation?'

Mother laughed. It didn't mean a great deal to her, nothing meant a great deal if people were content. Everything in her world had looked as if it were changing. Now she began to recognise it again. It didn't mean a great deal to her. The matter was as good as closed. He was practically baptized already.

He played for them. He played what they requested. When Uncle René suggested Mozart, he played Mozart as well. It wasn't good, but Uncle René had wanted it. He thanked him once more for the reproductions. They were detachable, you could hang them up.

Uncle René looked horrified.

But he wouldn't hang them up. You shouldn't see everything all the time.

Uncle René sighed, relieved.

Uncle Martin sat there with his whisky. Wilfred raised an imaginary glass to him across the table, he mouthed his thanks and winked. So he had said it again, more than enough. He could feel that he was beginning to make too much of it. He felt like making too much of it. When Aunt Klara asked him about school, he said it was going well, it was going alarmingly well, there must be something wrong with that school. They laughed. They liked him to be happy. They had contributed to it. They deserved it. It was the least he could do for them, to make too much of it.

'The fact is, I'm quite gifted,' he said. 'We're a gifted family, look at Uncle Martin's twins, they're positively English now.'

Yes, he was making too much of it now. They weren't so relaxed any more. Two aunts looked at each other, at least. He wandered into the dining room and drank a couple of glasses of what was open. It was really very convenient that they were left there like that. He went back and sat still and was intensely well-behaved. Was this not a family party – the least they could do for one another was to be happy, happy and well-behaved in suitable proportions. And a great deal of it.

Yes, he wanted to make everything right again. He wanted to make it better and better. You couldn't make too much of it when you wanted everything to be good. His manners became so perfect that it began to get out of hand, he created an air of expectation with his silent reserve. Was this not a family party, a reunion party for all those who had got through it! No doubt they had plenty to get through – all of them, maybe. Every single one had their own little thing. He sat down by them in turn and looked at them, he distracted his aunts in their board game. He knew all the possible moves and planned it for them, so they got a confused feeling that they were moving the small round cardboard counters according to an alien will. He stared at Uncle Martin's whisky glass and was at his elbow at once with the soda siphon. It made Uncle Martin nervous, he drank a full glass without noticing. He showed Uncle René a trick with two rings and a silk handkerchief. He performed the trick three times; he had learnt it at school. Mother and Kristine were talking quietly to each other, they were talking quietly and intently about nothing, like people do when they want to distract attention. He adopted a listening expression next to them, so that they faltered and stopped. He stared at Kristine, undressed her for a moment with his eyes. He fetched Apollinaris mineral water for the ladies – it was really not necessary to bother Lilly for such a small thing. He made two trips of it, and each time he drank a small glass as he passed through the dining room. He fetched glasses for them, he had forgotten that. He drank another glass, and another. He had forgotten Aunt Klara and made another trip.

Mother said: 'Can't you sit down for a bit, you're making me nervous.'

He sat down. He sat down so pointedly and studied Aunt Charlotte's tiny patience cards that it was like a blast of silence around him. Yes, good would be done here. Good would be done to such an extent that the goodness would deafen you. For was he not the youngest offshoot of the family tree, who could set an example even for his high-achieving cousins who had become English to boot? Was he not raised to perfection in the art of pleasing – he would please them to death right now. He strolled quietly in and drank a couple of glasses, and no-one could say he was fussing around making people nervous. On the contrary, there was a magnetic calm over all his movements; he felt his mother's glance – discreetly during the interminable conversation about nothing and nothing – it rested on him, that glance, it was hypnotized by his slowness, which he'd adopted at her request. He sat down like a wall and felt his numerous small glasses rising within him, as if they were ascending miniature steps towards greater and greater heights.

The telephone rang in the hall, but he didn't leap up, he rose slowly, with a deprecating gesture – and so that no-one should be troubled he closed the door behind him. A deathly quiet spread over the room. He could hear the silence behind him as he went to the phone and lifted the receiver.

'The boy's drunk,' said Uncle Martin.

Fru Sagen got up to fetch cigars for the gentlemen. 'Rubbish,' she said. 'Would anyone like to play croquet in the garden?'

'If we can see the balls,' said Aunt Charlotte accommodatingly. Wilfred was on the phone for a long time. They found themselves listening. Kristine said: 'We could put our coats on …'

She went towards the door, but stopped. She didn't want to meet him alone out there, and anyway he was on the phone. It was as if they were hypnotized by this phone conversation, by his absence. When he came in again it was like a release. When he heard what was proposed he fetched coats for the ladies at once. They were going to play croquet, a peaceful game, a guarantee of a mood of harmony. He brought all the clothes he could find in the cloakroom, piled one on top of the other, coats and throws, he helped them with everything. 'Good Lord,' said Aunt Charlotte, 'we're not going to the North Pole!' Mother asked: 'Who rang?' 'Andreas,' he said, 'he'd forgotten his homework again.' Uncle Martin said: 'Andreas – isn't that your friend with glasses, the one who looks a bit stupid?'

The ladies were fully kitted out now. They paraded out onto the veranda and down to the croquet pitch like liberated prisoners. Wilfred passed round the croquet mallets politely and went in again. His feeling of happiness had disappeared.

'Andreas isn't stupid,' he said coldly.

Uncle Martin was taken aback: 'I thought he was the one – you said yourself …'

Wilfred felt his temper rising. 'Andreas is a very able boy,' he said. 'All right,' said Uncle Martin.

'Very able,' Wilfred repeated. 'He's going to evening school. He's going to be someone.'

Uncle Martin carefully clipped the end of his cigar.

'His father is really hard up,' said Wilfred.

Uncle Martin lit up and blew out the smoke.

'And his mother is ill!'

Uncle Martin said, trying to end the discussion: 'A pity. That's very sad.'

'Incurably ill,' he repeated stubbornly. 'He has two brothers, one of them stuffs birds, he uses arsenic.'

Uncle Martin twirled his glass gloomily. He suddenly thought about that letter from the school his sister had once shown him. There was something about that ink …

'Perhaps you could pass me that ashtray,' he said.

'He sells them to the museum – the birds. Besides, I think the father drinks.'

It had never occurred to him that Andreas' father drank. All the gladness had gone out of him. He wasn't Lucky Little Lord any longer. It was the headmaster on the phone, wanting to speak to Mother. He'd said she wasn't at home. There had been a few small irregularities at school recently. He'd been expecting a phone call, or a letter. Would he never get out of those small things …

'Really hard up,' he repeated stubbornly, 'really terribly hard up.'

'Listen, my lad,' said Uncle Martin quietly, 'you should never get drunk at a family gathering.'

Wilfred looked at him open-mouthed.

'You can drink a little, and you can go to family gatherings, but not both at once …'

Uncle René approached on his unending tour of objects to be examined. 'Ridiculous place to put it!' he said about the icon over the entrance to the oriental bay window.

Those small things. They spun around you. It was something like that he had wanted to tell that doctor down in Vienna – about all the small things which came back again and again and wove themselves around you like a net.

'Thank you for the reminder,' he said to Uncle Martin, as Uncle René wandered away again.

'Not at all,' said Uncle Martin genially. 'You're rather advanced for your age, you know, with everything as I understand it …'

Wilfred looked dully at him. Uncle Martin was a man of the world, he knew what was in the air, he was moderately liberal. He had two sons with whom he had avoided difficult conversations. He was the man who knew what was what and expedited matters.

'What if I am?' said Wilfred defiantly. Uncle Martin shrugged. Uncle René joined them and suggested a walk before supper – 'we three gentlemen?' Uncle Martin agreed. He was not a man to prolong discomfort. Mother's brother, thought Wilfred. He said: 'I think perhaps I'll go up to my room for a bit.'

He pushed his fingers down his throat and took two aspirins. Uncle Martin was right. You shouldn't get drunk at a family gathering. You shouldn't get drunk at all. That episode from school – there were three of them who'd gone to the woodwork room in the break to drink. Wilfred had brought something in with him. It was innocent enough, but one of the boys had mutinied in religious instruction and said that Jesus was a socialist.

Headmasters like that – couldn't they keep order in their own schools? Why did they have to blab to people's homes? He was too old for this, too grown-up. He would go and see that headmaster tomorrow and have a word with him so that the matter ceased to exist.

He lay down for a while. Yes, all those petty little things must cease to exist. Cease to exist – that was the word. Either all the petty little things must cease to exist, or you must. You could cease to exist yourself if it came to that. If all the petty little things refused. Or if there were more petty things, more and more and bigger tiny little things which refused.

He glanced quickly across at the portrait of his father before he fell asleep – then you could cease to exist.

21

There were ants crawling over him, and he was naked. He had pine needles in his wounds.

He turned over slowly onto his knees and tried to crawl further into the forest. But his head was just shattered glass. He lay down again and let it come. Indistinct shadows rode like heavy horseback riders through his brain and left behind craters of light.

These wounds … He felt cautiously with the fumbling fingertips of one hand along the other arm, from the elbow down. But his fingers pulled back in horror from what they touched. One hand fumbled around near his eyes. It was like someone else's eyes, or someone else's hand. Little dark blue flickers of memory shot up through his groans and left behind islands of open fire. *That* could not be true. And *that* … His memory heaved and tossed furiously, like an angry sea. Then everything faded away mercilessly – until something popped up again, and he clung on to the odd remembered fragment of a gentler kind.

Kypare! Somewhere along the way he had decided to

pretend he was Swedish.* He had called for a *kypare*, whatever that was. Men in black had hurried over. It must be … it must be – where?

He had talked about his father. That's it! Of all things, about his strict father – oh, if they only knew how strict he was. When he put his cufflinks down on the desk and picked up the cane behind the mirror … They had thrown him out – no, wait, they had asked him to leave. A manager with ginger hair and a precise parting – but that wasn't there … He prayed to God for gentle sleep without end, and it came, but was not gentle – in flashes of red lightning it came, full of soundless visions; and not without end, for it was succeeded by white seconds of a clarity that blazed with limitless pain.

At one moment he sat up and looked in amazement at the spruces around him, but then he sank into unconsciousness, broken by painful shudders.

Those small public houses with stained tablecloths and white waiters, like sprouting potatoes, with pimply skin – it was somewhere like that where he had summoned a *kypare*. There were several of them: cafés with silent men with small bottles, or flushed, deathly tired, fat men behind large glasses in booths. There had been several of them, those cafés like deep caves burrowed into houses, populated by fathers. He had observed them, curious, greedy for discoveries. He had behaved well, drunk a few small glasses and been quiet. Once he had felt like shouting a bit … Where was that? When? Oh yes – Mother was in the country, he was alone in town, had come in by boat, was going to go back again, it was – well, perhaps it was yesterday, though that didn't seem likely.

The Freemasons' Arms. Right. He had investigated the secrets of the brooding fathers behind their glasses in the small public houses, he had behaved well. Then he went into the Freemasons' Arms restaurant. Here he was the well-dressed young man. He ate several courses and drank an expensive white Bordeaux. He spoke with a French inflection and had conferred with the wine waiter. He had enjoyed his food and drink very much.

It was really over coffee that things started to go wrong. The tables had got busy, well-dressed people, he was well-dressed himself, all was well, he ordered cognac.

The manager had arrived. He bent over the table so that you could follow the straight parting in his ginger hair, he bent discreetly over the table and enquired about the young gentleman's age.

Age? Twenty-one. He was often taken for nineteen, it felt good to increase it a bit. – Would he possibly be able to document that – they were bound by regulations, he apologized – some paper or other? What sort of paper? Well, a certificate. Did people carry certificates around with them? Well, in that case … What sort of certificate, a birth certificate? But excuse me, he was a Muslim, perhaps they didn't serve Muslims? It was the Muslim Sabbath, had the manager heard of that? Then he faced towards Mecca and drank cognac … But he had not been thrown out. The man with the straight parting had listened indulgently to his nonsense and asked him to settle his bill. After that he had stood imperiously by the entrance and looked meaningfully at him. He had left the Freemasons' Arms in a dignified manner between tables filled with people who smiled a little and maybe turned round.

After that. After that it was full stop. A cellar in Vaterland? A cellar full of hulking men, a beer cellar. A walk along the quay. Yes: guessing boats! He had walked along Tollboden, crying a little, and seen *Kong Ring*. Then he had caught sight of the white swan *Kongshavn* with its nobly curved prow. He had gone on board. Yes, right – that was where he had finished up. Kongshavn Baths' variety show.* That was where it had started.

Foggily he remembered the small round tables beneath the canopy of trees, and the stage with the energetic artistes, who paused in their song and dance routine as the train thundered by, yes, good God, it thundered straight through the park, between the audience under the trees and the stage. And the singers stood there open-mouthed as the train roared through, and the pointed bows of the two violinists paused like spears in mid-flight, until the last carriage had passed, and everyone carried on where they had left off. That was how it was … The strings of electric lights between the trees shone more and more brightly as the darkness fell, and above them: the dark velvet of the August night with stars between the foliage. Oh, debasement – he remembered it all now, he clung to this memory because it felt good.

The other things were not good. Two men arrived …

Two men arrived. He had noticed them at once. They didn't sit together, they were sitting at different tables where other people sat. But they were together nevertheless. He knew it from the first moment. He himself was still sitting alone. But more people came along and joined all the tables as the darkness fell. Those two men – first one of them came over, a lad of his own age, of his assumed age – eighteen, nineteen, he had a peaked cap, raised it, sat down, drank beer. A little later the other one came, he was older, dark, wearing a boater with a blue band.

They had asked whether he was taking anything. He didn't understand at first, the dark one had pointed at his glass, he was drinking wine. Wilfred was drinking red wine too. Then he had realised, they were asking whether he would stand a round. The men grinned at each other at that expression, the one with the peaked cap stuck a thumb in the air and ordered a bottle. It didn't taste good, he let them drink most of it, but they were friendly, they wanted him to join them.

On stage Isa Dahl was singing a song about lilacs, interrupted by the train from Bekkelaget, it was fun.

It was fun, they were fun to be with. A little unfamiliar to start with, but fun after a while. He was happy to pay for another bottle. They drank and had fun. He let them drink most of it, he'd had enough.

But they were fun. They wanted him to join them. On stage there were acrobats from Malaya making a pyramid. The train passed. Perhaps they ordered another bottle, they talked about many things – the one with the peaked cap – he didn't remember, they got him to talk, he talked about his strict father who took off his cufflinks before he hit you. They leant towards him over the table.

Did he hit hard?

I'll say he did! Wilfred demonstrated a single one of his blows, the bottle fell to the ground, the table tipped up as they tried to catch it. It was all great fun.

Have you heard about my father?

Yes, yes, you've already told us about your father. He hit you.

Have I told you about his revolver? He carried a whip.

He carried a whip?

Yes. He travelled in many countries. He rode. He had sixteen horses.

Jesus. The men looked uncertainly at each other. What did he want with them?

Sixteen horses. And ten wives.

Ten wives? The men were winking now.

He had ten wives. Actually he was a Muslim.

The men nodded. A Turk, then?

Muslim. It wasn't the same as Turkish. He had a castle in Bengal and commanded an army.

Castle? He had a castle?

In Bengal. And a house in Hurum. His favourite wife was called Annasus.

Annasus, Annasus. The men tried out the name. The dark one knew a girl called Lispet. He could fetch her if the others wanted. The one in the peaked cap wanted. Wilfred wanted.

Lispet must have been nearby. She had a sore at the corner of her mouth and cat's claws. She asked the dark one to take a bottle of wine. The dark one looked meaningfully at Wilfred. Wilfred looked at the one with a peaked cap. He also looked meaningfully at Wilfred, more than meaningfully. Lispet got her wine.

Oh yes, now he remembered a great deal. He kept a grip on himself. He sipped his drink slowly. Then suddenly he wasn't drinking so slowly. He wasn't keeping a grip on himself any longer. A roof of leaves on a velvet background with stars above, on stage a fire-eater, the train speeding through, hooting by

Bekkelaget, thundering past. Lispet who wanted to hear about his father. She had one attractive tooth at the front and one tooth which was not so attractive. She guided his hand to her thigh under the table. He sat there with his groin aching and ordered herring and dark bread. A caterpillar fell down into it from the leaves. Lispet removed the caterpillar from the onion rings with all the elegance of a woman of the world … Later?

Things had moved on. He'd called her his Lucielille, he declaimed ballads in her praise. Smutty, she said, sucking her tooth.

Something had moved on. He wanted to go.

But the gravelled garden was like an enclosure now. It had gone dark on stage, people must have left. There was the girl Lisbeth or Lispet, she must be somewhere. He had wanted to go.

But they were there. The one with the peaked cap, the dark one with the blue hatband. They and others – they were there, they were hanging about round the exits. He'd wanted to go. Every move he made, he bumped up against someone.

Yes, that was it. The peaked cap, him with the peaked cap. He asked him to sit down. He told him to sit down. They talked together, told a story.

The pictures it was pleasant to think about began to give way to ones which made him groan. One of them had said something about a sneak, a sponger. He told a story from Rodeløkka. Once he'd known a sneak like that, a crafty bastard who surfaced every now and then in Rodeløkka and got the lads up to mischief. Just such a one as Wilfred, he looked like him but was much smaller, a shrimp from the West End. Once he'd beaten an old Jew to death …

To death – ?

To death. Jew-hater, upper-class sneak … if he could get hold of him! German spy presumably. Only a kid. He did know that the Germans were planning to go to war? That Kaiser Wilhelm was planning to go to war? Capitalists were German sympathisers, didn't he know that? He for his part was a socialist. That was the one with the peaked cap. Lisbeth wasn't

321

there then. The dark one listened, threateningly.

To death? Beaten to death?

Beaten to death. A poor old Jewish bloke with a tobacco shop. He didn't die then. Not straight away. Later.

Beaten to death? To death?

The shock. Shock or something. Poor old Jewish chap from Galicia or some such thing. The Germans had driven him out. Or the Russians, he wasn't sure. There'd been a big funeral. His niece – his brother's daughter, he was a Jew as well, he'd done well for himself, poor bastard – she still came up to play the violin for them, in the hall at Dærnenga.* God's own angel from Jewry, Miriam she was called … That's what it was like in Rodeløkka …

But this was whilst they were still having a good time. While the chap with the peaked cap talked; he had drunk quite a lot. Sat and talked in an undertone. The dark one listened. Lispet! He had said into the leaves. Lisbeth had appeared again with a sore in the corner of her mouth, she smelt of onion. He looked for the caterpillar, to see if it would come out of her mouth.

No, no, no, no, no.

Lispet, he had said. The dark one – he could say things without moving his lips. Lisbeth had come out of the bushes. He wanted to go. He'd got up. It was dark on stage. Empty. He had paid a lot of money.

He wanted to go, but they were there. There were no people on the gravel under the leaves, but they were there – at the exit. They were at the other exit as well. The electric bulbs were extinguished in the leaves. They were there, the dark one. First at one exit, then at the other one. The one with the peaked cap talked and talked. A sneak just like him, but smaller. Beaten that old Jew bastard to death …

The dark one was there, at both exits. Lispet, he said out of the corner of his mouth, as if he was spitting.

And Lispet was there, emerging from the leaves, everywhere.

He was friends with Lispet, wasn't he? And Lispet was willing.

Lisbeth was there with her red arms, squeezing his hand. His groin was alive, everywhere else was dead, but there it was alive.

Lispet and he could go into Ekeberg forest …

Lisbeth and he – up a precipitous dusty road, and then on the paths. They were alone now. Or were they? Lisbeth hung on to his arm. Heavy and a bit drunk, she dribbled and burped herring gently as they climbed. Yes, now he remembered: wallow in the dirt, go down and be swallowed up. Down, down into deep pits. The trees rustled. The others? Probably gone home. The one with the cap? Probably gone off. The dark one with the straw hat? Oh, *him* – ! Lisbeth was willing. Lisbeth smelt of onion. She knew of a place up in the forest. A bit further up. She was pawing him here and there. She pawed.

To death? To death – ! What had he been talking about, the one with the cap.

Oh him, nothing, he was crazy. Socialist or some such thing. She knew of a place up in the forest.

What Jew was he talking about. Tobacco shop – ?

He was crazy. Nothing to worry about, not for him, for Wilfred. *He* was a gentleman. She, Lispet, only liked fine gentlemen, couldn't bear such common people. They struggled upwards in the dark. The path was slippery with dust.

He had spoken of a funeral – someone who played – ?

Just a sort of demonstration, they said. A Jewish girl, a do-gooder. She knew a place up in the forest. Pawing.

But there were eyes between the trees, little bushes with evil spirits behind them.

She was strong when he wanted to run. She was strong as a man when he tried to pull away from her. The trees rustled. They appeared. Him with the straw hat. They appeared from several directions. Faces like glowing ovals in the night. The stars above – a great whispering. And then – a rain of sparks in the night …

Ants were crawling over him. That was what had woken him. There was an intense pain in the cut beneath his eye, pine needles had got into it. He could hear church bells ringing.

Sunday. It had been Saturday. He was supposed to take the

half-past-six boat home. He had done a circuit of the small cafés. He tried to raise himself up on one arm, but it gave way. He lay on his back and held his arm up. There was clear sunshine now. The arm felt as if it were broken. It was brownish-black with blood from the wrist upwards.

The wristwatch – the wristwatch from Berlin, the new Swiss watch. He lifted one painful arm with the other whole one. It was gone. His body ached. He was naked. He was lying on a root. He could hear childish laughter, turned round painfully. There they were between the trees – a little girl in a blue cotton apron and three boys. One of them had a catapult. He hit home. Then they laughed. He hit again. Wilfred tried to stand up, but sank down again. A howl.

Stark naked!

Naked! P'lice!

Church bells the whole time. It had to be at least half-past nine. He was lying naked on Ekeberg hill at half-past nine on a Sunday morning. The bits of the mosaic moved painfully into place. Lisbeth ... had he – ? He looked down at himself. Couldn't remember. The sore in the corner of her mouth. Dr Strønen in Youngsgaten, the boys at school had spoken of him. They read adverts for a skin specialist as pornography. Smacked their lips. Dr. Strønen in Youngsgaten. Open on Sundays. Gave injections. Strønen the cobbler they called him.

Youngsgaten? He was naked. There were ants crawling on his thighs. He wiped pine needles out of the cut under his eye.

P'lice! howled the girl behind the trees hysterically. A man's voice. People everywhere. Bushes full of eyes.

He rolled over onto his side and got up. The bushes were alive now, laughter behind the trees, stifled boys' laughter, and a single man's voice. Police. The girl howling. P'lice! P'lice ...

He managed to stand, and ran into the forest on the other side. He saw people on a road, they were strolling. He saw the fjord down below, Sunday blue, small boats floating deep in the blue. He ran the other way. There was a rustling in the bushes. He ran.

He ran inland, moaning. He held his broken arm firmly with

the other. A hammer was pounding and pounding under his eye. He ran for his life, emerged in a clearing. There were tents there, a shooting range … He ran in behind a tent flap, but was met by a scream. A dark woman was in there washing. He ran back, out onto the clearing, hid behind the tent at the shooting range. But there were people behind him, behind the trees. A keeper came quickly out of the forest, braid round his cap, a stick in his hand.

P'lice! Someone shouted. The girl howled in the bushes down the slope. Bushes and trees everywhere. The keeper came closer.

He ran from the shooting tent straight across the clearing, ran to the merry-go-round, crouched down behind a cow painted green with a saddle for sitting on, hid behind the cow. The keeper was coming. P'lice! Someone shouted. P'lice! P'lice! Laughter and screams behind bushes everywhere.

Now the keeper was getting closer again. He stayed hidden and pulled the cow along with his good arm. The cow followed, the merry-go-round followed, began to play. *Ach, du lieber Augustin, Augustin.* Faster and faster as he dragged the cow along, hidden behind it. The keeper jumped on to the merry-go-round and came towards him from one animal to the next. Now he was swinging round the winged white horse. He let go of the cow and ran.

He ran from the fairground down through the forest, through berberis bushes, out onto a path. There were no people there. The church bells were ringing. He ran down the path and caught a blue glimpse of the fjord between the pines. There was a pounding and pounding beneath his eye and everywhere. One arm hung and swung uselessly, but it didn't hurt any more.

P'lice!! – He heard the cries far off, behind and to one side. He tripped over a root across the path, fell with his dead arm under him. Pain shot like lightning through his body. They were after him now, he was in a closed world where he was not in charge.

Was this his world?

Thoughts crowded through him as he ran. They were after him everywhere. Ahead were the steep slopes down to the fjord. He saw the roof of the brownish-black tar-burner between Grønnlien and Kongshavn. He plunged down the slope. But there were people there, sitting on benches, strolling. Now a woman turned round and screamed, a man turned round, they all turned. The shouts came from closer behind him and from the sides. He had stopped in fright. He ran again, downwards, but to the other side, towards the boat harbour at Grønnlien. He could see the red buoys floating in Bjørviken. He saw them from above, he had seen them once before – from above. He ran that way, slipped on the slope, fell and rolled over, got up, ran. He saw some iron railings ahead, swung over them with one arm and fell down on the other side, fell, fell …

There was a hill with sparse grass. The water ahead, behind him a fortified wall with a cavity under it. He crept into the hole, there were newpapers there, someone had slept there; an empty bottle of Siemens punch with a paper bung; he crawled in on his knees and the good arm. His back was hurting after the fall. He couldn't hear any shouts behind him.

He lay on his stomach groaning, biting on some stones which were sticking up. He experienced a feeling of greatness, the rushing of a mighty power. Pain took the place of his body and let it rise towards the clouds; pain remained behind and *became* him. Greenish visions rose and fell within him. He had lain in a cave once, he remembered that. He'd been inside a glass egg. The glass egg was shattered! It was no longer snowing inside an egg. It was snowing sunshine from everywhere, he was the singing star in a space without borders; the rushing, singing star in space. There were no voices around him now. Just the song of airless space against his skin which was bleeding into the blue.

Fru Frisaksen! He met her in the rushing, he was a disembodied rushing in space towards her. She was floating in her boat in the golden sun and there was beauty around her, there were rays around the boat, a halo of sanctity. And the sun darkened on that wrinkled face which was turned towards a land. He couldn't see the land, but he could see the reflection of it in her face, which became smooth and fresh in the reflection of coasts with scattered islands with dripping sunshine in seas of blue. Now she pulled in a whiting. There was a glint of silver. There was an ethereal grace over the hand which held the fish.

That icon – a ridiculous place to put it.

You shouldn't get drunk at a family gathering …

A grace which raised its light over all things, and vanished.

'Fru Frisaksen!' he groaned with dumb lips. They were swollen after the blow, there was blood in his mouth. He couldn't speak, he was dumb.

Everything, everything little Mozart had done for them, his father's pride and apple of his eye. Those small fingers had run like frightened animals over the keyboard. The applause from the court poured like silver from the hall.

Ridiculous, ridiculous place …

A little girl's head appeared in the mouth of the cave, making it dark inside. Light fell slanting across her cheek. She looked like Erna when she was small. Erna with the silk ribbon. Erna with her misplaced devotion over bowls of healthy cereal.

A scream. A shout. Police! Police!

The voices of reasonable men. 'The water, he must be down by the water …'

The egg was shattered. It was snowing dark sunshine inside him. Miriam – she played for poor audiences, she was good. A cigar seller had died of shock. I'm a socialist, let me tell you. New times – change, said mother. Uncle Martin: war …

They were outside the cavity now, couldn't find the way in, kept on searching. An arm. A long pole was thrust in. A boathook for the wild animal. It groped in the dark and scraped along the cave wall. 'No – .' The boathook disappeared. A spider lowered itself silently from the roof, spun a thread and then another, climbed rapidly upwards and dived down – a thread, a net.

The net. Soon it would be the last chance. He could still break through it. The spider climbed up, dived down. It grew before his eyes – a net over the opening. He crawled on his knees and one arm towards the way out. There were voices out there, voices searching upwards and downwards. The spider was industrious. It had a cross on its back and evil eyes. It stopped its spinning and looked at him. They looked at each other, one who was spinning a net and one who wanted to get out.

He tried to get up, his head banged on the stone roof, he felt dizzy and sank to one knee again. The spider was industrious. It was spinning more quickly now. It was urgent.

It was urgent, he got up again and pushed forward, broke through, the net stretched and broke, it felt sticky on his cheeks. He had the water below him. The light blinded him. Now the voices met in a collective shout. They saw him, he was there, in front of the wall. 'He's bleeding!'

He was bleeding from his eye, his hand, from the many cuts he had sustained. He ran. They had collected now, a body of people which became one person.

He swung himself over the fence by the railway and lay still on the cool rails. If a train came now – he would not get up; it would be a relief to feel the first weight of the wheels.

No train came. A marvellous exhaustion seeped into him – like nightshade in his blood; an exhaustion that would last the rest of his life. No train came. But his pursuers had been stopped by the fence. The roads … there were so many roads in the world, they divided, rich in possibilities. But so what? You didn't choose your road, as he had thought, that he was choosing roads to the kingdom of possibilities. But you didn't choose. There came a road – and there you were. He lay bleeding on his road, which was closed. He had chosen wrongly.

'Quickly! The boat …'

They were behind and beside him. He pulled himself over the fence below the railway line. Behind him they had begun to climb over. There were people down below. He twisted to the right, ran along the fence, threw himself down the slope with bushes sticking up out of the dust. Straight ahead by the water stood a group of men in their Sunday best, ready to catch him.

He twisted to the right again, towards the boat harbour, towards the sewer which ran like a greenish-black river out into the blue. There was no-one there. He ran through voices. There was blood everywhere now – blood in his mouth, he gurgled and fell, got up, ran diagonally above the boat harbour and down the last hill. Then he jumped. Greasy slime from the sewer filled his mouth. 'Father!' he gurgled.

On land it went deathly silent. People were leaping along the shore, but stopped. A nimble man with a club foot had loosed a boat with an extravagant gesture. Seagulls rested on heavy air filled with the ringing of bells.

His head came up, slimy with ooze. He was swimming. One arm trailed dead behind him. The shouts from land became one single shout. A bristling forest of arms pointing. Two other boats appeared and formed a barrier.

'There!' roared the shout from the crowd on the hills. The men in the boats worked steadily. One had a blue tunic and moustache. His small eyes gleamed alertly at the glistening head in the sewer water.

'There!' roared the shout.

The man in the tunic lifted a reassuring arm. Then he leaned out over the gunwale, making the boat tip.

'We've got him now,' he said.

Notes

Notes are marked with an asterisk in the text.

34   *Morgenbladet:* a conservative newspaper. Founded in 1819, it was the leading newspaper in Norway in the late nineteenth and early twentieth centuries; by 1912 it had lost much of its influence.

36   *Frøknene Wollkwarts' private school:* i.e. the Misses Wollkwarts. *Frøken* designates an unmarried woman, *Fru* a married one.

41   *Bretteville Jenssen and Sven Svensen's version*: S. Bretteville Jensen and Sven Svensen's *En liden bibelhistorie* (A Short Bible History) was published in Kristiania in 1899, and used as a study aid in schools.

44   *Skillings Magazin*: an illustrated weekly magazine with articles of popular interest.

44   *Christiania Nyheds- og Avertissementsblad*: an independent newspaper with a focus on announcements and advertising, dating from 1861. It later became *Morgenposten.*

51   *Christiania Intelligenssedler:* founded in 1763 as *Norske Intelligenz-Seddeler*, this was Norway's first regular newspaper. From 1890 it was an organ for the Liberal Party, and was bought up by *Verdens Gang* in 1920.

51   *a miniature stabbur:* a wooden storehouse raised off the ground on posts or stones, traditionally used on Norwegian farms for storing grain and other food.

55   *Borghild Langaard:* a popular Norwegian opera singer (1883-1939), who performed mostly at the National Theatre.

57   *that poet:* a reference to the poet Olaf Bull (1883-1933), who published his second book of verse, *Nye Digte,* in 1913. The collection contains the poems 'Elvira'

and 'Gobelin.' The former is about a little girl whose excitement at attending her first ball turns to misery when she finds she is not attractive enough to be asked to dance. 'Gobelin' is addressed by a father to his little girl who is dressed like a boy. He is tired and disillusioned, but she leads him by the hand into a magic kingdom where his sorrows are cured. Then the lovely dream vanishes and both are back in the everyday world.

57   *Folgefonnen:* a steamship which was wrecked after running aground near Skånevik, with the loss of 27 lives. This event occurred in 1908.

62   *the number of dead from the Titanic:* the *Titanic* was sunk on 15 April 1912. The article Martin is referring to, together with the account of the court ball, was in the edition of *Morgenbladet* for 18 April 1912.

62   *Social-Demokraten:* a radical left-wing newspaper, started in 1884 as a flagship for workers' rights. From 1894 it was owned by the Labour Party and the editor was one of the leaders of the party. In 1924 it became *Arbeiderbladet*, the name it still uses. The fact that Martin reads this paper is a clear indication of the gulf between him and his more conservative sister.

63   *Edvard Munch was going to fill the university with his daubings:* during the years 1910-16 the artist Edvard Munch painted the large historical frescoes for the main auditorium at the university. There was considerable opposition to his designs, which nevertheless won the competition for the commission.

66   *Oscar Mathisen:* Norway's greatest speed-skater, who broke the world records for all distances and was world champion in 1908, 1909, 1912, 1913 and 1914.

67   *B.W. Nørregaard's thoughtful article:* Nørregaard was for many years the military correspondent in *Morgenbladet,* and wrote a weekly column on military affairs.

67   *the Kiel Canal:* the canal in Slesvig-Holstein which links the North Sea to the Baltic Sea and saves the voyage around Jutland. It was finished in 1914.

68   *the fire service's new automobile:* Kristiania fire service got
      its first battery-driven fire engine in January 1912; but
      the batteries ran down very quickly and even on its first
      outing it had to be pulled by horses.

70   *Turkish-Italian war:* the Turco-Italian war was fought
      between Italy and the Ottoman Empire in 1911-12, and
      resulted in Italy capturing the province which became
      Italian Libya.

70   *brutal automobile bandits:* the Bonnot gang, a group of
      French anarchists which operated in France and Belgium
      in 1911-12.

70   *Messrs Amundsen and Scott:* on 14 December 1911 the
      Norwegian Roald Amundsen's team was the first to
      arrive at the South Pole, narrowly beating Scott's British
      expedition. The news of his success reached Kristiania in
      March 1912.

107   *like a Blériot over the Channel:* the French engineer Louis
      Blériot was the first to fly over the Channel in 1909.

118   *At the Mercy of the Farmer's Daughter:* 'I Bondedatterens
      Vold', a medieval Danish ballad.

121   *Ole-the-Flower-Seller by Jørgen Moe:* 'Ole the Flower Seller'
      ('Blomster-Ole') is a poem by the nineteenth-century
      folktale expert Jørgen Moe. Andreas' misunderstanding
      here relies on the close similarity between the words
      'tigger' (beggar) and 'tiger' (tiger).

121   *'The Devil's Tune', 'Koll and his axe', or 'Dyre Vaa':* 'The Devil's
      Tune' ('Fanitullen') is a traditional air from Hallingdal,
      collected by Jørgen Moe, about the devil who plays the
      fiddle whilst two men fight to the death. 'Koll and his axe'
      ('Koll med bilen') is a poem by Johan Sebastian Welhaven,
      about a man who lives by his axe and dies by the same
      axe, swung by the son of a man he has killed. 'Dyre Vaa',
      another poem by Welhaven, tells of a seventeenth-
      century farmer in Telemark who ferried a troll over Totak
      Lake.

129   *where little Gudrun disappeared:* alludes to the
      disappearance in June 1907 of little Gudrun Klausen. She

was thought to have been the victim of a crime, but her body was found six months later; she had fallen down a shaft to the underground sewer system and died of exhaustion and hunger.

130 *Bio Cinema:* Bio-Kino, one of the first cinemas in Kristiania, founded in 1911 by Gustav Berg-Jæger, the pioneer of Norwegian film criticism.

132 *Die Angst, die Axt*: in his feverish state Wilfred is trying to distract himself with a list of German nouns learnt at school: die Angst, die Axt, die Bank, die Braut – feminine nouns which take an umlaut in the plural (Ängste, Äxte, Bänke, Bräute).

133 *Bengal lights:* a kind of firework which burns with a vivid blue light.

147 *Skammel he lives in Thy:* 'Ebbe Skammelsøn' is another medieval ballad about a warrior whose brother steals his bride, pretending that Ebbe is dead. He returns to kill them both and is outlawed.

168 *Like a merry bridal procession they set out to sea:* an allusion to the frequent custom in rural areas of rowing the bride to church, which would make most Norwegians think of Adolph Tidemand and Hans Gude's famous painting 'Brudeferden i Hardanger' (The Bridal Voyage in Hardanger).

181 *The grown-ups always said 'Madam':* 'Madam' was the title given to a married woman of the lower classes. To call her 'Fru' suggests a higher social status.

184 *this scout movement from England:* the Norwegian scout movement was founded in 1911.

189 *the visit of the British fleet:* the British fleet visited Kristiania in 1908 – again a slight displacement in time to fit the story.

189 *Elias Tønnesen's latest escape:* Elias Tønnesen (1888-1950) was a career criminal and safe-cracker. His escapes from prison aroused much public interest, especially the one from Møllergata 19 in 1913.

206 *Ideas … aired in the country's parliament:* the so-called

Castberg Laws, which gave illegitimate children the right to take their father's name and the right to inherit, were proposed to the Norwegian Storting in 1908 by Johan Castberg and passed in 1915.

215 *The French aeronaut Pégoud:* Adolphe Pégoud was a French flying pioneer, the second man ever to loop the loop. He became a flying ace in the first World War, and was shot down and killed in 1915.

217 *all the different taxis:* Kristiania got its first two automobile taxis in 1908.

223 *It was 17 May in September:* 17 May is Norway's National Day, celebrated with processions and flag-waving. It is the anniversary of the drafting of the Constitution in 1814.

249 *the Berle school in Professor Dahls gate:* founded in 1894 as a girls' school. It is now a Steiner school.

278 *CIF and FOB and invoice:* terms learnt at business school. CIF: Cost, insurance and freight (ie the seller arranges all of the above). FOB: Free on Board Destination (the buyer takes delivery when the goods arrive at the receiving dock).

307 *their game of Go-Bang:* a board game invented in China which was very popular in Norway.

310 *just in order to have Stub officiating:* Kjeld Stub was the vicar of Garnisons Church, Akershus, from 1912 onwards. He was a well-loved preacher and local politician.

317 *to pretend he was Swedish: Kypare* is Swedish for waiter.

318 *Kongshavn Baths' variety show*: Kongshavn was a nature park on the fjord to the east of Kristiania, beneath the Ekeberg forest. Kongshavn Baths was Kristiania's oldest tavern, and had an open-air theatre in the summer. The area is now a container port.

322 *Dærnenga:* a dialect term for Dæhlenengen (now Dælenenga), an area just northwest of Rodeløkka in Kristiania.

A Divided Mind, a Divided World.

Johan Borgen's *Lillelord* is the story of the adolescent Wilfred Sagen, nicknamed Lillelord (Little Lord) by his mother, who is growing up in Kristiania, later to become Oslo, in the years just before the first World War. The novel focuses on a period of about 18 months, from early 1912 to autumn 1913, when Wilfred is 14-15 years old, although there are many flashbacks to his earlier life. He is a precocious only child, the darling of the family, intellectually far ahead of his class, a gifted piano player and sophisticated art lover. Yet behind this polished façade there is another Wilfred, an adventurer who seeks out risk, who steals out of the house at night and roams the streets of Kristiania, the leader of a band of boys who steal, capable of violence and of arson. As time goes on it becomes increasingly difficult for him to keep the two sides of his personality distinct, and he eventually has a breakdown, which leaves him incapable of speech, literally silences him. He is taken to Vienna to see a psychiatrist – whose name is not mentioned, but who bears a striking resemblance to Freud – and is seemingly cured, though the psychiatrist warns him that his neurosis needs long-term therapy if he is to be properly healed. Wilfred returns to his old double life, but his desperation is only repressed, not resolved, and eventually the past catches up with him and he runs out of places to hide.

There are many clues in the novel as to why this boy, who seems to have all the advantages that money and loving care can provide, is so catastrophically damaged. His father died when he was very young, and it becomes clear during the novel that he was a man everyone loved, and who let

336

everyone down, including his son, when he shot himself. His mother froze in her grief to the extent that she wanted time to stop, and focussed all her love on her little boy who must remain her little boy; she doesn't want him to grow up to the extent that he still wears his long blond curls flowing down over the collar of his sailor suit as a teenager. His aunts and uncles all see different things in him, and to each he must respond with a different, well-rehearsed performance. Where is the real Wilfred, one of them asks, behind all this desire to please? The perceptive psychiatrist suggests that he resembles Hans Christian Andersen's 'The Nightingale' – not the artificial bird which has been wound up by the courtiers to pretend to be real, as Wilfred supposes, but the *real* one who is banished from the court. In Andersen's story the real bird regains his rightful place at the end – and that is what might happen, it is suggested, if Wilfred can be cured of his psychosis. But that is not to be.

Borgen's novel is a *Bildungsroman*, a study of a young boy growing up and his intellectual, emotional and sexual initiation into adulthood. It is a study of psychosis, and a portrait of the artist as a young man. It is a city novel; the reader can follow Wilfred's excursions around the map of Kristiania/Oslo from the comforts of his upper-middle-class home on Drammensveien, across the bay by ferry to the pastoral idyll of Bygdøy, by tram to the East-End poverty of Grünerløkken or in Uncle Martin's automobile up to the open-air display ground in Etterstad. It is also a cultural and historical study of a whole society, one on the brink of a devastating upheaval which will change the lives of all its members irrevocably.

All levels of society are represented in the novel. We get the fullest picture of Wilfred's own milieu, the elegant bourgeois home with family dinners on Sundays, maid service, summers in the country and an innate sense of entitlement. Fru Susanna Sagen, Wilfred's mother, is the foremost representative of this class; she expects her maids to know their place, reads accounts of the latest balls at court in *Morgenbladet* and refuses to take any interest in the rumblings of war in far-off countries or the number of dead on the *Titanic*. Her brother Martin is more aware of current developments; as a businessman he reads the left-wing newspaper *Social-Demokraten,* keeps an eye on the family's investments in the stock market and is concerned at the way his nephew is being educated. But he too watches the activity in the streets from the privileged private space of his own automobile, and is too fond of his own comfort to exert himself excessively. His brother-in-law René is an aesthete who can afford to indulge his passion for fine art and music. Aunt Kristine, an aunt by marriage, is therefore accepted as one of the circle, yet is slightly suspect as an outsider who is unsettlingly different and liable to behave in a scandalous fashion.

We get an insight into the life of the petit-bourgeois stratum of Kristiania society through Wilfred's classmate Andreas. When Wilfred visits his home, he is intensely aware of the different smells in the hallway and the different look of the furniture. The piano is out of tune, the remains of the 'best' dinner service are kept in a cupboard and never used, and Andreas shares his bedroom with two older brothers. His father works in an office and dozes in an armchair after lunch with a drooping moustache. Andreas is a loser in Wilfred's eyes, someone he can use for his own ends. Yet a year later Andreas is going to evening classes and studying to become a businessman. He is going to become someone, he is the future.

The working class is seen mostly through Wilfred's eyes in this novel: the rough, unkempt, aggressive, yet easily impressed lads he meets in Grünerløkken, and the maids back home – though we do hear the occasional comment from fru Sagen's maid Lilly, who has sharper eyes than her mistress and is not impressed by the superficial charm of the golden boy. In the final chapter we hear more from the two working-class men Wilfred meets at Kongshavn restaurant, one of whom is more politically aware than most of the other characters in the novel; he declares himself to be a socialist and asserts that capitalists are German sympathisers and Kaiser Wilhelm is planning to go to war.

The authenticity of the portrait of pre-war Kristiania is reinforced by the proliferation of documentary material on which the novel is based. Borgen has done his research thoroughly, and references to contemporary events like the sinking of the *Titanic*, the Amundsen and Scott expeditions to the South Pole, the arrival of the new Kristiania fire-engine and the escapes of the convict Elias Tønnesen allow the reader to pinpoint precisely the time frame for each chapter. You can visit the newspaper archives and find the articles in *Morgenbladet* to which fru Sagen refers. Occasionally Borgen has taken slight liberties with chronology; for example, Oscar Mathiesen's speed-skating world records were set in 1913-14, and Uncle Martin mentions them here in 1912. And the demonstration by the aeronaut Pégoud at Etterstad in September 1912 is not a historical event, it is a fictionalisation of a similar event at Etterstad when the French aeronaut Chevillard flew upside down over the heads of the crowd – in October 1913. But it *could* have happened; and Borgen clearly needs the incident to occur at this point in the novel, when Wilfred's flight over Kristiania is followed by his first fully realised sexual encounter – a double initiation into adulthood which marks him out as a lover and a loner, mature beyond his years but adrift afterwards in a world where such ecstasy is ephemeral.

There are not only many references to documentary material in *Little Lord,* but also a network of references – both explicit and implicit – to other literary texts. The novel is suffused with intertextuality. The clearest reference, obvious from the title itself, is to Frances Hodgson Burnett's novel *Little Lord Fauntleroy* (1886). Here, as in *Little Lord*, the central character is a fatherless boy who is idolized by his mother, a clear model of what fru Sagen hopes her 'little lord' will be. But Fauntleroy is a straightforwardly good child, who recovers his father's lost estates and lives there happily ever after with his mother. The distance between this ideal and the real Wilfred underlines fru Sagen's wilful blindness to the reality of her situation.

Wilfred's fascination with erotic Danish folk ballads is not incidental. His choice of ballad for the school recital – 'At the

Mercy of the Farmer's Daughter' – reveals his preoccupation with sex and violence, as well as providing a wonderful excuse to scandalize teachers and parents. (Andreas' choice of text, a sentimental poem about a beggar, is equally revealing of *his* literary taste, and gives Wilfred the chance to put Andreas in his debt, something the resentful Andreas will not forget.) And later, when Kristine comes to visit in the summer holidays, it is the text of 'Ebbe Skammelsøn' which runs insistently through Wilfred's mind – a ballad of thwarted desire, as the beloved object is stolen by another man. It is in many ways a prophetic text, as Ebbe was cheated – by his brother, but also by his bride and his parents who concurred. Later Wilfred will feel betrayed by Kristine who takes another lover just after their union, and by his mother who tries to force him together with the innocent Erna and to block his involvement both with Kristine and with Miriam, an independent musician who is Jewish and therefore also threateningly 'other'.

Other more passing cultural references provide an implicit comment on the action. The statuette of Leda and the swan, for example, which Wilfred watches Uncle René's fingers caressing in the first scene, gives an early hint of his curiosity about the mysteries of sex, and later in the novel the silent swans on the lake are both a provocation and an echo of Wilfred's own silence. There are many parallels with *Hamlet* – the disturbed boy trying to find out the truth about his vanished father, the mother who wants to avoid facing up to the truth, the well-meaning uncle figure etc. And there are also many references to other texts by Borgen himself. His works are interlinked, with the same incidents and sometimes the same characters reappearing in different contexts. Furthermore, many details of the events of Wilfred's life are taken by the author directly from his own experience of growing up before the first World War, as he recounts it in his autobiographical essay *Barndommens rike* (The Kingdom of Childhood, 1965).

The different sections of the novel are also linked by recurring images. One of the most predominant is that of the net. Real nets play an important part in the narrative; fru

Frisaksen's husband, the light-house keeper, was found dead
trapped in his own nets, and it is fru Frisaksen's net that Wilfred
crawls into for warmth when he is stranded in her cottage in
winter. But he also has the constant feeling that nets are being
laid for him, in order to trap him; seemingly artless remarks,
especially by his mother, conceal a desire to pin him down, to
define and control him. When he is hiding from his pursuers
towards the end of the novel, the web spun by a spider across
the opening of the cave becomes the meshes of a net, the
bars of a cage. The glass egg is a related image. Here again, it
is at once a real glass egg which belonged to his father, with a
little house in a snowstorm, and a representation of the place
of solitude he seeks, a refuge which can then suddenly turn
into a death trap. Ambiguity is of the essence of the novel, as
it is of Wilfred's character; a terror of being caught, of being
known. His life is one long flight from definition, at the same
time as he longs for it. He is incapable of choosing, but always
wants to keep all his options open. By the end of the novel he
still does not know who he himself is. The final remark of the
boatman who pulls him from the river, 'We've got him now', is
full of irony.

Little Lord was published in 1955, by a writer who was already
well known as an author of novels, plays, and short stories,
as well as a journalist and literary critic. It was an immediate
success, and the reviews were overwhelmingly positive. Borgen
had not intended to continue the story of Wilfred, but public
demand to know what happened next inspired him to write
two further novels, *De mørke kilder* (The Dark Springs, 1956),
and *Vi har ham nå* (We've Got Him Now, 1957). The trilogy
broadens into a study of twentieth-century Norwegian society.
It follows the lives of Wilfred and those around him through the
first World War, in which fortunes are made and lost overnight,
the twenties and thirties, with international speculation, social
unrest and artistic experimentation, and finally into the second
World War, where the German occupation of Norway provides
the ultimate challenge to a character always inclined to be

on both sides at once: will Wilfred be able finally to make a commitment?

Janet Garton

Norwich, May 2015

Bibliography

Borgen, Johan: *Lillelord* (1955). Gyldendal, Oslo 1967. Introduction by Willy Dahl.

Birn, Randi: *Johan Borgen*. Twayne Publishers, New York 1974.

Buvik, Per: 'Om kommunikasjonstemaet i Johan Borgen's *Lillelord.' Norsk litterær årbok* 1976, pp. 70-87.

Christensen, Bente: *Johan Borgens Lillelord. En studie i kreativitet og kommunikasjon*. Aschehoug, Oslo 1993.

Flatin, Kjetil: 'Intervju med Johan Borgen'. *Norsk litterær årbok* 1973, pp. 116-25.

Lagesen, Ole Chr.: 'Tid, miljø og historisk bakgrunn i Johan Borgen's *Lillelord.' Edda* I, 1970, pp. 17-27.

Longum, Leif: *Et speil for oss selv*. Aschehoug, Oslo 1968.

AMALIE SKRAM

Fru Inés

(translated by Katherine Hanson and Judith Messick)

Fru Inés is a city novel, vividly evoking the sights, sounds and smells of nineteenth-century Constantinople. The city is a hub, a meeting point of East and West, where privileged Europeans enjoy a cossetted existence screened from the tumult and misery of the streets. One of the privileged is Inés, a Spanish Levantine from Alexandria, whose marriage to a Swedish consul has brought her a life of enviable luxury; but behind the polished facade she is lonely and unfulfilled, trapped in a loveless marriage. Her yearning for passion leads her to embark on an affair with a naive young Swede, Arthur Flemming; but their love is threatened from the start by portents of disaster and the threat of discovery, and Inés is inexorably drawn to seek rescue from the sordid dealers from whom she had been so careful to keep aloof.

Amalie Skram was a contemporary of Henrik Ibsen, and like him a fierce critic of repressive social mores and hypocrisy. Many of her works make an impassioned statement on the way women of all classes are imprisoned in their social roles, contributing to the great debate about sexual morality which engaged many Nordic writers in the late nineteenth century. Her female characters are independent, rebellious, even reckless; but their upbringing and their circumstances combine to deny them the fulfilment their creator so painfully won for herself.

ISBN 9781909408050
UK £11.95
(Paperback, 170 pages)

JONAS LIE

The Family at Gilje

(translated by Marie Wells)

Captain Jæger is the well-meaning but temperamental head of a rural family living in straitened circumstances in 1840s Norway. The novel focuses on the fates of the women of the family: the heroic Ma, who struggles unremittingly to keep up appearances and make ends meet, and their eldest daughter Thinka, forced to renounce the love of her life and marry an older and wealthier suitor. Then there is the younger daughter, the talented and beautiful Inger-Johanna, destined to make a splendid match – but will the captain with the brilliant diplomatic career ahead of him make her happy? With great empathy and affection for each member of the family Lie evokes the tragedy of hopes dashed by harsh social and economic realities.

ISBN 9781870041942
UK £11.95
(Paperback, 210 pages)

HELENE URI

Honey Tongues

(translated by Kari Dickson)

The honey tongues of the title belong to four friends in their thirties who have known each other since school. They make up a 'sewing circle' where no sewing is done, but much exquisite food is lovingly prepared and consumed and increasingly bitchy gossip exchanged.

The novel follows their three-weekly meetings over six months, as they take turns to entertain each other; we are privy to their thoughts and memories and discover how apparently innocent actions are motivated by emotional hang-ups with their roots in childhood traumas. The tension builds towards a gourmet trip to Copenhagen to celebrate their friendship, where during an eight-course meal the masks drop and undisguised fear and loathing are revealed. Shocking secrets are unearthed as the balance of power subtly shifts from one member of the group to another. Brilliantly observed, this is female bonding at its worst, manipulative and psychotic, exposing the dependency and deceit behind the compassionate and affectionate façade.

Honey Tongues is the second adult novel by a young Norwegian writer, Helene Uri (b. 1964), and was acclaimed on its publication in 2002 as a lively and entertaining read, whose seemingly frivolous subject matter is based on acute psychological observation.

ISBN 9781909408050
UK £11.95
(Paperback, 170 pages)

Lightning Source UK Ltd.
Milton Keynes UK
UKOW06f1540070317

296050UK00001B/23/P